Penguin Book 2093

_1965_

The Birthday King

Gabriel Fielding is the pseudonym of a doctor who practises in Kent. He was born in Hexham, Northumberland, in 1916, and educated at St Edward's School, Oxford, and Trinity College, Dublin. He completed his medical studies at the Medical School of St George's Hospital, and became a Member of the Royal College of Surgeons and a Licentiate of the Royal College of Physicians in 1942. During the war he served in the R.A.M.C.

In 1948 he entered private practice in Kent, and since that time has also worked part time in the Prison Medical Service. He published his first book, _The Frog Prince and Other Poems_, in 1952, and this was followed by _XXVII Poems_, and four novels, _Brotherly Love_, _In the Time of the Greenbloom_, _Eight Days_, and _Through Streets Broad and Narrow_. Gabriel Fielding is married and has five children.

The Birthday King

Gabriel Fielding

Penguin Books

by arrangement with Hutchinson of London

Penguin Books Ltd, Harmondsworth,
Middlesex, England
Penguin Books Pty Ltd, Ringwood,
Victoria, Australia

First published by Hutchinson 1962
Published in Penguin Books 1965

Made and printed in Great Britain by
The Whitefriars Press Ltd,
London and Tonbridge
Set in 10 on 11 pt Baskerville

This story is dedicated to my wife
Edwina Eleanora Barnsley

There is something in every eye which warns
us not to trust it infinitely; greatly perhaps
we may trust it, but not to the uttermost. It
is the feeling of being at the mercy of this
cruelty, which makes us shrink from sorrows
that come as if directly from the hands of
creatures. Our sense of security is gone. We
do not know how far things will go. Strange
to say, it seems as if we know all when we are
in the grasp of the inscrutable God, but that
when creatures have got their hands upon us
there are dreadful things in the background;
undiscovered worlds of wrong, subterranean
pitfalls, dismal possibilities of injustice magni-
fied like shadows and to appearances in-
exhaustible.

FREDERICK WILLIAM FABER

There is an unfelt pause between mere being
And of being good. There is a lapse in time
And an extension both unseen – unseeing,
While within, the gamut of the bad is run
Like many raging scales, ramping in their
    climb
To contrary variety through all
That can be done
In murder, theft and harmful jealousies. . . .
The pause lifts up the self-condemned to grace.

ERICA MARX

Chapter 1

At ten minutes to nine o'clock, silence everywhere; the instrument-room of the observatory interpenetrated by it as by the motionless mountain air, as by the soundlessness of outer space where only the hydrogen atoms 'speak', cheeping like chicks in a limitless incubator: the crepuscular buzz of the universe seeping down through the ionized layer whose depths it was the observatory's purpose to measure.

But at five minutes to nine o'clock, Professor Erwin Lillesand, the old man in the room above, the not-so-old Director of Research, aged about fifty-five or so, would sit up in his truckle bed and lower first one foot and then the other to the floor. He would sit there on his rump in his flannel night-shirt and rub his fresh grey face before starting to dress for the night's work.

Below him, his assistant, Ruprecht Waitzmann, also of the Aeronautical Institute, Berlin, was enjoying the last minutes of silence as he recorded the previous night's findings in the log book; collating the latest data neatly and not thinking about them overmuch at all, his mind flying about over a dozen different considerations as restlessly as one of the main transmitter's signals over the Heaviside layer. The Director, he knew, would grunt over this pabulum, fitting it somewhere into the broader project he had in mind. Later, the 'old man' would bully Schmidt the technician and then go to the equipment shed to feed his owls and, in a better temper, return to make his nightly report to Berlin.

'But tonight I shall feed his owls first,' Waitzmann assured himself. 'It's the weekend; and as from nine o'clock I'm officially on leave.' He ruled off his column of figures. Tomorrow morning I enter a different world; and, in the

7

meantime, as always, I have myself. He closed the log and looked out through the signal-room window. There was no sign of Schmidt returning for night duty and this pleased him; for he wanted himself to himself for at least another hour. He was very much enjoying being himself that evening; in fact, he found that he could think about nothing that was not intensely original and interesting.

He checked the instruments, left a fairly courteous note for his superior, tore it up and rewrote a rather more arrogant one:

23 August '39   Herzogstadt Observatory.

Herr Direktor, Sir,

I have had to go off duty a little earlier than usual as I have certain matters to attend to in the village.

The Baron von Hoffbach is calling for me at 08.00 hrs tomorrow and should you wish to contact me over the weekend I may be found either at my home in Bergedorf or alternatively chez my friend von Hoffbach at Schloss Schönform.

I fancy that the discrepancies in last night's readings are due to a condenser overheating or else to a fault in one of the relays. No doubt the good Schmidt will check both before you yourself take over.

                  Heil Hitler!

                     Waitzmann R. Chief assistant.

He particularly liked that 'the good Schmidt'; it did not strike him as callow at all until he was half-way down the mountainside when it was too late to return and alter it. Even then, he assured himself, Professor Lillesand, being himself ambitious, would understand how fortunate he was to have such an influential assistant as his junior; that, in such circumstances, the unspoken might occasionally be spoken without loss.

He stepped out now into the summer's dusk. It was precisely nine o'clock. The hands of his wrist-watch, set by the observatory's clock, confirmed it as did the bells of the entire landscape. From the valleys below, from towers across the lake, the clocks of several churches struck the hour, their notes and keys mingling and clashing as they drifted up into the last light of the August day.

8

It was brighter up here, keen; a late hawk hovered over the dark floors, drifting over the lights of the two nearest villages. It hung delicately on its wing-tips then slid across the face of the lake and fell abruptly into the darkness rising like a tide up the sides of the valleys.

Sometimes, at this hour, Waitzmann would go up the steps to the weather shack on the extreme peak of the Herzogstadt. From there, as inclusive as his thoughts, his eye could sweep the northern horizon to take in the whole country of his youth: in the foreground the monastery in which he had been educated; further north, Onkel Fritz's one-time castle on the peninsula jutting out into the Tegernsee; and beyond these, Munich and the plain on which the Waitzmann factories smoked as they had smoked for the last seventy years.

But tonight he did not wish to think about either the past or Onkel Fritz. He was in a hurry, hurrying towards those smoking factories as a prince to a cathedral. Quite distinctly he saw this prince, or it might have been a bishop, heading for some large building. Even as he himself walked across to the 'stores' the image suddenly possessed his mind, rising from what he supposed was his 'Culture', the legends, pagan and Christian, on which he had been reared and which no amount of scientific training had been able wholly to destroy.

Pleasurably, he followed up the implications of his vision. The prince, he realized, had many dangers to overcome before he could possess his inheritance. The young aspiring bishop, a figure dredged perhaps from the pages of Stendhal, whom he had read when he was sixteen, had many powerful elders to outwit before he achieved his consecration. But each ultimately would overcome all obstructions and distractions and enter into the closer embrace of destiny; obstructions, perhaps, such as Onkel Fritz, distractions like 'the Angel', his elder brother, Alfried, whom he would be seeing again that very weekend, on their return from the United States.

Glancing back at the main building to assure himself that the professor's bedroom light was still on, he entered the

9

'stores'. The 'old man' was by now shaving in cold water, his flat grey eyes confronted by themselves in the wall-mirror, the stubby hands smoothing out the skin-folds in his heavy cheeks for the touch of his cut-throat. There were fifteen minutes in which to feed the owls; and tonight, as opposed to a leg of rabbit or mountain hare, it should be a mouse. The owls enjoyed mice and the observatory kept a supply of them for research purposes.

Ruprecht closed the door of the shed and switched on the light. As always, he ran his eyes over the spares, checking each shelf to see that neither Schmidt nor the Professor had left anything out of place. He made a swift inventory of everything there: electrical components to the left, each valve and condenser stacked neatly in its carton; to the right, weather-gear; mittens, winter helmets, defrosting equipment, mercury jars and glycol. On the upper shelves, the tinned duty rations; below these, chemicals for the latrine, washing soap and disinfectant. Against the remaining wall, the three labelled lockers: the Professor's, Ruprecht's own and Technician Schmidt's.

Satisfied, he moved over to the window beneath which the two cages stood on a bench. 'The Mousery' had always fascinated him. It was a charming conceit of Schmidt's father, an Oberammergau wood-carver whose calvaries sold for the highest prices. As a compliment to the Professor he had fashioned it as a perfect miniature of a medieval cottage: the frame exquisitely carved, the little window-boxes filled with paper flowers and even a minute Madonna of Succour poised in a corner niche between the first and second floors.

At the back, through a plexiglass window, the twenty-odd mice could be seen going about their daily affairs: chewing up paper to make their breeding beds, nibbling oat-ears in the dining-room and scurrying up and down the little balustraded staircase which connected the two floors. For some seconds, Waitzmann, quite forgetful of his purpose, gazed in at them, then he lifted off the roof-section with its over-hanging eaves and selected three mice: a piebald, a pure white and a dun-coloured. They trembled in his hand, their snouts and sharp yellow teeth gnawing at his palm as they sought a means of escape.

His intervention had caused the customary pause. For ten seconds not a mouse was to be seen. They were all hiding in their bednests, which quaked and quivered like boiling oatmeal. Then, quite soon, the veterans began to emerge; one by one, the bulls, the cows and the young pushed out into the open, questioning and investigating just as they did when their feed-bowls had been replenished.

In the other larger cage, zinc barred for three-quarters of its height, but with a deep glass tray at the bottom, Professor Lillesand's two owls stood stiffly on their perches: breasts and faces paper-grey, their amber eyes so placed at the bottoms of their immaculate craters that they seemed to be a separate creation altogether: as solitary as single drops of dew. Waitzmann opened the cage door and dropped the mice one by one into the tray. He saw them start on their immediate investigations, their rapid circling tours and brief councils, then stood back from the cage and looked at the owls. Since their eyes were so set that without moving they could see each pattern traced by the mice on the shining floor, the birds did not even incline their heads to look downwards; and the mice, conferring now in a group, never once looked upwards at the wooden perches just above their heads.

As the first owl, talons outstretched, dropped from its perch, Waitzmann switched off the light and set off down the mountainside to Schorgast.

In the morning the Baron was hallooing from beside his open car long before the appointed hour. Ruprecht heard his cries from a turn in the path when he was half-way down the Herzogstadt. He shouted back and saw the shrunken sun-bright figure get back into the front seat and level a pair of binoculars at him. He waved and made signals and the Baron blew morse on the horn and semaphored with his arms.

When Ruprecht reached him he leapt out of the car again and said,   .

'Don't I look the better for it? Aren't the rewards there for all to see? For the first time in years I've a clean tongue in the mornings; my bowels are moving superbly.'

'You look magnificent, Baron.'

'It was very arduous, my boy.'

'What was the treatment?'

'Expensive; particularly the singing.'

'You had singing lessons?'

'Every morning before breakfast. Half-an-hour of it, with breath-control to mobilize the diaphragm. It was all explained to us in a series of lectures; most interesting.'

'And what does that do?'

'It helps to discharge the juices of the gall-bladder and the sweetbread. One has no idea what a lot there is to the digestive processes until one has attended a good clinic. And I, I might tell you, was one of the star performers, Ruprecht. The doctors told me I had a particularly fine baritone, good enough for Lohengrin.'

'And the food?'

'Food, my dear boy! In the accepted sense, it wasn't food at all. We lived entirely on vegetable juices, minerals and fruit pulp. We had hydrotherapy four times daily: scalding hot hosings followed by ice-water baths. My urine turned white as water and my skin tightened up like an athlete's.'

'And you feel the better for it?'

'Ten years younger! In Berlin now I shall speak to some purpose – and not only in Berlin.' He flashed Ruprecht a straight glance. 'I am even ready to deal with your mother.'

'And my brother, Alfried.'

'Ah yes! Your brother. Your mother tells me that he and your uncle are due back from the States this weekend?'

'You've heard from her?'

'She telephoned me two days ago. But let's not get to that just yet. There'll be time enough when we know exactly what's what. Tell me instead how you are yourself; how's the ionosphere behaving? I trust you're getting on well with Lillesand?'

'Oh, he's not too bad. We don't take much notice of one another.'

The Baron laughed. 'What self-confidence you have. I wanted his opinion of you, not yours of the Professor.'

'I don't think he's displeased with me. But really since I've no intention of making a career of physics I'm not greatly interested.'

'Then you must become so. It will make things easier for myself when the time comes.'

This was the Baron's way. He would be an open-air man and jolly for most of the time; but behind the presentation, or so Ruprecht was beginning to think, was a harder fellow, as calculating as a father. Yes, looking at him as he sat beside him, he saw this older man as strong and seasoned: square knees, behind the green hunting breeches, as heavily boned as a bull's, thick sinews, a massive skull. Not in his prime, admittedly, already beyond it; old enough to have sired a full-grown man of Ruprecht's own age, old enough to have sired Leo von Hoffbach who was in fact a year older.

But I'm in no need of a father, Ruprecht told himself as this splendid creature impelled his old car along the tortuous mountain road. No, no, I don't need a father at this stage. I've got on without one for years. But I can do with a man of his age behind me to be used. I'll use his strength, his ageing bones and his knowledge of power until I'm in a position to dispense with them.

But immediately after he had thought like this he also began to decry the Baron as a dusty old squire essentially out of practice in dealing with anything more complex than his crumbling castle and its neglected acres. Though he himself might imagine he was grooming Ruprecht to his own advantage, in reality Ruprecht was pushing the older man forward like a stalking-horse and watching his progress far more narrowly than he could ever have supposed.

'What scenery!' exclaimed the Baron as they came out on to the main road. 'You can have no idea how it moves a born countryman like myself to be overshadowed by trees again after the rigours of Karlsbad. Trees do something for the soul, my boy, and the body too. The smell of our native resin does more for me, I assure you, than all the imported incense of our monasteries.'

'I know exactly what you mean.'

The Baron was not a fine bull any longer. He was a grizzled boar such as his son Leo loved to shoot. A wily old male snuffling about for acorns in the forests of Schönform.

'We'll stop here,' he said, 'and take a look down through our native trees to our fair Isar. We'll hasten slowly, Ruprecht, and we'll be all the better able to deal with anything your Onkel Fritz may have in store for us.'

They got out of the car at an official viewing place and stood for a few moments trying to see down to the green water which at this point flowed through a narrow ravine. The beech trees were in full leaf and awkwardly placed; whichever way they looked they were prevented from even a glimpse of the river. The Baron inveighed against the city fathers and, turning his back, 'christened' the slope. He said it was unreasonable and inept to make a parking area and go to the trouble of erecting rustic seats and notices when the view for which they were intended was not at all times visible. With what Ruprecht took for 'old man's stubbornness' he walked up and down the retaining wall and then, in his smart breeches and white stockings, clambered over the parapet and went noisily downwards, stopping every now and then to do some breathing exercises. In a few minutes, when he had disappeared from Ruprecht's view, it must have occurred to him that he had parked his car incorrectly and he called up to ask if the rear wheel was in proper alignment with the edge of the road. Ruprecht called back good-humouredly that all was well but the Baron was not satisfied and instructed him to look again.

'Then I will measure,' Ruprecht assured him.

Without moving from the seat, glowering into the trees, he waited the necessary time and then once again called down into the valley that all four tyres were off the metal.

The Baron returned slowly, grunting as he scrambled up the steep slope. He refused Ruprecht's offer of help in climbing back over the parapet, and then, as suddenly, apologized for his ill-humour.

'It's Carin,' he said. 'I can't tell you how I worry about

my wife, especially when she's staying with her mother, Frau de Luce.'

Ruprecht, who had only met Carin von Hoffbach once, and had only heard accounts of her mother, Frau de Luce, from Leo, agreed that it was a pity for a mother and daughter to dislike one another so much.

'It's not merely a question of dislike,' the Baron corrected him. 'They're a bad influence on each other, my boy. They bring out the worst in one another. My mother-in-law, Eva, disapproves of Carin and the poor girl can't stand it, yet she cannot keep away from the old woman; she's always running off back to East Prussia to renew the quarrelling. When she eventually returns to Berlin she spends more wildly than ever and the cycle repeats itself.'

Ruprecht was interested. Carin von Hoffbach, the Baronin, French on her father's side, had been a glittering figure of his adolescence who had for a time haunted his boldest fantasies. Even in those days, he remembered, her breath had smelt of French drinks, her laughter had been harsh and she had painted her finger-nails violet. It was well known that she had always, as she might have put it herself, had 'a *penchant* for young men'.

'And then,' the Baron was continuing, 'when she has come down to her last mark of credit, what does she do but return once more to the old widow at Rastenburg to renew the very mood that causes all the trouble? And this, my dear fellow, when she might be living peacefully at Schönform with Leo. In confidence, it would not only be more economical but it would be much less embarrassing for us all.'

'I suppose the Baronin has expensive tastes, sir?'

'You should see the bills I get. Every month vast sums at the Adlon and the Kaiserhof, to say nothing of a sheaf of papers from Paris and Rheims for perfumes and champagne, and most of it for the benefit of young subalterns from my own regiment.'

'Disgraceful!'

'I'm glad you agree. What on earth d'you suppose is the matter with her?'

'I haven't an idea, sir. I suppose it might be something to

do with the fact that her mother disapproves of her. I find myself that this can have a great effect on one, even though, of course, I'm so much younger than your wife.'

'Of course, of course,' said the Baron in sudden excellent humour again. 'I'm very glad I've confided in you like this, Ruprecht. Everything will work out well in the end. One mustn't let these personal affairs drain one's energies at a time like this.'

'You're sanguine about the situation?'

'On the whole, very. Mind you, I had my doubts to begin with; but you've got to give Hitler his due, the fellow knows what's wanted.'

'How would you say the atmosphere compared with the last affair, sir, nineteen fourteen?' Ruprecht asked gloomily.

'No comparison at all,' said the Baron a little irritably. 'Those were very good times, Plumes, my dear fellow!'

'Plumes?' Ruprecht repeated in some surprise.

'Sorry! I was in my own thoughts, Ruprecht. I was young then, you realize? In fact, I wasn't old enough to join the family regiment until the early part of '14 but I remember the feathers and I can't think of that business without seeing them. It all started so innocently; whenever the Kaiser held a review the whole parade ground positively sprouted feathers like an ostrich farm. The generals wore them, the top echelons of the best regiments and the women too – a magnificent sight. Feathers and bicycle-croquet, my boy. That's how I think of that affair.'

'Really?'

The Baron was plunged in a nostalgia inseparable from those boyhood recollections. Visions of his walrus-moustached father, his veiled and beautiful mother, his fierce courtship of the half-French Carin, assailed him like a flock of bright-faced ghosts. Lost innocence and the confidence of his youth contended once again for recognition in his least-visited memory.

'Even the early cannon,' he vouchsafed, 'blew out feathers of cordite in August of '14; but it was different at the end of course: that was the trouble.'

'You mean the mud and lice, the howitzers and chlorine?' Ruprecht prompted him.

'Mere symbols of what was to come,' the Baron replied contemptuously. 'We entered the present sordid age; scarcely a shot fired on German soil but a wilderness just the same. All the best gone – with the plumes and glory. In its place; inflation, ignominy and influenza! After the death of my dear mother in that appalling epidemic I buried myself down here in Schönform. It was the only thing to do.'

'But you emerged again after Munich. Why was that? Was it because you'd regained your faith?'

'Tradition, mainly. Realized it was time I did something. I wasn't fooled by the trick played on Hindenburg. As a matter of fact I was damned sceptical and still am; but the key to it all is that extraordinary defeat, the wash of corruption which followed it. When you fall into a cess-pit, my boy, you grab at anything that shows signs of floating and, as I was telling you, Hitler has organized things. He's made something where formerly there was nothing. In a sordid age one doesn't care to examine one's leaders too closely, it's not aristocratic. These are not the days of Bismarck. We have to sink our foundations where we may if we're to bring off any sort of a reconstruction.'

'Aha, I see!' thought Ruprecht who, whenever he could, was always ferreting about such persons as the Baron to find out just what was going on at the top. 'We're prepared to back them up as long as they get results. We'll secure the turrets first and examine the foundations later. Very sensible!'

The Baron took a look at the young, flesh-green face beside him. A shrewd young man but a bit of a brooder. Not altogether trustworthy. Too quick with his questions to be that.

As they headed out of Munich along the Dachauerstrasse, he began to talk a little more jovially and lightly about the Führer himself: spicier conversation, more calculated to disarm; not so near the bone of his real conviction.

'I never cease to remind myself that *au fond*, of course, the fellow has the N.C.O. mentality and is, like ourselves, a

Southerner.' The Baron always resorted to French phrases when he was being less than sincere. 'When ill-bred, Southerners are always noisy and often disgruntled, Ruprecht.'

'Very true,' said Ruprecht.

'You realize, of course, that so far he has simply been scampering round the European barrack-room frightening everybody?'

'Yes, I suppose he has.'

'And to very good effect.' The Baron waited for a military convoy to cross the entrance to the new autobahn. 'One only wonders how much longer he'll get away with it.'

'Or how much longer we shall,' Ruprecht suggested.

'Ah, very good,' said the Baron, putting his foot down and keeping his hand on the horn as they overtook the convoy. 'The other danger, of course, is that Hitler has never been abroad and, more important, that apart from Ribbentrop in his capacity as a commercial traveller, none of his intimates have either.'

'You think it important?'

'My dear boy, of course it is. If an élite is to be truly *haut monde* then it should have friends in London, Paris, Stockholm and Washington. If you've never stroked the cat, how do you know which way he will jump?'

'That is certainly the way a successful business is conducted,' said Ruprecht, thinking of Onkel Fritz. The Baron too was thinking of the Waitzmann interests a little greedily.

'But surely,' said Ruprecht, circling round the obstruction of Onkel Fritz, 'for the Führer, such mundane contacts aren't necessary? People even think that he has powers of divination.'

Even if he were not, the Baron pretended to be astounded. 'You haven't fallen victim to that bungalow nonsense, surely? My dear fellow, if that sort of opinion's becoming current amongst the younger, more intelligent, industrialists we are indeed undone. Berchtesgaden and that eagle-nest of his are playthings only. They make the Führer feel Bavarian rather than Austrian. They provide Herr Goebbels with a little light copy and everyone else with the most delicious cakes provided they can stand the Führer's monologues.' He paused. 'Divination indeed! You can't be serious!'

In the driving-mirror Ruprecht saw that the jolly blue eyes had become thoughtful. A speck of dust evidently irritated the tissue in one of them for the Baron mopped at it quickly with a silk handkerchief which he kept, English fashion, up his left cuff.

'Personally I've always thought,' said Ruprecht, 'that there was a smell of Vienna about him. I can't really take him seriously in the social sense. Have you noticed, for instance, that whenever he's photographed with women, they're nearly always wearing those short arm-pitty white blouses one associates with the Viennese housewife?'

The Baron was delighted. 'Capital! Capital! You've hit the nail on the head; but then of course if the truth be told, he's a eunuch – and that is disturbing. There's something about a fellow who has no use for women, barring decadents of von Schirach's persuasion, that is alarming.'

'You don't think, then, that we shall ever be able to compare the Führer with Napoleon?'

'I think it's extremely unlikely. He is not of the same calibre at all. As I've told you, this is a cheap age we're living in. Even a man with mediocre powers of leadership must seem remarkable in comparison with such contemporaries as the last war left us, with jumped-up business men, if you'll forgive me saying so, like your Onkel Fritz.'

'Is that your opinion, then, of Chamberlain, the English premier?'

'Certainly! Roosevelt and Daladier too. Who are they, if not provincial upstarts who have made the most of their opportunities in an age of decadence? There's only one man with whom the Führer has seriously to reckon and that is Herr Stalin, the leader of the Soviets, and I don't think he'll make the mistake of underestimating that gentleman!'

Ten minutes later they drew up outside the Waitzmann House inside the factory grounds.

Let them get all the greetings over, all the posturings that the simplest human encounters require, was Ruprecht's thought as he led the Baron up the shining staircase to the drawing-room. Everything depends on what six months in America with Onkel Fritz have done for Alfried.

'Discretion, my boy!' the Baron counselled him within hearing of Frau Waitzmann's servant, Kegel, who was following them with Ruprecht's nightcase. Kegel was a little old now and deaf, though no less interested in these family goings-on. 'Don't forget that, Ruprecht,' repeated the Baron, 'be discreet and leave things to me.'

'Entirely, sir.'

Yes, yes, indeed. Everything should be left to the Baron; everything weighty and boring, the political considerations with which the drawing-room would be filled the moment this grizzled old boar caught sight of Onkel Fritz. Let those two get in a corner with an American cigar apiece and contend for their advantages beneath the nearly blind eyes of Mama, who like some wooden effigy in the forest, high upon the bole of a pine, would miss not a single tussle of their meeting nor speak one real word until she was alone with her sons.

Kegel pattered across the landing, smiling sidelong at Ruprecht, as she crossed the main light with its frieze of chimneys and pygmy figures of men unloading a trailer at one of the factory's ramps. Ruprecht smiled back at her and then with easy duplicity opened the tall white drawing-room doors and showed the Baron in, doubling away behind him to follow Kegel up to his bedroom. As he had anticipated, von Hoffbach hesitated, framed in the doorway, smiling on those others within who were gathered about Frau Waitzmann's sofa and the thin wine she drank at this hour. He paused and strode forward in the certainty that Ruprecht was following him, was for a moment nonplussed, then swept on to kiss Frau Waitzmann crookedly upon the right wrist at the same moment as Ruprecht was saluting Kegel's hollow cheek in a room above.

'Dear Emma,' said Ruprecht, taking his case from her. 'I could have saved you the climb up the stairs if I hadn't been so preoccupied.'

'You could, but you didn't.'

He kissed her again. 'It's living in the mountains entirely in the company of men. One's manners fall from one like the leaves of autumn.'

'Go on with you. What's it you're after?'

'Time!' he said aloud.

'We all want that, but not at your age.'

'But I do, Liebling. Minutes are vital to me.' She was fussing round his bedroom. Pointless twitchings at curtains and pillow slips.

'Well, go on then, what's it you want to know?'

'What's for dinner tonight?'

'Soup; a parcel of brown trout from Schönform – arrived this morning; ice-cream with nuts, coffee and Normandy cheeses.'

'Delicious! And "the Angel" and my uncle, when did they get here?'

'Last night about ten. Höth fetched them from the airfield at Frankfurt.'

'So she sent a car but didn't go herself and von Hoffbach sent his trout ahead of him and never mentioned it to me?'

'The fish was sent with the compliments of Herr Leo, if it matters.'

'But of course it does; everything matters, and nothing more than foresight. Don't you realize that being first with a box of matches has been known to win a man a wealthy bride?'

'You're not getting married? Now don't tell me that!'

'Oh no, not yet; but what about Alfried? Any news of a tie-up between him and one of my uncle's girls?'

'Not that I've heard.'

'Now come on; I've only a few minutes. What did she say last night in her bedroom?'

'Your mother was very tired.'

'Why?'

'The mistress doesn't tell me everything.' Emma was getting towels from a press. 'Now you get on down to the drawing-room or she'll wonder what's keeping you.'

'But what was she worried about? Has Alfried got himself a job over there?'

'Master Alfried's done nothing. He's looking thin; all at sixes and sevens; just as he was when he left.'

'No job, no women! Perhaps he's written a book then, or published some poetry?'

'Not that I've heard.'

'What on earth has he been doing?'

'Thinking too much, I'd say.'

'Good old Emma!'

'It's what I think. He worries the mistress something dreadful, him and his angels.'

'He's still on that tack, is he? What's he going to do? Have another try for the Oratorians?'

'I'm sure I don't know. Nobody ever did know with him.'

'But he walked out on them. They won't take him back at this stage. He'll have to try a different Order if he tries anything.'

'Not that I've anything against him,' said Emma. 'He's a sweet boy.'

'Go back with Fritz and lock himself up with the Yankee Franciscans?' Ruprecht ran on.

'Much sweeter than you ever were; gentler, better altogether.'

'Agreed! Agreed!'

'And no fool. But he ought to be making up his mind what he's going to do with his life instead of coming back here and upsetting everyone with his American propaganda.'

'He's become political, then? His trip's done that much for him, has it? What's his attitude?'

'I didn't listen.'

'Please, Emma. What does he accuse us of? Making money? Putting the Jews out of business or just war-mongering?'

'I don't know what he said. I only know he's upset the Frau Kommerzienrat, your mother, about everything and won't say whether he's going to stay and help her with the business or go off back with your uncle to help run the branch in Baltimore.'

'So we're really no further on than when we started?'

'It doesn't look like it.'

'You're certain he's met no beautiful girls?'

'Some nun or other.'

'A *nun*?' Ruprecht stopped still in the middle of the room.

'It was that girl that followed your uncle's daughters over there. The one he called his Beatrice. She's a nun now or she will be next year. He's been seeing a bit of her by all accounts; but it's come to no more than it ever did when they were children.'

'Ruth Lubbe! God in Heaven, as if he hadn't enough to bewilder him without falling in love with an exiled quarter-Jewish postulant!'

He could no longer wait to see Alfried again; all other considerations were temporarily driven from his mind by the sudden intensity of his curiosity and affection.

Affection, certainly! He assured himself as he left Kegel and hurried down the stairs to the drawing-room. Though I've sometimes detested him, essentially I've always been fond of Alfried; though I remember wishing him vanished or suffering sufficiently for me to be able to forgive him for something or other, I've never wished him any absolute harm. What a curious fact this is; particularly since, now that he's back and being as troublesome as ever, I feel guilty at the thought of anything but the most complete acceptance of him. I must really take care to be more consistent in my emotions or I'll end up by betraying myself.

He slowed his pace and entered the drawing-room looking thoughtful. He was indeed being thoughtful, therefore it was simplest and most disarming to look thoughtful. In the pause he kissed his mother thoughtfully.

'But where have you been, Ruprecht?'

'He's as capricious as a goat,' suggested the Baron genially. 'One moment he's in front of you and the next he has vanished.'

'Doubtless it's the mountain air,' said Alfried coming forward. 'He looks matured by it. Years older.'

'My boy!' Onkel Fritz took his hand for a moment gazing with his moneyed green eyes into Ruprecht's face.

'How are you, Uncle? Have a good flight?'

'Excellent.'

'Some wine?' Alfried asked him. 'Not Mama's pathetic stuff; but your favourite Niersteiner? I got it from the cellar myself for you. The second bin on the left, yes?'

'Correct.'

Affection for Alfried stole upon him like the symptoms of a subtle illness. The glass he had handed him was itself misted round the oval prints of his finger-tips, the perfume of his body mingling with the drift of the grape.

'I gave Emma a hand with my case,' he told his mother belatedly.

'That was good of you. Now, Baron, where were we?'

'Well, we were discussing the advisability of a change of name. Petty, admittedly; but, as we agreed, under the circumstances – politic.'

'Ridiculous!' said Onkel Fritz. 'The man's a maniac. The company has traded under the family name for over a hundred years.'

'Two hundred years if one includes the banking,' said Ruprecht.

'When we were indeed wholly and safely Jewish,' added Alfried. 'I often suspect that my right eye's not quite Aryan. It has a nasty way of lighting up when I make money.'

'Oh, capital!' said the Baron, who thought this was in bad taste. He turned to Frau Waitzmann. 'No, my dear Frau Kommerzienrat, appreciating as you will the anomalies of my own position, in return for your very great kindness in admitting me to the Board you asked me to find out what was required by our friends in Berlin. I did so; and this suggestion of a name-change, not my own I assure you, is the fruit of my most tactful enquiries. The Party cannot stand discrepancies.'

'Always the mark of villains,' said Alfried.

'Now, please don't make things difficult for the Baron,' Frau Waitzmann told him.

'But discrepancies are the hall-mark of the Creator,' Alfried insisted. 'I'm sure that's why absolutely nothing moves in a perfect circle.'

'Alfried, Alfried, come here. Sit beside me and be quiet.

The question at issue is whether or not we accept this hint from Hitler.'

'Not the Führer, I beg you! Let us blame "certain quarters".'

'Nonsense, Baron! Of course it's from Hitler.'

'Well, within these four walls.'

'Microphones!' said Alfried in broad American. 'Make sure we haven't been bugged by the Gestapo in our absence, Ruprecht.'

Everyone laughed and none louder than Onkel Fritz who used this loud instrument to suggest that a change of name would involve considerable expense.

'And better contracts,' put in the Baron quickly. 'I'm told the firm's going to be kept very busy indeed in the event of a Polish contretemps.'

'We'll vote on it,' said Frau Waitzmann with finality. 'Ruprecht, you may have a proxy seat on the Board for the occasion.'

'Cousin Levi's,' said Alfried. 'Since he's half Jewish and lives in Lille, he's unlikely to be able to cast his vote for the next ten years.'

'Very well then, we have a quorum. Those in favour? Count for me please, Alfried.' Frau Waitzmann herself raised her hand.

'Four in favour. One against, Mama.'

'And whose is that?'

'My own, Mama.'

'You're a great nuisance, Alfried.'

'But the vote's carried, just the same. Consider me merely as a wasp in Eden. There would have had to have been just one for Adam and Eve to appreciate one another's nudity.'

'Oh, you're impossible,' she said.

'But how lovely it is to have me back, isn't it, Ruprecht?'

'Of course.'

Alfried got up from his seat beside Frau Waitzmann and strolled over to the netted window. Standing there leaning a little crookedly as he looked down into the busy street, he appeared to forget everybody. Ruprecht, watching him, shuddered inside his clothing: his shirt, trousers and jacket separated themselves from his body as this tremor of disquiet ran through his muscles as swiftly as a cat's quiver.

As he had foreseen, Onkel Fritz and the Baron were now discussing larger issues: the question of American neutrality in the event of war with Poland.

'In that event, my dear Baron,' Onkel Fritz was saying, 'if your informants are in good faith, it strikes me it would be an excellent idea for someone to pay a short visit to Stockholm to fix the prices of our raw materials on a long-term basis. Don't you agree, Wilhelmina?'

'I've already pegged the prices with Malnë – by correspondence! It's so much cheaper.'

'You have!' Onkel Fritz's face fell into the immediate apathy of satisfaction.

'I signed the new contract a month ago.'

'Mama, you're superb,' said Ruprecht, taking his eyes off Alfried for a moment.

'You never cease to astonish one!' said the Baron.

'It was perhaps an obvious precaution,' she said modestly. 'I shall be fifty-eight next October and although it's no great age I find my blindness a great burden. Though I've the strength to manage our affairs during a second war, I no longer have the will.'

'Quite understandable,' the Baron agreed. 'It's time you were relieved of the heaviest burdens. Even my wife, Carin, who's fifteen years your junior, finds, of late, that she's slowing up a little.'

'Understandable but regrettable,' said Onkel Fritz. 'There's no one like Wilhelmina. My cousin's more like an American woman than a European. In middle life, they've a quite remarkable flair for money. I move that Wilhelmina be ruled out of order on the question of her retirement and that we consider the next item on our agenda.' He leaned across over her and took her hand, patting it as if it were a little cake of dough and he the baker. 'You understand, my dear? I, for one, could not return to the States knowing that anyone else was at the helm in such a crisis.'

'Hypocrite! Your hand-pat gives you away,' Ruprecht

told him silently. 'You know very well you've only come back in order to put Alfried in Mother's place.'

As if she sensed this too, his mother withdrew her offended hand and covered it with the other. In her roundest voice, a tone full of her vanished girlhood, gentle, firm and courteous, she said:

'Nevertheless, Fritz, I've decided. Alfried will have to take my place. I hope that he will?'

But from Alfried there was no answer. Of course they all, with the exception of his mother, turned round to look at him as he stood behind them lolling crook-backed at the window, lost in whatever observation he was making. He had, in fact, pulled the stuffy netting to one side the better to see the people in the street.

'Alfried, my dear, what are you doing over there? We're all awaiting your decision.'

'Mama?' his hand dropped and the netting sprang back into place. He moved over to the sofa, his long head slightly on one side, his eyelids fluttering down whitely over his pale green eyes. He walked with the immediate lop-sided concern of someone too suddenly aroused from a doze.

'How healthy they all look,' he said. 'Anyone else noticed it?'

'Alfried!' cautioned Onkel Fritz as if he were his trainer. 'Have you not heard our discussion?'

'Every word. You were talking about the war and so forth; but what fascinates me is the people. I don't know whether it's entirely the evening light, but they seem to glow with appetite like children coming home from school.'

'Yes, my dear fellow, but at the moment . . .'

'They've been got at, that's obvious,' Alfried interrupted him. 'Someone's been telling them delicious lies. It's astonishing how much better one feels for an authoritative lie or two. I remember myself someone telling me one Christmas, when I was very young, that I was going to be given a large steam locomotive – one it was possible to ride in – and for weeks I walked about as dreamlessly as if the future had already come true.'

'Now please do stop this nonsense,' pleaded Frau

Waitzmann. 'I told you earlier you were to sit beside me. What's your answer, Alfried? It's very important for us all to know and we can't keep the Baron waiting.'

'You have decided, Alfried?' Onkel Fritz asked him.

'Well, obviously it would be rash to throw in my hand altogether just now. One never knows what's going to be required of one. And after all, what excuse have I? If I had a good reason I'd love to hand things over to Ruprecht for the time being. He knows that?'

'Drivel!' exclaimed Ruprecht as the last of his affection crumbled. 'If what you really mean is that you want to have it both ways, why not say so?'

'Calm yourself, my boy,' counselled the Baron. 'We must try to appreciate your brother's difficulties.'

'I spent my childhood and adolescence doing that and I don't intend to spend my manhood too. It's like dealing with an idiot. Alfried never knows what he wants either of us or of himself.'

'Alfried is a little different. Ever since he was a child—' began Frau Waitzmann.

'Mama!' Ruprecht interrupted her. 'If we're going to go back to that damned angel, I for one, suggest that the meeting be adjourned for biscuits and lemonade. Let's all relax while Alfried tells the Baron, the only member who hasn't already heard it a hundred times, how when he was a sweet and simple child he saw a pretty little angel floating round the ceiling.'

'I think that Ruprecht, if impatient, is right,' said Onkel Fritz. 'We mustn't waste time on inessentials. On the other hand, we all know that, though Alfried's inherited this somewhat poetic temperament, he has great practical ability.'

'Excellent, Herr Waitzmann,' said the Baron. 'Let's give Alfried a day or two to make up his mind. I'm sure Ruprecht too is feeling the strain, or he wouldn't have spoken so violently.'

'I'm tired of indecision: that's all.'

Frau Waitzmann, who had remained silent for so long, delighted by this clash of wills, and to be so significant and alive, gave Ruprecht the little 'push' he no longer needed.

'Take your thousand paces, Ruprecht, before dinner,' she said. 'You'll miss nothing of importance.'

He left them and went quickly down the staircase, and out into the open. The familiar smells of the factory and the town mingled in the evening air as he moved away from the house along the cindered path to the Waitzmann memorials; for that was how he thought of them. Though there was not a corpse or a family bone buried in these spare acres his forebears had furnished, their ghosts seemed to him to linger slow and prosperous behind clumps of ivy and sooty pergolas, within Grandmother's grotto and Great-Aunt Rebecca's summer bower; heavy ghosts strolling through the middle of the town whose people skirted the gilt-topped railings so noisily.

The ground itself shook to the passing of buses and diesels, pulsed day and night like dark flesh to the rhythm of the factory's turbines; and the ghosts, safe in their heartland, moved on as he himself moved, gaze-down and meditative, detached from and at no peace with the living.

He remembered strolling here with his grandfather on many evenings between wine and dinner nearly twenty years ago. He remembered the scent of the old man's cigar, the bulge of his eye-level waistcoat with the bottom button undone, the sound of his eructations and the crunch of his stick on the cinders:

'Take note, little Ruprecht,' he had said once at the Dog's Ground. 'This patch of land alone is worth ten thousand marks! A monument both to foresight and sentiment.'

'Yes, Grandfather.'

'Well, what do you see?'

'Pictures – all the dead dogs.'

'And the dates of burials?'

'Just dates. The times they died.'

'Then I'll tell you, my boy. There's not a single schnauzer or pomeranian to my great-great-grandfather Aron Waitzmann's name. He was a Spanish Jew and an aristocrat who spent his fortune on land and property. His conversion to Christianity at the turn of the last century evidently did not influence his attitude to the animal kingdom; but with my grandmother and my mother this nonsense reached its climax. They buried three or four court favourites here every seven years of their lives. Just look at them! Chows, alsatians, borzois, dachshunds and poodles by the dozen; and all interred between eighteen hundred and sixty and nineteen fourteen. Be warned!'

'Why, Grandfather?'

'Of your Jewish heritage. This little Folly is a fable of our family's decline. As our Jewish blood was watered down by intermarriage with these romantic northerners the number of dead dogs went up as fast as our investments went down until I myself came along.'

'And what did you do?'

'I forbade dogs, I started the pulp-mill and I practised my religion.'

'Mama says religion should always come first.'

How Grandfather had laughed; but his laughter and any word that he might have replied were gone. If he did, in fact, still stroll these three or four dingy acres dotted with Mama's statues, then he borrowed only the remembrance of the living for his substance and was silent as the dogs beneath their granite and grime.

Ruprecht paused now by their Ground, looking up at the Biedermeier statue of St Francis, drooping-eyed and silly on his plinth round which the creeping willow herb and white jasmine climbed and bushed. The willow-herb had smothered Grandmother's rock-plants and alpines. It crept over the mildewed glass-encased photographs of pomeranians and short-nosed schnauzers; an eye here, a snout there, shining deadly between its leaves. Ten thousand marks, thought Ruprecht. You may double that now, quadruple it, and if you care to include the rest of the land then you may multiply by a hundred, even without a victorious war.

What would he not do with it when his chance came? A new factory extension rose in his mind, glass-walled and gleaming. New machinery in place of the outmoded Krupps stuff put in by Grandfather, oil-fired colour kitchens and overhead conveyor belts, rolling silently day and night.

He moved on, afire with plans, looking kindly on St John Nepomuk, patron saint of tongues and oral cancer, who jutted white from a mound of ivy slowly strangling a bush of daphne. He paused, as the Baron might have done, to take a few deep breaths before the entrance to Grandmother's grotto and then, smelling the gardeners' urine, became immediately angry again. Doubtless inside, the place was now an outdoor servants' latrine; and who could blame them? Why! The house itself needed new lavatories. The central heating and hot water, supplied direct by underground pipes from the factory, was all outmoded and unreliable. A fresh hand was needed, hard and energetic, an eye colder and more Jewish than Onkel Fritz's, less dreaming and confused than Alfried's. Less Jewish also? That depended on what one meant by the word. Grandfather had equated it with both spirituality and materialism. It would be the sort of question in which Alfried delighted. Later he might put it to him.

At that moment Alfried came in search of him. He did not call him, it was not his way. He took pleasure in catching people unawares.

'Ah! There you are.'

Ruprecht dropped the key-ring which he had been unconsciously jingling. 'God in Heaven! Must you do that?'

'I thought you might be missing me.'

'There's still no need to play childish tricks.'

'But you wanted me, for a hundred questions or just one?'

'What happened in the house?'

'Not very much, everything slowed up after you left. Mama wound things up in her usual masterly way and von Hoffbach asked me to remind you about your luncheon at Schönform tomorrow. He has a pretty girl for you.'

'They didn't succeed in tying you down?'

'No, I floated round the ceiling with my angel.'

Alfried smiled suddenly into his brother's bitter face. 'I thought you were amusing about that.'

'It bores me.'

They turned and began to stroll back together beneath the birches, beside the lavender hedges, black barred by the shadows of the railings. Alfried plucked a handful of flowers and sniffed them crushed in his palm.

'I see Mama still keeps her clippers going,' he said. 'I think she must love the gardens as much as I do.'

They had paused before the little statue of St John Nepomuk. The figure was balanced on a concealed pedestal in the hollow of the ivy bush, the packed leaves rising black behind the head and mantling the feet like the pediment of a breaking wave.

'That's how you see things here, is it?' Ruprecht asked him. 'As aspects of Mama's sentiment?'

'Has it ever struck you that in a cemetery one is likely to meet only women?'

'I've never considered it.'

'They start us off inside them and when we're dead they tend us still. Generations of dead men under the ground; and the women with their clippers and watering cans.'

'What was decided after I left?'

'Mary Magdalen, for example,' went on Alfried, inhaling the fragrance of his lavender. 'Certainly she had a pot full of flowers with her.'

'What did Fritz say?'

Alfried dropped his lavender. 'You'd rather consider the question of the factories?'

'Yes.'

'They may well fall to you.'

'When?'

'That depends on how greedy I'm feeling. I like money. I enjoy being the heir. It's one thing to give away something you'll probably get; but it's quite another to discard a certainty.'

'If you don't make up your mind soon we'll all suffer. Once I know where I stand I could start immediately instead of leaving things to Fritz and von Hoffbach.'

'Supposing I were to waive my claim. What would you collect?' asked Alfried.

'How do you mean?'

'Well, you'll obviously have to go in for something. Rich men always do. First of all you'll have to find a wife, preferably someone well-connected, some delicious drifting thoroughbred of a girl with a slightly large nose and spiritual eyes. After that you'll want to start investing your money in something you can handle in the daytime.'

'I wish you'd cut out the facetiousness.'

'But I've thought about it often. Myself, for instance, I'd go in for books and medieval carvings. But you, I imagine, would be more attracted by yachts and Ferraris, a villa in Italy?'

'In a few minutes she'll be sending Fritz out to us. Why can't you answer my question? What'll you take for the business? What promises do you want from me to use your influence with them to make them see they'll lose nothing if you take a back seat?'

'I want only your happiness,' replied Alfried with a vicious smile. 'Promise me you'll be the birthday king for the rest of your life, growing nobler and more generous as every year passes, and I'll sign the papers tonight.'

'That joke's wearing a little thin.'

Alfried took his arm, one of his sudden moments of contrition. 'I'm sorry, I'm getting a bit tired of the whole problem; but I'll tell you what I'll do. I'll make you a promise that if you'll be patient I'll give you a final answer in two years at the latest.'

'Why not sooner? Why not tonight?'

'I can't.' He was looking overhead, following something in the air. 'Ah, the bats are out.'

A pair were circling the birches high in the evening sky; silent black mice, more soundless than leaves in their flight, chinking like little chains as they weaved their way round the tops of the trees, disappearing into the swathes of smoke which the mists had brought down from the chimneys. As the brothers stood there, faces up in the sharp shadows thrown by the arc lights of the yards, a sooty dew fell on to the parched grass and the dry shrubs of the garden, pattering like the onset of the thinnest rain.

'Why the two years' delay?' asked Ruprecht again.

'A question of poison amongst other things. I've been catching up on my reading. Fritz has a good library and

I've been following the origin of the Führer's thought. I don't like it.'

'Fritz seems to have survived it.'

'And your friend von Hoffbach?'

'He doesn't read, he's a straightforward opportunist, which is more than can be said for Fritz, who's a crooked one.'

Alfried laughed. 'I see your point. The hungry middle-aged?'

'Mama's no fool, Alfried, but she's getting older. If we're not careful we'll find we've both been by-passed.'

Ruprecht moved on. 'Why can't you be honest and admit you're waiting as we are to see how far the Third Reich fulfils the Führer's prophecies and promises.'

'Because it's not strictly true. As you've probably heard, I'm in love. I don't want to discuss it now because it's not the real cause of my difficulties. My trouble is that I want everything; all the money I can lay my hands on, a particular woman, a family, and Heaven as well."

'Couldn't you have chosen someone else?'

'Someone other than Ruth you mean?'

'In a year or two, even now during this visit, you could take your pick. Why select a penniless Jewish exile with a vocation?'

'Let me put it simply. While I want everything the world has to offer I'm quite unable to believe in it and while I reject all of the accepted ways to it I cannot cease to believe in Heaven. Ever since I saw that wretched angel in my childhood I've had the sensation of having lived my entire life already. I seem to know it all and yet I can't help hoping that if I hang on long enough I'll become reconciled to things as they are and find them credible.'

'Then you've got a vocation. Why don't you see Pater Lippich?'

'I did, before I left.'

'What did he say?'

'He advised me to see a psychiatrist.'

'He was joking.'

'Exactly.'

They were silent. In the distance they saw a sudden shaft of light from the house as the front door was opened.

'Two years then?' asked Ruprecht. 'Before you can decide?'

'I'm afraid so.' Alfried paused. 'All things considered, primogeniture and the providence of God, it's not such a bad bargain, is it?'

'I suppose not. But why the devil couldn't you have been like other pious types? All those smooth-faced sixth-formers who revelled in Father Jeremy's penance walks and always chose to miss the Easter holidays?'

'I've told you. Greed and uncertainty. You'd better pray for me.'

'If I prayed for anyone I'd pray for your little Jewess. I presume that if she does take her vows instead of marrying you, you'll give me my chance?'

'Immediately.'

'What about your present plans? Are you going back to Baltimore with Fritz?'

'Next week, before the Führer's patience is exhausted. I think we'll find ourselves at war within a month.'

'That might change everything.'

'But not necessarily for the better,' said Alfried. 'You realize we may not get the chance to talk like this again. You'll keep it to yourself?'

'Of course.'

They could see now that someone was standing by the entrance to the house. They saw his big head, the tip of his cigar glowing with each puff, the shape of his solid well-clothed little body dark against the white pillars of the portico.

'The old man himself,' said Alfried. 'Trying to read the future, watching us and wondering.'

'You couldn't manage either of his daughters?'

'No, not for me. They'll do all right provided someone continues to make enough money to endow them. There are quite a few Americans in the offing.' Alfried raised his voice suddenly, 'Well, can you hear them, Fritz?'

'Hear what?'

'The bats.'

'What have you two been up to? Your mother's getting impatient.' He searched the sky, his cigar smouldering between his teeth, his heavy face frowning upwards into the dusk. 'Bats you say?'

'Yes, a pair, just above us.'

'No, no, I can't hear the little beasts. I can't even see them.'

'Not even now, when they're so close?'

'Of course not. One doesn't hear these creatures after one's twenty-five. My specialist tells me that the joints in the ear-bones grow stiff, the membrane coarsens.'

'So?'

'So!' agreed Onkel Fritz, looking suddenly sagaciously into their two faces. 'Whatever else the future holds for me it doesn't promise the squeak of a bat. I heard my last a quarter of a century ago.'

They went into the hall; a flood of light from the Viennese chandeliers falling into the scented air, air scented by pot-pourri, by cigar smoke and the faint aroma of trout cooking in the kitchens.

'Your mother's worried about you,' said the older man as they ascended the stairs. 'It would be as well if you were to have a few minutes alone with her, I think.'

'He means you, you troublesome blighter,' Alfried told Ruprecht.

'Well thank God she's sufficiently interested in me.'

Onkel Fritz paused at the top of the stairs and looked at them a little coldly. 'You may be sure that as long as she's alive your mother will never cease to be interested in either of you,' he said; and he went along to his room to change.

After dinner when they were seated again in the drawing-room Alfried said casually to Ruprecht: 'Oh, I forgot to tell you; the Baron had news for Mama. The Party have offered to let her keep the title of *Frau Kommerzienrat* provided she agrees to the change of name.'

'Have you accepted, Mama?'

'What choice have we? If it pleases them, it can certainly do no harm to us.'

'It certainly pleased von Hoffbach,' said Onkel Fritz. 'In the absence of a monarchy these petty squires hate to be in anyone's debt. The fact that we've given him a seat on the Board so that his wife will be the better able to subsidize her young lovers without getting off her back, is doubtless less galling to him now that Wilhelmina has been allowed to retain a title they had no authority to revoke.'

'Whatever's upset you?' she asked.

'You forget perhaps that before Hitler the von Hoffbachs had no use for any of us. When I bought Schloss Tegernsee and started to launch Anna and Hildegarde – none too easy for a widower – that lot, from the Hohenheims downwards, always cold-shouldered us. We weren't quite rich enough, my dear Wilhelmina, and what was worse, we were a little Jewish.'

'He's right,' said Alfried. 'No brown trout or saddles of venison in those days. D'you remember how Mama schemed to get the young Leo to your birthday parties, Ruprecht?'

'And now,' said Onkel Fritz, 'one hears the poor fellow's developed a patch on the lung and can do little more than waste his time hunting.'

'What bitterness!' said Frau Waitzmann. 'You're all over-looking the real issues. At a time like this, the Baron's in-fluence is cheap at the price of a few thousand marks and a little graciousness. And as for Leo's misfortune, Fritz: you yourself have high blood pressure while I grow blinder every year.'

'True!' said Alfried to himself.

'True, true!' agreed Onkel Fritz, becoming suddenly patriotic and hard-headed. 'Our fortunes are with Greater Germany. We've managed to stick it out, and with dis-cretion and foresight we can survive this time too.'

He began a long speech on this subject, alternately rub-bing his fine hands and gesticulating with his cigar. They were all amused by him, and even Ruprecht, treasuring the memory of his conversation with Alfried, warmed to him, seeing him suddenly as a potential ally who might one day come in as useful as the Baron.

Glowing with after-dinner comfort, the little man went on to point out that the Baron's influence was only matched by his financial stupidity, that thus he would make an admirable negotiator with the new men in Berlin.

'Payment by results,' he elaborated. 'We'll doctor his commission to suit his contracts and any advance information he provides. It's quite obvious that whether or not the Führer invades Poland, the Party will tend increasingly to interfere with private property. We've not the stature of a Krupp or a Thyssen; and we're vulnerable in other respects, our inheritance. One's only hope of remaining wealthy is to *be* wealthy, and our only hope of that lies in suffering, amongst other things, the patronage of a nincompoop like von Hoffbach.'

'But that doesn't help the others – even our own relatives,' said Alfried. 'We should start a fund for those who can't afford to get out of the country. We should have done it long ago when the first shops were shut down.'

'Too risky,' said Ruprecht.

'My God!' went on Alfried. 'What a damned idler *I've* been.'

'My dear, you could have done nothing for anyone in those first years. We were in an impossible position. Our duty, as Ruprecht says, is to survive this crisis and then do all we can later.'

'Alive!' said Onkel Fritz suddenly, inspired by some fresh taste of his fears. 'Persecution's always subtle to start with and that's where most of us went wrong. It's like a flooding river. A few inches and you get wet feet, a few more inches and your goods are ruined. An inch or two beyond that and you're fighting for your life.'

They all saw his strength, his foreignness and exoticism. On one of his short fingers a ring with a single flat-set diamond flashed at them and above it, his eyes, narrow and calculating in relaxation, widened and flashed too. Beside him on the sofa, Frau Waitzmann rustled with concern. In her turn she now put out a hand and groped for one of his, patting it as he had done; making him seem immediately less powerful and sagacious.

Alfried was smiling. He poured a little brandy into his uncle's empty glass and handed it to him.

'A flood, Onkel Fritz! The only question is, how many of us will it drown before it recedes?'

'Only those who are unprepared.'

Frau Waitzmann, who had been searching at first to try to see Alfried's face, following his movements about the room eagerly, now expressed her anxiety by going over to the Madonna and Child which stood on one of the bookcases across the room.

The statue, about two thirds of a metre high, and a Spanish heirloom of Alöis Waitzmann's, had originally been gilded. But now the gold lay only in the deepest folds of the garments and so thinly that it was best discernible by its smoothness to the finger. Elsewhere it had long since been rubbed away, leaving only some reddish pigment scarcely different from the naked wood, scored and scarred by the myriad accidents of piety. The faces, too, had at one time been delicately painted but were now so nearly bare that their expressions appeared to be constantly changing. Only the black glass eyes, shallow, dust-filled in their settings, gleamed clear from the shadows of their sockets. From the arm of the Infant hung Alfried's first wooden rosary, which he had insisted on presenting to the statue at some time in his childhood and which no one had ever thought of removing. Whenever she was near it, Frau Waitzmann had a habit of fiddling with these beads. In the old days, when Kegel brought them down for their night prayers the little boys would often find her standing beside it pulling the beads round the Infant's elbow, as a rope round a pulley. Then she would light the candles and kneel with them to lead the prayers and the singing of festival hymns. This evening, however, she did not grasp the rosary but contented herself by revolving her wedding ring round her finger. She told Onkel Fritz it was obvious there would be no decision that night and that it might be better to carry on the discussion after Mass on the following morning.

Then she asked Ruprecht to go downstairs with her to her bedroom.

'You seem strained,' she told him as they went down the stairs. 'I hope Professor Lillesand hasn't been working you too hard.'

'We keep late hours; but I enjoy the life. At this time of the year I consider I am lucky to be living on a mountain.'

'You must take back with you some fresh eggs and butter. Perhaps tomorrow you might ask the young Leo to let you have some provisions from the farm.'

'Who is this girl they have staying there?'

'A Fräulein von Boehling. The father was in the diplomatic service.'

'One of the old school or one of the Führer's men?'

'A friend of von Papen's. His wife is a Catholic but he himself is a Lutheran.'

'Have they money?'

'I really don't know.' By the door of her room Frau Waitzmann paused. With her clouded eyes she gazed into his face and put a hand to his forehead. 'Why, you're so damp! Whatever's troubling you, Ruprecht?'

He stepped back quickly. 'Nothing, a warm night, that's all. After the Herzogstadt the plain seems like a Turkish bath to me.'

She clucked her tongue twice, vexed by her blindness, then moved into her room without troubling to switch on the light.

'Ruprecht!' she called from the darkness. 'It's not good for young men always to be calculating.'

'But I'm not, Mama.'

'All the time,' she said, moving about in there. 'Like some animal I read of in my girlhood who eats his own tail in the winter time. Do you hear me?'

He switched on the light and followed her in. Indifferent to the light or the dark she was moving things on her dressing-table; the precise accustomed movements of a routine. He watched her unclip her collar of small diamonds and place it neatly in its case.

'Munch, munch, munch!' she said. 'At the bottom of your little hole.'

He trembled. 'With a war in the offing anyone would be tense. Don't you realize I might have to die before I've done anything, Mama? If we invade Poland I might find myself put in the Luftwaffe before Christmas.'

'Of course you may, darling.'

'Before I've done anything,' he repeated, infuriated by her endearment.

'And why not?' she asked. 'If I myself had known that I was to lose your father within seven years of my wedding day and grow blind twenty years later, I might have been tempted to wear black rather than white.'

'If it were Alfried you'd say something. You'd not be so indifferent.'

'And what has Alfried done that is so final?' she asked him, still at her dressing-table.

'That's the whole point. He's done nothing because he doesn't know what he wants to do. But I do know, I know exactly what I want to do and to be.'

He was infuriated by the affection with which she was now looking at him, not even listening attentively, slipping her feet out of her black, low-heeled shoes as if she were a young and capricious bride.

'Oh I know,' he went on. 'You're going to tell me that I *am*; that I owe the gift of life to God, that I must love Him and love my neighbour. That may be all right for Alfried if he's been made that way; but it's not so pleasant for me to have to await his whims, his angels, his cock-eyed visions of the world when my own future is involved.'

She was taking the pins from her hair so that it fell, tress by grey-black tress, to her shoulders and down her broad back. His voice rose as he told her that Alfried could take his, Ruprecht's, place.

'If he's so eager for reality why doesn't he take my place? Let him remain here and join the Luftwaffe and get himself shot down in flames. Then we shall all know where we are.'

She came over to him smiling, framed in her black dress and the canopy of her long hair. But he moved away from her, embarrassed by his sudden sense of her marriage night.

She sat down on her dressing-stool. 'You make me feel so old,' she said.

'I'm not a child, Mama.'

Her face followed the direction of his voice gravely. 'Of course not. I have to deal with a man – a man who is pale with greed.'

'I want only what I believe I'm entitled to.'

'Your birthday?'

'I no longer find that funny, Mama.'

'Won't you ever see that there's only one, that you *are* your birthday, Ruprecht – now and for ever.'

She pressed the bell to summon Emma and turned away from him. He suspected that she might be smiling to herself and asked her why she was laughing at him. For a moment she did not reply. Absurdly, since she could not see her reflection, but from long habit, perhaps, she was looking into her mirror. He could see only half her reflected face.

'I'm not laughing at you, Liebling,' she said, then hearing Kegel enter, changing her tone to one of brightness and amusement, she went on, 'The Ruprecht is angry with me, Kegel!'

Kegel paused by the door, taking everything in with the hungry never-satisfied curiosity of the lonely. She looked at Ruprecht expressionlessly; a cancellation of disapproval, of resignation, of affection and disdain, all in those menial eyes. With a little shrug, in her harsh, respectful voice, never meaningful until she was alone with a single individual of 'her family', she said, 'He always rested the better for his rages, Madam.'

'The Ruprecht is angry because there's something he wants to see and cannot, or else because he knows he could, but he doesn't wish to.'

'Yes, Madam.'

'But one day he will, Kegel. He'll forgive me because he'll see after all, that if anyone did, then I gave him his birthday.' She turned. 'Now go along with you, Ruprecht! Take your anger to bed with you.'

'Good night, Mama.' As he kissed her hand coldly she

suddenly hugged him, her lips touching his cheek before she pushed him away.

Emma switched on the little lamp beside the bed, turned down the summer sheets and pulled out the prie-dieu from the side of the wall to face her dead master's, Herr Gottfried's, wedding gift of the Infant of Prague which stood on a wall plinth facing the bed, a candle flickering beneath it.

As Ruprecht left the room he heard their voices, the first sentences of the trivialities with which they always began: the placings at breakfast, the menus for luncheon and dinner, the times of the Masses. In five or ten minutes, no doubt, they would be discussing more important matters; Onkel Fritz would grow young again in their conversations, his daughters no older than Madam's boys. Briefly, even the Herr Direktor himself might walk again in that quiet room, coming in from his dressing-room bathed and rosy. The two women of Aachen, northerners still, would console and advise one another out of the acknowledged past.

Lights left on all over the place, Ruprecht was complaining in the drawing-room above. The glasses not cleared from the table nor the ash-trays emptied.

Cigar stench, a hollow in the sofa where Fritz had been sitting: books pulled at random from a bookcase by Alfried and not replaced. From Fritz's bathroom the last of the water running down an outside pipe and, doubtless, in an adjoining room, Alfried already sitting on his bed with whatever book he had chosen, reading in that casual way of his, forgetting even to undress.

Ruprecht emptied the ash-trays into a waste-paper basket, put the books back into their shelves and returned the glasses to the pantry. He switched off all the lights and went upstairs to his bedroom, pausing on the nursery landing beside an oak chest on which a night-light wavered in its little glass cup.

Emma again! Two night-lights a week for nearly thirty years. A tiny flame shining not for me nor for Alfried; but for her own loneliness. In front of it, the winter-swing hanging on grey ropes from one of the roof timbers. Were I to sit on it now the hooks would rend the wood. There would be a great noise, cries from Mama and Emma. Alfried would interrupt his reading and Fritz in silk pyjamas would appear in his doorway like an hotel guest on the night of a disaster.

He gave the swing a kick and watched the high-backed seat move past the night-light on the wooden chair, past two black family portraits and an inlaid musical box into which they had long ago slid pfennigs for waltzes and mazurkas. It hung momentarily against a locked door and then swung back to cross, one by one, black height lines ruled by Mama: 'Alfried, May 1914, Philip and cousin Helma, August 1916: Ruprecht, May 1917' and, returning, counterpointed a pile of rapiers and fencing masks straddling two ugly chairs.

Nothing had changed, not even his own desires which were no stronger now than they had been fifteen years ago when Alfried had given him fencing lessons on wet afternoons. He had wanted this house then; to own the Waitzmann House and all that went with it. The same pictures, he now noticed, hung against the wall-paper, the same house-heat accumulated under the roof, the same secrecy and quietness captured him.

Love for it all; she should realize that, he thought. I was the one who put everything back into its place at the end of the day and opened the front of the musical box to save the same coins in my tin. Mama forgets the years of depression when we nearly sold out; she forgets Onkel Fritz trying to raise money and keeping me awake with his talk of disaster and inflation! While Fritz with his wailings and breast-beatings only amused Alfried, to me he was as terrible as a drunken conjuror!

He took the sense of the house again, assuring himself that all was well: Mama and Emma saying goodnight now, Onkel Fritz with his teeth out and a sheaf of papers spread out over his blankets; Alfried, probably at his devotions, lying like a pillar of marble, on his back with his eyes shut. Outside the house, surrounding it on three sides, the sleepless factory, and beyond that, the town, the forests and rivers and mountains of the Baron's 'Greater Germany'.

Inquisitiveness grew in him at this thought. Hesitant as an eavesdropper, it centred about his mother and Alfried and moved on out into the dark countryside. It was true, as he had told her, that there was 'a tremor in the air'. Even Alfried had hinted at it in his remark about the people in the street. All Germany lay under this fiery spell; faces glowing at dusk, the old, resigned at first, but now, like the Baron, stirring to the memories of plumes and cannon. The young, like Technician Schmidt and himself, like the youth of a hundred towns, tasting this spell as if it had been promise of death at some moment of most intense desire.

He changed his mind about going to bed and went downstairs again. He strolled over to the locked garages and roused Höth, the chauffeur who lived over them with his young wife and child.

'Which one, sir?'

'The Mercedes.'

'Going far?'

'Frankfurt. You might tell the Gate I'll be back pretty late.'

'You won't disturb the house. The Mercedes has a full tank and I can top up first thing before I drive the mistress to Mass.'

Ruprecht gave him ten marks. 'Why the uniform?'

'Drill night; looks as though I shan't have to be putting in for training leave this autumn. Going to be the real thing this time.'

'You think so?'

'We had a lecture with films tonight down at the Barracks. There's no doubt the Führer won't take much more of it.'

'What reserve are you in?'

''40 to '41, sir.'

'We'll be losing you, then, if we do decide to teach them a lesson?'

'I'm afraid so, but it shouldn't take long to knock the Poles out. They've got nothing; no discipline, no weapons. I'll be back here in my job in no time.'

Höth saluted him as he drove down to the main gate. The gatekeeper, eating bread and sausage behind his plate glass, saluted him too. That was as it should be. If anything, factory discipline had improved a great deal in recent years. The gatekeeper pressed his switches and the lights blazed out briefly. The long gate slid open and Ruprecht drove off through the town to the North-south autobahn.

In Frankfurt he made straight for the station. If he went to one of the hotels he would not only run the risk of being recognized; but he would also have to take a room for the night. He wanted an easy girl, not some demi-mondaine to whom he would have to lie skilfully and preserve the appearances of earlier acquaintance. He wanted someone fresh, a woman as complicit as one of the mice he had fed to Lillesand's owls, someone nameless and unidentifiable.

In the event, he was lucky. Carrying out a search on foot of half-remembered streets and addresses, he found a small bar with a dance floor in the second street he entered. It was called 'The Rose Garden', a perfect period survival of the early thirties: unobtrusive, seedy and suggestive; so far overlooked by the Party in its unremitting clean-up of indoor vice. In the window a placard advertised:

AMERICAN JAZZ. ALL THE LATEST TUNES.
DANCE HOSTESSES AVAILABLE.
COMPREHENSIVE TARIFF.

Ruprecht opened the glass doors and pushed through a pair of heavy black curtains into a deserted cloak-room space. A middle-aged woman from a nearby table rose and came forward to meet him. The bodice of her black, sequined dress was dusty with face-powder. She had a perfectly smooth face and eyes as expressionless as burn-holes in a sheet. She handed him a bunch of paper roses of different colours and told him that each of them entitled him to dance with any hostess of his choice at five marks a time.

At the far end of the room there was a small dance floor, in front of which there was a bar with a photograph of the Führer behind it, whilst on the opposite side there was a jazz band of four sick-looking men playing out-of-date tunes.

A group of students were drinking cheap wine at one of the tables. There were half a dozen couples dancing, a few middle-aged men sitting at the bar, and in the darker corners patrons and hostesses whispering together over more expensive wine. The students shouted to Ruprecht and made a place for him on the wall-seat. The woman with the smooth face came over and smiled at them. Looking up at her, Ruprecht was reminded fleetingly of his mother and experienced a satisfaction so intense that it was almost as tangible as a hand passed across his forehead.

'You must dance,' she told them. 'If all you wish to do is to drink you should have gone to a beer hall.'

'I'll dance if you'll dance with me,' said one of them.

'You're not too old, is she?' said another, patting her on the buttocks.

'I'm not too old; but it's not my job,' she said automatically.

'But there are other things?'

One of them got up and put his arms round her. She kissed him lightly and then expertly detached herself and walked away.

The students resumed a political discussion, half-drunken, not wholly bored and spiced with references to their immediate intentions. They kept eyeing the hostesses who were not already dancing, chattering about them with the awed familiarity with which most young men discuss prostitutes. On the surface they appeared to have accepted Ruprecht immediately; but he was determined to give nothing away to them.

'I tell you, the Polish army is as disorderly as a Polish household,' one of them was insisting. 'The Wehrmacht will clean it up in six weeks at the outside.'

'That's inevitable. They've not only got their own Jews now to undermine their economy, but they've got a lot of ours too.'

'Oh God! Politics all evening,' complained the young man sitting next to Ruprecht. 'I'd rather talk about Trottie. That's a shocking cough she has. Whoever takes her home tonight will have to stop at the chemist for throat lozenges.'

But the first speaker suddenly rounded on him. 'Can't you think of anything else?' He turned to Ruprecht. 'What's your opinion? Should we go into Poland or should we wait for them to sell it to us without a struggle?'

'Depends on the price.'

'Well, we got Czechoslovakia for nothing. British Jewry instructed Chamberlain to give it away. Why shouldn't the same thing happen over Poland?'

'If only I had twenty marks,' said Hans. 'I'd take Trottie home, germs and all. I'm not so high-minded as Peter and if there's going to be a war I want to enjoy myself first.'

But the student named Peter ignored him; drawing on his cigarette he leaned across the table and asked Ruprecht what he thought of 'the Jewish problem'. Didn't he think that before the Fatherland fought for its living-space, all the non-Aryans should be thrown out of the country so that they should not weaken it?

'But who would take them?' Ruprecht asked him.

'No one, that's the trouble. The Jews are by nature subservient. It's well known in the modern world that the Führer's right. It was Jews and Jewish religion which corrupted Rome. Christianity's a slave religion.'

'He doesn't want to talk about religion,' said Hans. 'He's come here like the rest of us – to get himself a drink and a girl.'

'Quite right!'

'There you are, for God's sake dry up, Peter, and leave him alone.'

'But I want to know. If you don't mind my asking, don't you agree that Christianity bears all the marks of Jewish subservience?'

'I want to know which girl you've got your eye on,' said Hans, tapping Ruprecht on the arm. 'I know them all and I can tell you which one gives the best value for the money.'

'What about the redhead at the third table?'

'That's Kyra, she's half-Italian. She's good but she always smells of garlic.'

'Where does she live?'

'That's the snag. She lives right out of town. If you want her you have a long walk back.'

'I've a car.'

'A car?' said Peter. 'Then you must have views on things.'

'Does it follow?'

'Yes; even at our age property and opinions go together. Now tell me what you think about religion, and then I'll let you get on with your own plans. D'you agree or not that Christianity's a slave religion?'

'Certainly.' Ruprecht was angered by his brooding persistence.

'You do? Why?'

'Yes, why?' they chorused.

'Because the Christian, like the slave and the Jew, has nothing to lose. He gets down on the ground before God so low that he trips up his masters.'

'Ah, good!' they all shouted.

'Yes, yes.'

'He's never content,' Ruprecht continued, momentarily believing it and thinking now of Onkel Fritz. 'Subservience doesn't satisfy him for long because it's still not little enough in face of this god-image; so he rebels and crosses the Red Sea, leaving plagues behind him.'

All the students became very much excited, one or two of them actually clapped.

'You speak well,' Peter told him. 'You hold forth as if you really believed in your theories. But you've missed out one essential.'

'You think so?'

'Yes, the biological aspect.'

'What about it?'

'I can't tell you here. You can't discuss serious anti-semitism in public places. But later, if you'd like to come out with me, we could have a real session.' He followed him down the room.

'I wanted to ask you. Are you a Party member? I'm joining the S.S. next month and I think you might have a big future in it. They're looking for new blood. If you gave me your address I'd send you some of the literature. We might go a long way together.'

'I'll think about it. By the way, what were these biological aspects you were talking about?'

Peter lowered his voice. 'It's a question of the Jewish germ-plasm. It contaminates the Gothic substance. That's what we've got to eliminate. Don't you realize that if man has Jewish blood in him he's corrupted before he starts? He can never stand up against the tests that History demands of him.'

'You really believe that?'

'Of course I do. It's been proved in this century. The Great War proved it; the stab in the back. But for the usury of the Jews we Germans could have fought on three fronts and still won the war.'

'That's a theory I've never been able to accept.'

'Perhaps not. But if we could meet again I know I could convince you. How long are you in Frankfurt?'

'I leave for home tomorrow.'

'Then you'll give me your address?'

'I can't, I'm afraid.'

'Why not?'

'Because my work is secret.'

'Are you on research?'

Ruprecht smiled at him. 'I don't want to have to be un-pleasant; but you're a little too persistent – and indiscreet. If you ask many more questions I might decide to answer them, and then you could be in trouble.'

'How in trouble?' Peter looked a little doubtful of him-self. Ruprecht withdrew a pace and smiled again.

'For persistence in face of discretion. I might find it necessary to have your motives checked. You don't sound to me an altogether ideal recruit for the S.S. One of the first lessons you should learn is that Security doesn't like people who mix business with pleasure.'

This had the calculated effect. Peter stood back from him and Ruprecht turned and left him. A few minutes later he noticed that with the exception of Hans, who was dancing with Trottie, all the students had left 'The Rose Garden'.

At midnight, Kyra disguised herself with a pair of spec-tacles and Ruprecht guessed that she must have her room in a fairly respectable area. In 'The Rose Garden' she had looked quite exotic; but now, in a limp coat, her hair in a bun on the nape of her thin neck, and her long ear-rings removed, she looked like some Party official's secretary returning from overtime at the office.

'Where to?' he asked her as he got into his car.

'I live out by the airport.'

'You'll have to direct me when we leave the main road.'

'Are you spending the night?' She was touching at her face, putting a stick of solid scent to her wrists, pressing at her bun with the thin fingers of her left hand. The smell of her scent reached him, mixed with that of benzine and a trace of garlic.

'I don't know about the whole night; but I don't like to be hurried.'

She kept silent as they passed through a heavily flagged area, the remains of a local rally or the preparations for one. There were slogans above the tram wires; the black, red, and white flags hung in scores from their standards beneath the yellow sodium lights and the green blaze of the moon, motionless or swaying slightly in contrary directions like the palms of giant, slowly clapping hands; each one tattooed in its centre with the ring and swastika.

'You didn't dance,' she said suddenly. 'The boss doesn't like us to leave with those who haven't danced. He'll start getting at me on Monday.'

'Then why did you accept me?'

'Because I wanted the lift. But you didn't buy enough. You didn't buy enough wine, you didn't even buy flowers or chocolates for me.'

'What time do you usually get home?'

'I catch the last bus to the Niederräder Depot and walk from there. It takes me more than an hour.'

'Tonight you'll be home in fifteen minutes.'

'That makes no difference to the boss.'

'He should have bigger worries than that. I can't understand why with the clean-up he wasn't thrown out of business months ago.'

'He's got influence.'

'He's going to need it if he hopes to keep open. Why d'you

51

stay with him if he bullies you so much? At a time like this you could do something better for a living.'

'It suits me. I've plenty of other worries.'

'Such as?'

'Money, for one.'

'Oh, money, there's more than one way of earning that.' He handed her his wallet. 'Take five notes. Four for yourself and one for the boss if you're really worried.'

She slid out the money quickly and handed the wallet back to him. 'I can tell you now. I've a little boy to support.'

'That's all right, but don't confide in me.'

'Everything costs money, you know. His shoes, his baby food. He doesn't live with me, he lives with my mother but we don't get on and she charges me the earth for looking after him.'

'You should farm him out then, or put him up for adoption until you get yourself a different job.'

'I've tried other jobs. I've worked in shops, I've worked on the land and in cinemas; but I want Hans Jürgen to have the best. I want him to have holidays in Italy with my father's people and this is the only way for me to find that sort of money; at least until I can get married.'

'Married? You don't really imagine you'll ever get married while you're doing this, do you?'

'Of course I do. We all do. The girls often get married, and besides, with me it was different. I got caught when I was seventeen. I only did it once and then he went off to the Sudetenland.'

'I told you – I don't want your life-story.'

'But you gave me advice.'

'No arguments. I've given you some money, double the amount you'd probably have asked me for. Now keep your eyes on the road and give me some directions.'

'Turn left at the end of this road. Then you carry straight on under the trees, turn left again at the end of it. It's a bad road, it peters out into the fields. My rooms are in the second half of the last bungalow.'

'Who lives in the other half?'

'Oh she's on night-shift in the new powder factory. She doesn't get in till six o'clock.'

'Good.'

He parked his car on the grass verge and waited while she unlocked the gate in the tall wire-netting surrounding the plot. A dog barked monotonously in the distance. Heavy lorries of a military convoy were passing down the main road three hundred yards away. There was no night wind. A web of cloud over Frankfurt, motionless as the leaves of the chestnut trees, reflected the glow from the town's centre.

As he followed her up the path to the house, her keys jingling in her hand, his shoes crunched on its surface and he looked up, involuntarily scanning the tree-tops for bats.

'Don't turn on any lights,' he told her. 'And don't undress. We'll stay out here in the garden.'

'I'm not doing that, not for anyone.'

'Give me the keys.'

She tried to snap them back in her handbag; but he was too quick for her.

'At least you might let me in the car,' she said.

'I'll get rugs. No one will see.'

She made no attempt to move but waited while he went back to the Mercedes and unlocked the boot, coming back to her with an armful of rugs.

'Why d'you want this?' she asked him from the shadow of a tree.

'More natural.'

'More natural than a bed? You're crazy.'

'I don't like beds.'

'What about me? Don't I count?'

'You don't want to count, do you?'

'I might, with someone.'

He kissed her and then drew her down beside him. 'I shan't keep you long.'

'You can spend the weekend if you like? For nothing. If only you'll come in the house?'

Alfried would be asleep. When he awoke he would have an exact continuity in his mind, the smooth transition from the evening before into the morning after. No self-questioning, no trial of his strength or weakness. He had said that discrepancies were the hall-mark of the Creator; but he did not invite them.

'What are you thinking?' she asked.

'Amongst other things I was thinking of those fellows in "The Rose Garden".'

'Oh them.'

'D'you know them?'

'I know Hans.'

'What about Peter?'

'I've never been with him. He doesn't go for us much. He's always on about politics.'

'And the Jews?'

'Yes.'

'What do you think of his opinions?'

'I don't listen to him. Jews are no different from anyone else.'

He put his arms round her and they lay down together on the rug. For several minutes there was no sound, the dog was silent. The last of the convoy had passed. He could hear her breathing and smell the garlic behind the cologne.

Chapter 2

'We live so damned uncomfortably,' Ruprecht told Onkel Fritz the next morning after Mass as they took their places in the Mercedes outside the Marienkirche. 'When we get in, Alfried will be sitting over a pot of cold coffee and half a dozen slices of toast. If we're going to start a war on this diet what on earth shall we be eating when it ends?'

'Something in that,' said Onkel Fritz, who was clattering through a newspaper he had bought on his way across the square.

From the belfry the carillon was thrashing out for the next Mass, an aggressive noise to Ruprecht's mind; he had taken a dislike to the tenor bell during the consecration on which act that morning he had cast an especially cold eye. Accompanying his mother to the communion rail, always an embarrassing task when one had to wait there without receiving the sacrament oneself, its notes had continued to echo in his mind like the ringing of an iron mountain.

'Why can't they keep quiet about it?' he had thought, dissociating himself from the priesthood and the congregation. 'Must all the motorists and marchers be reminded every Sunday that the faithful are at their mysteries?' Boom! Boom! Boom! The priest holding up his wafer faithfully, the fabulous cup glittering in a sun-shaft; the snap of the Host; the covert nibble and swallow as one man consumed God in the species of solid and liquid.

'Alfried's is an excellent idea,' he advised Onkel Fritz and his mother. 'By going early to the Jesuits he not only gets the best of our breakfast but a cup of coffee with Pater Lippich as well. I can see I shall have to take my religion more seriously.'

But Frau Waitzmann, grumpy and hungry herself, was

watching nearly sightlessly through her window. She told him he'd feel better when he'd had something to eat.

'Had I known you weren't taking communion this morning I would have asked them to give you something before we left.'

'I preferred my bed, Mama; and besides, I always hope the Sunday breakfast's going to improve.'

'It's difficult for them, dear; Kegel is getting old and those two girls are only half-trained.'

'No servants at all in the Northern States unless you're as rich as Croesus,' Onkel Fritz put in.

'That's different. Over there they have labour-saving devices; but in Bavaria we get the worst of both worlds: incompetent country girls and antiquated kitchens.'

Höth was having to drive very slowly. The Square and the surrounding streets were full of pedestrians and youth-marchers. Pigeons flung themselves high in the morning wind. Cold white clouds swept fast across a bright sky.

'Anything in the papers?' Ruprecht asked.

'A Goebbels editorial on the Warsaw Government and some violent border clashes.'

'But we're not at war?'

'Not yet, but I think I might be wiser to leave on Thursday whether Alfried is joining me or not.' Onkel Fritz folded his newspaper neatly across his knees. 'I'm beginning to think that on the grounds of his uncertainty it might be best if he returned with me for a time. He's in no condition to handle things here at present. As he said, he can always get back later on and it may even be possible for me to accompany him.'

'If he's had a talk with Pater Lippich he may well have reached a decision. No doubt he'll tell us when we get in,' said Frau Waitzmann, making it clear that she wanted no further discussion in front of the chauffeur.

They remained silent as the car threaded its way through the narrow streets of the old town and entered the factory gate.

As Ruprecht had prophesied, Kegel had laid the circular table in the dining-room with an assortment of cold sausage, ryebread toast and a silver pot of tepid coffee. Alfried was lounging in there on the bearskin sofa reading the newspaper. He had his long legs up, the feet crossed at the ankles showing his American silk socks. The morning sunlight striking through the netting enmeshed him in a froth of folds barred with the shadows of the lattice. A band, heading a parade of the local regiment, was approaching down the Schellenstrasse. The click of the side-drum, like that of a large clock ticking somewhere outside, penetrated the orange light thrown from the wooden floor and the pale gold walls. Alfried rose to kiss Frau Waitzmann and then sat down again.

'So we're to have no more lemon juice,' he said. 'It's not grown in the pure Aryan soil. One crosses the Atlantic to learn that rhubarb juice is more healthful and natural for the true Germanic blood.'

'Cheaper at any rate,' said Onkel Fritz.

'Guns instead of butter,' put in Ruprecht, helping himself to some.

'I resent a diet of lies,' said Alfried.

'But there may, after all, be something in it,' Ruprecht suggested. 'The Chinese don't eat potatoes, the British can do without rice. Discrepancies in dietetics may well be part of the divine plan.'

'No doubt; but such jokes are dangerous if one has to travel long distances in order to find someone with whom one may share them.'

'One doesn't have to lose one's sense of humour just because one is coming to believe in the historical destiny of the Nation, surely?' replied Ruprecht.

'Historical destiny, what nonsense! History's no more than the actions and discussions of a few families. *This* is history! This sitting together round a meal discussing principles.'

'Politics shouldn't be discussed on empty stomachs,' Frau Waitzmann told them.

'Alfried hasn't got an empty stomach,' Ruprecht retorted. 'His ill-temper's entirely due to early Mass. There's nothing like it for making one surly.'

'I'm not surly.'

'Then perhaps it was your conversation with Pater Lippich. Jesuits for breakfast are even worse than continued fasting.' Ruprecht drank some coffee noisily. 'What's the trouble? Did he tell you your vocation's still in the nest? It must be damned uncomfortable for you sitting on a doubtful egg like this.'

'Ruprecht, you mustn't be so spiteful.'

'But I'm feeling spiteful, Mama. I rather thought the air would have cleared overnight. I'm not particularly spiritual myself; but I'd imagined that on his return to his first father confessor's church, the Holy Ghost might have tapped Alfried on the shoulder and that we'd have come in to find him looking serene and radiant.'

'As you would yourself if you'd suddenly decided you'd make a good physicist?' asked Alfried. 'What a romantic you are. Why on earth should a vocation make one look any more serene than the decision to become a vet or an industrialist?'

'It's not the same thing. For myself I'll admit I should probably never smile again.'

Over the noise of the marching men and the band which had just struck up outside the window, Frau Waitzmann interrupted them:

'What did Pater Lippich advise you, Alfried?'

'I'm sorry, I can't hear you, Mama.'

'She wants to know what Pater Lippich suggested,' Ruprecht repeated. 'Are you going to go back with Onkel Fritz or stay here with Mama?'

'What a frightful noise!' Alfried got up and started to circle the table. 'The Father thinks I should give myself another year in the States, attached to one of the universities as a post-graduate.' He had raised his voice in a crescendo to overcome the noise of the parade.

'Very sound advice,' bellowed Onkel Fritz. 'Every foundation should spend as much or more on research as it does on new plant.'

'New what?' asked Ruprecht.

'Plant!' shouted Onkel Fritz.

But at that moment the loudspeakers in the square and the main streets were switched on to relay an official party address on the Polish situation by the gauleiter. Blurred, iron-tongued, phrases mingled with the receding strains of the band and resounded through the room. Alfried jumped on to the sofa and swung the shutters across in front of the windows, plunging them in half-darkness. He switched on the light:

'We're becoming a nation of shouters. Do you know that this town is now as noisy as New York?'

'It's a question of confidence,' Ruprecht said with the idea of goading him into further political admissions. 'If a nation doesn't make itself heard at a time like this no one takes it seriously.'

'A really confident government never needed gagging,' insisted Alfried. 'All this bellowing and strutting's a bad sign.'

'Then you should give Pater Lippich the hint. When he gets on his feet in front of a microphone he yells his head off.'

'His motives are a little different.'

Ruprecht smiled and slightly changed the subject. 'You missed an excellent sermon at the Marienkirche this morning, didn't he, Mama? The necessity of patriotism and obedience to the temporal order.'

'Under all circumstances?'

But Ruprecht ignored the question. His late night and the accumulated vexations of the past twenty-four hours gave him a malign and satisfying self-confidence. Alfried seemed to him this morning an inconsiderable figure, quite different from the man with whom he had discussed things at twilight the evening before.

'Yes,' he went on. 'We were advised on resignation to the providence of God and told that prayer was the key to our dilemmas.'

'Prayer is never shouted,' said Alfried. 'I don't mind betting that if one voice was raised on Calvary it was that of the unrepentant thief.'

'What about Christ? He's supposed to have shouted with a loud voice.'

'Only at the end, at the moment of death.'

'A shouted prayer, nevertheless.'

Frau Waitzmann made some small movement and Onkel Fritz wiped his red lips with a napkin.

'They should have passed Him up, not vinegar, but a lighted cigarette,' Ruprecht said. 'That's the way *we* may have to die if there's a war.'

Frau Waitzmann put down her cup. 'You've both said quite enough. Ruprecht, if you're going out to Schönform you'd better get started.'

'He doesn't mean it, Mama. He's worried about his future; that's all.'

'Since it doesn't depend on my own decision but on yours, I have to be worried about it. I wouldn't mind being a second son, I'd accept the wretched providence of God if only you'd make up your mind about things.'

'Ruprecht, since you're behaving like an adolescent you shall be treated as one. You're to have no further discussions about your future until you've shown signs of maturity.'

Ruprecht ran up to his room to change into clothes suitable for an afternoon with the aristocracy.

The head forester's daughters were playing on the forecourt quay when he reached Schönform. He saw them as he drove past the water-gate, a wide archway opening between the courtyard and the ornamental waters which lapped the castle's pink walls. Going slowly to avoid picnickers already awaiting the afternoon's tour, he saw the two little girls with their white pigtails crouching quite still over some pebble-game, their starched dresses held out as stiffly as the folded wings of the swan floating in front of them.

In the stable yard, Leo von Hoffbach was in conversation with Wempe, their father; the two of them standing slackly in the thick sunshine filling the valley. Leo waved to him casually and then went on talking to the Verwalter, who gave Ruprecht a salute of some sort. As he approached, Leo's eyes followed him as alertly and disinterestedly as if he had been some beast that was out of season. He greeted him and then went on talking about his neighbour Prince Hohenheim's potato crop, not troubling to lead Ruprecht anywhere, nor yet, by his manner, suggesting that he was welcome to overhear the discussion. 'This is breeding,' Ruprecht told himself, standing blackly between them. 'This fellow behaves as though it were not a year since we last met, but five minutes. He gives nothing of himself away, not even his hostility!'

'You could get a sack or two off his bailiff and we'll roll them in the long stretch just above the lake,' von Hoffbach was saying. 'If that doesn't fetch them in a dry autumn, nothing will.'

'No good,' said Wempe, who rarely called Leo 'sir'. 'He'll realize what we're after.'

Leo's thin cheeks, faintly tanned, tensed and relaxed beneath the shadow of his green hat. 'Then we'll do some gleaning one evening. For some reason the boars prefer his crop to anything I can grow or buy. We've asked him for seed a dozen times; but he always makes excuses.'

'That auerhahn last winter?' suggested the bailiff.

'Oh, just on the borders, Wempe.'

'Then maybe the tree was walking that morning? From where I was that bird looked to be fifty metres inside the Prince Hohenheim's boundary.'

'You're planning a boar shoot?' Ruprecht asked.

'First get your potatoes, Waitzmann. For three seasons now, ever since Hohenheim started growing some Danish variety, the Schönform sows have chosen to farrow in his woods. Somehow we've got to tempt them back as soon as the main crop's harvested.'

'A weighty affair. Have you any idea where your father is?'

'Oh, he's about. You'll probably find him in the lake-room listening to the news.'

Leo and Wempe moved off with Ruprecht a little behind them.

'He's expecting you,' Leo told him. 'It would be a good thing if you could take his mind off Berlin for an afternoon.

Since you interested him in your factories he seems to have no enthusiasm for anything but politics and finance. Isn't that so, Wempe?'

'The Herr Baron hasn't lifted a gun in twelve months.'

'In industry, guns are only an embarrassment,' said Ruprecht.

But the Baron, who was restless, had winded Ruprecht from afar and came clattering out of a turret doorway as they crossed the courtyard.

'Ah! My dear chap; you're on time.'

He was bluff with surface health and impatience, an autumn man in the bright sunshine; to Ruprecht's eyes, a tree heavy with fruit and not too sound in the limb. He was obviously longing to find out how things had gone with Frau Waitzmann at the morning conference but must not divulge his anxiety until they were alone. He cast his blue eyes round the courtyard and the pink walls of his castle, espying the two little girls who were hovering like white butterflies round the group of men.

'A splendid day, Leo, we shall have a lot of visitors, I think.'

'As long as they don't disturb the pheasants, they can do what they like.'

'I'll see to that, sir,' Wempe assured him. 'We don't get much trouble since I put up the notices.'

'Ah, they're tired of the newspapers,' reflected the Baron. 'If they prefer the works of nature and of art, who can blame them? Undoubtedly there's not the same enthusiasm as in the time of the Hohenzollerns; but if it comes to it they will, of course, stand up to it. We can't provide them with bloodless victories indefinitely.' He looked at Ruprecht. 'There comes a time when it may be good for one to have a bluff called.'

'Why the switch?' Ruprecht wondered. '*We* have evidently provided the victories but *one* has put up a bluff. He identifies himself with the Party when it comes to the victories; but when it comes to my own battles he's cannier. Is he thinking that it's up to me to deal with Alfried – without his assistance?'

'You might take a turn round the lake this afternoon,' Wempe was advising Leo. 'I saw a group of buck there last night.'

'At the water?'

'Yes, sir. The Prince will be praying for rain soon or there'll be nothing left for his winter shooting.'

Leo's jaw muscles were tensing in and out. There was a coldly vacant look in his delicate eyes; the green of shadows beneath spring larches. He's like a dreaming dog, Ruprecht thought, behind his eyes he's chasing something all day long; but his whimperings he keeps to himself.

'Even Hohenheim will have little time for hunting this winter, I think,' said the Baron with satisfaction. 'But we must not antagonize the old man. We must be honourable in small matters as well as large. I've no doubt whatsoever that when the time does come, he'll acknowledge his responsibilities to the country just as I have had to do.'

The two little girls had grown bolder. At first they had not wished to be noticed, but now they did; so they abandoned their old game and played a new and more provocative one. The ten-year-old Friederike began to march round the courtyard keeping close to the rosy walls. She was joined by her sister and together they chanted: 'The Princess is coming, the Princess is coming!'

'I shouldn't be too sure, Father,' went on Leo, ignoring their clamour. 'Wempe tells me that this year the Prince has doubled his potato acreage and is leaving plenty in the ground for his guests.'

'Guests?'

'*Our* boars, Father. There'll be work for Waitzmann, too, this afternoon if he wants it. He can help us borrow and roll a bag or two of the little potatoes into our own land.'

'The Princess is coming, the Princess is coming!' shouted the two little girls who had now forgotten why they had started this game and really did believe that a princess might appear at any moment.

'What!' exclaimed the Baron, frowning over the Hohenheim business and only too ready to be distracted by the children. 'A Princess, little ones? What Princess? There is no Princess coming to Schönform today.'

'But she has come,' Friederike called back, so cheekily that her little sister Irma grew bold too. 'Yes, Herr Baron, the Princess is upstairs in the Lake Room. She came last night and only we saw her – from our bedroom window.'

'She is from Rome,' added Friederike, 'and she has a hundred pieces of luggage.'

The Verwalter, their father, was pleased and embarrassed at the same time. 'Ah, they mean the Fräulein von Boehling, Herr Baron. They've been listening to some nonsense of Maria's.'

'But, of course! How slow of me.'

'Their heads are full of fairy stories, Baron.'

'So they should be, Verwalter, at their age. Come here, Friederike, and tell me what sort of a carriage this princess drives.'

'Oh, it was a golden coach,' said the child, 'drawn by six Windsor greys.'

'Well! Well! And what are Windsor greys?'

'Special horses, from England, Herr Baron.'

'They've been looking through old magazines from London,' said their father. 'They muddle everything up.'

'We don't, Father. The English kings are all Germans. All that is good in England is from Germany.'

'Bless my soul!' said the Baron.

'Shakespeare, the poet, was a German,' said Friederike.

'But the Prime Minister is a Jew,' said her sister.

'Ach! They've been listening too much to that wireless,' insisted the Verwalter, who was now feeling apologetic. 'Run along in and get washed before your dinners.'

'What a thing!' said the Baron. 'These children never cease to surprise one. Such memories. We must tell Alexandra that she is a princess from Rome. I believe I mentioned her to you yesterday morning, didn't I, Ruprecht?'

'You said something to Alfried.'

'A charming girl. Her father asked me to put her up on her way from Rome. They themselves will have to remain there for some weeks and he tells me that at this time of the year the heat is quite appalling. Alexandra was wilting like a mountain bloom.'

'A nervous, anaemic sort of girl,' thought Ruprecht, in rebellion against the Baron's poetry. 'Cannot stand heat or spaghetti.'

'She's on her way to Berlin, you say, sir?'

'Yes, I'm taking her with me by road tomorrow morning. Unless she decides to take up quarters in a hospital, she may well be my wife's, Carin's, guest for a year or two and that would be a good thing from many points of view.' The Baron broke off a little brusquely and turned to Leo. 'I'd be glad if you'd tell Maria that we'll be in for luncheon in ten minutes. You might give Alexandra some wine and apologize for our discourtesy. Ruprecht and I are going to take a little walk before eating.'

They made their way through the back of the courtyard to the water-garden.

'You mentioned a hospital,' said Ruprecht, who had been brooding over this trifle.

'Yes, yes, maternity work or something of the sort.'

'She's not a nun, then? No vocation?'

'Vocation? What on earth put such an idea into your head?'

'I was thinking of Alfried,' said Ruprecht with all the blandness of truth. 'I discovered last night that my future depends almost entirely on the course of his love affair with a postulant he's met in America.'

'Indeed!' The Baron, only minimally reassured, was still unable to wrench his suspicions of Ruprecht's oddness back into his pocket. 'Well, there might be worse reasons from your point of view.'

'From ours you mean, sir.'

'Oh, you're too generous, my dear boy. Now tell me: how did it go last night after I left? How did your uncle take it?'

'That's immaterial, sir. I thought you'd understand; Alfried and I have reached agreement – privately!'

He told the Baron of their bargain: that if Alfried did not marry his postulant within two years he would waive his claim to the factories; and that in the meantime he would suggest that Ruprecht be given a free hand with their management.

'Capital!' exclaimed the Baron sincerely, for he was confident he would be able to handle Ruprecht profitably. 'We could scarcely have hoped for more. With my connexions in Berlin and your eagerness we should be in a position to do an excellent job of work for everyone – not least, of course, for the Fatherland. I'm not decrying your brother at all when I say that I feel that he lacks the necessary aptitudes for such a venture.'

'Bit of a dreamer,' said Ruprecht comfortably.

'Exactly!' The Baron's self-confidence was entirely restored. 'If your brother's hesitating about the responsibilities at this stage, then your control is as good as won. I have a dread of eccentrics, you know,' he went on with surprising candour. 'Especially in time of war. It seems to me that your brother . . .'

'He's too innocent, sir.' Ruprecht repeated the remark in order to make himself quite clear: 'Alfried's whole trouble is that he's too innocent to be greedy. But at least he has the wit to know it.'

'Greed, you say? Why yes, I suppose you're right, Ruprecht.'

The Baron's gaze passed over the water-garden, the shining streams and the clear surfaces of the pools, the weeds smothering the alpines planted so long ago by Carin. The sweetness of home betrayed him to intimacy.

'Now that's what I miss in Leo. I can't persuade him to take any interest in these affairs, nor see any connexion between them and our home. Anything that creeps or flies will absorb his attention; but the affairs of men and of Germany; no!'

'Not so different from Alfried, perhaps,' suggested Ruprecht.

But the Baron would not be parted from his moment of sentiment. 'I'm a very lonely man at times, Ruprecht. I have such thoughts! Though I've seen so much both in the small way and the larger, I've accomplished so little. All this, for instance.' He waved a hand at the castle, the garden, the floor of the valley and the still dark pines. 'Propped up on what? Promises that I myself have never fulfilled. Germany in microcosm.'

'An excellent image!' Ruprecht's judicial tone effectively concealed his yawn. 'After the confidences comes what?' he was wondering. 'Each one is a victory for me; and, after all, what's a little boredom?'

'It is true,' continued the Baron with one of the Führer's long oratorical pauses. 'Everything is here. It is why the people come out here Sunday after Sunday. Who can grasp the Matter of Germany save a Friedrich or a Bismarck? But who, standing where we stand, could fail to catch its spirit?'

'You are excited then, sir? There's something new in the wind?'

'There is indeed, and from what I've heard it's a warmer wind than we had any right to expect; and it's blowing, of all places, from Moscow.'

'Now we're coming to it!' thought Ruprecht, as his companion, sunk in melodramatic thought, gazed at the pines on the far side of the valley.

After a moment, the Baron, taken aback by his affected indifference to this astonishing hint, became voluble and even more indiscreet.

'I'm persuaded, almost,' he said, 'that we're entering an era in which anything may happen, Ruprecht. And what happens, I ask you, if at the right time one jumps free of political conscience and adopts instead a doctrine of expedience?'

How flattering it is of him to bore me like this, thought Ruprecht, saying, 'You mean the wind from Moscow, Baron? One hears so many rumours; but even Alfried, who has been swallowing a lot of America propaganda, has made no mention of this one.'

'*Rumour*, my dear boy! Do you think I've brought you out here to feed you on rumours? What I have to tell you this morning is not yet a half-day old. I received a telephone call from the Chancellery only two hours ago.' The Baron did not even glance round suspiciously, nor trouble to lower his voice. He was magnificently the proprietor of his confidences. 'I refer to the march *with* the East, a Russo–German entente.'

Ruprecht said, 'Ah!' and kicked a pebble into a pool. The Baron stood stock-still.

'Then you're bewildered?' he suggested, with satisfaction. 'I thought you might be, quick as you may be. No, no, please don't interrupt me. We understand one another well enough. What I want to tell you – and you must for the present keep it to yourself – can be said very shortly. Within a few hours or days at the most, the little winesalesman who represents our country abroad will secure his biggest contract yet – in Moscow!'

The ripples from the stone were spreading smoothly over the surface of the pool. Uplifted by a sudden broadening of consciousness beneath the feathery Bavarian sky, not looking at one another, the two men watched them. Their differences vanished; for the moment they were united in vision and mood. They saw men hurrying, hand-shaking. They saw papers being signed; the movements of armies, the murmur of war, thunder, lightning and gain. Then they turned and went back through the courtyard to luncheon with Leo and the young Fräulein von Boehling.

'And what a charming girl she is,' Ruprecht decided as they sat in the Lake Room after luncheon; 'like that dark mountain honey in which there's a flavour of iron beneath the sweetness.'

The Baron had gone to his study to rest and they were sitting in this cool room, full of the scent of pines and flowers. Reflections from the water wavered over the ceiling and a wall of portraits in the shadowed end of the room. Since at present it was too hot to stir out into the garden or woods, they sat where they were, awaiting the coffee which Maria would bring at three o'clock.

Leo von Hoffbach sat keenly, ridiculously polite over his impatience. Fräulein von Boehling sat as though she had never yawned or felt sleepy in her life, turning first to one of the young men and then to the other, with a hardly perceptible movement of her head. Ruprecht sat closely back in his chair as the sole proprietor of the well-guarded secret he knew himself to be. They talked of Italy, Leo of its hunting, Ruprecht of its Galleries and Fräulein von Boehling of its churches. Leo suggested that the art galleries were a great waste of time and extremely tiring.

'I can't understand why these droves of people come here every weekend to gaze at the murals in our chapel.'

'If nobody came,' asked Ruprecht, 'to whom would you show off your antlers and your boar's snouts?'

'Ah, but the chapel is so beautiful,' sighed Fräulein von Boehling. 'That fountain by the piscina's quite unique, I think. This morning at Mass . . .'

One could see her checking herself over so intimate an indiscretion; and her cheeks burned a little in the hot room. Both men came to her rescue as she concluded reticently, 'It was so beautiful.'

Agreeably, Ruprecht said, 'My mother thinks it's a direct link with Rome.'

'Ah, yes, they liked always to build their villas by running water. What more natural than that the spring of Christianity in Europe . . . .'

But Leo interrupted her. 'Our priest here, who's an Italian, says it's German romanticism to have that thing bubbling away through the Consecration.'

Ruprecht laughed and Fräulein von Boehling was fascinated. Indeed they were all three fascinated, tasting justification in this sudden criticism of themselves from outside.

'Really?' asked Fräulein von Boehling, drawing the word out in the cooing innocent way of a wood-pigeon.

Leo put his hands to his mouth and imitated this sound immediately. A brooding wood-pigeon might have been in the room with them.

'He fools all the game like that,' Ruprecht told her. 'By whimpering into his palm as if he were its young I've seen him fetch a buck from the woods and then shoot it.'

'How talented he must be.'

'Not talented enough to teach Waitzmann any of it. In the woods he stamps about like an elephant at a mousehole.'

69

'Oh, surely not,' she said with virginal sympathy. 'I wouldn't have thought Herr Waitzmann was at all that sort of a person.' She had avoided the word 'man' and sat not looking at Ruprecht with her hands most peacefully in her lap.

'You've formed an impression already, then?' asked Ruprecht.

She smiled at him. She was so very well-born that she contrived to turn the conversation without effort: 'But how can the old Italian Father say such a thing of us? Has he not been in Bavaria long? Does he not like it!'

'He's honest, that's all,' replied Leo. 'He says exactly what he means and he's astonishingly innocent. One Lent, my cousin was staying here when she was about four months pregnant. She never missed her confession and she couldn't understand why she got such heavy penances. Then, just before Easter, she fainted at Mass and Father Guardini told her he'd noticed how much weight she was putting on and that he thought her health would have been a great deal better if she'd kept the fast!'

Fräulein von Boehling had the prettiest way of laughing, the light sounds of her merriment seeming to mingle with the reflections on the ceiling; as she poured coffee from the silver jug, that too shook in her hand, emitting additional reflections.

'What a sweet story. I'll write it to my mother this evening. It will encourage her in that dreadful heat. But surely your cousin told Father Guardini the reason?'

'No. He still believes that, like the rest of us, she over-eats.'

'But surely he cannot think that that's still a German failing?'

'The Jews, at any rate, no longer find it so easy to grow fat,' said Ruprecht.

She was immediately distressed. All her eagerness vanished. She thought but she did not know what to say out of this dream of castles and Roman fountains; for she sensed that the remark was not merely in bad taste, but a little malicious too.

So Leo, sensing her embarrassment, told them a joke: 'I heard a good story about that when I was last in Berlin; somebody accused someone else of getting richer and richer despite the taxation, and he said, "*Sh!* Don't tell anyone; but I keep a Jew in my attic."'

How grateful she was to him for his quickness and gentleness. Even Herr Waitzmann had to laugh. Not knowing how rich he might be, but suspecting from his name and from something Leo had said earlier that he might well be a little Jewish, she now felt very much safer with Leo than with Ruprecht, and from then on treated him more formally. She took unconscious care, too, always to give him six more inches of physical distance than she gave Leo. There was no longer any possibility that in going through a door, or in walking through the woods and gardens, they might inadvertently touch.

'How I love the Berliners,' she said. 'They put everything into perspective.'

'Everybody loves them,' said Ruprecht. 'All over Germany the people laugh at the Berlin humour; none more so than those who are most reluctant to live there.'

'So?'

'The Baron, for instance, tells me that even Hitler feels uneasy when he's there.'

'It's true; he detests Berlin.'

'Do you know him, then, Fräulein von Boehling? Have you ever met him?'

'But yes. I didn't care for him at first. Not at all. I don't think I like fanatical men; but the second time I met him, his strength overwhelmed me. It was a marvellous experience.'

'In what way? How can a man be more than a man – a pair of eyes, four limbs, a moustache?'

'But surely there's such a thing as human greatness, Herr Waitzmann? The Führer's eyes and handshake thrill one. They are heroic. It's the Berliners' loss that they don't appreciate this quality, I'm sure. They object to being pushed; and that is bad.'

'So do we, don't we, Leo?'

'It depends in which direction,' said Leo lazily, but with a most energetic glance at Fräulein von Boehling.

'It is, after all, a capital city and should set an example,' she said. 'Sometimes it's good for us to be pushed.'

'Good?' said Ruprecht. 'Not good? What clear distinctions you seem to make!'

'Oh yes I do. Perhaps it's simple of me, but that is the way our mother brought us up.'

'Admirable! If one can accept a parent's ruling.'

'It is the way we were brought up,' she repeated.

The children were right, thought Ruprecht, irritated by her assurance. They saw her as a princess because it's her own self-image; even if it were only a third-class carriage, any child would see her stepping out of a golden coach into an island of flunkeys and luggage. Yet he was delighted by her hostility. It pained him more vividly even than her breeding and virginity; and, as they went out into the courtyard into which groups of people were moving for the afternoon viewing, he purposely kept as near to her as was politely possible.

They walked out through the courtyard into the water garden; Fräulein von Boehling in a not-very smart English style hat with a floppy brim. From behind she looked a little ridiculous, walking so gracefully on her well-bred legs, with their long ankles showing beneath her over-long skirt. On her little finger she wore a signet ring which glinted in the sunlight. The unstiffened lavender-coloured brim of her hat hid the nape of her neck, disguising her beauty effectively. It hid her hair, too, which though carefully plaited and coiled was so fine that indoors he had seen it only as the hazed coiffure of a very young girl.

Her signet ring was a touch of masculine grotesqueness. And, surely, the narrow finger, puffed a little by the constriction, occasioned her, too, a small but constant pain? The hat spoiled the line of her narrow shoulders and she had an unbecomingly modest neckline from which narrow tucks, broadening as they descended, flattened out all clear definition of her breasts. The hem of her skirt really was unfashionably deep; half an inch above the swell of the calf, so that although she walked with a long stride it was difficult to catch more than a glimpse of the pale mauve hollows behind her knees.

A little dust rose from the white, shadeless path and Leo, walking beside her, began to cough undramatically but persistently. Not acknowledging the cough he increased his pace and said he wished to go to the sunflower-field to find the best place in which to set his pheasant-trap.

No matter how hard he tried to hide his discomfort, the poor young man could not overcome the obstruction or irritation in his throat. His eyes shone with unshed tears; yet he would insist on continuing to talk about his project as though nothing were the matter with him.

Fräulein von Boehling was obviously distressed by his fortitude. Pretending she was tired, she leaned against a gateway, sweeping off her hat and fanning her face with it; but at that moment Leo heard a buzzard crying and, with his binoculars to his eyes, hurried on ahead, while Ruprecht waited with Alexandra until such time as her deception should be concluded.

The buzzard was crying coolly over an open group of pines, very old and tall; and Fräulein von Boehling followed its flight with innocent eyes. She wore no make-up of any sort, a smudge of red on her upper lip being apparent only because she must just have bitten it out of sympathy for Leo. She wore no eye-shadow either but had probably slept badly in Rome to give herself the delicate prints above each cheek, just below the lower eye-lids.

She did not look at Ruprecht but watched the buzzard soaring on a wind current in a wide, leisurely circle. Its cry came out of the sky to her like a question. She had come so far and this was her first grown journey; there was nothing else in the sky, only the haze of sunlight and the wild bird. She really did hear its call as a question, eerie, provocative and perhaps beautiful. But to Ruprecht, who, though he heard it, scarcely bothered to differentiate it from any other country-noise, it was if anything a remote statement, too often repeated.

Leo had stopped some distance away from them, coughing

as if he were encased in plaster and gazing upwards through his glasses.

As though she were speaking of an unruly child, Alexandra upbraided him to herself: 'Ach! He really ought to rest for a few minutes.'

'Then you should tell him so.'

'You persuade him, Herr Waitzmann; please!'

'But the delicate have always to be untiring. He wouldn't thank me.'

'Then let's *all* sit down somewhere. It's so hot.' She left him and went off towards Leo. 'What a beautiful call that bird has. Please might I borrow the glasses?' But she was too late, the bird was drifting away fast in a high current, floating far away over a horizon of pines. 'However do you follow them when they move so fast?'

Leo put his fingers to his lips and blew out a buzzard cry; the mewing of some companion not too far away and not too near, plaintive but encouraging. In a few moments the bird returned and Leo repeated his call three times in quick succession.

'Now you'll see him if you're quick,' he told her as the bird swept over them, its rounded wings swinging against the sky as it circled and dropped into full view, brown and black, short-necked.

'Oh, thank you. How beautiful he is and how fierce. Does he think he may find his mate?'

'Not his mate – he'll know where she is – but another male. They have their own territories and will allow no rival into them.'

'Then there's a difference between their calls and you can imitate a male or a female at will?'

'I've practised since I was young.'

'To think that no one ever taught me that.'

Ruprecht joined them.

'Never taught you what?'

'Oh, it's not important. What does the buzzard eat, Leo?'

'Anything small that he sees moving, mice, voles, and the fledglings of other species.'

'The observatory owls eat mice,' said Ruprecht. 'One

74

drops them into the cage when it's growing dark and the owls ignore them. It's very boring waiting for something to happen.'

'But you said they ate them! In a cage!' she exclaimed.

'They do eventually, but it's no good waiting. They don't like an audience. The other night I might have been late for an important appointment if I'd waited to watch the slaughter.' *Beautiful women always make me tell lies* he was assuring himself. *But since I know when I'm doing it, it's of little importance.*

Alexandra was quite unable to decide why leaving the mice without watching made it so much worse and longed to accuse him of the most horrific sadism; but, on the other hand, she did not want to get any further involved with him. 'It's so hot,' she said. 'Let's go over to the trees and sit down in the shade.'

'Yes, let's roost,' said Ruprecht. 'We can pretend we're a colony of buzzards, weary of crying and rearing little buzzards to be spied and fired upon by Leo.'

Leo said, 'I'll be back soon. It's better if I go alone as we don't want to make too many tracks in the plantation.'

'But, Leo, I want so much to watch you. How do you trap the wild pheasants? Won't you please show me?'

'It might ruin any chance I have; but if you insist. . . .'

'I must be brave,' Alexandra decided. 'After all, what harm can Herr Waitzmann do me?'

'You must be brave,' Ruprecht told her. 'If my conversation's upset you, then let me explain myself at leisure; or if you like, we'll talk of Italy. I intend one day to spend a lot of my time there.'

Leo left them. *Pheasants*, he was thinking, *red pheasant cocks, dull hens, little sandy fledglings, fat grain. Peck! Peck! Follow the trail into the trap of sun-flowers; then in the morning in a day or two from now I shall come early and there they will be, scuttering about on the dry soil; a whole clutch caught.*

He did not care in what confusion the other two might be. He told himself that Alexandra must wait and that Waitzmann, in any case, was a boor.

As it happened, when he had left them, she was refusing to sit down beside Ruprecht who was sprawling on some dried-up moss, looking at her ankles as she leaned against a pine-trunk. She watched Leo disappear into a neck of the woods. When he had gone, when it was quite impossible for her to distinguish his green hat bobbing away between shades and shadows of blues and greens, she noticed Ruprecht's scrutiny and crossed her legs as if to protect them from it. He smiled up at her.

'You find something amusing?' she asked him.

'Leo's enthusiasms always amuse me.'

'Like yours for the owls?'

'But you noticed that he couldn't say anything? That, at least, he's logical? Why d'you think he studies the pretty ways of birds and beasts if not in order to be more certain of killing them?'

'It's only his way of escape from his chest trouble, and in any case he's not cruel by intention.'

'You think it's a question of motive? Tell that to the boars and the bucks; they'll be no more comforted than my mice.'

'But surely you see it has nothing to do with the animals themselves but only with the men who do the things to them?'

'You're not only beautiful but clever too,' said Ruprecht smoothly. 'Please tell me your views on suffering. If it's necessary, is anyone to be blamed for inflicting it?'

'That's for one's conscience. In doing only what is good we should cause as little pain as possible; and that's why I think we should persuade Leo to rest in all this heat. He's doing himself harm.'

'But he's happy.'

'I don't like to see anybody suffering.'

'But how should we show our concern? You believe he needs boredom and rest, and I believe he should cough and be interested.'

'You're only being clever. You know I couldn't possibly have hurt him by trying to make him rest.'

'No, but you've hurt *me*,' said Ruprecht sincerely. 'Very soon after I met you, I became angry about something. Anyone beautiful always affects me like this. I can't explain it, but it's true. At first I'm excited and silent and then I become talkative and unpleasant. Lastly, I fall into jealousy.'

Alexandra said nothing. As Ruprecht, with the arrogance of a man making a bad confession, became evermore unnecessarily truthful, fear and delight fluttered inside her like trapped pheasants.

'For two hours I've been wanting you to think about *me*. Instead, you think only about buzzards and pheasants; yet you don't care for them, you don't even particularly care for Leo – who does appreciate them.'

'You're being ridiculous.'

'Let me look only at your foot, please, and I promise you I'll see more beauty in it than a huntsman sees in a lifetime. Really, for several moments I was spellbound by my thoughts of it. I realized that just as it had brought you here so it might take you away again before I'd had time to tell you I was jealous.'

'I think you must be mad.'

'No, you're wrong. Always when I fall in love I feel unusually sane for minutes on end. The world no longer excites me! It seems so small in comparison with myself that I suffer inexpressibly.'

Alexandra walked out into the sunshine. The shade from the sheltering trees slid from her like the shadows of clouds and she stood pathetically for a moment as she tried to make up her mind in which direction she should go.

'You're making the mistake of thinking my extravagance implies insincerity,' Ruprecht told her. 'Why are you so quick in matters of logic and so slow in those of emotion? All I've done is to tell you the truth about your effect on me, and because it's not some physical disorder I'm describing, you've no sympathy for me.'

Alexandra was telling herself who she was; 'these are trees, this is a field, this is a Sunday afternoon and I am on my way to take up midwifery in Berlin. Once I'm there, I shall have to deal only with mothers and babies.'

'Well?' Ruprecht demanded. 'D'you wish to add to my suffering by making me feel embarrassed?'

'Doctors are different,' Alexandra was continuing to herself. 'And I'll have no difficulty with husbands at such times. Leo too is sick. Oh! if only he would come back.'

'Leo!' she called. 'Leo!'

'He'll only think it's a buzzard,' Ruprecht said. 'And in any case, you're going in the wrong direction.'

She allowed her hand to rest in his as he led her through the woods, trampling down young spruce and pine, so that her stockings should not be torn.

She hoped so much that by this concession she might have ensured his silence. She said a prayer that he would not continue to excite himself by talking in this mad way. Almost immediately he released her hand and began to apologize.

'I must tell you before we find Leo that I've behaved in this way only because I think there's going to be a war.'

'I'm afraid it's very likely.'

But Ruprecht's mind had gone off on a tangent. The word 'war' had conjured up the word 'Industry'. For a few moments he forgot all about Alexandra in realizing that this might be a good opportunity of finding out what her father was doing in Rome. No one had thought of share movements at the Board Meeting. It might still not be too late to make some advantageous changes in the Waitzmann investments.

'Is that why you're going to Berlin?' he asked her.

'Oh no! I am going to Berlin to study midwifery, a two-year course.'

'I only wondered if your decision to go now might not be connected with the Polish business? Does your father, for example, feel it can only be a matter of a few weeks?'

'He thinks the Führer will not wait beyond the end of this week.'

'And the Italians agree with him?'

'My father didn't discuss that. Perhaps I ought not to have told you so much as I have already.'

How sad she sounds, he thought. I must return to the attack at once. I'm not an insincere man. I'm a realist. I was thinking only about money in relation to Alexandra herself.

'As I was trying to tell you,' he went on, 'I felt I couldn't afford to wait. No, that's a lie of course! I admit I'd have acted as impulsively if this were the millennium.'

'Really?' she said non-committally.

'Yes. Ever since I met you, I've felt as if Time were contracting. The minutes in which we were alone together were sliding down like sand in an hour-glass, burying me before I could make any impression on you.'

Alexandra picked her way along the rough path he was beating for her. She wore no scent; but in the hot sunlight the perfume of her skin and hair came to him mixed with the resinous smells of the pine trees.

'You do believe me, don't you?' he insisted. 'You can understand the feelings of someone as impatient as myself?'

'I know nothing about such things. I'm not used to such conversation.'

Ruprecht took her hand in his again, holding it gently but forcing her to remain where she was.

'Do you imagine that I thought you were? Of course not, or else why should I have bothered to give you your first experience of it? I too have waited as we all must. We make these speeches many times in advance. We long for an adequate occasion to present itself. Why, even my brother, Alfried . . .' But he broke off. 'Fräulein von Boehling, I've declared myself. I can do no more. Let's play safe inside the conventions we both so rightly respect. I'll be patient.'

They were nearing the boundary of the plantation and could see the yellow of the sunflower-field glimmering like fire beyond the trunks of the outermost trees.

Alexandra smiled at him coldly and carefully picked burrs from the hem of her long skirt. The fire of the sunflowers, yellow and shaking in the waves of heat rising from the cracked soil, was only an illusion caused by other illusions, as, for instance, that the moss in this particular area of cleared forest swarmed with hares, when in fact they saw only one, redder than bracken, running silently away from them, as if it traversed a soundless vacuum of colour; or that the pine bolts were violet at the base but foxglove-pink where the sun struck at them; or that the foresters were working on a Sunday. At any moment, they felt, a tall tree might shudder and fall, the sound of the axe blows being caused only by a black woodpecker striking the hot timber in the silence.

Alexandra was the first to see Leo; his green hat, with the feather in the crown, moving amongst the heavy heads of the flowers. She did not hesitate to move out into the crop, her skirt swinging to her long stride, her hat held loosely in her hand, her pale face finely studded with perspiration.

Ruprecht waited where he was, angered by her eagerness to get to Leo.

'We've seen hares, but no pheasants,' he called to him.

'They're out of season.'

'You should not have left us, Leo,' said Alexandra, 'when the flowers are such a sight. This field is really exotic. What enormous black faces they have.'

'They're only suffering from the drought. Even their leaves are turning yellow.'

'Did you find a good place for your trap? I do hope I'm not walking in the wrong places. Heavens! Some of these flowers are taller than you are. Aren't they beautiful? And each one of them following the sun?'

'Yet they never get giddy,' shouted Ruprecht.

Leo ignored him and explained himself to Alexandra. 'I've found a good place here, you see, not too far from the edge. Now I've only to bleed a sack of wheat every other night in the early autumn. To begin with I'll stop short of the cage-door until the birds are accustomed to following the trail. Then on the seventh night I'll scatter my wheat over the floor of the cage itself which will be covered in with fresh flowers. Please watch your step. We'd better go back a different way or we'll make it too obvious to the birds.'

'But these are nearly ripe already. Surely it will be too late if you wait until the early autumn?'

'We'll cut this part of the field last; if necessary, we shan't cut it at all.' He was looking at Ruprecht. 'So you saw hares, Waitzmann? How many?'

'Oh, dozens, galloping in all directions as though possessed of evil spirits.'

Leo frowned: 'That can occur only in March.'

'Then it must be an abnormal year. Alexandra was quite alarmed. Two or three of them got up just beneath her feet.'

'Impossible. At this time of the year the hare is always solitary.'

'Herr Waitzmann saw one hare,' Alexandra said in a tired voice. She turned pointedly to Leo, 'Please tell me what you're going to do with the pheasants? Re-stock your breeding pens for the season?'

Leo made his way over to her. 'I don't understand this about the hares. Did you see them as well, Alexandra?'

'I tell you she was too frightened, my dear fellow. I saw them all right. Didn't you hear me clapping to disperse them?'

'Herr Waitzmann's quite impossible,' said Alexandra. 'Please let's drop the subject. It's far too hot to argue and I seem to have been doing that all afternoon.'

'What a waste of such a day.'

'Oh, but some parts of it I've enjoyed enormously. You mustn't think I've failed to appreciate your lovely home. After the noise and heat of Rome, Bavaria seems like a dream to me.'

'You see!' said Ruprecht. 'Alexandra's enjoyed herself; and I too am feeling extraordinarily exhilarated, in fact I've a presentiment that today's been of tremendous importance for me. When I arrived I was in a bad mood; I was even expecting to be bored; but now, after that wonderful lunch and this peaceful walk, I feel as full of optimism as the Baron. My head's completely cleared and I've quite made up my mind to return to headquarters in Berlin next spring.'

Alexandra ignored him and begged Leo to take her to see the lake where the animals came down to drink. 'It would be so pleasant,' she said, 'to sit down beside water.'

'All the same, in this drought I shouldn't risk the Schönform mosquitoes,' said Ruprecht. 'If I were you I should make for high ground. There'll be an evening breeze by the time you get there. Buzzards and pheasants will be settling on their perches to spend the night peacefully above the ground. Stars will appear and if you wait long enough you might see the full moon coming up. I'm only sorry I can't stay with you, there are so many interesting things we might discuss. But I promised I'd see the Baron before I left. Now that I've decided to get back to Berlin I must get him to use his influence with my chief, Colonel Udet, about my next move.'

Leo watched something through his binoculars – he dissociated himself from these plans, and Alexandra supported him.

'What is it? What do you see, Leo?'

'I thought I saw a kestrel. They don't usually come so far north, they prefer the hill-country.'

'As I told you,' said Ruprecht. 'Try the high ground, you might find it swarming with wild life.' He kissed Alexandra's hand gracefully. 'Good-bye, Fräulein von Boehling, or may I continue to call you Alexandra? Leo, thank you for a delightful afternoon.'

'You may call me by my first name if you wish,' she said, 'though since we're saying good-bye it seems a little pointless.'

Leo dropped his binoculars. He smiled at Ruprecht. 'Try the high ground, Waitzmann, that's my advice. One has only to be a good climber and the rewards, as you say, may be great.'

Ruprecht laughed, but he was angry to see her amusement; angrier than ever when, as he turned and left them, his head full of the pressure he was going to bring upon the Baron, he realized how much she had tried to conceal it.

He walked back to the castle slowly, making plans for his future. Fräulein von Boehling would be in Berlin for at least two years; the guest, initially of the Baronin, Carin von Hoffbach. Even if he could not soon get a posting back to the headquarters of the Aeronautical Institute he could at least take his weekend leaves in the capital. He could keep an eye on the Baron; and the Baronin, too, might provide some useful contacts, social and political, if he handled her cleverly. Why should he not himself become one of her followers? He had as much to commend him as anyone. If she were a snob – and he did not particularly remember her as such despite Onkel Fritz's remarks – then his relations with the Baron would amply compensate for his mixed lineage.

He ran up the stairs to the Lake Room.

Chapter 3

It had taken Ruprecht nearly fifteen months to get back to the Berlin Institute. In fact, he did not return there until November 1941. Unexpectedly, the Baron had done little to help him, telling him always that he would be better advised to avoid any direct contact with what he called 'The Jackals of the Hierarchy, the minor officials who surround our Führer'.

'Leave it all to me, my dear fellow,' he had said, often enough. 'In view of the double threat to your ambitions – not only your brother, who might return at any time, but the military situation too – you'd do much better to keep out on the flank of the jungle.'

And even though in many respects he had been proved right, his stubbornness, inasmuch as it had influenced Frau Waitzmann, had angered Ruprecht. He had realized that since his emergence from his long retirement, the Baron had indeed been very quick to relearn the twists of prevailing policies.

The Party's quasi-military conduct of even the most civilian affairs had suited him admirably. He had obviously made a good impression both on the army and the bureaucrats and had even become more soldierly in appearance, cropping his hair short and wearing a moustache beneath his fine bone of a nose.

Largely due to his influence, the factories were working overtime, supplying thousands of uniforms which at this moment were breasting the freezing winds of the Russian steppes. Only a few months after Ruprecht had arrived in Berlin, the Baron had presented him with a magnificent order for five hundred thousand yards of striped denim for use in the camps in Poland and East Germany.

He had proved right about Alfried too. Unaccompanied by Onkel Fritz, who wrote that he shuddered at the persecution of the Jews, and sent photographs of himself looking bored and angry in his New York hotel, he had returned on a 'flying' visit in the autumn and had settled indefinitely in the house in the Schellenstrasse.

'A bad thing, my boy,' the Baron had said at that time. 'You know what you must do?'

'What can I do, sir? Alfried has no plans. He's bristling with criticism of the country. He can't or won't bring himself to take any part in the war. He carries his return ticket with him everywhere, but doesn't use it. If he were called up he'd at once claim that he must take things over for us in the South.'

'Precisely! And if it were arranged for him to receive his call-up papers, you might defeat your own ends. Therefore you must, as I was going to have told you, leave it all to me. I'll explain to your mother that I cannot afford to be embarrassed at this juncture. Her devotion to your brother is so great that at the right time I'm sure she'll persuade the boy to rejoin his uncle before it's too late.'

'No hurry for you, perhaps,' Ruprecht had thought. 'You're doing very well out of it. Even if Alfried were to outwit me, I doubt if your interests would suffer now; and no doubt you could always find ways of concealing from him such matters as the orders secured through the Reichsführer S.S.' But he had replied non-committally and continued to betray no impatience, seeking instead some other means of securing Alfried's return to America as soon as possible. In fact, for months prior to his Berlin posting he had never failed to bring the Baron's wife, Carin von Hoffbach, some small but expensive present whenever he called on Alexandra, who was staying with her indefinitely. He had sent her tasteful messages, thanking her for her hospitality and had even begun to confide in her, suggesting that she was not so much an elder sister as a mature and beautiful woman who would well understand the shortcomings of young girls.

If he had known of the effect his attentions had had upon

Carin, he would have been delighted; in fact, on occasion, he did suspect the pleasure he was giving; but had not the inclination to dwell on it, preferring to calculate its advantages without being greatly interested in what she herself might feel when, as on this particular evening, she was waiting for him at her flat.

Ever since she had realized that Ruprecht might be in love with Alexandra, Carin had thought her ridiculous to resist such attention and to be so young that she did not resent her own infatuation. It should have been clear, she thought, to any sensible girl, that she herself intended only to swallow Ruprecht whole as soon as possible. This should have put such a girl on her mettle. It should have been equally obvious that once she had done this, a woman of Carin's sophistication would have been content to disgorge him undamaged, and leave him to his contemporaries.

As the months passed she grew ever more irritable over Alexandra's refusal to see the situation in this light. With her sweetly stony face, her stubborn absences, and her dedication to her studies, Alexandra had so far prevented anything developing at all and there was not even a 'situation'; nothing whatsoever to discuss, however subtly. And as week succeeded week in that bitter winter of 1941, Carin became ever more desperate and malicious. She found her mind fastening on trifles like Alexandra's flat heels.

'Don't you think that a slightly higher heel might be more becoming, Alexandra?'

'But they do not like us to wear them in the hospital.'

'My dear, I do not mean at your work; but here in the flat. With all the presentable men in boots one can afford an extra quarter of an inch.'

'But my work is with the women,' Alexandra said with sweet diffidence. 'High heels can be quite dangerous at a confinement.'

'But surely one needn't look like a district nurse all day.'

Alexandra had looked startled and the Baronin, feeling her own cheeks reddening unbecomingly, hastened to apologize.

'I was only saying to Herr Goebbels last week that he

really ought to do something for the women. I know, of course, that the Führer in that sense doesn't share the tastes of Napoleon; but surely with all these charming regimental uniforms it's not beyond somebody's wit to give the women auxiliaries something more than a shirt and a bun.'

Alexandra helped herself to a petit four. 'You think it matters?'

'Oh,' said the Baronin with a little laugh. 'It depends on one's values. Though that little biscuit you're eating is a mere trifle it does represent five hundred years of French culture! And from my point of view the conquest of France was worth it for that alone. I'd rather have one Paris biscuit factory than the whole of the Renault plant.'

'But we have both!'

'That's not the point; it's not what men fight for. They fight in the last resort to impress their mothers.'

'Really?' Alexandra was thinking of Leo.

'They marry for the same reason; and since, of course, they never succeed, they never tire of trying. The least we can do is to provide the greatest possible incentive. If you'll forgive me for repeating myself, low-heeled shoes do not explain the Wehrmacht's love of a French posting.'

Alexandra laughed and promised that she would get a permit for a pair of high-heeled shoes the next day. Carin rang for her servant to take away the tea-things. It was the hour for their evening war-work and Alexandra went to her room and came down with a knitting-bag bulging with comfort socks for the troops in Russia.

She was having difficulty in turning the heels. She was always intending to get someone to show her how to do it; and, in the meantime, starting on yet another pair. She had decided that when she had completed her twelfth and lightest pair, which she secretly intended to send to Leo, she would turn all twenty-four heels together and send them to her brother's regiment somewhere on the steppes.

Carin, however, who had less conscience about the troops, had a different preoccupation. In her desk she kept a set of dinner mats she was making for Frau Goering. They depicted hunting scenes taken from a sixteenth century manual belonging to Nicholas' grandfather. There were stags being disembowelled by hounds, hounds being savaged by boars and foxes being smoked out and speared by men. She had touched them up with water-colour most effectively and was framing them between sheets of glass held together with green passe-partout. Since it was no use giving Emmy Goering anything less than a set of thirty for her Karinhall parties, Carin found her commitment increasingly dismaying; but she had promised them and despite the English air-raids on Berlin which had affected the Reichsmarshal's standing in recent months, she was still intent on finishing them.

A few of her friends had secretly suggested that they would do nothing for the Goerings' appetites and she had laughed loudly, thinking it more than ever a pity that she had made up her mind not to give them to Emmy until the war was won, by which time it might be more politic to give them to someone else. For the same reason she deplored her son Leo's fairly recent infatuation with Alexandra and never tired of telling Nicholas, her husband, that he ought not to commit himself to marriage until victory was assured.

She was in a great muddle with her mats. They were like Alexandra's socks, an apparently simple project: sixty pieces of glass, thirty old prints, twenty yards of passe-partout. But some of the glass had to be kept in the cellar, some was in her bedroom, while the remainder was still at the depot, as yet uncut from the bombed sections in which it had originally arrived. Then too, there was the question of the borders of the engravings. At first it had seemed a good idea to enhance these by colouring them bottle-green; but later she had had her doubts. Might it not be more amusing to paint them in different colours in sets of six or five? Should she leave them bare between their sandwiches of glass, or give them backgrounds? Should she back them with baize to prevent their scratching Emmy's Versailles table, if that was where they were due to end up?

She did not know; yet whenever she was most irritated by her affairs she set to work. She manipulated her scissors and ruler, her yards of tape and paint brushes, while in the meantime she measured and weighed the multitude of her intentions and preoccupations, criticizing herself amiably and making a great deal of noise.

Alexandra sat bolt upright on the sofa with her socks. Unless Ruprecht arrived sooner, Carin knew she would go to her books at six o'clock exactly. If he dined out with them, as he might, the girl would excuse herself and go off to the hospital canteen at seven, letting herself out so silently that only Carin would hear her go. This evening she would be in early to write her letter to Leo. Eventually, and too soon, she might become engaged to him and Ruprecht would cease to call at the flat. His comings and goings apparently depended entirely on Alfried's decision between his still smouldering vocation and the claims of his inheritance, or as Carin herself had put it, 'Between God and Mammon – and I know which I should choose!'

'A conscience in a young man is so unattractive,' she had decided of Alfried. 'Though he doesn't realize it yet, Ruprecht has very little. When one's with him there are no disparities at all.' But longing for him to arrive, she took off her spectacles just the same and slid them as far back in the pigeon-hole of her desk as if they had been false teeth. Then she thought: 'How absurd!' and put them on again to tell Alexandra through them that she was going to change.

'Be pleasant to Ruprecht and tell him I shan't be long.'

She looks so sweet in her spectacles, thought Alexandra, saying: 'But I mustn't wait. I've so much to do this evening.'

'You can perfectly well be warm to him for ten to fifteen minutes. It's so much more effective than running away. Nothing so discourages a man as the feeling that he's been fairly sampled and still found unsatisfactory.'

'But I find him detestable, I do really,' said Alexandra, clacking away at a particularly long winter sock. 'It's not that I'm trying to provoke him; it's just that he makes me feel uneasy, and with my examinations so near . . .'

'Nonsense! Have a little game with him. Ask him how Alfried is and he'll look so gloomy that you'll begin to feel quite sorry for him.'

She heard the Mercedes draw up outside and glanced at

herself in the mirror above the mantelpiece. She took off her silly spectacles. How old and hopeful I look. Great blanks in my face; all the things that have already been taken away.

'You're a naughty girl,' she told Alexandra. 'Working far too hard. Little lines on your forehead.'

'Oh, dear!'

'That lady-doctor look already when you're still so young and pretty. Now you must promise me you're going to be less earnest.'

Hurriedly, for she was really in a fuss to reach her room, she kissed the girl on the forehead, hearing Ruprecht's knock on the front door as she did so.

'Forgive me dearest, how detestable I'm being.'

'The war worries us all, I think.'

Carin assured her distractedly: 'I've neglected you terribly I'm afraid; but as one grows older it's so hard to attend to everything.'

She fled along the hall to her room, pausing behind her door, absurdly flustered, hearing Ruprecht's careful tread across the carpet and the closure of the drawing-room door behind him.

She concentrated on doing her hair, wondering which way to sweep it so that a dawning thinness over the temples might be best concealed. The silvering of the undercurls over her narrow ears saddened her and she realized she was growing tired of having to be so perpetually busy with herself.

'My body's more trouble even than a mother,' she decided. 'I have to wrestle with it like the most devoted daughter.' Then, catching herself in this involved attitude, she changed all her clothes in front of the three photographs of previous escorts. Hansel, bearded and a little beastly in his U-boat uniform, Christian, gaunt and gentle-looking in his S.S. black, and 'kleine' Rudolf grinning beside the propeller of his Messerschmidt. How unbearable even healthy men were when once they were past fifty. What a bore this evening would be were it not for the prospect of Ruprecht!

It would be cold in the car and fuggy in the restaurant. Nicholas's Chancellery friends would be blowing over her hand like horses and crunching away at the dismal food like horses too. She would have to think of a creditable excuse to get him away early; one that would embarrass nobody, least of all Ruprecht. So moody, she thought. 'Little Jew!' She had even referred to him like this to her mother on her last trip to Rastenburg and the old lady had licked her lips. Later, Carin had taken herself to task for her unfairness; but it still amused her to call him like this to herself: 'Little Jew', and secretly she told herself it was his own fault for being so sensitive about Alfried and Onkel Fritz.

He at that moment was questioning Alexandra about God. His tone was facetious, he did not seem in the least pleased to have found her, for once, both alone and mildly warm in her manner. He was so angered by recent events, a letter from Frau Waitzmann about Alfried and a dull day in the laboratory, that to begin with he did not even resent her use of the formal 'Herr Waitzmann'. He waved his mother's letter about so pointedly that Alexandra became ever more nervous of it, wondering when on earth he might refer to it and to what purpose.

'Women are by nature better than men,' he was saying. 'So perhaps you can tell me what is a man's duty to his mother if he feels bound to give his life to God?'

'Surely there's no difficulty? Less than if he gave his life to some other woman?'

'You think so? You yourself would like God as a daughter-in-law?'

Alexandra frowned: 'I've no experience either of marriage or of vocation.'

'But you're devout, aren't you? You're certain of yourself in these matters of religion? You trot off to Mass every Sunday just as you trot off to the hospital every evening.'

'But what else is there to do? Naturally, I behave in the way I was brought up.'

'So did I when I was young; but I'm no longer at home in the world. There's the war. Everything is changing.'

'Ah, yes, that's true.' Alexandra picked up a stitch as if nothing had changed at all.

'An inner order, I suppose; that's what you're hinting at? It doesn't matter in the least if by rushing into a German monastery Alfried might embarrass his entire family and endanger everyone's interests?'

'You seem to forget that I've never met him. Could his decision really endanger you all?'

'Certainly. He could perfectly well enter an American order where his political opinions would pass unnoticed. He'd then merely be keeping everyone waiting.'

'Oh, I'm sure he'll be quite safe.'

'Quite safe!'

'And you too!' Alexandra picked up another sock. 'I think you must be over-tired to be worried about anything so – good. The Sister always taught us that vocations can't be hurried and that it's the person himself who suffers the most. Though I'm not really very devout I can understand that.'

'Not devout!' he said, irritated by the attention she was giving her work. 'Just look at your knitting.'

'But we're all doing it. We've been asked to.'

'Exactly! All over Europe factories are being blown up, and hospitals bombed. In Russia and Africa men are dying like rabbits and what do you do? You knit.'

Alexandra dropped Leo's uncompleted sock into her lap and started to collect the others pairs together. They looked suddenly ridiculous to her, and some instinct bade her hide them away in the old striped brocade bag given to her by her mother as a night-dress case during the last term at the convent. But Ruprecht moved over from the mantelpiece and seizing her latest sock exclaimed upon it.

'True, you've not yet given this one a heel; but I suppose that will follow.' He ran through the bundle exasperatingly, holding up the socks as if they had been something she had stolen.

'But they're none of them complete; they're anklets.'

She became as frantic as if the socks had suddenly become alive; and, with the exception of Leo's to which he had taken an absent-minded fancy, began to stuff them all back into her bag.

'A vocation, as I understand it, would make one calm and decisive,' he went on, sliding the sock over his hand as if it had been a mitten. 'If one were going to be a nuisance to anyone it would be only to God.'

He had transferred his cigarette to his mittened hand and stooping down was pretending that this same hand was a half-naked foot with the cigarette held upright between its toes. She watched him fascinated and whereas she had originally really longed to escape from the room she was now only determined to do so.

'If you'll give it to me, please? I have to go in a few minutes.'

But Ruprecht assured her it was an excellent idea. 'The only question is how, if one had lost both arms, one would get one's foot to one's mouth to smoke the cigarette? For which of your patients did you knit it? Was it for some air-raid victim?'

'As it happens it's not for a patient, it's for Leo.'

'Ah!'

'I'm going to turn all the heels together when I can get a moment to myself.'

He saw that she was nearly weeping with vexation and became instantly contrite: 'I'm sorry. I admit I'm in a foul temper but it's only because I'm worried myself.'

'I didn't notice it.'

He stooped over her: 'Alexandra, please forgive me. Let's forget it all – leave your books and come out to dinner with me.' He tried to take her hands but she withdrew them and he saw that she was trembling.

'You poor little creature! Do I frighten you?'

'Not for myself.'

'You're frightened for me?'

She hesitated: 'I think sometimes that it's you who are in difficulties, in more danger than your brother, that's all.'

'Yes?'

She was backing away from him. She had heard Carin in the hall.

'But that's wonderful!' he said. 'Like an angel hearing one's cry.'

'Carin is coming.'

' "Who if I cried," ' he quoted swiftly, ' "would hear me amongst the angelic orders?" You know that line?'

'Yes.'

'Rilke's longing must have been great. Change your mind, Alexandra. Come out with me before it's too late. We'll drive out into the country.'

They turned as Carin came in and Ruprecht, effortlessly as ever, went forward to her and kissed her hand: 'Dear Carin, we've been waiting for you.'

'And you've had an interesting talk?' she asked. 'Your Colonel Udet is being more helpful?'

She moved over to the marquetry cabinet, bringing out a little tray of glasses and a bottle of San Raphael which had arrived with the shoes and the lovely Parisian stockings.

'We insist, don't we, Ruprecht, that tonight Alexandra joins us? Nicholas won't be back for at least half an hour and he'll have to change, so you'll have nearly an hour for your dreary books.'

'I simply daren't.'

'Then at least you'll take an aperitif with us. There, that'll give you an appetite for the hospital food.' She looked at them quickly, 'Now what have you two been talking about?'

She was thinking how unruffled the girl was, far away, quite lost in her own affairs. Could it be that she was not anxious to escape at all?

Ruprecht told them both about his latest brush with Colonel Udet: 'We've at length caught up with the English radar and just completed a most effective prototype. We present it to this clown and what d'you think he says? He says, "Thank you, gentlemen; but we've no need of mouse-traps in *our* planes!" '

Carin laughed harshly: 'That's always the trouble with veterans. They distrust technical advances. I'm always telling Nicholas that they should never be given command of research units.'

Ruprecht went on to describe his interest in electro-statics. He became so technical and boring that Carin had to listen with the closest attention while he gave them a long description of a device he was working on for dispensing with the cable in synchronizing transmitters. Alexandra rose to go in the middle of it and, still talking, Ruprecht conducted her to the door, bade her good night and went on talking as though he had not another interest in the world.

Carin, despite all her resolves, became first alarmed and then angry. How infuriating he was! Surely she could not have been mistaken in him? Perhaps he was only trying to impress her in advance of the older men he would meet later; or had something vital taken place in his conversation with Alexandra?

'Oh dear, dear,' she exclaimed aloud. 'I'm quite lost in all these details.'

'Then I'll explain more clearly,' he said, taking a piece of paper from her desk. 'Now if this line represents the ionosphere, which, of course, is an inconstant, and these two points represent my transmitters, and this the signal, then it should be possible, despite the variables, to work out an average for the time taken between the despatch and return of any individual signal.'

As they leaned against the white mantelpiece over which their heads and his rapid hands were reflected in the mirror, she studied her own face more than his, since it pained her to think that the possessor of such looks might be nothing more than an incipient bore. She looked at her eyelids; they were a little gelatinous; her hair, too harsh; the bones of her breast, too prominent. Then she caught sight of his eyes watching her and became instantly aware of his anger. His eyes were blacker than her own and he was smiling at her confidently. They moved over to the sofa and she stroked his left hand while he vented his grievances about his future. She read Frau Waitzmann's letter with half attention and encouraged him to talk about Alfried.

'Two years is a long time for you to have to wait. But surely you should tell your mother of Alfried's promise to let you take over completely unless he gets married?'

'She doesn't trust me. She would think I was trying to force his vocation. She has a superstition about him. Nothing, least of all my own plans, must be allowed to interfere. In his two years as a novice he mustn't feel subjected to any additional pressure; and, for my part, I'm not going to take over if I'm only to be thrown out the moment he changes his mind.'

She did not care about all this in the least, these clear grievances of the young. If only they could see that it was merely a question of survival and not waste their energies in brooding at thirty over what they would probably have at fifty.

'Your mother's your real difficulty,' she told him. 'You should make more fuss of her. At this moment, dearest, you should be with her instead of wasting your time on me.'

But he grumbled on and she was exasperated by his failure to notice her inference.

'Two months, no a month,' he was saying. 'That's the fuss I'll make of her. I'll join the Luftwaffe and get Nicholas to see I'm posted to the hottest spot going. She'll be without either of us then. A little death might warm her up.'

She thought of Rudolf with his surgical photographs, burned and grafted in the Lichtenstein skin clinic; and turned her attention idly to a consideration of Alfried. She kissed Ruprecht and asked him if it were not the case that Alfried had taken out his papers for American citizenship late in 1939? And whether or not his little Jewish nun was still 'playing' with him? Was Alfried not a trifle indiscreet? She thought someone had told Nicholas he was one of those belligerent, anti-Party, croyants influenced, no doubt, by the propaganda of a neutral country. She even remembered that the Führer was becoming increasingly touchy about industry, the Waitzmann factories with their Jewish connexions were a source of embarrassment to him. Certain quarters were pressing him to make an example of them and so rid himself of any charge of inconsistency.

Ruprecht was as glum as any half-traitor, as any husband discussing his wife with another woman. What she was saying was all the more indelicate because it was so much what he wished her to say. Women lacked true sentiment. It was obvious she had not realized how devoted he was to Alfried.

96

He told her this gently, kissing her on the cheek. As he did so he had a most curious swift illusion that it was Alfried's cheek he was saluting. He saw vividly the Schellenstrasse garden, lights beyond the trees. He heard the hum of the machinery and saw Alfried pausing to look at one of the statues as, at that instant, he himself planted this most compassionate kiss on his cheek.

The presentiment disturbed him, it made him suddenly angry; and, as he withdrew, protesting afresh how good Carin was and how fond he was of Alfried, he saw her smiling to herself. A quite violent emotion seized him. Believing momentarily that he hated her, he saw her now smiling quite openly as she leaned her head against the back of the little brocade-covered sofa. More images flashed through his mind, corporeal and most unwelcome; the upper part of her white arm, her smooth lips, her violet, almond-shaped nails and her eyes searching his unease like a beam; unifying all these physical fragments with a certain fearfulness.

'It seems to me,' she said, 'that it's you who must make up your mind about Alfried.'

'But you must realize that I love him.'

'I'm sure you do.'

'No, no that – not love perhaps; but I accept him. He's always been an essential part of my life.'

'One can have an affection even for ugliness if it's been with one long enough.'

'No, it's more than that. Alfried's a danger to himself.'

Was she about to laugh, she wondered.

'There's an epileptic quality about him,' he went on. 'I'll tell you that he gives one this unease of certain religions, of priests. You don't know where they begin or end. When you try to reach them you suddenly find yourself talking into an empty space as though they'd hidden in a cave.'

'Surely he should be in his monastery?'

'Of course he should, if one could rely on his remaining there.'

How easily that could be arranged, she was thinking. A word from Nicholas that anyone so unsound was likely to take over the Waitzmann Group and he would never be released. But she said only, 'What an awkward creature your big brother sounds. Whatever are you to do about him?'

'I'm serious, Carin. Alfried's not just a clown. Have you never met anyone who emphasized the defects of an entire family? Well, he's like that. He confirms one's night-fears.'

'Then he must be protected. His hand must be forced.'

He drew back, scowling: 'I was a fool to confide in you.'

She smiled. 'Haven't I understood you very well? Don't you realize I intended nothing? I was only reflecting aloud – and your secrets are as safe with me as Nicholas's.'

'Then please forget them. There's no need for anyone to be concerned at present. Probably he'll change his mind again and return to Baltimore.'

'And if he doesn't? If he breaks his promise and continues to harry you both for another two years?'

'You say "both". Is Nicholas worried too?'

'In some ways he has more reason than you, Ruprecht dear.'

'That makes it easier. Between us we'll think of something fair and convenient. But leave it to me. Alfried's my brother and I can't bring myself to force him.'

She gave him the truest of smiles. 'You feel warm towards him?'

'Why, yes, nearly always.' He said this with astonishment, seeing her again as a whole, most attractive person.

'And so do I,' she said, and she wrapped her fingers round his hand. After a moment, as if in some well-rehearsed tableau, they rose from the sofa together and Carin patted the cushions deftly back into shape.

On Nicholas's return they went off to their dinner party. Really a lugubrious meal; she could not at all remember the beginning of it. One drank, seated oneself, drank again, made faces and conversation with Herr von This and Admiral That. There was a common little Party man too, a Herr Luthmann, who was far too anxious to admire her. She noticed that every time he made any remark he always took a quick diagnostic look at her face as if to see whether or not she were impressed by his having opened his mouth. But she was not deceived; within his stubby bank-clerk's body with its far too short legs, there lurked a most smelly little beast; and it was tiresome and injudicious of Nicholas to have invited him.

People like this were always jumping up into the hierarchy, she knew; but was it necessary for everyone to placate them even in the interests of victory? When the war was over they would quickly be driven back to their own places, only the most exceptional among them retaining any vestiges of power. So, in the meantime, why could it not be made clear that the amnesty for the Führer and his veterans did not extend to all these later boors as well?

She was particularly annoyed about it this evening because of some antagonism she discerned between Ruprecht and the man Luthmann. He quite boldly claimed acquaintanceship in a winking fashion, mentioning some restaurant he owned, or had owned, in the village of Schorgast. 'Your days at our local observatory, you remember, Herr Waitzmann?'

Just when she least desired it, Ruprecht was thrown off balance by the incident. He showed Herr Luthmann his teeth and became silent for a while. She noticed that he started finger-twisting from that moment onwards and trembled a little for the impression he might make on Nicholas's more important friends. I do so want him to enjoy himself this evening, she believed. He's so charming when he's happy; so open. He'll disarm everyone and make it so much easier for me to deal with them when the time comes. So, very soon, when Luthmann returned to the subject of Bavaria by asking Ruprecht if he had enjoyed his time in 'our local observatory', she joined in the conversation with a remark about Schönform. 'My husband's always telling me, Herr Luthmann, that as a Prussian I'm incapable of appreciating the beauty of Bavaria.'

'But you have French blood, Baronin?'

'On my father's side only,' she admitted, concealing her annoyance with a smile.

'And the French are very sensitive to beauty,' he said in his country accent which was not at all pretty. 'I have letters from my son in the Wehrmacht describing the mannificent chateaux in the Loire country, and a postcard of the Palace of Versailles which he visited on a forty-eight hour pass.'

'Ah, Versailles!' she was thinking that at any moment he would pull out a wallet of letters and photographs.

'Yes,' he went on, clutching the table-cloth with a brown hand. 'A little garden of Marie Antoinette with a dairy and a miniature farm where lambs played in the fields.'

'And they cut off the poor girl's head,' said Carin with an unbidden shudder. 'I can't bear to think of it.'

The men laughed loudly at something in her tone and she tried to explain away her suddenness.

'I've just been reading a book about her. And any mention of the Petit Trianon upsets me dreadfully.'

But how inadequate this was. How could she explain that the acidity in her tone was her fury at this square-fingered lout even knowing about such things? Ruprecht, she noticed, was sawing away at his pork as though he were decapitating it slowly. Feeling his ill-ease, fresh anger escaped her in a little jet as she told Luthmann:

'But you've proved nothing at all. Marie Antoinette was not a Frenchwoman. Surely, Herr Luthmann, you remember your history books? The French never liked her; they always referred to her as "the Austrian".'

Ruprecht put down his knife and fork.

'You take Herr Luthmann too seriously,' he said. 'He certainly wouldn't be disturbed by the fate of the Queen or of the lambs. He's a man of many parts. For years he ran the best butchery in Schorgast.'

'Quite!' put in the Baron uneasily to Luthmann. 'No time for history, my dear fellow! Leave that to idlers like Carin and Marie Antoinette.'

But the man was not in the least disconcerted. He glanced round the table first, and then, insolently, at Carin herself; all deference gone.

'Present day history only, Herr Baron. And if the Austrian herself had had more of an eye for her own times she might have lived a lot longer.'

He was evidently quite well aware of everything connected with that Princess. 'My own parents, like the Führer's, were Austrians. Who but an Austrian would have troubled with that little farm set-up? We're romantic folk, we care about beauty. But that doesn't mean that more materialist races can exploit us indefinitely.'

He went on to talk about blood-hatreds and became boastful about his son's part in the Battle of France.

'Compiègne!' thought Carin. 'Why he's a fanatic! Anyone would think it had been his personal victory; that he too had danced the Führer's peasant jig beside the railway carriage; or, that in place of his own son, he himself was deflowering the Normandy girls.'

Nobody else at the dinner-table liked this display of Party ethic; and the devil rose in her. Did they expect her to eat with such a creature merely because he was a new protégé of the Reichsführer S.S.? Seeing herself as his hostess she began to flatter him grossly, as if he had been such a misfit that he could only be excluded by politeness. She reminded him that Bavaria had been the cradle of National Socialism and that she had heard Hitler himself say that in the end the truest understanding of his aims would come from the South. She asked him gentle and admiring questions about his son, exclaiming over his Iron Cross second class and asking him whether or not the young man would seek a commission after the war?

To her astonishment Luthmann did not respond to this treatment. He looked at her in a calculating way and smiled at his hand, as much as to say, 'Go on! You're doing fine; but your flatteries are of less consequence than your hostility.' She knew in fact that this was exactly what he was thinking; and for the second time that evening experienced fear. Was it class hatred? She wondered. Do we really scent one another out beneath all the uniforms and jewellery? Or is this some association in my mind between Marie Antoinette and the little garden where the lambs once played?

Certainly, 'the Austrian' would never willingly have entertained the new France at her table on an equal footing. That was not the way Revolution was accomplished. There was something obscene about this breaking of bread together in a good restaurant.

Luthmann, she sensed, had dropped her from his immediate consideration. Dismissing her, he had returned again to the subject of Ruprecht's affairs. He harried both the Baron and the younger man with great boldness, circling round his subject expertly. He spoke first of the new labour force made available by the successes in the East, showing by his casual enumeration of facts and figures that he was a master of his subject. Then he touched on Herr Speer's emphasis on the responsibility of employers; they must make the maximum use of foreign drafts in order to release more of the Fatherland's sons to the fighting fronts. In this connexion he wondered what precisely were the plans with regard to the future direction of the Waitzmann Group. It was essential that the factories should be energetically managed; and, in view of this local connexion, he hoped that everyone present would understand his interest in the matter.

'I hear, for instance, Herr Baron, that there's some doubt about Herr Alfried's plans. Perhaps being so well up in things he finds it hard to decide about them and about the country's best interest?'

'Since his latest return from the States,' lied the Baron, 'I've had no direct communication with Frau Waitzmann; so we're a little in the dark. But there's no doubt at all that Herr Alfried will do the right thing in the end.'

'He's lucky, Herr Baron, to have a choice. Most of us don't. But you wouldn't think that he could do much good by returning to the States now that they are so hostile?'

'One has to think of the future. Foreign connexions, you know, shouldn't lightly be abandoned; we don't want to be caught napping in the season of victory.'

At the speaking of this word all the other guests became merry. They drank hastily with quick, grey-haired smiles; then, just as suddenly, they became heavy again. The elderly 'desk' admiral puffed out his cheeks and leaned back against the spine of his chair and then forward again as if he were stretching an aching muscle. He used his napkin to cleanse a moustache he must have shaved off years ago. Another man, whose name Carin had forgotten, developed a thick vertical crease between the eyebrows; and Luthmann, the only person present to be unaffected by this moment of weakness, became suddenly brutal.

He dominated the table; and seeing him, as it were, stepping into a knacker's yard with his pole axe in his hand, her fear of him became hatred. He smiled at her and then looked directly at Ruprecht.

'Perhaps you are more fully informed, Herr Waitzmann?' he suggested.

'What's that?' asked the admiral. 'I can't follow this business at all.'

'Production, Herr Admiral. What the Herr Baron always refers to "as the sinews of war".'

'Oh, quite! Very important.' The admiral too turned to Ruprecht.

They all turned towards him and Luthmann lighted a fat little cigar as Ruprecht began to discuss his brother's plans.

He did it lamely. Carin longed to prompt him; but she was, for the moment, wordless. I should never have come, she was thinking. There are occasions when men must be left to scar themselves. A woman's only chance of inadequacy! But as if forest animals met, she could not help her curiosity and loved her predicament.

Floundering between anger and guilt, Ruprecht was explaining that there was really no problem at all, since the Board as at present constituted was quite capable of dealing with all eventualities. He waxed and waned so much that at some moments she despised him, while at others, as when his eye fell on Luthmann, on that 'village butcher's' judicious cigar, his anger gave him such weight that she saw him as some 'great' man in the making, and was absurdly mollified.

He'll get away with it, she thought as he began talking

about Alfried's potentialities. This is where Ruprecht will suggest something to his own advantage. After all, with the exception of the admiral, they would none of them be in the least surprised; as a businessman they'd expect it of him.

But Ruprecht did nothing of the sort. He began to hesitate and 'run down'. He talked more and more carefully as does a man who has lost all track of what he's next about to say. His fingers found that grey piece of bread left over from the soup and for an instant he came to a full stop. Then with a horrible effort, he concluded:

'In any case, I think that my mother –'

Everyone waited. But he left it like that for moments on end. She could stand it no longer; she was forced to ruin the whole atmosphere with her feminine voice.

'Your mother?' she prompted him.

He was looking straight ahead of him at one of the waiters. 'Yes, my mother.'

There was no further silence.

'What do you say?' asked the admiral turning to Luthmann as though he were deaf. 'Did he say his *mother*?'

But the Party official did not answer him. He was watching Ruprecht with the closest attention; and Ruprecht was quite oblivious of him; no anger at all in his face; as nauseated a bewilderment as if he had drunk too much wine earlier or had for long been overworking. Because they thought he was ill, they were all immediately aware of his brilliance. He had become pale in the face. He got up, as they thought, to go and be sick somewhere. He said 'Excuse me!' and left the table.

The admiral said, 'He looks seedy. Probably it was the fish – breakdown in the refrigeration due to the raids.' Then, as if this did not quite cover the incident, he asked of no one in particular, 'What was he saying about his mother?' And the Baron put in quickly: 'A very capable woman. They're both devoted to her. I wonder if you'll excuse me, also? Someone ought to see if the poor fellow's all right. He's been constantly overdoing it lately. Doesn't realize his own limitations.'

But Herr Luthmann only smiled over his little cigar: 'It's

in the family, isn't it? I've heard that Herr Alfried is also highly strung.' His glance was on Carin since she was now the only person present who might claim acquaintance with the family.

What impulse overcame her at this moment? She could never afterwards analyse its nature. She could scarcely indeed remember Alfried's physical appearance; but malice, springing from nowhere, gave her a most clear picture of him; and how distasteful. A clown, had Ruprecht said? Then, whitefaced. Something priestly? Then, in black. A confirmer of a child's night-fears? Then, stammering and egregious; a non-conformist to that world of men which she understood enough to covet and despise.

'Highly strung, Herr Luthmann?' she asked emphatically. 'Why, that's putting it mildly. He's pathologically unstable. Not quite "responsible" perhaps; and they all know it, even though, like my husband, they may be too loyal to admit it.'

'A family always sticks together,' said the admiral.

'You said irresponsible or unreliable, Baronin?' Luthmann asked her.

'Oh, not unreliable. No one takes him sufficiently seriously for that. He had visions as a child. Like some epileptics, they've had to nursery him all his life. I've no doubt at all they've longed for him to take Orders so that he might be happy. But probably Frau Waitzmann's torn two ways, as one is over a delicate son. I know the temptation myself, even though our own boy, Leo, is no embarrassment to us in any political sense.'

'Herr Alfried still has those opinions then, has he, Baronin?' asked Luthmann familiarly.

She saw Nicholas returning and hurried on. She even appealed to him before he had sat down again.

'We've both thought, Nicholas, haven't we, that Frau Waitzmann ought never to have exposed anyone so suggestible as Alfried to the American propaganda?'

'Have we, my dear?' Nicholas was looking at her as gently as if she might have confessed to him the most perfidious of her adulteries.

'But of course,' she said, 'you know that he refers to the

Führer as an upstart heretic and is always saying that victory can never be won under such leadership.'

'I think you're exaggerating,' said Nicholas. 'I've heard no such specific report of Waitzmann's opinions. He is, after all, perfectly responsible.'

'But how can you be so cruel?' she demanded, plucking at the sleeve of her dress, as nicely as a bird at its plumage. 'That's just what I was explaining to the admiral when you left us. The whole point is that he's *not* responsible! Why, to suggest that he was, would be to present him as a traitor instead of merely a harmless case of some sort.'

She paused, as if she were politely concealing a yawn, and said to the admiral, to whom she had been pretending to address all her remarks since Nicholas's return: 'Believe me, my dear Admiral, if only this young man would make up his mind to go to some seminary where he might nurse his eccentricities in peace, no one would be more pleased than my husband and myself. Since we interested ourselves in the Waitzmann Group we've had more worry about its eventual management than the entire course of the war.'

'Understandable, Baronin; it certainly doesn't do to have crackpots in charge of industry during a war.'

But the Baron had recovered himself. 'I fear my wife has exaggerated. Everything's well in hand. I'm in the closest possible touch with the Frau Kommerzienrat Waitzmann and we've nothing to fear so long as she remains in charge.'

'Yes, for so long,' agreed Carin, now permitting herself the smallest of open yawns. 'But who's to say how long that will be? Now really, you mustn't allow loyalties to betray you. Disloyalties we all understand, unfortunately, even without reference to Alfried; but –'

'That will do I think,' said the Baron. 'Let's leave it at that if you don't mind, my dear. These affairs are best not discussed in any detail at the dinner table.'

By now she was amused by his discomfort. 'Here I am doing for you what in fact you've been longing for me to do ever since you emerged again,' she would have liked to say to him. 'And then, like Macbeth, the moment you see the dagger in my hand, you start having scruples. But it's not a dagger, Nicholas dear, it's only a paper-knife! These are desk-men; a few forms will be filled in and your problems will be solved. Nothing very drastic will happen at all.'

She smiled warmly at Herr Luthmann as if they shared this secret and said: 'Nicholas is quite right. It's all dreadfully boring. For my part, if Alfried Waitzmann's ever wise enough to return there, then America may have him, if only in order that we may have a change of conversation. That, of course, is what's the matter with Ruprecht. It was no bone in his throat, he's worried grey by his loyalties.' She rose from the table. 'Nicholas dear, I do really think you ought to go and see again what's happened to him.'

'Of course.'

'Well do go, please.' She must really conceal her asperity. 'I too have a headache. It really is most oppressive in here.'

A siren sounded in the distance. A faint cry first of all which no one was sure they had heard; then a nearer repetition of it which could not be ignored. Talk dropped, the crowded room was stilled; noises filtered through from the kitchens, a cascade of knives and forks on to a steel tray, a chef's expletive. The moving waiters appeared to be tiptoeing, women fondled their furs as if caressing babies' heads and men thumbed the buttons of their uniforms. Then conversation was resumed louder than before, threaded with wicked shrills of laughter.

Luthmann had fixed on her phrase about treachery and this she had not actually intended; now that she had spoken she was quite aware that Alfried was not 'as bad as all that', but Luthmann was talking about the famed Jewish 'stab in the back' after the 1914–18 war, giving the whole conversation a Party historical flavour; and, more dangerously, lighting up the question of the Waitzmanns' antecedents.

She tried to turn the conversation by talking about the approaching air-raid: 'A few of their Wellingtons, I suppose! But the fact that even one bomb is dropped on the capital must cheer the British breakfast table.'

The admiral alone followed her up. He looked at his watch and said: 'They're early tonight. Must be a full moon.'

But Luthmann was not to be deflected. 'Not a single pork-hater within a hundred yards of us,' he was saying. 'That's a good thought.'

'What, sir?' asked the admiral.

'Herr Luthmann was discussing the Jewish question,' said the Baron distastefully.

'Oh! Never had much to do with them myself.'

'On the other hand,' went on Luthmann, 'if a bomb fell on this restaurant, not a single Jew would be killed. That's another thought.'

'I can't say that it disturbs me,' said Carin. 'After all, if we were all dying ourselves – even a headache's enough to make *me* oblivious of my company.'

'Then you can have had no dealings with them,' said Luthmann, who was drinking greedily. 'That's the real test. Ask anyone who's a good word to say for them only one question; ask him if he's ever had any business dealings with them, not meeting them at garden parties and so on; but business. If he says he has and can still support them, then he's a liar or worse, and that's all there is to it.'

'Garden parties? How quaint.' Carin gave him another warm, disgusted smile.

'We might as well discuss our love-affairs in public,' she was thinking; but she saw that the creature was smiling to himself as if greatly pleased by the exchange and realized that he would be saying, 'Never trust a good-looking woman – that's another of my rules.'

'I really must get some fresh air,' she told Nicholas. 'Perhaps Ruprecht would take me home? He's still looking very queasy himself.'

For he had just returned and was standing behind the admiral; obviously making an effort not to appear tired or ill.

'You don't mind, do you, Ruprecht?' she appealed. 'There's nothing you particularly want to discuss? Because Nicholas could perhaps take me.'

'In the middle of an air-raid, Baronin?' asked Luthmann, looking round the table for laughter. 'A headache's not so severe as being blown to pieces, you know.'

'You don't know my headaches. They're worse than Marie Antoinette's.'

Luthmann picked up a table knife; he neatly severed an apple and again looked round for applause. Receiving none, he got to his feet and made a great show of kissing her hand.

Nicholas accompanied them to the door.

'You went too far on the question of Alfried. Heaven knows what troubles you may not have caused us.'

'In the morning,' she said furiously. 'I was trying to help you all and my head's fiendish. I don't know why I came...'

She drove with Ruprecht through the wide, nearly empty, streets. High above the dark buildings, searchlights and flak; another Berlin over them between whose exploding lights and clear stars men swarmed in their tiny machines.

'What is this you've said about Alfried?' asked Ruprecht, heavy over the steering wheel.

'Heavens, I can't remember. I was thinking about you, dearest. That revolting little Luthmann and his questions. You had gone, Nicholas was being old-school and someone had to fill in. It was a crisis.'

How confident she was. The essential thing now was to lie so successfully that he would never feel guilty. She must protect him.

'You made everyone so suspicious,' she told him. 'The only possible thing to do was to be more or less truthful. Not easy when one knows so little about poor Alfried. Perhaps I was a little too facetious. I doubt if my comments will even be remembered; but at least I succeeded in making them laugh.'

'You did?'

'Of course. With the exception of Nicholas, that is. He feels himself too much involved with your mother – and then again there are his traditions. He does like things to be open and soldierly; a charge sheet, witnesses, corporals' evidence.'

'You think nothing will come of it?'

'They might perhaps think it wiser if someone else took over – they might approach Nicholas with some useful suggestion as to your brother's future. But I can't honestly be sure I've helped as much as that.'

'How am I to know what to believe?'

'You're tired. Now do think back for a moment and tell me why it was you stopped short at your mother.'

'She had been in my mind lately. I don't know if I care for her.'

'Silly boy, of course you do. Now drive me to the park and we'll go for a little walk. A good night's rest and everything will seem much better in the morning.'

He parked his car beside an entrance to the Tiergarten and together they walked under the trees.

She took his hand: 'How noisy it is! It must be quite their biggest raid so far.'

It sounded as though there were a select rain shower deluging the shrubbery just ahead of them. Leaves of the evergreens detached themselves in the moonlight and slumped to the soil. Weighty drops fell into the earth. A pool started to life as though a handful of pebbles had been thrown into it; then something ploughed into the asphalt just behind them.

Ruprecht pushed her: 'Run for the summerhouse!'

'But it's shrapnel, come with me!'

'Oh, let him walk!' she thought, 'it may change his mood.'

In the summerhouse, so bare and pretty, clean swept of peacetime mess, cigarette packets and chocolate wrappings, she was calm. Looking out into the silvered park over which flares flew and metal still fell like rain, she lighted a cigarette. She had the oddest feeling that she was wet and young; a dash through sudden rain, her own scent filling the confined space. Was there not some language in which she could make this clear to him?

But he was standing outside watching the barrage from a nearby battery and she came closer to him. They stood looking up at the cold sky, the quick fire-bursts under the moon, the blue-white ladders of searchlights reeling over the city.

'What is it, Ruprecht?'

'I've told you. I love my brother.'

But she misheard him in the firing of the barrage.

'Put her out of your mind until you see her again. You must grow up.'

He looked at her with hatred; worse than Luthmann's discerning glance.

'My *brother*, I said; not my mother.' His voice was venomous and he moved away as if he was stepping back in a prosecution. 'I don't know what you've done interfering like this. Dangerous.'

He went on speaking through the crashes of heavy salvoes; 'Destiny ... Alexandra ... A betrayal of confidence; coarse-mindedness. I didn't mean anyone to do anything. I was only talking. He was an additional obstruction. I was being opposed in too many directions at once.'

The anti-aircraft shells directly overhead cracked like near thunder; not a blunt noise, but sharp, as if the upper air were being rent apart.

So it's Alexandra after all, she thought.

'What a coward you are!' she told him. 'You'd have preferred not to know about it. You were waiting for it to happen – as it certainly would have happened sooner or later – behind your back. And now, because you've gone on bullying everyone until they felt they had to do something, you start talking of Destiny.'

She clicked open her handbag: precise, fascinating movements: lighting and drawing deeply on a Gauloise in a mannered nineteen-twentyish way; so that he saw her age.

'Heavens!' she went on. 'Are we to fear disturbances of Destiny only when we know about them? A dozen people are probably betraying me at this moment. And what do I care? I shall find out about it when I get there.'

'Kiss her!' He was thinking, watching that ardent, moon-bright, face. 'Alfried'll be all right. I'll write to him the moment I get back and tell him the truth.'

He smiled at her. She saw him visibly relax and was astonished. She smoked unconcernedly while he confided in her yet again:

'A cable from Fritz. A warning from myself, and he'll take the first available plane. Technically, the States is still neutral. Alfried still has time.'

'Much the best,' she agreed, 'and of course you'll be telling him the truth. A confession, my dear; so comforting.'

'You're right. It was bound to happen sooner or later. Much better to bring it out into the open.' He paused. 'Really, I should apologize to you.'

'Sweet Ruprecht!' She dropped and ground out her cigarette. 'You're so scrupulous, darling; grumble, grumble like a little boy. Why, you even grumbled at Alexandra after I'd spent half an hour persuading her to welcome you. Supposing *she* had written to her father about your difficulties? Would that have made it any easier for you?'

'I didn't go to the same lengths with her. We talked principally about her knitting.'

'Oh, that knitting.'

'She's knitting for a regiment of cripples?' he said. 'Twenty-three pairs of socks without a foot between them.'

'Twenty-four,' she corrected him. 'One pair is for Leo.'

'So she told me.'

'Poor Ruprecht.'

There was that little pause of the glance, of eyes, of swift appraisal. So much amusement, such a relief; the comedy of sexual complicity. Without a further word they moved into the summerhouse.

Chapter 4

For Kommandant Grunwald of the Albrechtstrasse Prison, Berlin, the preliminary interview with Alfried Waitzmann was a profound shock. For he had expected that, to carry off the affair satisfyingly, he would have to simulate the optimism which was not in his nature.

He had imagined himself stepping easily away from his varnished pinewood desk as he told his chief officer, Halstedt, 'You may go, Halstedt. No need, my dear Waitzmann, for formalities between *us*. Your friend, the Baron von Hoffbach, was particularly emphatic that you should be incommoded as little as possible –' or words to that effect; though probably subtler when the time actually came. The Kommandant could always rely on the exquisite manipulation of his words and feelings to suit the occasion, because of the deadness inside him, the thorny despair of his home life.

Indeed he was quite looking forward to this envisaged encounter; the suggestion of moistness in his own eyes at the sight of this forlorn man of wealth and influence thrown temporarily into his charge; a victim of ridiculous indiscretions who had jeopardized for himself a future of silver and gold to which the Kommandant could never have aspired.

There would be more fencing; putting the man at his ease. A cigarette from the silver box, attention drawn to the homely touches of the office in the new administrative block: photograph of his son Hubertus at the age of fourteen, flashing: photograph of Gudrun, his wife, in an 'up-phase' – white velvet, piled-up hair, Nuremberg 1936. Then, after enquiries, half social, half official, the reassurances: 'Can't do anything about the food, of course; but since the wheels will soon be turning in a reverse direction, that shouldn't worry you, Waitzmann.'

Ah, but would they? In his fantasy the Kommandant had always stopped at this point. It was a question of who was turning the wheels. Indeed, they very seldom ever stopped; and he doubted if they had once been known to reverse. Very well then, Herr Waitzmann, in his black suit with already a little of the pallor of uncertainty on his face, should now be pitied. More sensations of liberal tears at the contemplation of the wheels continuing to turn. A sudden reassuring image of Officer Halstedt, blotting them out. Never anticipate. But a hand on Waitzmann's shoulder at this moment, a glance of the Kommandant's blue eyes across the distances separating them. The unspoken never to be spoken admission, 'Tortured, my dear fellow, all of us. I too. Germany. Destiny. The grip of forces we – Come, come. I understand you have had doubts. Haven't we all! But *you* acted upon them. I, as a man, understand this. Never certain of Heaven, but Hell! Aha, that's not made so difficult for us.'

All this and so much more would have been said by that warm hand or by an equivalent gesture – even a glass of wine or the passage of Hubertus's photograph. 'Bright boy, works in the Ministry of Propaganda. Not my choice, but –'

Then, unobtrusively, the toe on the concealed bell which would bring Halstedt back. Just time to say a few things about the prison library, visiting privileges, interviews at a moment's notice. 'At any time you like, you have only to let Halstedt here know. Halstedt will look after you admirably. There will be the doctor, of course, but that is mere routine – like the army. Now don't forget, Waitzmann, I'm here and your friend von Hoffbach, the Baron, etc., etc. All letters censored, of course; but –'

So he had imagined it; but in the event, the prisoner had not waited for any sort of manoeuvring. Even before Halstedt had been dismissed, this pale, black-suited man had sprung across the floor to the desk and put out his hand to shake that of the Kommandant.

'How do you do, sir. I'm so sorry to – No, no, I'm not. After all, it's your work, you're used to it. But I find it extraordinary.'

'Yes, yes, extraordinary. No doubt,' said the Kommandant, looking at Halstedt without seeing him, 'you mean the fact of –'

'Of?' questioned Alfried, waiting courteously but with a leaning kind of eagerness which made the Kommandant step hurriedly out from behind his desk. 'Why, the fact of my imprisonment, sir, quite extraordinary! I'm *here*, in Albrechtstrasse. After all, sir, everybody at some time or another has imagined themselves imprisoned. It's like rape or suicide. There isn't a man who hasn't contemplated such things – or finding a burglar in the pitch of night. Why, we've all –' He broke off and began again: 'And to tell you the truth, lately I'd begun to think about the possibility rather more often and in more detail. I've a powerful imagination! But to find it actually happening after picturing it so often seems to have made it all the more surprising!'

The Kommandant looked at his photographs on the mantelpiece; his eye wandered to various trophies made by past prisoners: statues of the Madonna, busts of the Führer and model U-boats. His gaze fell upon Halstedt, heavily discreet, it moved back to Alfried, who had paused with the fearfulness of having been impolite to talk so much.

'Halstedt, you may go,' he said unwillingly; and Halstedt obeyed with equal reluctance.

The Kommandant collected himself; he looked up at the beerhouse-style rafters spanning the ceiling and was reassured by memories of peacetime Bavarian holidays.

'Not at all, Waitzmann. On the contrary, I'm glad to find you in such good shape after the shock of your arrest.'

'It may be deceptive, sir, it occurred to me that perhaps my excitement's a bad sign – I'm always talkative at a dentist's, for instance. Really, though, I mustn't keep you. I suppose there are rules and so forth? Perhaps it would save your time if you were to give me a handbook?'

'Oh, you'll find that in your cell. Now do sit down. Here, have a cigarette?'

'Thank you, no. I've recently given it up. Since my return from the States in fact.'

'So? Well, perhaps you're wise.'

'I shall probably weaken, of course. It all depends on how long I'm here, and I suppose that'll depend on many other factors.' He looked round the room again. 'How strange it all is. But for the Japanese attack I could have returned to the States, as I suppose you know? But something stopped me. Most odd. D'you think it's possible for a man to want to lose his freedom?'

'I suppose it's possible.' The Kommandant was thinking of his wife.

'I hope I'm not wasting your time, sir.'

The Kommandant slid an arm down the mantelshelf and told himself aloud: 'To listen to you is the object of the interview, Waitzmann; my duty. But apart from that, it's from these affairs that I hope to continue to learn.'

'You've very patient. I can tell you that for a time I imagined I had a vocation – a combination of loneliness and intense greed, I suppose. Yet I'm by no means solitary; I like people and enjoy the world enormously. I'm constantly in love but always baffled by my own limitations. I don't think I could remain faithful to one affair or even to fifty, so I've delayed over marriage. I've always believed I was a liability and that's why I went to the United States.'

The Kommandant was a little lost. 'Restlessness?' he suggested.

'No, no,' said Alfried. 'Well, perhaps – it was a woman, a nun as a matter of fact, a postulant. There was still time for me to marry her; but she was fairly safe I think, I mean really convinced of her vocation – safe in her castle, so to speak. One wonders if all the castles weren't convents and all the maidens postulants. You'll admit that such passion-ate innocence is a powerful attraction in a girl, sir? All that was lacking in our case was the dragon.'

'The dragon? Quite.' The Kommandant again saw his wife without meaning to, in one of her down-phases. He was disturbed and began to count mentally on his fingers: library, visiting privileges, censored letters, the Baron von Hoffbach. Herr Waitzmann had a most expressive face, he noted. The electric clock made a small click each time the pendulum touched the terminals.

'I may talk freely, I suppose?' went on Alfried. 'I know that's the reason I'm in prison so perhaps it's an impudent question under the circumstances.'

The Kommandant felt a little safer. 'Once they're sentenced thieves still continue to thieve – if they can; though there are punishments.'

Alfried picked a model liner from the mantelpiece. 'In that case, perhaps I'd better say no more!'

But the Kommandant did not want him to leave. 'What you say to me is confidential,' he assured him. 'It may even assist me to help you; but outside –' he indicated the prison itself, 'you'd do well to be discreet.'

'No microphones?' asked Alfried, shaking the model.

'No microphones as yet,' said the Kommandant.

'One hears of such vicious developments.'

'I must advise you, of course, Waitzmann, that neither officially nor personally can I countenance any disloyalty to the Party. We're both aware that the crime with which you are charged is sedition.'

'And rightly so,' Alfried agreed. 'Though I didn't think I'd gone quite as far as that. I'm so much of a coward, in fact, that this might turn out to be a good thing for me. In some ways I look on it as an involuntary retreat.'

The Kommandant smiled a little sourly and Alfried attempted to reassure him.

'It's not that I'm fond of retreats, but sometimes they do force one to come to a decision.'

'In a sense I agree with you.' The Kommandant had a sudden desire to smile as at the death of a friend.

'After all, if one has doubts about a government, there's no point in staying in the middle. One must either get up to the top or sink down to the bottom.'

'You're not suggesting that you came here voluntarily?'

'By no means; it was most unexpected.'

The Kommandant again remarked the brightness of his eyes and two perceptions passed through his mind, swifter than swans in the sky: that those eyes were like his son Hubertus's: that this young man was not after all sure that he had not been imprisoned by his own election.

When swans have passed there is always sadness and the Kommandant was at first irritated and then disposed to be cheerful.

'Well,' he said. 'This has all been most interesting, Waitzmann. I only hope you're not going to be disappointed in us. The monotony you know – although I've no doubt it won't be many days before your friend, the Baron, looks in to see how you're settling down.'

'I suppose not.'

The Kommandant picked up something from the mantelpiece and studied it with interest. He had a headache, he felt cramped and confined. He must stretch his legs. Where the devil was his coffee? He took his hands out of his pockets and stood a little straighter.

'Unfortunately, Waitzmann, unlike the present conversation, all others with any visitors whatsoever must be recorded. I'm sure you'll not embarrass us by any indiscretions.'

'I'll guard against it, though as a matter of fact, with von Hoffbach it won't be very difficult. Somehow all my ideas seem a little dull when I'm with him; but I'll do my best to reassure him about myself so that he can pass it on to my mother.'

'Good,' said the Kommandant, treasuring this remark of reassuring the Baron. 'Well, now I have to get on my rounds. Are there any questions you'd like to ask me before I hand you over to Halstedt?'

'Only the usual one, sir, how long?'

'Impossible to say. As you know, it might have been a very different business, shorter, sharper. In cases like yours, I think I might say that the length of your sentence is at the discretion of the Führer, that's all.'

'Thank you, sir, you've been most kind.'

The Kommandant returned to his desk and pressed the bell under the carpet. As Halstedt came in and waited by the door he stood up again with the intention of returning to Alfried. He wanted to put that hand on his shoulder and shepherd him across the carpet, past the three large photographs of the Führer, the Minister of Propaganda and the

Reichsführer S.S.; past the smaller group photographs of the prison staff, with his year-by-year younger self sitting in the centre. But at the last moment he found that the gesture would be distasteful, so he took one more look at Alfried's eyes, then he gave the prisoner a little bow; and Halstedt, with harshness, commanded:

'This way.'

The Kommandant then reseated himself at his desk which lay mid-way between the barred windows facing out into the prison entrance yard. He had the solid rectangle of the desk in front of him and a square of wall directly behind him, so that from the outside his office always appeared to be empty, even when he was in there; and for some reason at this moment he found this especially comforting. Awkward customers, he told himself. A brick or a shot in the back of the neck.

He found the report on Prisoner Waitzmann difficult to complete so he put it off for a few minutes whilst he drafted a letter to Himmler:

Albrechtstrasse Prison,
Albrechtstrasse,
Berlin.

23 February, 1942.
Herr Reichsführer,

Sir, your esteemed directive to hand. The prisoner A. Waitzmann, No. 0654 was received into this establishment for ultimate transfer to the special observation wing today, Feb. 23rd, at 19.30 hrs. He was interviewed this morning. (Transcript to follow.)

As you have requested he will be given special consideration pending your further advice, and visiting privileges by such persons as are named on your pro forma. All personnel in direct or indirect contact will submit confidential reports to myself on his behaviour. Similar reports from the medical side will also be submitted. The prisoner's next-of-kin, the Frau Kommerzienrat Waitzmann, will be suitably advised in terms previously approved by yourself and the Baron von Hoffbach at the Chancellery.

On a separate sheet of paper he added a note in his own hand and sealed it in a separate envelope:

I thank you, Herr Reichsführer S.S. for your most benevolent enquiries regarding the health of my wife, Gudrun. Alas! Her gall bladder continues to torment her at regular intervals. I have the greatest difficulty in obtaining supplies of unsaturated fatty acids to render the contents of her colon more fluid. I greatly regret that the doctor here has pronounced it more than unwise for her to have to submit to the calcium-impregnated waters of the Auschwitz plateau. At the same time I am sensible of the honour you have done me in offering me this post and of your continuing warm interest in my own and my wife's behalf. Heil Hitler!

> Felix Grunwald, Colonel Kommandant.

Now for the actual report, he thought. Extremely tricky. Perhaps it'd be better to put it off until the evening. For he always worked better in the evening. He might do the round, drop in on the doctor and have a cup of coffee. But if he did that he would miss the post. The Reichsführer would at once become suspicious. Very well then, what the devil had Waitzmann said? What was the total impression? *Must not get involved.*

He took a report form out of his drawer and compromised by jotting down some notes to draft out later:

Interviewed 11.00 hrs to 11.30 (*? add fifteen minutes for conscientiousness: could not have stood more at the moment*).

Waitzmann is a gentleman not markedly Jewish-looking (*? Harmless ass: thoroughly dangerous?*).

Suggest, my dear Reichsführer, that in this instance, the medical reports will be of considerably more help to you than anything I myself can –

He appears to be resigned (*? positively sanguine*). Made no demands. Talked principally about his religion and love-affairs. No political asides: (*was this true?*).

At this point the Kommandant snatched up an internal report form, one that would be seen only by the senior staff of the prison itself. Now what was that nonsense of dragons and castles? Perhaps the fellow was musical. (*? Wagner: Sibelius.*)

Location? Well, that was settled: double cell to himself on A Landing – under officer Halstedt.

Exercise: Medical officer decides: but in isolation to begin with.

Visits: full privileges *pro tem.*

Letters and interviews: close censorship of all records by myself.

Recreation: prison band.

Employment: Library – Political section.

He thought to himself: *Might be damned useful at home just now. Could fix wireless, cheer up Gudrun. No, no. Too risky –*

At this point he was interrupted by Halstedt who asked whether or not the new prisoner was to be allowed writing materials: 'He asks permission to keep a journal, Herr Kommandant.'

'See that he's supplied with foolscap and then join me over in the hospital. I'm going over to have a word with the doctor.'

'Very good, sir.'

They drank ersatz coffee together in the hospital office. Dr Lütgens was a fierce young man with a cold grey face and luminous eyes; though recently invalided out of the Medical Corps with a duodenal ulcer, he had managed to retain his uniform and always wore it. He was a keen amateur strategist and this morning gave the Kommandant a long talk on the implications of the bad news from the Russian front. He spoke coldly on behalf of the Führer and the Generals, running his fingers all over the morning's maps in the *Allgemeine Zeitung* as he did so.

The Kommandant sat patiently waiting for him to finish. He knew the sequence exactly: the narrowing down from global strategy to domestic affairs, the philosophical interlude laced with eugenics which preceded any discussion of prison business. And when, finally, the Kommandant himself broached this subject, Dr Lütgens invariably became uncommunicative. He seemed to have no opinions whatsoever on such matters, or only written ones. He was very fond of saying, for example: 'I'll let you have it all on the relevant forms, Herr Kommandant,' or 'If you don't mind, I'll deal with that on paper.'

This morning he said only, 'Ah, yes, Waitzmann. I read through the reports last night, I'm due to see him after lunch. I'll see that you have my minute –'

But the Kommandant interrupted him: 'You've no idea how long he's likely to be with us?'

The doctor looked up, visibly recalling himself from larger questions. 'You mean with you, Kommandant, or with *us*?'

'I thought perhaps you might have had medical instructions that conflicted with our own.'

The doctor removed his newspaper and opened a file. He looked hard at the Kommandant: 'It's possible, as you realize, sir, that the matter might be taken out of my hands too. In any case, my own first impressions as to his responsibility will depend on my interview this afternoon.'

There was a pause; as if to emphasize his reticence a red light flicked on behind the doctor's head on the indicator board. Simultaneously the internal telephone rang and he picked it up.

'Security is calling me. I think we'd better say that you'll have my full report within twenty-four hours.' He pressed a switch on his desk to summon his chief hospital officer and a few minutes later the Kommandant, accompanied by Halstedt, began his morning rounds.

That evening, after Halstedt had personally served him his supper of soup and bread, Alfried sat down at his cell table and began a journal. He headed the page: *A Record of my Imprisonment*: and, then thinking that the personal pronoun looked wrong, substituted the word '*an*' for '*my*'.

He wrote for several minutes, said a prayer, and then began again at the top of the page:

My difficulties began when I saw something which perhaps I ought not to have seen. I was six years of age at the time and our house seemed to me to be both large and beautiful—

Outside his cell, somewhere in the prison courtyard, the clock struck six, the hour at which the angel had first appeared to him. It had clung about his room, he remembered, in a most impersonal fashion; never replying, scarcely glancing at him, seeming content only to be seen; yet contriving by this means alone to reassure him. He had understood from the beginning that he must keep quiet about it, but had later grown bold and boastful and told Kegel. Kegel had told his mother who had questioned him eagerly. The news had spread through the household and amongst the factory employees.

'What colour was it?'

'All colours.'

'But what colours?'

'All colours in one.'

'Where did it first appear, Master Alfried?'

'In my bedroom.'

'By a crucifix?'

'No, above my bed – at the head of it.'

This, of course, had been a lie to protect the angel. For, in reality, it had clung to the picture rail which was only half a metre from the flat of the ceiling, which would imply that it had been small. But the angel had had no size at all, neither had it been serious, solemn, nor gay. It had been, in a sense, comical and that was its greatest secret; the fact that it had had no sense of its own importance.

When his mother had asked him why he thought it had appeared, he had said: 'Because I wanted it to.' And this had so satisfied her that she had foolishly told everyone, even the Jesuits, who had been as much taken in as everyone else and so had not thought of asking him why he had wanted it.

That summer, Kegel had had her younger sister, Elizabeth, to stay for a town holiday. She was a country girl of eighteen and she had slept in the other bed in the night nursery. He had fallen in love with her. Each morning he had climbed into her bed at day-break, and at first she had always pretended to be asleep. He would lie down beside her under the great pile of feathers within which her body softly breathed and moved. The skin of her neck was soft, curls of dark hair feathered above its hollow; and as she lay still, pretending that she did not know he had come, her back to him and a long arm over the coverlet, he would put his lips to this hollow and breathe against it, tasting back his changed breath.

She would start, say, 'Oh, who is this in my bed?'

'It's me, Alfried.'

'What? A man in my bed?'

'Yes.'

There would be a silence in which he knew that he was indeed a man. He would not forget that she dressed him and put him to bed, could lift him in and out of the bath and must kneel down in order to dry him. He would only see that a man lay inside him to be called awake by this game, a being in scale with Elizabeth's beauty. Then she would put her arm round him and hold him, saying: 'Sh! Little one.'

He would kiss her wrist and play with her fingers passively to begin with, then forcing them far apart with his own, trying to hurt her. She would say that he was so strong; she would weaken, he would pull her fingers further apart until she pretended to scream with the pain when he would kiss their tips and bandage them all together, saying: 'There, there, now, little Elizabeth.' But she would become violent and strong. They would wrestle there on the big bed. She would weigh him down with her legs, straddle him for a moment like a bird with a breast of finest down, pressing against his hot cheeks as he struggled beneath her trying to throw her off; but she would hold him there, stronger and stronger, laughing at him and saying: 'What sort of a man is this? Why, it's no man at all, it's only a little, weakly, boy.'

He would start biting her gently, and then desperately. She would kiss his eyelids and allow the coverlet to slip off the bed to the floor and then follow it herself so that his pride should be restored. He might leap down upon her, upon this soft cocoon of Elizabeth and the duckdown carpeting the bare, shining, floor.

Then she would stretch herself, carry him to his own bed, yawn about the room singing a little, saying: 'Listen to the world awake.' She would pluck tiny feathers out of her hair. She would put on a dressing-gown to go down to the kitchen and fetch him up a slice of the buttered black bread favoured by his grandfather.

But one morning he had offended her. She had stopped

playing and looked in his eyes with what was perhaps a quickly concealed amusement. He had felt the secret which each successive night and morning had been slowly growing inside him, drawn out of his mind. He had noticed how, that morning, she had brooded upon it, not singing, but sitting for long minutes on her own bed watching him in a way that filled him with anxiety.

When, after all, she had brought him his bread and milk, had smiled at him and forgiven him with a somehow generous caution, he had been so sick with guilt and sorrow that he had called on the angel. It was in this way he had earned the nickname which Ruprecht had never allowed him to forget, and which, not indirectly, had been responsible for his present imprisonment.

Thinking how dangerous nicknames could be, he picked up his pen again and added to what he had already written:

I was quite at home in the world of my garden and family. Though I was by no means wholly innocent and could never remember having been so, I saw an angel of some sort; it was this experience which began my imprisonment.

He paused, thinking what to add to this paragraph, when suddenly the light was switched off. It must be six-thirty. He had forgotten that Halstedt had told him that from this hour the prison was in darkness. He sat where he was for a few moments and then, hearing footsteps crossing the court-yard outside, climbed on to the table to take down his blackout and admit some fresh air. He looked out between the bars and saw someone, the Kommandant, he thought, crossing the yard; the moonlight casting a short shadow behind him. Momentarily, he was tempted to call out good-night to him but then thought better of it and lay down on his bed.

For the sake of his health, the Kommandant always walked the kilometre to his home, this evening a little faster than usual.

In peacetime he had always paused in the drive to see which lights were on and thus determine any slight change in his wife's mental condition. If she were nearing the end of a 'down-phase' there might be several: the bathroom or the drawing-room, for example; if the end of an 'up-phase', only one: the kitchen. At the zenith of her optimism his house in winter would have been ablaze with lights; at the nadir, dark and silent, as now in the blackout.

Opening the front door he switched on the light in the hall and went to the downstairs cloakroom. His son had been in and gone out again: the little room was still warm with his presence: highly scented brilliantine, the silver-backed brushes askew in front of the mirror, a used hand-towel. On the tiled floor there were two parcels from the Mono-store in the Kudamm with an ill-spelt note in Hubertus's handwriting on the back of the clothing coupons.

'She wanted underwear, pair stockings, also a white blowse, O.S. Your turn. Back late I expect. H.'

The Kommandant washed his hands scrupulously and studied his sad face in the mirror. He determined that it was sad despite his quiet exhilaration over the affair Waitz-mann. He told himself that this was the face the prisoner had seen, sad and cogitative, giving the lie to some of the hearty words he had been forced to speak. But, he assured himself, 'We communicated'; and, feeling even more cheer-ful, he screwed himself up to the evening's encounter with his wife.

He would treat the whole thing as the execution of an unpleasant duty, he decided. He would go straight into the kitchen where she would be waiting to watch him cook his supper. If she were not there then he would go up to her bedroom where, unmoving against the headboard of her bed, she would be awaiting the new clothes and the oppor-tunity of making the one remark on which she had been meditating all day.

The duty of an unpleasant execution, thought the Kom-mandant, overcome by some last-minute reluctance. No preliminaries; a squad; slender man blindfold against wall. Command! Fire! Falls dead. No doctoring. Momentarily, he caught himself disliking Doctor Lütgens intensely; then, with a last glance at himself in the cloakroom mirror, he caught up the parcels and went through to the kitchen.

As he had anticipated, Gudrun was sitting in the wooden chair against the wall; but she was a little larger than he had imagined her, a little stiffer. He gave her the parcels and kissed her on the forehead, noticing as he did so that the two flattish boxes lay across her black lap and that her hands came up automatically to retain them. Otherwise, save by the exclusion of her smile, she did not acknowledge his salute at all.

In the small refrigerator on the other side of the kitchen there was washed tripe in an enamel bowl, the usual selection of war-time sausage-meats, some tinned milk and some egg substitute and half a kilo of white fat. Carefully the Kommandant re-washed the tripe and put it on the stove to boil. He sliced onions and long sausage, mixed a roux of fat and brown flour ready for the tripe juice and then washed his trembling hands once more. He cut bread and toasted two pieces beneath the grill, while all the time Gudrun watched him, following each of his actions with fractional movements of her head on its broad neck.

Before he broke away to the dining-room, to the solitary place laid for him by the day woman at the head of the polished table, he had himself to say something to her. It was necessary to have broken the silence with a word; as essential as the kiss. Even though she might not reply she would certainly not go upstairs until he had spoken to her. 'Things went well today, my dear.'

She glanced at him royally; her hands reassuring themselves of the two draper's boxes on her lap.

'We took in a new "political", a friend of the Baron von Hoffbach's in whom the Reichsführer is interested.'

'So?'

'I've been rather worried about it, but things went well after all. He'll settle down quickly, I think, and there should be no complications.'

She lifted the boxes and placed them on the table beside her. She smoothed the heavy stuff of her skirt over her thighs and stood up. Holding the parcels like a tray in front of her she took short steps to the door and waited for him to open it, then, still smiling to herself, she crossed the hall and ascended the stairs to her bedroom.

The Kommandant took his supper through to the dining-room and ate it in the midst of his many possessions. Some, like his few pieces of old silver, he had inherited, some he had been given by wealthy prisoners or their friends or parents; others he had collected in street markets and antique shops. All of them he loved. They were the furniture of his achievement and of a kind of safety. Surrounded by them, it was possible for him to believe that at some time he had been loved, that his father and mother must have cherished him in their bequests; even, that in their death, that 'must' was 'now'. He was happy to eat in such comfort; his things gave splendour to his loneliness.

The meal finished, he drank a little good wine from an engraved glass and restoppered the decanter. Then he walked round his table, enjoying the glimmer of light on glass and silver. Outside the dark house he was aware of the greater darkness in which the prison lay: the men in their cells who supported him like five hundred turbulent sons. He switched off the lights and went back to the kitchen to wash up. Before he could reach his bedroom and the book-cases in which his week's reading was already mapped out, he had one more hurdle to cross; the final word with his wife.

He knocked at her door, waited the customary seconds for her 'No', and when it was not given went in to her.

He saw that the parcels had been opened and rewrapped; they lay at the foot of her bed on the luggage trestle with only the pair of stockings extracted. These lay on her quilt and she herself brooded beyond them, comfortable, her still-black hair scrupulously combed down to frame her neck and face, the breadth of her cold white shoulders. Her reading lamp was switched on and her small hands, with a ring on each, rested on the stuffed coverlet easily, with no book between them nor anywhere in sight.

'Hubertus shopped badly then?' he began. 'My dear, I'll find the time to get you what you need tomorrow. There's no chance of your being well enough to come with me, I suppose?'

'No, there is not.'

'You feel no better at all?'

'I am, as we all know, perfectly well; a good deal healthier than you are yourself, Felix.'

'Yes, dear.'

'I am in full command of myself. At these times I see most clearly.'

'I know you do.'

He had picked up the parcels and was reading the note in her spreading handwriting:

A brassière of the German type. *Reinforced*. No Parisian lewdity. Drawers from my dressmaker with *broad* elastic. A white blouse with low but not immodest neckline of fine cotton and *lined*. Full length sleeves buttoning at the wrist. If these cannot be found for me I shall have to retire entirely to my bedroom for the time being.

She had so many drawers full of blouses, all white, all with sleeves buttoning at the wrist; she had boxes full of old-fashioned brassières and cami-knickers packed between camphorated tissues. She had two or three dozen pairs of plain knickers or 'drawers' as she called them, never worn. In her cupboard there were squads of blunt-toed shoes and black pleated skirts; the mission-wear of her girlhood when she had done church-work in the merry slums of east Berlin. He remember her vividly, her correct black and white; a strong crusading girl behind tea urns or in soup kitchens during the post-war depression. He remembered how they had danced together in dusty halls, drunk Schnapps at Christmas time and, in summer, caressed antiseptically on rivers' banks with a prayer book in among the picnic things.

'You mustn't hurry, Felix,' she said now. 'A husband should always conceal his eagerness to leave his sick wife.'

The Kommandant sighed.

'Well, won't you discuss it?' she asked. 'After all, there's nothing wrong with me really; yet I'm such a heavy cross to you both. Wouldn't you like to tell me how much you regret it, or are those days all over too?'

'What days?'

'Battles!' she said.

'My dear, you don't realize that I have a great deal to see to in the morning. There may be important visitors and I must get some sleep.'

'I think you read too much,' she said with a faint smile.

'The Reichsführer will probably telephone. I must be fully prepared.'

She stroked her cheek with one of her ringed fingers. 'Indeed you must.'

The Kommandant took up the parcels to shield himself a little. He knew she was about to say that one thing on which she had decided.

'For if you're not careful, you may let your special prisoner betray you.'

He looked at her, at her small blue eyes in the big face. His hands were shaking again. Feeling himself threatened he cast round for something hurtful to say and remembered her note.

'If Herr Himmler does telephone I may well ask his permission to employ this particular man in the house. It will depend on how quickly you're up and about again. I find these depressed phases of yours an increasing strain.'

She smiled indulgently, and he went on:

'I know you dislike having prisoners about the place, but I have to think of my own health occasionally; and under these rather particular circumstances the Reichsführer would not forbid it, I think.'

'He would welcome it,' she said.

'I'm glad you agree.'

'He would welcome it because it would be so unwise, so very unwise.'

'Nevertheless –'

'I'm tired,' she said, waving at him. 'Please don't waste any more of your evening on me.'

He left the parcels on an oak chest outside her bedroom where he would see them on his way to the bathroom in the morning. In his room the blackouts were already in position. He drew the curtains together and switched on the light above his desk. This week was to be devoted to reading hagiography and he sat down in the chair to run through one or two of the letters of St Teresa of Avila.

Bookcases surrounded three walls of his bedroom. From his bed his view was almost exclusively of bindings. To his father's library over the past twenty years he had added a complete set of the German Historians, books of philosophy, mystical theology and a collection of the important military strategists. He had a dozen reputable text-books on psychology and criminology; treatises on physical culture, physics and eugenics. In addition he had a history of torture, all the more important works on diabolism and the Caballa and a shelf full of the world's classics in translation together with the complete works of Goethe and many miscellaneous volumes of sermons and missionary endeavour in various parts of the world. Only his wife knew that, although he continued to buy and collect, he no longer read more than a page or two at a time.

It interested him to pick a book from his shelves and see his pencilled comments in the margins; the date on which he had started to read it, the underlinings, the question marks and cross references. By this means he could trace the decline of his interest in any particular subject; for the more recent the date in the book the fewer the number of pages read and marked. But still he pecked at them, still hoped, read eagerly a section or two, or, as tonight, sat absorbed for half an hour by the extraordinary character of the nun of Avila.

By reading in this manner, by constantly collecting and never giving up, he persuaded himself that behind all else his real and secret progress went on. Ultimately, from his weariness would come wisdom, power, unification; at some final moment the books would be no longer necessary, outward experience would conform to inner necessity; an explanation would be his at the last.

But this evening as he enjoyed his nightly cigar and made unhappy comparisons between the Spanish nun and his tormented wife, Hubertus, who had been in his mother's bedroom, suddenly rushed in upon him. He was wearing one of his smartest uniforms and had obviously had too much to drink.

'Hello, still reading? How's the cigar?'

'You're very late.'

'Tremendous night, Father. Party with my chief.'

'Herr Goebbels?' How much longer, the Kommandant wondered, would the Reichsminister put up with the boy?

'No, not old clubfoot. He's junketing with his woman. I was with my departmental boss, Ulrich! Christian names already, you see!'

'On both sides?'

But Hubertus ignored the thrust and went on to describe the party: 'A gaggle of youngish girls in backless frocks and rather spotty. I longed to powder their backs for them and freshen up their hair-dos. They all seemed to have dandruff. Everyone drank masses and there were some interesting men on leave; *they* thrilled me – the mark of the warrior, you know. In between drinks I watched their eyes. You could see they had seen terrible things.'

What would I feel, the Kommandant was wondering, if Goebbels did get tired of him and he had to do some fighting himself, were killed? Goodness me! The death of Sarpedon! For he could see that grey-eyed Hubertus, glittering in that uniform, was not quite noble.

'They're all heroes, every one of them,' said the boy, as if some old fool had challenged him on this point. 'I'd defend them to my death, Father. We ought to blazon it out in headlines once a week, *Heroes all*, or something to that effect.'

'Very patriotic, but not very practical.'

'Good old Father! You've seen more than I have, is that it?' He came over to the desk. 'What are you reading tonight? Military history?'

'Please don't fiddle with my lamp.'

'But I've never noticed it before. It's delicious. French Empire, lovely little Nubian boy!'

He danced briefly with it, a step or two between the bookcases and the end of the bed as his father watched him, his cigar shaking slightly between his fingers. How similar he was to the young Waitzmann – how unlike.

'Father, promise me you'll write to Goebbels and get me posted to our new African empire.'

'Please put that lamp down.'

Hubertus rolled on to the bed, stretching out his black uniform with its silver insignia to its full length, like a young hero lying in state. The Kommandant studied him; he felt old, he seemed to be seeing him over a foreground of rubble, of demolition.

'Sit up, sit up!' And with a yawn the young man sat up, not because he had been asked to do so but because he was going to have done so in any case.

'There's something I wanted to tell you. Dammit! Mother and her shopping-list have put it right out of my head. How was I to know she'd want *broad* elastic? That sort of thing would be up to you if you were giving her what she wanted.'

'*Enough!*'

'Sorry! But it's so obvious what's the matter with the poor darling. At her age a woman needs –' Hubertus broke off. 'Of course, I remember now. Carin von Hoffbach was at the party with her latest; a splendid fellow, Ruprecht Waitzmann. I was dying to know him but she completely monopolized him.'

'Well?'

'Waitzmann was more than charming whenever madame la Baronin allowed us a moment together; but he was on edge from the moment I told him about you. Until I had a chat with "Musch" ' – this was Hubertus's name for his mother – 'I had no idea why my connexion with the prison might have alarmed him. Father, is it true we've just taken in his brother?'

'It is.'

'Good God! No wonder the poor fellow was so tense. He must have felt I had a hold over him. How rotten and how terribly funny when at the time I'd not the least idea.'

'You realize, I hope, that this is a confidential matter?'

But Hubertus jumped off the bed: 'Then I could meet him! There must be a tremendous story behind it all.

What's he in for? Is it something frightful or just a little prophylactic surveillance?'

'You know very well that I never discuss prison business with anyone.' The Kommandant took off his heavy tortoise-shell spectacles. 'I'm extremely tired, Hubertus.'

'Poor old Father! Let me soothe your troubled brow.'

'Go away!'

'Just give me an inkling, that's all I ask, and I shan't trouble you any more tonight. Is Waitzmann grande luxe, one of the Führer's guests? Or is he here for treatment? You know, the bang bang in the early morning?'

The Kommandant's hand jerked as though it had been pulled by a string. His spectacles clattered on to the face of his desk, and Hubertus became conciliatory at once.

'I'm not being merely frivolous, Father. When it's someone one practically knows one simply has to make a joke of these things. But quite apart from that it's a question of my career. One never knows when first-hand information isn't going to be vital later on and if the von Hoffbach's are involved. Well!'

The Kommandant was shocked. His ambition for Hubertus, his sense of his own duplicity in his handling of Waitzmann, not less than his contemplation of his death several times that evening, alternately soothed and ruffled him as though he had been a cat stroked by a chancy hand.

'Please leave me,' he ordered. 'I've had an extremely tiring day.'

'But I only want to meet him, casually, in the library or somewhere.'

'He's not working in the library. Nothing has yet been decided.'

'But he will, won't he? The V.I.P.s always do. I don't want to rush you or anything. But, as you know, I always get my own way in the end and "Musch" would agree with me over this. It's a question of my future.'

The Kommandant stood up and Hubertus helped himself to one of his cigars. 'I don't want to have to involve her in this,' he went on. 'She gets so terribly difficult when she's worried about me. But if you won't help me, what else can

I do? She'd write one of those marvellous letters to the right quarter and get permission for me to see him.'

The Kommandant felt his lips flickering. He thought he might even be a little faint, a recurrence of his low blood pressure. For an instant he found it extremely difficult to distinguish between the new prisoner and his son. He had an idea that his wife was standing between them and that they were pointedly ignoring him.

'Kindly leave my room,' he said distinctly. 'Where is your respect for me? For your home, your country?'

'But Father, dear, you know I've none. I've none for myself even. I'm too young, I suppose. After all –'

'Quite apart from that, your tongue, you young fool! It'll betray us all.'

'Never.'

'I beg of you to learn to control it. This is a time of danger. Things are not going well.'

Hubertus was unmoved by his father's trembling fits. Indeed, he quite enjoyed them. 'I know! I've frightened you, haven't I? Well, I'll tell you something. I'm marvellous at keeping secrets until the right moment; it's the whole essence of journalism. I shan't say a word about all this to anyone. You can trust me absolutely, Father.'

The Kommandant was silent. He folded away his spectacles, snapping the case shut; he opened a drawer in his desk and marked the place in his book.

'After all,' went on Hubertus, 'we've got to learn to trust one another some time, haven't we? I *am* your son.'

The Kommandant smiled to himself and Hubertus rushed up to him and kissed his cheek; 'I knew you'd come round. Don't worry about Mama's shopping. She's only trying to rattle you. Really, she approves of everything I bought.'

Leaving a little eddy of cigar smoke behind him, he ran out of the room. There was a spring in his step, supreme confidence. He left the door half-open behind him as if to signify that there were no longer any separate divisions within the household.

The Kommandant stood for a moment by his desk and

then took out his handkerchief and absentmindedly wiped his son's kiss from his cheek. He called out, 'Please do not disturb your mother again tonight, Hubertus.' But there was no answer.

A week later, seated in his office at the prison, the Kommandant found himself wondering if his son's whims had not become a way of life. The house was littered with their reminders: a silver-plated clarinet in the landing chest, his jazz phase; a collection of nineteenth century walking sticks, interest in antiques; one or two sticky-looking oil paintings in expensive frames in the drawing-room, art; a slim volume of poems. He remembered too how he had been lewdly tattooed all over his chest and abdomen: the most grossly suggestive pictures in imitation of a friend. Was it perhaps significant that the Führer had ultimately had to imprison that friend, a perverted Saxony princeling in Oranienburg, where he had shortly died of sexual exhaustion? The Kommandant did not know; he shrugged off these thoughts and returned to the present, feeling momentarily proud of the young man as he watched him through the window of his office.

Hubertus was re-crossing the courtyard from the visitor's block. He had had the good sense to absent himself from the interview between the Baron and Waitzmann and a moment later was irritating his father afresh by fiddling with things and cocking eyes at himself in the mirror. He had evidently been much impressed by the prisoner.

'What eyes! He's better looking even than his brother. He moved me profoundly. Such reticence. So perfectly at ease in those ghastly prison clothes. I simply can't understand how such a man could have been such a fool.'

'Keep your voice down, Hubertus.'

'Seeing him in there like that, a man of such obvious distinction, I got an idea for a tremendous article on loyalty.'

'Classified material. You can't use it in any way whatsoever.'

'It was only a general idea. I'd have to know the facts first. Incidentally, I've already done a little research in that direction; but it's damned hard to find out anything definite. Couldn't you give me just an idea?'

'Hubertus, I don't know how you contrived to meet von Hoffbach this morning; but I must warn you for the last time that if you continue to interfere in prison-business —'

'But it's all to your advantage, Father. I'm in with the right set. I meet everyone; and as it happens I get on particularly well with older women, women like Carin von Hoffbach.' Hubertus swivelled away from the mirror. 'Shall I go on, do I interest you?'

'Keep your voice down!' The Kommandant was by now himself fiddling with his 'In tray'. Hubertus waited for him to look up and then smiled at him significantly.

'I feel sorry for such women, Father. Need I say more?'

'Leave your mother out of this!'

'No reference intended! I was talking about Carin. I've pumped her dry but still, at this stage, she won't say much. I've an idea, though,' and he in his turn now whispered, 'that it's *money*. They both reek of it, the brothers Waitzmann, I mean. There's one of those delightful tie-ups going on somewhere and I simply have to find out what it is.'

Hubertus put a hand into his breast pocket and passed his father an imported cigar.

'Here, have one of the Baron's Havanas. He gave it to me in the car.'

'Put it away!'

'He's invited me to lunch afterwards, too. I'm going down pretty well with him. A good thing for all of us. Mother will certainly appreciate my adroitness.' He returned to the mirror and asked himself. 'Father, don't you want me to succeed? Wouldn't it gratify you if I were able, for instance, to get you a nice soft job somewhere when the war's over.'

'If you wish to know the truth, the greatest service you could do me would be to leave me to manage my own affairs.'

'What a ghastly job you have. I know I couldn't do it. I feel things too deeply. What in heaven will happen to that man? How far did he go? I noticed he'd picked up a slight

American accent; but if that's the extent of his disloyalty he can't be shot for it. He was so civilized, gentle. Father, you can't let him just vanish like Iggy.' Iggy was the tattooed princeling and the Kommandant blanched. He looked at his son with quick loathing.

'The Prince von Hartz und Hanau did not just vanish. He died whilst serving a well-merited sentence for corrupting the country's youth.'

'But Baldur von Schirach, who's as queer as they come . . .'

'No *names*!'

'He's even been after me. He gets you drunk and then leaves two or three hundred marks pinned to your jacket, or gets you promoted.'

The Kommandant brought down and fractured a glass paperweight. It had been sent him from Brazil by a successful ex-prisoner and held an azure butterfly. His son's beautiful-eyed face wrinkled and shifted as though clouded water had suddenly flowed over it.

'Death, you puppy!' whispered his father. 'Look out for yourself! I won't look after you if you let this poison destroy you. We have to remain loyal, loyal to something inside.'

He had caught sight of the Baron and Officer Halstedt recrossing the courtyard. 'Now wait in the outer office until I send for you.'

They straightened themselves in front of the mirror, doing this not self-consciously but as though for reassurance against the conspiracy of the room itself. The mirror seemed to be a window which might reveal their indiscretions.

The Baron was in a poor mood. He had not been impressed by his interview with Waitzmann. When he spoke he omitted the Kommandant's rank:

'He wasn't in good shape at all, Grunwald.'

'But yesterday he was in excellent spirits, Herr Baron. I saw him myself at some length. Daily reports are called for, you know. Officer Halstedt, I think, will bear me out?'

'I regret, Herr Kommandant, that the prisoner was somewhat discourteous to the Herr Baron.'

'Waitzmann was not impolite,' the Baron contradicted. 'He was uncommunicative. I had hoped he might want me to pass on some messages to his relatives and friends. There were certain matters of national importance which he refused to discuss at all.' He glanced at Halstedt. 'I'd like to make some suggestions.'

'Halstedt, you may leave us.'

'It's up to you, of course,' went on the Baron more warmly as soon as they were alone. 'I'm not trying to teach you your job, Colonel, but it occurs to me that whatever you may yourself decide will be approved by the powers that be.' His gaze took in the photographs on the wall. 'You'll no doubt remember those difficult devils in the last war, the "Awkward Squad"? Whether one relaxed or tightened discipline wasn't always a matter for one's senior officers – and things haven't altogether changed.'

'Not yet.' The Kommandant was waiting for something more definite.

'I myself,' said the Baron, 'will take the matter up with the right quarters at the first opportunity and I think you may assume that whatever you decide will be approved of by the powers that be.'

'Thank you.'

The Baron was again looking at the photographs; the Führer, the Reichsführer, the Kommandant in full uniform, 1917. 'We must hold firm,' he said a little shakily, 'A watching brief. We're about of an age, Colonel.'

'I imagine so.'

'So we should understand one another. I take it you'd like me to confirm my suggestion by telephone?'

'And in writing, too, if it's not inconvenient? There are wheels within wheels. As a friend of the Waitzmann family you'll appreciate my position.'

'Only too well. You shall have something in writing within twenty-four hours. If you can think of something that meets the case I'll be extremely grateful.' He paused. 'In better times, Colonel, we must meet again. I was talking to your son about Schönform. He tells me he once painted it.'

'Just before the war. On a holiday.'

'A talented young man, he should go far. I've invited him to luncheon with me today. My own boy, Leo, unfor-

tunately, is out of the running at present. A gammy chest.'
By the door they shook hands. 'If your son would like a
little shooting on his next leave he'd be very welcome at
Schönform. Leo gets a little lonely.'

'Hubertus would be delighted.'

'I'll see that Leo drops him a line.'

Accompanied by Hubertus, sizzling with self-confidence,
the Baron left for his luncheon at the Adlon.

In the next days, telephone calls, messages on the private
line from S.S. Headquarters followed in quick succession.
The Kommandant, attending the complex machinery of
his administration, found the wheels he had so often envisaged noticeably slowing, being braked from some point
not quite definable, turning scarcely perceptibly, temporarily even halting. He considered every aspect of the
situation. He covered himself by a number of minutes and
entries in his official day book, carefully involving the
names and reputations of as many other people as possible.
Eventually he decided to employ Alfried in his own household.

Five days a week, at ten hundred hours, the prisoner
should be driven unescorted to the house in the Bergenstrasse to catalogue the private library and generally make
himself useful in the house and grounds. In the evening, at
seventeen hundred hours, he would have a tea meal and be
returned in the same van to his cell.

Chapter 5

Alfried worked hard in the Kommandant's house, obeying meticulously the instructions left for him on the desk in the upstairs room:

Tuesday. March 1942.

10.15 to 12.30 hrs.	Cataloguing.
12.30 to 13.00 hrs.	Mid-day meal and cleaning.
13.00 to 15.00 hrs.	Outdoor work. Kindly prepare potato bed.
15.00 to 16.00 hrs.	Saw and stack logs in woodshed.
16.00 hrs.	Coffee. Please complete report on day's work.

To such instructions, typed by the Kommandant's secretary, there would often be a hand-written postscript:

Frau Grunwald may or may not have additional instructions for you. I would be grateful if you would oblige her.

Felix Grunwald.

But to begin with, Frau Grunwald never appeared; and Alfried, being continually stirred up by references which he felt implied more than they actually said, had difficulty in not thinking about her too much. Out of hours he was often tempted to question Officer Halstedt with whom he had become quite friendly; but he never did so in case it might seem ill-bred. He kept on telling himself that it was no business of his: 'Keep to the work in hand,' he decided. 'What does it matter what she's doing? She's an invalid. She's confined to her room. The poor woman can't bustle about arranging flowers or baking bread in her own kitchen. She's lying in her bed all the time. It has a blue counterpane and she's used to hearing prisoners about the place. I must trespass as little as possible.'

But he could not rid himself of an idea that she was

taking an interest in him. Every time he went upstairs he found himself pausing on the landing and eyeing the other doors, even looking for worn patches on the carpets that might indicate those in most frequent use. He was determined not to let this habit get too much of a hold on him and vowed that next time he would go straight ahead without pausing. 'Vulgar curiosity!' he thought. 'How would I like it if some new servant at home were constantly prying on my own mother during an illness? I must use this experience to overcome all the difficulties of the servant-master relationship. I can learn a lot from it.'

After about a fortnight he believed he might be making progress. He had succeeded in ridding himself of speculation either about his 'mistress' or the third occupant of the household, her son Hubertus, whom he had not even remembered seeing on that one occasion in the prison. He was keeping his eye directly on the next thing to be done and only smiling at the Kommandant's increasingly peremptory postscripts:

Frau Gudrun is distressed by your silence which she interprets as stealth. She is in a highly nervous condition and would prefer you to make a little more noise in going about the house.

Accordingly, he began to whistle occasionally and to run up the stairs and drop a few books. He closed doors firmly behind him, reminding himself that his own mother had always been made uncomfortable by what she called 'creeping jennies'. He began to see that in some way he was perfecting this other relationship. His position in the household, apparently fortuitous, was part of a design and he must do his best to fulfil it perfectly, so that indirectly he might 'comfort' his own mother for whom at present he was able to do so little.

But in the third week, the atmosphere changed. Frau Grunwald began to move about upstairs. He would hear the lavatory being flushed and the sound of wireless music from her bedroom. Just as he was settling down to his cataloguing, the set would be switched on loudly in the middle of a programme of dance music. It would play for five or ten minutes and then, as capriciously, be switched off again in the middle of a bar. Occasionally, if old music were being broadcast, tunes of the Fourteen to Eighteen War or the early twenties, it would remain on until the end of the programme and Alfried would think: She's re-living her youth; and he would long to go in to her and introduce himself.

He would hear a door being quietly opened, naked foot-steps on the landing and that peculiar kind of pause which ensues when someone stops to listen. He decided that she was not 'playing fair', and, until he remembered that this could be a further test of his humility, became indignant. He would look at the clock and encourage himself by thinking that in a short time he would be going down to the kitchen and that afterwards he would be doing outdoor work, when her presence would no longer distract him.

'It's a tremendous battle,' he decided. 'Bigger than my imprisonment, and it involves the whole relationship be-tween a man and a woman. Probably Potiphar's wife behaved in the same way to Joseph; and the fact that I've never even seen her makes it an even greater test for me.'

But when the time came for him to go out into the garden he would begin to imagine he was still under observation. A dozen times he would pause in his digging or weeding to turn and look at the windows of the house. Although to begin with he was never confirmed, he kept up the habit since he now believed he must have some facts to go on. It's different from the landing business, he thought. Once I catch her at it I can come to a decision. I'll give myself three days to find out whether this is imagination or not.

On the second day, quite certain he was being watched, he went on with what he was doing. He shook the soil from the weeds carefully and piled them into the wheelbarrow, working at a steady pace as if totally absorbed; and then, after two or three minutes when he thought that he might have put her off her guard, he turned round suddenly and caught sight of a face in an upstairs window. She moved quickly to one side behind a curtain; but the curtain swung and went on swinging. He was sure she was standing behind it and that she would not be able to resist another glance; so he remained as he was for several seconds, smiling back at the window.

From that day onwards Frau Grunwald started to leave notes for him in the kitchen:

Be so kind as to leave a supply of logs beside the stove;

or:

I'm grateful to you for your help. Empty tins should be deposited in the waste-bin.

On the fifth day, a triangle of Swiss cheese wrapped in tinfoil accompanied her note and the morning dance-music gave place to propaganda. The upper-floor of the house would be filled with patriotic lieder sung by male choirs and marches played by massed bands. There would be extracts from political speeches delivered at the full volume of the set. As before, the programmes were never complete in themselves. They would be switched on and off quite haphazardly so that each item had a cryptic quality about it as if Frau Grunwald wished to question him from a distance. He could not escape the idea that she was addressing him through a megaphone from a hilltop.

Despite all his efforts to remain detached, his secret prayers to accept and interpret the situation profitably, his nerves became affected. Through Halstedt he sought an interview with the Kommandant to ask him about the religious facilities of the prison as he felt it might help him to make confession. The Kommandant sent him back a message to say that he must submit his request in writing and, later, left a further postscript for him on his desk:

I fear that under present circumstances our facilities in this respect have been curtailed. Such consolations as you request are extended only to those under a more final sentence. I will do what I can but promise nothing. No doubt your own convictions will fit you for any difficulties you may experience. You have my sympathy. F. G.

He began to suffer from prison insomnia; getting 'off' to begin with, but waking repeatedly, oppressed by absurd fears and preoccupations. In the little hours he found himself devoured with desire for Frau Grunwald. At first he persuaded himself that he only wanted to meet her in the normal way; but later he had to admit that he longed to make love to her. He imagined that one day she would leave a note for him asking him to come up to her bedroom, or that the very next morning he might look round to see her standing in the doorway of the Kommandant's study wearing only a transparent American-style negligee. At other times his speculations became almost mystical and he thought of her as 'The Woman'. She merged with his mother, a figure in the wisdom of mourning for the war and the slaughter, an earth-priestess who might bless and liberate him.

At such times he longed to confide in somebody; but in the mornings, as soon as it was light and he heard Officer Halstedt approaching to unlock him for breakfast, his fantasies would quickly resolve. He would realize that his intention of trying to get a letter through to Pater Lippich was absurd and would set off quite cheerfully for his day's work in the Bergenstrasse.

In the event, his first meeting with Frau Grunwald was prosaic. Coming in from the garden at four o'clock one day he had found the kitchen filled with the smell of war-time coffee; a tray laid with the best china and a plate of damson pastries, the bottle in which they had been preserved already washed out and placed on the draining board. Beside the tray there had been a note:

I shall be glad if you will take coffee with me in my drawing-room at a quarter past four this afternoon.

Gudrun Grunwald.

Alfried washed hurriedly and combed his hair in front of the kitchen mirror. Frau Grunwald had not asked him to bring in the tray and so he left it. He left the coffee too, simmering on the stove, and went through to the drawing-room.

This rarely used room was filled with the scent of old pot-pourri and camphor. Frau Grunwald, in a black dress with a coarse cameo pinned on the bodice, had extended her hand for his kiss and he had noticed its soft whiteness and bitten little nails. He had hardly dared at first to look at her face. He had experienced difficulty even in sitting down beside the tiny electric stove she had switched on to warm the damp fabrics and cushions. For minutes, while she saw to the coffee in the kitchen, he had stood uneasily, his eyes wandering over the profusion of Biedermaier patterns, the oil paintings signed by Hubertus and the illuminated address commemorating her missionary work in old Berlin. But on her return he had been able to relax, to look unabashed into her strong white face with its neat, ear-ringed, ears and small blue eyes.

She had managed the occasion exquisitely, conducting him through a 'polite' conversation and constantly offering him the little tarts in which the halved damsons were embedded beneath a dusting of saccharin and sugar. They had talked of music, of her missionary work during his childhood, of picnics, home-cooking, education and foreign travel. At half past four she had offered him a stained cigarette from a small silver box and thanked him for his company, saying she was sure he would appreciate the fact that her life was not an easy one.

'Normally, Herr Waitzmann,' she had said, 'I'm not at all the kind of person who's sorry for themselves. I've always led an active life. As a girl I was never still. The days weren't long enough for me. I was never given to self-pity; I'm sure you understand that? Even without anyone having told me so I can see that you're a sympathetic person.'

'But I'm afraid I'm not, Frau Grunwald.'

'You must allow me to know,' she had insisted. 'I'm very sensitive to people. I'll make a confession to you; I dreaded the thought of you in my house. I know I should have grown used to such treatment down the years; but this time, in my present state, I was more upset than anyone except my son Hubertus could possibly have known.'

'If I could have done otherwise –'

'I know! I'm not so unsympathetic myself that in my

present state I can't appreciate the troubles of others. Of course you have to obey other people's instructions. We all do, it's a charge laid upon us by being in the world at all; and so often, as in this case, it proves to have been for the best.'

'For the best? You're right. Everything perhaps is always for the best.'

'Not everything, I'm afraid, Herr Waitzmann. There's ill-health, the wickedness of people, the grievous lack of sympathy between us all. These things we must never accept. We must remember that there *is* evil in this world and the identity of its prince. You read your Bible, I'm sure? I trust that things have not yet changed so much that such consolation is denied those who still believe and whose need is amongst the greatest?'

'Regularly.'

'Then you'll know what I mean, for we must remember, whether we are orthodox Christians or not, that we wrestle not against flesh, but against the dark spirits that drive men and women into error.'

As if she had not expected him to reply she had risen to her feet and smoothed out her stiff skirt. A few moments later she had taken her leave of him with a last smile, waiting while he opened the door for her and pausing by the foot of the stairs:

'We'll have many more discussions, I know. One must never give up when one knows something more is being demanded of one.' She gave a little cold laugh as if she were denigrating her own nobility. 'I'd thought for so long that nothing more was to have been asked of me by the powers that be; and now here I am entertaining again after such a difficult time. Life is very unexpected, isn't it?'

But she was not interested in his answer. She was holding the seam of her stiff dress as if about to curtsy to someone. It would not have surprised him if she had tossed her head.

'And later you'll meet Hubertus!' she said. 'I stopped him from seeking you out, you realize? I had to deceive him a little in a way of my own; but now that I'm sure of my ground, of what God's doing, I'll see that you do get to know one another. Hubertus is very sympathetic. A person after your own heart.'

'The Kommandant won't object, Frau Grunwald? I don't want to abuse his trust.'

'My husband's trust in his son or in myself?'

'No, in me.'

'That's a matter for your conscience, isn't it? My own is quite clear.' She held out her hand. 'My husband, I believe, still has a little respect for me. My wishes are not altogether ignored.'

Her fingers tightened momentarily on his hand as he raised them to his lips; then she turned and ascended the stairs to her bedroom with a stiff back, humming softly some phrase of a hymn.

'Mad!' thought Alfried. 'Grotesque! What's God playing at, throwing me into a mess like this? I don't want to meet her son. He sounds dreadful.'

His hand shook so much that he could scarcely hold the pen with which he was attempting to write the report of his day's work for the Kommandant. He wondered if he ought to convey to him some hint of this new development in his life and played with the idea of forfeiting his privileges altogether. Then he decided that he would ask Halstedt's advice and waited eagerly for the opportunity; but as soon as he mentioned Frau Grunwald's name, the officer became excessively courteous and Alfried realized he was jealous.

So that's what's the matter with him, he thought. He doesn't like my going there at all. For the last few weeks he's been getting more and more formal. What a fool I was not to realize it sooner.

He became bitter. He slept scarcely at all and dreaded the regular conversations with Frau Grunwald even more than the long black nights in which he carried on a great battle of prayer and introspection.

'Like Frau Grunwald,' he told himself, 'I've tried to accept things and to reach some sort of truth with everyone I've met; but I'm not mad. I've looked upon the whole thing as a test of my own sincerity and resisted the temptation to resent all these people from the Kommandant downwards. This is my Judea. I've to pick my way as Our Lord did between the customs men, the soldiers and the betrayers. If someone were to cut off Halstedt's ear I would immediately want to stick it on again – or run for the doctor. Yet when I ask for his help he won't give it to me. He's incapable of caring for me in the way I care for him.'

For Halstedt had fathered Alfried from the beginning. Like many officers he was inclined to get attached to certain prisoners and would not, as he might have put it himself, have been able to 'stick it out so long' if it hadn't been for the fact that 'you still find a man or two who'll take advice'.

Alfried had given him no trouble. So far, he had sought no privileges and had never tried the sort of bribes that other wealthy prisoners were given to. He took a polite interest in Halstedt's health and yet never tried to get round him. Sometimes he even made jokes about his chest trouble and his confidences about his flirtatious young wife; and one day he had gone so far as to tell him that he was an old humbug who enjoyed his jealousies. He had said: 'You know what you ought to do, Halstedt? You ought to put the whole thing to the test.'

'And how would I do that?'

'Run up A Block stairs, get a heart attack and then see whether she cares or not.'

'It would be a fine thing if I dropped dead, wouldn't it?'

'She might be delighted. She'd be free then to marry a younger man and you'd never feel jealous again.'

Without meaning to, Halstedt had laughed immoderately; and then, remembering his position, had drawn himself up, shaking his head in as much self-disapproval as if he had caught himself guffawing in the middle of a burial service or an execution. After one or two such exchanges he had been quite unable to resist confiding in Waitzmann. He found himself unconsciously seeking the prisoner's approval, looking forward to being tricked by him into some further private indiscretion. 'It's like the old days,' he told himself, 'when politicals were politicals, and a man wasn't expected to exceed his duties by acting as go-between for the doctor and the Kommandant.'

Yet, at the same time, whenever things went wrong at home or when for no particular reason he found himself wondering if he had not wasted his life, he was glad of his double rôle and congratulated himself on the 'softness' of the reports he had hitherto made. When he noticed Alfried's increasing absorption in the affairs of the Kommandant's household he began to climb back to a more normal relationship with him, becoming tight-lipped and formal.

Alfried wounded him still further by taking no notice of this change in his attitude. He made no attempt to press him for a resumption of his confidences and was as courteous and open with him as ever. A day or two after he had asked his advice about Frau Grunwald, Halstedt had felt bound to warn him of his dangers in his own way:

He had said, 'It's a bad thing for a prisoner to accept favours before the end of his sentence, Waitzmann.'

'I'm sure it is, Officer Halstedt. But under the circumstances, how can I refuse them?'

'You can only take it from me that the wise prisoner distrusts friendship more than enmity.'

After this Halstedt had felt he had done his duty and decided that his years of discipline in the service had not been wasted. 'I should have known better,' he had thought, 'than to trust one of 'em after only four weeks.'

Alfried met Hubertus for the first time about three days later. He came into the Kommandant's study one afternoon when it was raining. Alfried had been asked to paste ex libris slips into the covers of all the books he had thus far catalogued and was hard at work when the young man interrupted him. Hubertus did not trouble to introduce himself or shake hands. He seemed to be devotely intent on making Alfried feel as welcome as some not-quite-old friend and started talking immediately:

'Sorry I couldn't manage this before; but, as my father says, there are wheels within wheels and I wanted you to settle down with "Musch", my mother, before I started in on it all. You've been coming here for a week or two now, haven't you?'

Alfried found it easy to accept this honest, busy, approach. 'Nearly five,' he replied, 'thirty-three and a quarter days to be exact.'

'There you are!' said Hubertus. 'Isn't life incredible? I could have sworn "Musch" only started talking about you a fortnight ago. Do you find that sort of thing?'

'Not at the moment, though your mother has been very kind to me.'

But Hubertus was thinking about her and was not quite sure what it was that had so surprised him.

'Incredible!' he said again. 'Privately, you know, she's fascinated by you. I've been quite jealous.' He gave a little laugh not unlike Frau Grunwald's and looked critically round his father's room. 'God, isn't it dreary in here? Let's get comfortable. Switch on the stove while I make some coffee.'

'I'd prefer not to, if you don't mind? I'm not particularly cold.'

'You're not alarmed by what I said, I hope? I'm not really jealous. I only say these things in case they might be true. With your own mother-trouble, I thought you'd understand immediately.'

'My own mother?'

'Oh, yes, I've heard all about it from Nicholas von H. and Carin. Not *all*, of course, but, as you know, I'm a journalist and we piece things together incredibly quickly. Just as you do yourself, I despise journalists. It's a feminine gift, don't you think?'

Alfried laughed.

'But then, so's flying a Messerschmitt,' went on Hubertus, 'so there's no need to be ashamed of it really, is there?'

'Of journalism, you mean?'

'Yes, I often pull my father's leg by telling him there are great similarities. After all, the best fighter pilots are light-boned. They have those observant, tender eyes that one sees in young girls. They're intuitive and absolutely absorbed in themselves, dying to shoot something down. I often imagine I'm one myself. I pretend I'm screaming quite silently through the sky, getting the sun behind me

151

and coming up on the other man from underneath. It's all over in a matter of seconds of course; but it makes you feel absolutely god-like at the time.'

'You're a poet.'

'D'you really think so? I wish you'd tell my father. He's always telling me that I'm only an actor and that I lack any true sensibility. I'm at the cruel age, I suppose; and, like you, I'm an individualist at heart; at least I would be if I had the guts.'

'Why didn't you join the Luftwaffe?'

'My mother! I'm her only hope and joy. We adore each other. Like your own mother she's a bit of a witch and she saw what was coming and got me in with Goebbels about a year before Poland. I'm grateful, of course, with one side of me; but with the other I rather hold it against her. You do know what I mean, don't you?'

'Fame?'

'Not exactly; glory, perhaps.'

Hubertus took something out of his uniform pocket. 'Here, have some French chocolate; a present from Carin. I know you don't smoke so I begged a slab from her last night. She has an ex-boy-friend in Paris who sends her a parcel every week. I didn't tell her this was for you because I don't altogether trust her yet; but I think she's on our side on the whole.'

'I'm sorry, but I don't quite understand you.'

'Don't worry, I'll tell you everything later. First, I'm going to make you your coffee. The fact that I'm a bit "cruel" doesn't mean that I never think of anyone else. As a matter of fact I've been thinking about you in father's gaol an awful lot. I've been wanting to make up for it if I could.'

'Why?'

'I don't know why.' Hubertus laughed again. 'In a way I've identified myself with you. I suppose you think that's just another journalist's trick, do you?'

'I think perhaps you analyse things too much.'

'But it's not entirely insincere. I was going to have told you: I was brought up with prisoners. For as long as I can remember we've always had the best of them about the place. They love children and you'd be astonished at the things they used to tell me.'

'Your father didn't object?'

'He never knew! And if you're worrying about our meetings, you mustn't forget you've got my mother on your side – and in this house that's not half the battle, it's the whole of it.'

'I see.'

'I thought you would.'

Hubertus smiled at him and then abruptly ran down to the kitchen. Alfried heard his light feet down the stairs, his hesitation half-way and his equally swift return. He heard him walk softly across the landing to the door of Frau Grunwald's room and was tempted to go to the door of the study to overhear their conversation but he resisted the impulse and forced himself to resume his pasting-in of slips.

Beyond the windows rain fell steadily from a low cloud-base. Lorries rumbled past the front of the house and everything in the big room shook to their passing: the desk, the cupboards, the Nubian lamp and the bookshelves all began to tremble at their approach. There were creakings and tickings temporarily drowned out by the noise of the engines but emergent again as soon as they had passed. The room seemed like a recording instrument, so sensitive that it abused its function.

'I must be careful,' Alfried told himself. 'Something is happening.'

But when Hubertus returned with a tray of coffee and one of the Kommandant's silver bon-bon dishes into which he had put the squares of French chocolate, he forgot his caution and told him a great deal about himself. Hubertus led him into a discussion about the nature of treachery, saying:

'You see, to me treachery isn't an absolute! It's only setting oneself against whatever happens to be happening at the time; and that's why I don't really take you seriously as a prisoner. We all know that you're really an idealist, a poet like myself; and that's why we're determined to get you back into circulation. You're going to be needed later.'

They went on to discuss their love-affairs and the nature of sexual desire. Alfried told him that ever since his unsuccessful pursuit of Ruth Lubbe he had felt as if he were 'living a sigh', and Hubertus was very struck by the phrase.

'It's beautiful,' he said. 'Poetry is obviously the force behind all religion. What a pity it is that you haven't yet found a way of turning your powers of expression to your own advantage. Can't you see that it's a poet's business to survive as long as possible? Where there's no vision the people perish. For the poet, death is the only evil.'

They talked for another hour. Alfried, devoid of any real ideas, sitting uneasily at the desk. As the afternoon wasted he became ever more convinced that the substance of what he heard was not Hubertus's at all but the fruit of adolescent discussions he had held with his mother in the years before the war. He was sure that these callow theories were as much a part of some private test of his character as the earlier ordeal by Frau Grunwald's wireless music.

In the following weeks, Officer Halstedt, who was still much drawn to Alfried and felt that there was something 'very decent' about him, became ever more irritated by 'his' prisoner's preoccupation with his job in the Bergenstrasse. 'He's only got one real trouble,' he decided. 'He's wrongly classified. He should have come in under Religious instead of Political. Then everyone would have known where they were.'

He resolved to mention this to the Kommandant in his next report. He had become very attached to Colonel Grunwald after his own disappointment over Alfried and hoped that he had made this clear by a slight change in his manner and by his warm tone every time he and his superior met. 'Everyone knows,' he thought, 'that the Colonel, like myself, has trouble at home and is made a monkey of by his wife and son. My first duty, after all, is to the staff here and the uniform I've worn so long.'

But the Kommandant was quite unaware of this new

sympathy and only wondered why Halstedt looked so deferential and eye-glistening every time he entered the office. He was worried about other things. There was a conflict of some sort at the Reich Central Security Office, the result of a divergence of opinion about racial and labour policies; and the Kommandant was wondering how it might affect his future.

Halstedt began to trust more and more in 'leadership at the top' and started to attend the Prison Officers' clubs in the evenings instead of going home to upset his wife and fuss over his youngest daughter. He became much more friendly with Doctor Lütgens too and started telling his brother officers that 'the doctor knew his job so well' they would soon be losing him to one of the camps. Yet, at the same time that he experienced this change of attitude he was still able to feel thoroughly 'fair' about Waitzmann; his reservations about the prisoner's character, the withdrawal of his trust in him, did not affect his judgement. In fact, since 'the business' had been taken out of his hands he was able, if anything, to be more patient with him than before.

For his part, Alfried had noticed the change in Halstedt's manner immediately but was so absorbed by outside affairs that he had no energy to deal with it. 'I must accept it,' was his attitude. 'In this case it's a poor devil of a man I'm wrestling with, not one of Frau Grunwald's wicked spirits.'

The coffee-parties in the Bergenstrasse drawing-room were now an almost daily event. Hubertus often found the time to help him with the work in the mornings as well as in the afternoons and had begun to convey messages back and forth between Alfried and his friends.

'I don't see much of your brother Ruprecht,' he said. 'Though I admire him intensely, he fights shy of me for some reason. I can't help thinking he might be a little jealous of you.'

'Of course he is.'

'You admit it!'

'He has every reason to be.'

'But you're not jealous of *him*, are you?'

'Not at present.'

Hubertus thought this over and then told Alfried that he loved him for his honesty, even though he realized that it was this quality which had caused him all his trouble.

'As a matter of fact,' he went on, 'I've quite won Carin round to my view. She sympathizes with you now and you have her to thank for keeping you in touch with your brother. She passes on all your messages to him.'

'But apart from telling them that I'm in good health, I've not actually given you any messages.'

'No, I've made them up for you,' said Hubertus. 'I've even told them that you've begun to modify your views and, of course, I did this to make sure that Carin passed it on to von H. Someone's got to help you even if you won't help yourself.'

Alfried prayed furiously. 'What sort of an imprisonment is this?' he asked God. 'I'm as willing to suffer for my faith as any loyal novice! But all that happens is that I get mixed up in a confusing domestic wrangle. You joke with me as if I were some weak character in the Old Testament.'

He became increasingly confused and unhappy. His inability to sleep properly, his loss of appetite and his doubts about his significance as a spiritual creature combined to make his days as wretched as his nights. He lay awake rehearing Halstedt's half-reproaches and running over anything the Kommandant might have said to him. He accused himself of an unhealthy curiosity and came to believe that if he had been more detached he would never have attracted Frau Grunwald's attention in the first place. To escape his perpetual self-accusations he tried to start a system of organized prayer, vowing that he would never say less than five rosaries a night; but whenever he tried to do it, he would experience a longing for some more tangible form of suffering and find himself on the verge of crying out for iron and staples, for a roughened pillar of wood against which he might be scourged by real whips. The presumptuousness of his tendency to see his suffering against the background of the Garden of Gethsemane disturbed him too; yet he could not get it out of his head and continually reminded himself that there were similarities. For at that time, he would think, nothing had so far happened except that some men, His friends, had gone to sleep.

Hubertus now began to involve Fräulein von Boehling in the situation. She too started sending 'that poor man' presents and messages. Though she had never met him she was remembering him in her prayers, she assured him. She begged him to read 'this little book' which she herself had found such a comfort 'in times of separation from my parents and friends'.

Alfried sent her back his thanks and took the book to his cell that evening. It was an expensively bound volume of St François de Sales' *Introduction to the Devout Life*, much of it in the form of letters to Philothea, an imaginary young girl in seventeenth century France. It was full of counsels about the dangers of the social life of the period and euphemized all spiritual dilemmas in elaborate and delicate metaphors such as the following:

Finally, Philothea, in the midst of our spiritual dryness and desolation let us remain courageous. .... If we cannot offer Our Lord a devotion that is sweet let us offer Him one that is dry. .... In fine spring weather the bees make more honey yet produce fewer young ones, for they are so busy gathering honey from the flowers in the sunshine that they forget about them; but if the spring is cold and cloudy they produce more young ones and gather less honey; unable to go out and gather honey they thus employ themselves at home. ....

Then:

Everyone takes it upon himself to judge and criticize rulers and other nations according to the way he feels about them. Never fall into this fault, Philothea, for besides offending God it will involve you in endless disputes. ...

Or:

The princess we have mentioned was not responsible for the dishonourable proposal made to her since we have presupposed that it was made against her will, but if she had in any way encouraged the man who courted her, wishing to make love to him, she would obviously be responsible for the very proposal; and even if she then drew back she would still be worthy of blame and punishment. ....

At first Alfried was captivated by the detachment of these admirable counsels and unable to stop reading; but later he became infuriated. Even more clearly than before, he saw that he had for long been avoiding the issues by taking coffee every day with his hostess, Frau Gudrun and by fiddling about with books and forming grotesque attachments to people who did not seem to be there. He became afflicted with strange reveries and dreams. He saw Hubertus as a dancer of ballet, Frau Grunwald as an immense and faceless chaperone, Officer Halstedt as a lackey standing at his coach-door as he himself descended the steps to enter the theatre of the young demoiselle of Paris. He told himself that he must in some way dispel this absurd charade and break through to the realities that lay behind it. 'I'm suffocating in that house,' he decided. 'Her rectitude! Her mad superstitions and madder certainties! There's something more behind them; and if I don't identify it soon, it will ruin me as surely as it ruined Hubertus.'

He prayed for guile; for a lance or a sword; a target into which he might plunge them. And the next morning he was told by Halstedt, who was more courteous than ever, that the Kommandant would be interviewing him early.

When he went into the office he was greeted warmly and offered a cigarette.

'Break your rule for once,' the Kommandant said. 'You mustn't bank on it, Waitzmann, but it looks rather as though your stay with us may be coming to an abrupt end.'

'Really, sir?'

'I can't tell you anything definite at the moment. I wouldn't even if I could; because it's against my policy. I want you to carry on quite normally until I've had confirmation from the powers that be.'

'Not my release, sir. So soon?'

'Carry on normally!' repeated the Kommandant. 'It's always best in the end, I find, whether the news is good or bad. Sanity and salvation lie only in Normality.'

Alfried was irritated: 'What do you mean, sir? What is it? I've never discovered what Normality is.'

But the Kommandant ignored the question. He was

thinking that occasionally, very occasionally, it paid to be young. He had lost hope some years before; but the young were never without it. They did not hope; they expected! Whereas he had never hoped to have such news as this. Dozens of these poor devils down the line, he was thinking. One had to give them hope out of the deadness. It was the only thing they understood: reprieve, petitions, amnesties, their food. After a certain stage in one's life, one never expected again to be larger than despair – but here today it was. 'I'm opening something,' he realized. 'I'm taking the lid off his heaven for him and somehow I know that he's one that's unlikely to come back.'

He visualized Alfried in a monastery, safe in the mysteries of his particular persuasion; one of those odorous Bavarian churches with bones and jewels behind glass: chantings of monks, suspect benedictions.

'By this evening we might perhaps celebrate, I think,' he said aloud. 'My wife will be delighted to preside. I've a lot to thank you for, Waitzmann; in a purely social sense you've done her good! For my part and in my turn I hope you'll realize that I've not been idle?'

'You've been extremely kind, Colonel,' Alfried assured him.

'I did my best. It wasn't always very much; but there are wheels within wheels in this job; one has to keep on the right side of the law, you know.'

He laughed at his joke. All had proved so unexpectedly pleasant. Von Hoffbach had obviously had even more 'pull' than he had given him credit for, though not, perhaps, more than Hubertus had discerned. That boy of his had an unhealthy guile.

'I'm glad,' he went on, 'that you should have got on so well with my son. Who knows that you may not meet again in happier circumstances? Do you ever visit Schönform?'

'I haven't been there for a year or two.'

'The Baron von Hoffbach has invited Hubertus to do a little shooting on his next leave. Not quite his style; but he'll enjoy the country life.' He paused, thinking, 'Oh well, I might as well put in a word for Hubertus too. He has his life to lead and Waitzmann is going to be an influential man.'

'What does it mean?' Alfried was asking himself. 'It's been nothing; a petty Calvary. Muddle, fear, ridiculous spiritual exercises. No dignity and now liberty again with nothing decided one way or another.'

'Hubertus asked me,' said the Kommandant, 'to give you an extra hour's grace this evening. My wife seconded the proposal strongly. I think under the circumstances one might stretch a point, Waitzmann.'

'Thank you, sir.'

'Hubertus is a talented boy. I worry about his future. I'd be glad if in happier circumstances –'

'When the war's over?' suggested Alfried.

'Right! One can decide nothing at present, nothing at all. We're all the toys of destiny, call it what you will. . . .'

Alfried was not taken to the Bergenstrasse until after the mid-day meal and found it as silent as on his first days there. He did not know what he had expected. Lights on to brighten that dull winter's afternoon? Music from the drawing-room? Frau Grunwald and Hubertus with a cake, candles for a birthday king? No, that would have been Ruprecht's fantasy. He must work, then, finish the cataloguing of the Kommandant's books. If he were efficient he might just complete it before it grew dark, before whatever had been arranged took place. That perhaps would be 'normality'.

But he found it hard to concentrate. The silence upstairs, the rumbling lorries, the closed doors worried him. He was a little light-headed. The clouds beyond the window oppressed him; February's weather in March, as if the year were standing still, a season arrested, the pause in hostilities that preceded the spring offensives anticipated by everyone. Nothing might have happened at all, he thought; it might have been his first week of imprisonment, the day of his introduction into the family when Frau Grunwald was yet to meet. It might be the first intimation of a pointless but remembered dream.

As he replaced book after book on the shelves he found he was expecting to hear the wireless at any moment, dance music, *Lili Marlen* being sung by the unfit. Frau Grunwald might appear in the doorway in a white nightdress with a black pectoral cross on her breast:

'You are busy, Herr Waitzmann?' she would ask. 'I thought I heard you call.'

'No, Frau Grunwald, I didn't call. I don't think I called.'

'Young men often do! My son Hubertus cries out in his sleep. He's not strong, you know; I never know what to do for the best for him.'

'What's the matter with him?'

'You too, I'm told, have night fears. To some they are given.'

'We must accept them.'

'Never, Herr Waitzmann.'

She vanished. He had imagined it all, of course, out of the sleepless nights and the excellent news. In a few hours, by tomorrow morning perhaps, he would be free. The dream need never be repeated.

In the bedroom, Frau Grunwald started to sing. It was not his imagination this time; distinctly he heard her moving about in there, a heavy woman whose body shook the floorboards. He gave up and went down to the kitchen, floating or seeming to float down the staircase. 'I should have shouted,' he thought, 'and instead I made a few remarks. . . . I was disgruntled. I temporized with Ruprecht over the factory management and advanced spiritual difficulties to him as my motive, when the whole time it was only that I liked the thought of the money! This, then, is an excellent punishment; an excellent absurdity. I start with an angel and I end with a fat woman prancing about in her bedroom. It was all my attitude was worth.'

On the kitchen table he found a note. Frau Gudrun had left it beneath a jam jar filled with cut celery.

My son and I are entertaining this evening. There is to be a *small party*. I shall be most obliged if you would set and lay the stove in my drawing-room with dry wood at *six* o'clock. There is a lantern in the back kitchen. Remember always that you have been helped. We have not been found wanting.

Gudrun Grunwald.

No wonder she's singing like a revivalist, thought Alfried. By that 'we' I suppose she means herself and her tea-leaves or some sign or other. She can't possibly mean her husband. He's merely the cross on which she likes to think she's pinned. People always provide their own.

But she had been busy. Besides the celery there was a tray-ful of plates covered with slices of bread, some of them spread with boiled beans, others with bottled tomatoes, pickled onions, sauerkraut, lozenges of cold sausage, gherkin and pumpkin with crab-apple jelly. There were six coffee cups and a large tin of Swiss milk from the store in the larder.

'I could like her if she stuck to this pathetic housekeeping,' he thought, as he lighted the lamp in the back kitchen. 'But it's not enough for her. She threatens me with her appalling mythology, her unbleeding righteousness. Dear God, what am I to do?'

The woodshed was some distance from the house and on his way to it, with the quiet rain falling, the lamp swinging over the soaking grass, he was suddenly aware of a goat. He caught a glimpse of its coarse yellow pelt in the hooded light of the paraffin lamp before it backed away from him into the shadow of Frau Gudrun's arbour. He heard it purr in its throat, a thick fleshy noise which he found attractive; and moved forward to see it more clearly. An eye shone, the purring became staccato and babyish. He saw the yellow head with the dancing eyes lowered for the charge and drew closer. He could smell the creature intimately, its odour blanketed the arbour, the rain and air foul with it. The goat's lips clapped up and down over its long teeth. As it ran for him, heading him away from the house towards the woodshed, he was triumphant. In the following minutes, before it ran out through a gap in the hedge, he was shaking with disgust and a simple terror yet, simultaneously, he was joyful too; for at last he knew how he would prove her.

She was awaiting him in the drawing-room. He saw the filled whiteness of her new blouse, the black hair piled stylishly on her head, the new but old-fashioned buckled shoes on her small feet.

'Herr Waitzmann!' she exclaimed, startled by the suddenness of his entry.

'Not my fault, Frau Grunwald. You have a guest in your garden.'

'But your clothes!' she drew back as she smelt him.

'A goat,' he said, with deliberate expressionlessness. 'Very strange. At first I didn't believe it. I thought I'd walked in something; but it was too subtle for that. It was in your arbour.'

'You've left all the doors open.'

'I've never seen such a goat. One eye permanently mad, focused on nothing, angry, surrounded by hair.'

'But Herr Waitzmann, you are soaking wet; you look ill.'

'I had the sense that it was measuring me in some way, as if I presented a peculiar problem.'

'Herr Waitzmann, you *are* ill.' But he moved over to her and she became larger. 'Keep away from me!' she commanded. 'What are you doing with that wood?'

'You should have warned me, Frau Grunwald. If you are going to play these tricks on people, how do they know where they stand?'

She was looking at him with hatred, her eyes taking in his white, vicious face and his dirty clothing.

Alfried smiled at her distastefully. 'But perhaps you don't know yourself? Perhaps you're in such a ridiculous muddle with the world that you can no longer distinguish between coincidence and the supernatural? Perhaps, after all, it was only one of your son's pranks.'

'Leave this room.'

'After all, your son is devoted to you. He'll do anything he imagined might please you, even though you have led him into such a ditch.'

'Go out of here at once, Herr Waitzmann.'

'What was your reason, I wonder? Perhaps neither of you knew anything about it; they say that goats are evil – like the Jews.'

'Enough!'

163

'This goat I saw was either a trick or it was something worse. Something from the other world perhaps, a spirit, an omen?'

'Leave me!'

'But you understand these things. Your son tells me you make prophecies and consult astrologists. Perhaps recently you dreamed of a goat?'

'You've brought disaster to my house,' she shouted. 'You're a traitor, Herr Waitzmann, and you wish to betray my son, I've been watching you.'

'Let us stick to the goat,' said Alfried. 'It's something we can both understand; a materialization, an evil spirit seeking to destroy the Thousand Year Reich. But it may only be seeking to destroy you. Perhaps you've called it up without meaning to and one day, next time, it may return to claim you.'

'Out of the kindness of my heart,' said Frau Grunwald, looking over his shoulder at her missionary certificate, 'I've allowed you to involve us all in your treachery, your giving and taking of messages. I know all about them; but now I know you for what you are! You've given yourself away at last. You're a Jew, Herr Waitzmann! An enemy of the Führer and of our country.'

'I'm a Christian, Frau Grunwald, a Jew and a Christian and a German all in one.'

She laughed. One of her small hands fluttered to her hair and stroked a coil into place. 'And your position won't protect you this time. *I* shall see to that. My son has had his suspicions for a long time and I too have my means of reading people's hearts.'

'You are squinting, Frau Grunwald. You've developed the National Socialist squint.'

'It will do you no good to try to escape. Only one person might have helped you and she has been saved in time.'

'I don't want to escape. I've no wish to. I shall wait in the kitchen till you send for the staff.'

She moved past him carefully. 'You may leave the logs on the stove,' she said. He saw her pick up the telephone in the hall.

Chapter 6

Throughout that spring Fräulein von Boehling prayed intensively for success in her final examination which she was due to sit in June. She also prayed regularly for Alfried, particularly after Hubertus had told her of the change that had come over him in March.

Hubertus now confided more or less intimately in Alexandra, because, once he had come under the care of the S.S., Carin had refused to allow him to discuss Ruprecht's brother at all. Carin told him that she greatly regretted ever having been involved in the affair and that Nicholas had been most put about by her meddling. She told Ruprecht that the mere mention of the name had been sufficient at one time to deprive him completely of his appetite. On occasions she had known him even to drop his spoon in the soup and go out for a lonely walk. So when he could catch Alexandra alone, Hubertus in his astonished, frank way told her all about what he called 'the night of the goat' and the disturbing effect it had had upon his mother. He was much given to this surprised type of confiding, as if, constantly exercised, it might eventually reconcile him to some strangeness within himself.

'It was amazing,' he said. 'I can't get over it. You see, in her own way, my mother always used to be gay. Even in her worst spells she would play little snatches of wireless music in her bedroom and keep abreast of developments; but ever since that beast alarmed her by trying to involve all his friends in his own treachery, she has retreated into a private world of her own.'

He increasingly used well-accepted phrases to describe events. He said that his mother's nights were 'a torment to her' and that she could not 'forgive herself' for having been so deceived as to imagine that such a man as Alfried might respond to kindness and even become a friend of his, meaning himself.

Alexandra responded to his excitement as well as she could. She thought and said that Hubertus seemed to be very disturbed and that he must try to put it all out of his mind, as she was sure that nothing more would come of it. Once or twice she was a little bewildered by the constant mention of a goat in connexion with the affair; but whenever she tried to find out what part it had really played, Hubertus became quite incoherent with description. He would say: 'Well, Mama's psychic, you know. She has a great sense of evil – it was her childhood in the Black Forest – and she saw this goat long before it arrived – in a dream. D'you know she even removed the Dürer engraving in the hall. Or she certainly meant to do so. The goat she dreamed of had a long, pale yellow tongue and she knew that it represented evil.'

'That is terrible.'

'She saw in a flash that it was something to do with treachery; but until that night she didn't connect it with Waitzmann.'

Alexandra was distressed. She told Hubertus how the devil had left his footprint in the Frauenkirche in Munich and from then onwards did not fail to pray for Alfried immediately after she had asked her patron, Alessandra di Rudini, to intercede for her examination results. She mentioned Hubertus's story to Carin, who laughed sharply and said that Alfried must be even madder that she had always supposed.

'I can't think why you should be alarmed by such nonsense,' she said. 'As a Catholic you must have been reared on stories of would-be saints being pestered by devils disguised as animals. I know poor Nicholas was. I sometimes suspect Ruprecht of being more influenced than he realizes. They're both obsessed by him.'

'By whom, Carin?'

'By Alfried, of course. You didn't surely think I meant the Devil?'

Carin herself was obsessed by Ruprecht. Things connected with him, no matter how intrinsically boring or disturbing, were now of moment to her; and she felt bound to refer to them. Probing him obliquely over this, she said that Hubertus, constantly upsetting everyone with his stories of his mad mother, was becoming increasingly 'a little pest'. 'It's a great pity Alfried could not have been sent to a normal prison where he would have been better protected against his eccentricities.'

Ruprecht looked at her angrily and then replied that he loathed all psychic people and none more so that Frau Grunwald.

'Why is it,' he asked, 'that people who make these claims are always so much more sensitive to evil than to good?' He became threatening and said that he still expected her to go on doing all she could to press the Baron to secure Alfried's conditional release.

'Don't be so *accusing*, Liebling,' she said. 'You know I've always done my best to see he was decently treated; but you must see that just at present it's far wisest for us all to lie low. The Party's getting a little sick of private pressure groups and Nicholas is genuinely alarmed by the repercussions from the Grunwald affair.'

Though she was becoming accustomed to such fencing she had to admit that Ruprecht was an even moodier devil than she had supposed. The affair with him, exciting as it was, had let her in for all manner of difficulties. Taking her husband's worries seriously, she had advised him not to meet her at the flat since it not only embarrassed him but it upset Alexandra who, she felt, might be writing anything in her letters to her parents.

'You mean?'

'Only that she's so young; so simple, if you like.'

'So innocent perhaps?'

'I don't use the word. At my age it has no claims on me.' She had thought it advisable to be a little more politically active and had managed to get herself appointed as a Sunday lecturer to the League of German Girls. Though she found it inexpressibly dull there had been advantages:

some respectable publicity through the Reichsminister, Herr Goebbels, who was always publishing her picture and, better still, had allotted her a Volkswagen with an extra ration of petrol.

'A godsend,' she had told Ruprecht, 'now that you're off the road.'

'We could manage without.'

'Not with such an unusual lover! I often wonder if you're not some sort of a fetichist, Liebling.'

She was referring to the deserted swimming-pool in which they had first consummated their affair. Officially a water supply against incendiary raids, it was disused only in the evenings; in the mornings the men of a nearby anti-aircraft battery made use of it for physical training. On their happiest evenings she would pick Ruprecht up at some discreet distance from the Institute. They would drive off to a quiet, rather shoddy, restaurant in the East End where no one would be likely to know them and she would see that he had enough to drink and make sad jokes about the food. They neither of them had much appetite at this time. The meal was only a gesture they paid to history and their social position. Quite often they lingered over it unnecessarily, drinking the coffee and smoking her Gauloise cigarettes. Then, so well could they time one another's inclinations, they would, without a word said, get up together and drive straight off to the pool.

There were gates to climb and locked turnstiles to negotiate which Carin enjoyed peculiarly. They made her feel so very young and, in some way, 'wicked'. She enjoyed his bad-tempered agility, the skilled impatience with which he bundled her over things. Sometimes, even in the middle of a raid he would keep her waiting intolerably, muffled up in his own vast overcoat, whilst he stripped and plunged into the black rectangle of water.

Getting out, he would say, 'The symmetry! It appeals to me as does physics. The tiles are all in line, the dressing rooms too and their reflections. I like to be the only person to have the idea and to make use of it with you.'

'Discomfort can be delicious,' she agreed. 'It's a luxury the wealthy and the unyoung needlessly forgo.'

Behind the locked door on either the Men's side or the Women's, depending on Ruprecht's impulse, she would be rewarded. They would make love, doze or sleep a little, smoke a cigarette or two, take powders if they had head-aches and drink from his flask. Then they would make love again and, quickly, a third time; chasing, through their exhaustion, images less substantial than their own reflec-tions in the unlighted pool. But they would persist. They had a pact that there must be no giving up of the goal once they had set their wills upon it.

Knowing his moods, Carin was careful never to take her full share of his flask. She would pretend only to swallow from it so that there would always be enough left for after-wards when disenchantment hit him or he became super-stitious. He has his brother's blood, she would think, when she felt him shudder in the darkness.

'What is it?'

'Something moving. Quiet!'

'Silly man.'

For she herself was never frightened: 'At my age it's the light one fears; to be old, Liebling.'

'No night,' he would say, 'passes without its event. There's always something: one footstep, a whistle or a whisper; some creature moving. Lacking our eyes to deceive us, we do well to be frightened.'

'There, there, lie down again!'

But one night he leapt out unsteadily, saying that there were rats, a hoard come to drink at the pool.

'They've been disturbed by the bombing,' she told him. 'Ignore them and they will go away again.'

But he persuaded her home; his expression scrupulous with distaste as if he were washing some defilement from his hands. He never brought her to the pool again. Instead she had to endure wet grass and thin spring woods until her rheumatism flared up and her temper with it. They met less often and ever more insistently Ruprecht bothered her about Alfried. Despite her warnings, he insisted on calling for her at the flat and, one evening, after a letter from his mother, he became so unreasonable that she silenced him with an outburst of truth.

'You fool! Don't you realize that at this moment he may be involving each of us? Write and tell your mother that they have him!'

'I shall lose everything.'

She was too astonished to laugh. For a moment she thought she might love him.

'But your *mother*!'

'Well?'

'Liebling, do you love no one? Would you really write as baldly as that if it were not for your future?'

'She is indestructible. Nothing can damage her; but she can still ruin *me*.'

'Ah, you again. Always that little birthday king. Everything! For a moment I was foolish enough to imagine it might have been me you preferred.'

'No man's to blame for his birthday and I'm not the sort of man who can love empty-handed. It's not my fault; but nothing's going to stop me correcting that situation.'

'And you have your mother's strength, you hope? Certainly there's no weakness on that side of the family, Liebling.'

He had seen the implication in that remark and forgiven her instantly If this is Jewish strength let me have more of it, he thought. Let me have as much as I hope Alfried has.

Alfried had replied to his S.S. questioners over and over again.

'I assure you that von Hoffbach passed me no messages. Herr Grunwald – Hubertus – is mistaken if he told you I sent any such messages. He is lying.'

'What did you discuss?'

'Poetry, sex, religion.'

'What else?'

'Religion, sex, poetry.'

'You discussed the régime?'

'It was too risky.'

'Ah.'

'But only because I wasn't sure either of my opinions or of Herr Hubertus's. My religion by tradition is authoritarian, Lieutenant. It's never been afraid of a dictatorship. After all, we have one of our own.'

'Answer the questions, prisoner Waitzmann.'

'I have answered them. Let me repeat; I know exactly what was discusssed, I know what books I catalogued and I know what messages my friends sent me. In your sense as well as in mine, all my activities and conversations were innocent.'

'How many messages did you receive from your brother, Ruprecht Waitzmann?'

'Three. He hoped each time that I was well, that I had written to our mother and that I should soon be free again.'

'The Baron von Hoffbach?'

'None.'

'His wife?'

'Two. She hoped I was well.'

'If you do not reply helpfully tomorrow you will be punished.'

'Very well, Lieutenant.'

Halstedt returned him to his cell and Alfried prayed standing up: 'No violent fools,' he demanded. 'If they lose their tempers please see that they do it gradually. You, after all, took your time over it. You even had supper first and a lingering scene in a garden. I very much doubt if even Judas had a face like that second fellow, the one that keeps so quiet; and in any case all the Jews, whether they accepted You or not, were essentially religious. That swine is about as spiritual as a pig.'

He had developed a fixation about this second man and always watched his face as he might in other circumstances have scanned the sky for that high thin cloud, iced and crystalline which promises convulsive weather in the settling of any given season. This officer, not always present and of senior rank, unthinkingly snapped matches in his fingers. His teeth occasionally grated on the lips of his cigarette holder and often he had cuts round the chin due to the rigours of his morning shave. In moments of cowardice, when Alfried looked at his face with that frightful innocence of affection which it is sometimes very difficult to repress, this officer's skin glistened like meat. It seemed his features were as adventitious as those that spring out of patterned things when one is tired and depressed; faces full of sadness, of mockery or malice. So after a time Alfried ceased to appeal to the face and yet remained more conscious of its owner's presence than of that of the other man.

The sessions to begin with were held in the mornings; but in the second week with the doctor's consent they took place in the afternoons and evenings as well. If on each occasion one or two new topics had not been introduced Alfried might have been able to repeat himself indefinitely; but the inquiry extended very slowly. It seemed to him sometimes that it was feeding on him, strengthening itself out of his increasing weakness, delicate as the lies of which it was so largely composed.

When the dossier was complete and Alfried had given such harmless information as he could about each of his acquaintances from his school-days to his return from the United States, he was advised by the doctor that he was classified as fit for all degrees of punishment. He was warned that the information he was withholding was of vital interest to his country and that if he did not co-operate he would be finally deprived of the privileges previously allowed him.

'You must realize,' Dr Lütgens said, 'that your health is at present good.'

'I am to be shot?'

'You will not be shot so long as you can work; but you can only work so long as you are in good health.'

'Then I am to be tortured?'

'That is not for me to decide.'

'In that case I can assure you that I am withholding no information.'

The doctor looked up. 'In future, Officer Halstedt will report your condition to me twice daily. As from today you will neither receive nor send any letters or messages whatsoever. Those are my instructions.'

The next evening when it was dark Halstedt marched Alfried along the corridors to the punishment cell. He was silently solicitous and gave his orders as considerately as if this were what he himself had sadly looked forward to all along. At times, in flashes, Alfried felt like trying to cheer him by saying such a thing as, 'Forgive yourself, Halstedt; the infliction of a just punishment delights us all. Acknowledge your pleasure and you'll feel better.' But he was always too frightened to do this; and, in any case, the impulse was one of so many that he had no real time to act upon it.

In the punishment cell the screen was arranged to conceal the officer who carried out the 'exercises' as they were called and Halstedt stood to attention beside it so that he might take Alfried's pulse and keep an eye on his condition. Alfried was strapped down in such a way that he could only turn his head in two directions; he could choose to look either at the ceiling which was high or else watch Halstedt's face which was full of gentlemanly affection. A third person whom Alfried never saw but presumed to be a stenographer sometimes interrupted the exercises to ask the answers to be repeated more slowly or for the prisoner to raise his voice.

A routine was quickly established: a question would be repeated three times, a punishment inflicted, the question repeated twice more, a more painful injury inflicted, until the question had been posed seven times in all. The wounds would then be inspected and recorded in the case medical history sheet by Halstedt while everyone else rested for a minute or two. Then a second question would be asked three times and the whole process repeated until not less than ten questions had been posed.

At the end of the session all the ligatures would be removed and replaced in the sterilizer by Halstedt. Alfried would be allowed to pass water if it were possible and would later be given a sitz bath if it were not. Halstedt, with surgical forceps and spirit, would remove the pieces of microfilm from his body and gently dress the small burns on his genitalia and between his fingers. His face was never injured at all.

During the first three days Alfried was given the ordinary hospital diet but on the fourth he was put on to the Number One punishment diet, sixteen ounces of soup and one cob of rye bread a day, as it was decided by Lütgens that his resistance might weaken faster if his calories were reduced. The pace of the interrogation was increased, as many as eighteen questions being asked and the session correspondingly lengthened. The punishment cell itself began to warm up; it was pervaded by a sense of conviction similar to that which fills a hospital theatre during a prolonged and difficult operation. The participants were by now consumed by such intense curiosity as to the mystery of Alfried's will and substance that they no longer had any ethical judgement left. For them he might have been one man or many; and Alfried sensed the change at once.

He noticed that Halstedt had now become as kindly as if he had found him absolved of anything he might have imagined him to have done. Often, he openly helped him down the stairs and on one occasion allowed him to step with his swollen foot on to his own bright boot at a particularly deep step. He patted him on the shoulders continually and on the back of the head as if he had been comforting a sufficiently sick prisoner; and, privately, he became amazingly cheerful about his own health and domestic tensions.

To begin with Alfried reproached himself for shouting. The sounds he made were ugly even to his own ears and he resented them; but no attempt was made to silence him; and when, through half-shut eyes, he saw that his cries had no visible effect on the one face he could see, he said to himself, 'That's good!' Since God had given him a voice with which to scream, he would scream as much as he liked, he decided; and found thereafter that he was much less inclined to scream, though he groaned rhythmically instead. He told himself later that he had somehow the intention of making each of his groans a prayer; but when the time came he thought to himself, this is not a prayer. It is the noise a baby makes at the breast. It is the sound of an old man dying. But perhaps these too are prayers.

Each night when he returned to his cell he took back his

intention of 'offering up' his pain and in the morning excused himself by saying to God: 'Since they must mean something, I've the will to make my cries a prayer. Please remember this even if I forget it.'

Soon afterwards a splendid thing happened; in the middle of a session he ceased to feel any pain at all. His whole body had become very malleable and pliant; it sweated more easily, the joints seemed to have loosened and the skin to have become as soft as a young girl's. Only the pain-sense had ceased to operate.

'I'm in the position of pre-anaesthetic man,' he decided. 'I've regained a forgotten bodily function.' Imaginatively, he seemed to have entered not a negative, pain-free state; but a grassy plain in which stood many great trees beneath whose shade he paused at each moment of torture. At first he was incredulous. He found it difficult to know even which particular method was being tried, feeling only pressures and withdrawals, brief sensations of heat and coldness which immediately became lost in his exhilaration. He foolishly forgot, until it was too late, to keep his secret to himself; and instead of continuing to groan and flinch lay perfectly still, his mind full of exciting speculations. His indifference was soon discovered and there was an immediate pause. The S.S. officer who was in charge of the session questioned Halstedt and then conferred with his colleagues somewhere on the other side of the screen. Cigarette-smoke began to drift up to the ceiling where it was silently sucked out by an automatic fan.

Someone tapped a typewriter. In a few moments all three officers moved out into an adjacent room and Alfried heard their voices and the tinkle of telephone bells as the receiver was replaced. On their return the screen was removed and Halstedt was dismissed. In the sharp light Alfried was confronted by the senior officer, the Captain. He had three small shaving cuts on his chin, one of which had recently bled. He leaned against the wall, the peak of his uniform cap at an angle over his blue eyes. His junior, the Lieutenant, stepped forward and touched Alfried gingerly with his gloved fingers. Their tips probed his stomach and then ran up his chest wall, circling a burned nipple and sketching the outline of the collar bones beneath the skin.

After a moment one of them said: 'You can see he's a Jew by the distribution of his skin pigment.' Then the Captain left his place by the wall and took hold of one of Alfried's ears and twisted it quite gently as if he had been a schoolboy. The Lieutenant opened a bottle of seltzer water and drank from its neck. Then he put the bottle down and lobbed a pair of rubber gloves across to the Captain, who put them on and said 'Catch!' as he threw back the dusting powder which the Lieutenant caught nonchalantly in his left hand.

As soon as he had put on the gloves the Captain began to examine Alfried fearlessly. At first he made jokes about sexual intercourse and excretion; but then he became silent. He moved round the table like a man playing bagatelle, making shallow incisions with a scalpel and forcing ligatures over different parts of Alfried's body. Suddenly he lost patience; in his black breeches he jumped astride Alfried's belly and with the seltzer bottle began to beat him in the groin. Every so often he would turn round to look at his face. The Lieutenant left the room and as soon as he had gone the Captain began to sing Party songs. He threw his cap into a corner of the punishment cell and ran amok with bottle and the knife, nearly severing one of Alfried's ears and sticking the blade through the skin of his stomach along the surface of the muscles. Then he went over to the wash-basin in which they washed their hands. He sponged his face carefully, retrieved his cap and put it on at the same tilted angle in front of the mirror. The Lieutenant returned and without any further conversation they rang the bell for Halstedt and told him to order a stretcher. When they had collected their papers together they went off duty.

Halstedt took Alfried down to the hospital theatre and dressed his wounds. He arranged for his admission to a side ward reserved for important political prisoners and told him that Doctor Lütgens would see him in the morning. Alfried remained in the prison hospital for three weeks pending a decision from Himmler's headquarters as to his further disposal.

Chapter 7

In the autumn of that year, 1942, Nicholas and Carin drove down to Schönform for a brief holiday. It was the first time they had travelled anywhere together for several years and in other circumstances the Baron would have been inclined to draw her attention to the fact. He would have enjoyed reminding her that, '*au fond*' their greatest happiness had always been in the country and that essentially they were country people. 'Must be, my dear, since we both enjoyed a rural childhood; you in East Prussia and I in the South.'

At the oddest moments he found such protestations leaping to his mind and never more so than at this time when the war was going so little well for the armies; retreating in Russia and at a standstill in North Africa. But whenever he expressed a hint of such sentiment to Carin she laughed at him: 'You're becoming as middle-class as the Führer, wanting to eat his cream-cakes in peace and take Fräulein Braun out to feed the Berchtesgaden squirrels.'

So now as they drove South on the sunlit autobahn, slipping swiftly through dark forests and broad valleys, Nicholas stifled such longings for reassurance and continuity and tried instead to keep his mind on realities. He riffled through his brief-case, full of disturbing memoranda and documents, and kept an eye on the back of the chauffeur's head through which he would have liked to put a single bullet.

Carin, had he told her of this wish, would have been as much amused as by his other impulses. The presence of this observer of Himmler's had ceased to interest her. Since she was quite certain that if anything had been going to come of it then it would have happened long before this, she was no longer 'in a state' about it. They had all been only a little indiscreet, she was sure. Since the spring, events had moved on so far and so fast that the Reichsführer had many more urgent problems to occupy him. She doubted if the name 'Waitzmann' would now mean anything to him at all; and, if only Ruprecht continued to behave sensibly, there was no need for him ever to respond to it again.

Poor Ruprecht! She thought tranquilly, 'I wonder if by now he's found his true vocation as a lover of money?' With a glance at Alexandra, who was sitting beside her, she assured herself that she herself could afford to be 'collected' since undoubtedly she had had the best of him. He will have altered already, she decided; that type does. These 'money-men' are like jugglers; the moment they get to their weights they begin to thicken quite horribly. Oh dear, how unsubtle they become!

But Alexandra, gazing remotely out of the window at the flashing countryside, was not thinking of Ruprecht at all. Her thoughts were divided between a longing to see her parents who were in Stockholm and a sense of great excitement at the prospect of meeting Leo again in his beautiful water castle. She was telling herself that really she lived in a fairy tale, journeying South as a Princess might have done to meet the Prince who had asked her father, in another country, for her hand in marriage. Leo had written to her so patiently throughout those Berlin months; delightful letters, a little wry, full of tasteful jokes about her work in the hospital and sprinkled with hunting stories such as that of the injured doe he himself had 'delivered of a fine pair in the forest'. Their friendship had progressed as nicely as if it already had been written for them, a medieval tale of love enclosed between the covers of a well-bred book, each chapter taking it a little further into the impolite unknown for which unobtrusively she longed. She wished, as she had earlier told Carin, she really wished so much that she might love Leo; and perhaps, at the end of these two or three days, her mind would be composed for her and her many prayers answered. 'It's not right,' she had repeatedly told herself, 'for us all to be so safe. No love story is complete without danger and although we move through a much more terrible world than our ancestors ever did, we never seem to get involved.'

She washed her hands a little in the clear bowl of water which she always carried with her. It was not a real bowl, of course, and the physical action of washing was no more that of evasion or cleansing than is the use of a finger bowl. It was merely a rinsing of the fingers in the lap, a delicate ablution in response to distasteful fancies such as that aroused by the back of the chauffeur's head, which reminded her of Ruprecht's; and, by association, of his brother Alfried. Herr Waitzmann had become a ghost, a gap in the air. He was never referred to, he had been unable to acknowledge the little book she had sent him and therefore she prayed for him. She hoped to pray for him in case, by his own foolishness, he suffered. She longed for her prayers for him to become as loyal as prayers for the dead; and in the meantime, whenever that 'gap' presented itself to her, she changed the subject and rinsed her restless fingers.

As it happened, the Baron too was thinking about Alfried. He alone had any idea of his present whereabouts and until today he had had no wish to discuss that notion with anyone else. But at this moment, had he been alone with Carin and quite certain there was not one of Security's little machines concealed somewhere in the body of the car, he would have started a discussion at once.

'How should we put it to Frau Waitzmann, do you think?' he would have asked her. 'Her references to the boy have ceased. She writes exclusively about factory matters and Ruprecht's handling of the labour problem.'

'Well?'

'But I am not a fool.'

He tried to fill in the pause which would have followed this imaginary assurance. What would Carin have replied, he wondered? It was quite impossible to say; and in any case, if he could have guessed that, then what the devil was the point in having asked her?

His eyes followed a line or two of print on one of his documents as he carried on his own end of this fantastic conversation, one that he would surely have with her as soon as he could get her to himself in Schönform, well out of range of any possible servant or microphone, any plant such as this oaf of the Reichsführer's who was driving the car at such a pace.

'When a woman like the Frau Kommerzienrat dries up over a thing like this,' he went on to himself, 'that is the time to make one's preparations, my dear. In recent letters I've given her a dozen openings; and what does she reply? That production's never been higher, that young Ruprecht has suggested we start putting in claims for war damage already.'

But Carin, he could see, was not, in any sense, attending to him. That strange woman was eating a bright green apple which would not even give her indigestion. He watched as she ate greedily for some seconds and then saw her absent-mindedly bring another apple from her pocket and offer it to Alexandra, who refused it politely. She did not even trouble to proffer it to him who was now silently advising her 'to make a clean breast of it to Wilhelmina. Tell her that Alfried's a hostage to fortune and that you yourself only intervened when you saw which way the wind was blowing and decided that he must be taken care of.'

No, no, that wouldn't do at all, he commented. Horribly ambiguous. Very well then, let him suppose it was his own son, Leo. What, in that case, would it boil down to? What would one want to hear? That he was happy? Courageous? That he remained himself, or more than himself? That he had discovered something? Why yes, he thought, one would want to learn that one's son had unexpected resources; heroic strength; that he had discovered that other reach of the brave. 'My dear,' then he would advise Carin, 'you must stress the fact that when we last heard, Alfried bore no ill-will to anyone. Convince Wilhelmina that this is true; because I happen to know that it is – and so will she; though you, my dear, might not.'

He glanced at Carin again, still busy with her apple, her expression as vacant as a child's, and thought that he might have been hasty. 'God dammit!' he swore to himself. 'Whatever your feelings for Leo, this business of Alfried is your doing, Carin! The result of your absurd infatuation with his brother. Left to himself, Waitzmann would have gone back to Baltimore or joined the Oratorians. He would certainly not now be in a camp. Those places are not for one's friends.'

To be quite sure that he knew what he was thinking, Nicholas went over this phrase once more in his mind: 'Those places, not monasteries – they're understandable if people are so minded – not monasteries, but camps, my dear Carin, are *not* for one's acquaintance.'

But Carin, crunching the last mouthful of her apple, her eye catching separate lines of typescript held between his square-tipped, manicured fingers, was relying on Frau Waitzmann's social susceptibility.

'My dear friend,' Himmler had written. 'Baa – Baah – Baah – time being, this Political is fortunate to have been relegated to our camp at—' But Nicholas had turned the page. It was as frustrating as trying to over-read someone else's newspaper. She nibbled out a pip and bit it in half with her own sharp teeth. 'When I was young,' she remembered, 'I used to eat the whole of an apple even to the little scales in the core and the dried flower at the end. I didn't worry about my teeth then, or worms.' She was quite aware that Nicholas was brooding over Alfried and Frau Waitzmann and, if only he could be made to realize it, it was all quite simple. The Waitzmanns were only rather 'recent' industrialists and no one of Frau Waitzmann's age, and as 'tough' as she obviously was, would have failed to make provision against suffering. 'Charm is wonderfully penetrating,' thought Carin. 'There's no situation in which it can fail to make things just a little more bearable; and that's my task. To be warm, to be quick, collected and quietly sincere. Now what does Wilhelmina Waitzmann look like? Unimportant. What must I look like? Vital. I shall wear for her benefit something quiet: navy blue, a suggestion of officialdom: a hard little hat. With my tightest belt I could still get away with my London suit; but Maria must lower the hem half an inch. Stockings are easy, thank God. Ruprecht loved my legs.'

She dropped her apple-core into the ash-tray and settled back. She sat forward again. 'My God! She's blind!

Wilhelmina can't see a thing.' At this recollection she was inclined at first to confide in Alexandra, next, to laugh artificially as at a party; but then her thoughts came to a dead end and she stared foolishly round the car and out through the windows, realizing for the first time in minutes that they were actually moving, that they were approaching the outskirts of some town or other. Alexandra, she saw, was miles away; brooding over Leo obviously. They were passing a military convoy halted for lunch: there were one . . . two . . . three more tanks drawn up in the lee of the trees. Young Panzer men everywhere.

'I shall dress for Ruprecht,' she decided. 'For his mother I shall rely on my voice, on what Bonne-mama used to call one's "address". After all, one owes it to a man to be as desirable "after" as "before". Does anything justify one more than that smile from someone with whom one has shared such precious indignities? It is what one has lived for, really; the secrecy, the fleeting certainty.' Inside herself, she sighed, saying quite unintentionally to each of her lovers and to all: 'Keep, I pray you, my grave green as I yours.'

'Nicholas,' she said aloud. 'Tell that man to stop in the town centre for coffee. I'm unbearably cramped and Alexandra's looking sick.'

'That would be so nice,' said Alexandra, 'but really, I'm enjoying the drive. The trees are so beautiful in the autumn time.'

'Nuremberg,' grumbled Nicholas as the chauffeur helped the ladies descend from the hideously camouflaged staff car. 'It gets uglier every year.'

'The poor people have had such terrible raids,' sighed Alexandra.

'As for coffee,' added Nicholas, 'we'll be lucky if we get a hogwash of acorns.'

'Shall I enquire, sir?' asked the damned obedient chauffeur, not looking at anyone.

'No, look to the car if you please, Corporal. It's badly parked.'

'Perhaps he'd like a little refreshment himself,' suggested Carin with a smile for the man.

'You may join us, Corporal, when you've seen to things. But we leave in twelve minutes.'

'Herr Baron.' He saluted and got back into his car as proprietorially as a taxi driver.

'Never get a minute to ourselves,' Nicholas told them as they went into the chilly, spotless, room where an ugly waitress showed them to a small table. Sprays of silver birch and berried mountain ash in tall vases hinted at a former elegance: the odours of peacetime, the thin furs and thick chocolate of the rearmament period.

'So sad,' said Alexandra to Carin. 'Even the berries look tired.'

But the Baron was still obsessed by Himmler's man. 'That fellow thrusts himself upon one without any encouragement. I fail to see why it was necessary to invite him to join us.'

'It would be as well for you to remember, darling, that the guilty are never charming and in any case it was not I who invited him.'

'Dear Nicholas,' Alexandra intervened to her almost certain parents-in-law. 'I'm sure he's tired.'

Over the coffee and some rationed scones heavy with rationed lard, they straightened themselves out in a variety of ways. The coffee was unexpectedly good, the cups restaurant-clean and the tinned milk delicious. The corporal even enjoyed the scones and Carin made him eat the last one, saying, 'I'm sure you must need it with all those convoys to overtake.'

The Baron was a little soothed by the hot coffee and lighted a cigar. 'Things are not so bad as they might be,' he admitted; and Alexandra, swallowing a last crumb of scone, agreed that they might be very much worse. But Carin sent the corporal off to the car to fetch a tin of her petits fours from the boot. She made the others feel humble and uncomplaining. The Baron, in fact, was thinking: 'This is the way we shall win, we are eating stringently to victory'; while Alexandra said suddenly that one should not grumble if one could possibly help it. 'Whenever I'm tempted to complain,' she said, 'I always find myself thinking of our men in Russia and Africa.'

'It's the ugliness I detest,' said Carin. 'Even motor-cars. Just look at the lines of that staff car. Not a single curve anywhere. Now who thinks of these things and what's the advantage?'

'The designers, my dear. It's a question of raw materials. Shortage of steel.'

'It's a question of men, Nicholas. They get together and they say, "now it is war! We must convince ourselves. We'll make the world masculine and everyone will tremble." '

'How funny you are,' said Alexandra. 'Used Leo to play at soldiers?'

'Never.'

'Hunting mad,' said the Baron.

'He is always so gentle that I can't imagine him like my brothers. Karl and Sigmund made such faces and noises that Papa had to build them a den in the garden.'

'You've heard recently?' asked Nicholas.

'Only through Papa, he sent me a letter on from Stockholm. It was already two weeks old when it reached him from Kharkov before the retreat.'

The corporal, standing by the table, butted in. 'You had a relative outside Kharkov, gnädiges Fräulein?'

'My brother, Captain von Boehling.'

'Ah.'

'Corporal!' said Nicholas. 'We must reach Schönform before the main convoys begin their night moves. Perhaps you had better start the car.'

The corporal lighted a cigarette and blew out the smoke. 'As I see it, Fräulein, the trouble at Kharkov was not the hedgehog defences; but the guerillas in the rear of our lines, the treachery of the Bolshevik population.'

'So?'

'You see what I mean,' said Carin as soon as he had gone. 'He's a bumptious young man. One can feel him filling out his uniform like a field marshal.'

'Then we'll quarter him in the stables,' said the Baron. 'He can eat with the forester.'

'Leo might give him a little shooting, perhaps,' she suggested. 'There's no point in antagonizing him.'

'On the contrary, he shall run Leo to the station on Monday morning. It might remind him of his rank.'

Alexandra was saddened and appealed to Carin. 'How dreadful it will be to have to say good-bye to Leo. I know I shouldn't say this; but today I'm almost glad he has such a weak chest. Is it very unpatriotic of me, do you think?'

'Of course not!'

'We can't all die in our boots, my dear,' added Nicholas. 'It's not the way Heaven works. On occasion I could have wished he was with your brothers; but when it came to it I'll confess I was damned glad I was able to get him posted to the Midi. Yes, damned glad,' he repeated stagily as he glanced out through the window to the car in which the corporal sat blowing smoke through his nostrils. 'Leo's doing his best. He might get stronger down there.'

'Be realistic,' said Carin. 'Were I even half a man there's nothing I'd like better than that sort of war. Fraternizing with the French Resistance and doing a little hunting on the sly.'

As they resumed the journey she reflected that one said these things because it was rather unbearable to say what one really felt. She hoped she had not hurt Alexandra but she did so dislike wrong sentiment. Certainly she was not, she supposed, over-devoted to poor Leo and never had been. She remembered that years ago someone, a baggy friend, had once told her, 'If you want to like them, have half a dozen. It's only the first one that's in danger of remaining a little stranger.'

But apart from the working class and a few papists, did anyone really enjoy their babies? As with one's house and one's body one had to partition off a whole section of one's mind if one was going to breed even once. How she had detested it: pills, moods, corsets, doctors, nannies. And at the end of it all, wispy little Leo with his consumptive's eyelashes and pointed bottom.

She glanced at Alexandra: she was looking hurt, eyes wide open so that she should not blink too often. Carin prised one of the girl's hands loose from its knot of fingers and briefly imprisoned it in her own mauve-nailed grille.

185

'But I wouldn't for the world have missed coming with you to say good-bye to my brave Leo. I really am going to worry about him as much as if he were on his way to the Africa Korps.'

Nicholas blew his nose most affectingly and Alexandra smiled bruisedly.

'Really!' thought Carin, who considered herself French. 'How right we are about the mushy German soul. It's about as civilized as plum pudding.' She glanced coldly out of the window again. Now that they had left Nuremberg behind they were journeying due west, crossing the vast plateau of South Germany. Against the hard, yellow meadowland distant houses and farms shone in the sunset like children's bricks left out on a lawn.

'In some ways, darling,' she resumed, 'it's a pity you couldn't have decided earlier. I blame Leo for not having asked you.'

'But it feels so strange,' Alexandra burst out, ready to laugh through the tears which she had not thus far shed. 'We don't really know each other. How could he have come to a decision without seeing me a little more often?'

'Then,' persisted Carin, 'we'd be on our way to a wedding instead of an engagement. There would have been the honeymoon, even a baby to look forward to.'

'Don't embarrass the girl,' said Nicholas.

'You'd look well in ivory,' went on Carin, unabashed. 'You might wear the veil I used, I think. It's somewhere in the West Turret. Maria will know. But there again you might look even sweeter in the Spanish. It was made for Nicholas's great-grandmother and was quite unspoiled last time I went through them.'

'But I can't begin to think of such things. Really, I've never considered them. To be Leo's wife, to have his child, however must it feel?'

'Like anyone else's; ghastly!' thought Carin, saying, 'Fibber! you know you've thought of nothing else from the time you went to school.'

'But I haven't. Why, the sisters don't allow one to have such thoughts, do they, Nicholas?'

'I shouldn't think so. The monks weren't too broad-minded, even about us.'

Yet, Nicholas knew what she meant: all that Bride-of-Christ thing the good sisters substituted for the realities of the business. Why, he remembered his own mother drumming it into his sisters' heads years and years ago; and how once, just before 1914, he'd caught Katrina praying a lily into flower. What a picture! The child in the water-garden when it was raining, crossing herself deftly before a blind plant and looking up to heaven in imitation of one of her holy pictures. Dead now. She'd married a sot and developed appendicitis in the middle of a pregnancy, rejoined Mama and Papa one hoped. What a sadness fell upon him at this moment with his bewildering wife beside him and Alexandra politely hesitant about accepting his son.

Ah, my religion! His mind was in a realm of incense and flowers, of waxen drops sliding like pearls down the ivory of candles, of bishops and their scarlet, of monks and chants, of cold schools and old confessions.

'It will all come right, my dear,' he told Alexandra. 'Corporal, I think you might switch on your headlamps; useless as they are they're better than nothing in this half-light.'

Carin raced on with her teasing, Alexandra with her happy denials; and he left them to it. There was no one she could not handle, given a chance. When the time came – tomorrow might be best – she would know just what to say. Frau Waitzmann's grief would be set at rest. That blind old woman would confide in him again and they'd be able to set their heads together as in the first days of their association.

He stowed the papers back in his brief-case as they traversed the high street of the last pink village. He saw with delight the piles of good Bavarian chestnut stacked before the cottage walls, the blackouts going up against lamp-lit interiors and the wine carts rumbling in over the cobbles. As they ascended the floor of the valley to Schönform he sat forward impatiently, blowing a little through his nostrils like an animal coming within sight of its hide. They circled the forecourt lake and drew up by the postern, the mass of the castle standing dimly over them; the dead, stone silence beyond their voices threaded with the insinuations of the water garden and the full culverts.

Scarcely noticing Leo's welcome, the insolence of the corporal's commands to his Verwalter, the Baron shook them all off and strode through into the courtyard where not a light showed, where swathes of wood-smoke laid by the chill hung bitter in the autumn air. Like a schoolboy returning he had a longing to leave them all and tour his home: to clump through each room with none of these people beside him, to set his tread upon the floors, to enter once again into possession.

'My childhood! What have I to do with this woman and her son who came unbidden into my life and have remained with me ever since? With that damned corporal and his insolence? I'd welcome only my own mother and father. I'd put the clock back forty years to nineteen-hundred and two, to Kaiser Wilhelm, to Ludendorff, Hindenburg; scarcely a factory in the area, government the business of the educated, and war of the Christian.

'Oh my mother and father!' he told a stag's head he could barely see, its antlers piercing the darkness against a charcoal ceiling. 'It's a good thing, after all, you are gone. You'd not have liked it at all. But perhaps, if for one moment you might, in procession – mama so slightly in advance of papa – greet me at this late hour, then perhaps you might say that word again of rightness and certainty, so effective and so forgotten.

'I'm not old, at all,' he told himself as he moved round the banqueting table, unused since Leo's coming of age; but each of whose carved chairs he knew by touch. 'For my age I'm in excellent shape. I can feel my body as it ought to be, well grown, a little heavy in the paunch; but not too heavy for my legs which have grown heavier too. In the morning I'll walk by the lake before breakfast and sort out all my problems. We'll conclude this business of Frau Waitzmann at a decent hour. *I'm* not a ghost, I've still my claims on time. It's they who are ghosts, my mother and my father. I shall find time to look in on their vaults on Monday after Leo has left, and leave a wreath for them. Father Guardini shall say a Mass.'

He ascended a stairway and moved down a corridor filled with vapours eddying through the open doorways of unused rooms. He climbed another half-flight of stone stairs in a turret and hurried to the living quarters over the forecourt lake. Lights burned in the ante-room; the silver photograph frames of his childhood, unpolished, shone dimly. A bear-skin rippled rank on the floor. By the doorway into the Lake Room, with its nail-studded sofas, old magazines and out-of-date wireless set, he paused, hearing the roar of the stove.

It reeked and roared from the hidden pine baulks blazing in its centre. A galvanized chimney took all of its flames and most of its smoke out through the wall, but every now and again subsidences of charcoal, sparks swifter than fireflies, flowered to the hearth beneath the grate. Acrid fumes escaped into the room and stayed there until the draught seeping round doors and windows dispersed them. The fuel burned fast and had to be constantly replenished. Everyone in there blew their noses at intervals or cleared their throats. Their eyes were as bright as those of people who have recently wept. No one stayed still for very long. They moved about pointlessly between sentences of their conversation, drifting first towards the bulk of the stove to get warm and then away to help themselves to food or to use their handkerchiefs.

The Baron, whom no one had ever been able to persuade to replace the stove, collected himself outside the room. Across it, Carin was drinking disdainfully milk that had once been hot. With her free hand she speared sections of cold breakfast sausage from a plate on the edge of a side-table laden with food. There were loaves of white bread and cakes of black, two jugs of milk from the farm, a saddle of cold venison on a stainless steel dish, three large local cheeses, half-a-dozen bottles of wine and two flagons of light beer from the Andaches monastery. Leo, in his green hunting-jacket, grey breeches and coarse-knit stockings was

189

dropping logs into the top of the stove with quick movements and Alexandra, trying to look warm and comfortable, was sitting stiffly on the arm of a chair.

The Baron embraced Leo. 'Splendid! If it's well stoked it doesn't smoke half so much.' He cut himself thick hunks of bread and cheese, then filled a tankard with beer. 'A famous occasion,' he began, then seeing Carin looking at him over her glass of milk he changed his mind and said instead, 'No, no, but it's damned good to be back. All would seem to be well.'

'You think so? I never felt so depressed in my life.'

'You're too much a stranger, my dear. It takes a thing like this even to make you set foot in the place.' And he looked at his son. 'A double event, Leo, we ought to have the flag hoisted.'

'A little premature, don't you think?' said Carin. 'With our men starting another Russian winter?'

'Alexandra,' Leo said. 'You're cold.'

'But no, this room is so beautiful.'

'She looks half dead,' said Carin.

Leo went over to her. 'Have my spare handkerchief. In this "beautiful room" one has only two alternatives, to weep or to freeze.'

'But where else can I go?' smiled Alexandra, mopping her eyes.

'If you take my advice,' said Carin, 'to bed. There at least one's tears are one's own.'

'But really this is so much what I like. I do like sometimes to be cold and a little uncomfortable.'

'Ah yes,' Carin agreed, thinking of Ruprecht in the swimming pool. 'Contrast is everything. But how I shall revel in my bed!' She kissed Leo hastily on both cheeks. 'You look so well, darling. No hollows now, and you're not even coughing, despite Nicholas's fiendish stove. Forgive me for leaving you so soon; but I must take off my car clothes. Does the bath water still occasionally run hot?'

'Maria and I have been stoking it all afternoon. Your bed's been aired and there's a plate of apples beside it and your little silver knife.'

'Sweet boy! I do believe you've missed your dreadful mother.'

'Of course he has,' said Nicholas. 'This place was built for women – a fortress. Never seems right when it's woman-less, does it, Leo? Now I'm going to follow your mother's example. Good night to you both, and don't give tomorrow a thought. Remember that all will come right in the end.' He paused. 'By the way, Leo, in the morning your mother and I have to see Frau Waitzmann so we'll leave estate business until after lunch.'

He looked round for Carin, whom he had imagined to be awaiting him by the door; but with a kiss of her hand she had disappeared in the middle of these remarks and he was left a little 'put out' with the glass of beer half con-sumed. He drained it at a draught and kissed Alexandra tenderly on the cheek before hurrying from the room.

'He's so sweet,' she said. 'I do wish he wouldn't worry so much.'

'He's lonely, that's all. By the way, I've heard from your father.'

Alexandra said nothing.

'I got the letter yesterday morning.'

'Yes, Leo?'

'He said that so far as he and your mother are concerned—'

'They would be so happy.'

'You knew what I was going to say?'

'I've thought about you so much, your letters.'

'But they're not the same thing as seeing me?'

'That would have been so much easier, Leo.'

'Then why don't you look at me?'

'You mustn't tease me, please.'

'You like only to look at me when I'm not looking at you, perhaps? That's true of hunting. Wild beasts can sense one's attention.'

'Sweet Leo!'

'I amuse you?'

'It's only that from your letters I've learned so much more about buck than I have about you.'

'Then have a drink with me, some wine?'

'I hardly feel I'm here. I've thought about it so much – all the way in the car. Oh, what a graceful glass this is, it reminds me that someone once told me – I can't remember who it was – but he said the glass is more important even than the wine.'

'But not than the occasion?'

'Oh dear!'

'It sounds like Waitzmann. I've often heard him say it – a businessman's phrase. He trots it out every time he gets a drink here.'

'Don't be angry with me.'

'Did you see much of him in Berlin?'

'Scarcely at all.'

'Which? Not at all, or scarcely?'

'Leo, you look so cross.'

'I'm in love with you. Tell me about Waitzmann. How was he – in Berlin?'

'I suppose he was much the same as he always is, but I saw so little of him.'

'He changes, you know. He has a triple personality. There's Waitzmann the industrialist, Waitzmann the lover of nature, no doubt there's Waitzmann the man about town.'

'He doesn't interest me. I never think about him.'

'Yet you remember even his most trivial opinions.'

Alexandra was so excited that she would have liked to go on with the discussion all night: it gave her 'hot and cold hands' all over her body. She did not know what she might try next and was quite astonished when she decided to hand back her empty glass saying, 'Please take it, and kiss me good night.'

He held her by the shoulders, touching her eyelids with his lips. She heard him whisper, 'To be in love is to be angry, that's all I can say.'

'Put your arms round me!'

Fleetingly she imagined she was something Leo had shot. How strangely he made love. He trembled yet he was steady. His fingers fondled her ears as if they had been furry and rare. He kept closing her eyelids and stroking the little muscles in her cheeks and neck. He caressed her hair as if it had been a plover's crest.

'This room is cold,' she said. 'So beautifully cold. Hold me to you closer. Oh, I think I must love you.'

His finger tips were like a cat's pads on her neck. His lips continually paused on her own and she decided suddenly that she had made a mistake. She should have waited until his anger was forgotten. But how was she to have known?

'Everything is so exciting,' she said, moving away from him.

'Schönform. You really like it?'

'I've longed for it.'

'For what?'

'For the courtyard, the lakes, the waters everywhere, even this strange, cold room.'

'And the woods, and game? The little bats and the jays, the scavengers?'

'It's another world. But it frightens me a little.'

'Then we'll be married here on my first leave. We'll ignore the war and be traditional. Nuptial Mass: all the tenants, an escort of foresters and as many of our neighbours as possible: Hohenheim, the Kordts, the von Plattenburgs – even the Waitzmanns.'

'But you must give me time.'

'You've had too much already. You must make up your mind by tomorrow evening at the latest. If it's sooner we'll go over to Father Guardini in the morning while the others are in the town. He can look out his vestments and choose the music.'

He put a hand over her mouth and turned out the oil lamps one by one, forcing her to accompany him round the room.

'Say nothing.'

'But Leo!'

He shepherded her along the chilled corridor to the door of a guest room, throwing it open so that he could see her face. He kissed her thoughtfully and left her there, moving as silently as if he had been in the depths of the woods. She was left with a close-up of his sharp little face: the brown stainings beneath his feminine, long-lashed eyes, the nearly concealed hollows which Carin had chosen to ignore. She felt she might weep for him or for herself and prayed formally on a rush-seated prie-dieu between the blacked-out windows. Then she turned the lamp right down and undressed as precisely as if she had been back in her convent at school. Yet she was still excited; wondering, believing that this was what a betrothal might be. A journey whose beginning was only apparent at its close. 'No one,' she thought, 'has every really tried to tell me, and if they had, of course, I should have been bound to stop them at once; but how sad.' She wept again in the slowly warming bed.

In the morning, Carin was made bad-tempered by the drive to the factory. She was never at her best in the mornings and had long since given up reproaching herself, believing she was too feminine to be at ease in these male hours of vigour and noise. 'Bonne-mama', her French grandmother, had never risen before eleven – oh, the scent of coffee and cosmetics in the guest room – and never dressed before midday. But her own mother, Prussian to her shadow, had always been an early riser and even now in her seventies was still called each morning at seven-thirty.

Those two should meet, she thought, remembering Frau Waitzmann, with whom so shortly she would have to deal. They'd agree about so much; and principally about me. They'd have little need of their tongues were I the subject of discussion. Like 'bonne-mama' I'm a Latin and therefore I offend. I lie about in my bed in the mornings and awaken in the evenings. I am given to all my little luxuries and have a Gallic attitude to men. How much these sisterly old women must pity Nicholas.

'But surely,' she told him, as they stopped at the factory entrance, 'this railway's new?'

'Not a railway, a siding, my dear.'

'And all those men in the trucks?'

'The day shift, I imagine. No comment, though, I beg you. The Frau Kommerzienrat is difficult.'

'But where have they come from?'

Nicholas sighed: 'Waitzmann anticipated the staff short-age and when the Ministry sited a labour camp nearby, we put in an application. We raised half the capital and quite quickly we got the siding and the labour – in a matter of months.'

'They're all foreign workers then?'

'Poles and Bolsheviks. Corporal! You might sound your horn.'

In front of them the train's diesel motor throbbed and the wagons jerked up the yard, their wheels screeching on the rails, their buffers ringing above the din of the mills. Carin took two headache cachets from a little silver tube in her handbag. She covered her ears with her hands as the car drove on into the factory yard. Men began to descend from the wagon on both sides of the line, some jumping, others, on nearly empty trouser legs, letting themselves down gingerly as winter bathers. They really had nothing apparent at all in their trousers and it seemed that they had a fool-hardy arrogance to hope to stand upon them. Half-way across the siding the car stalled, the corporal pulled at the dashboard levers, the back of his neck reddening over his uniform collar.

'What a fool the man is,' she said.

'Corporal,' said Nicholas, 'if you can't get your engine to go, we'll walk the remainder of the way.'

'A moment, Herr Baron.'

He blew the horn again and shouted out of the window. A few of the prisoners turned round and one of them detached himself from the lines they were forming and ran forward until he was stopped by a charge hand in a white coat. This man himself started forward to see if he could help; but the gate-keeper came out of his box and started to shout instructions to the corporal who, by this time, had the bonnet open and was jerking at something inside the engine. The car jerked to his movements. He pressed the self-starter and the engine made a wailing noise. Carin opened her door.

'For heaven's sake, let's walk, Nicholas.'

The Baron gathered up his brief-case and flung the fur

rug across the front seat. The engine of the car suddenly started and the corporal slammed the bonnet shut and got into the front seat. The two other men stood looking and behind them the column of prisoners moved off on its long coalescing shadow; but as the car moved forward the men of the night shift started to stream out of one of the factory's many wide doors. They straggled out, dazzled, looking incuriously at the car or perhaps unable to see it after the relatively dim lighting within the shops.

The corporal pressed his horn and drove past them and between them to reach the entrance to the private drive of the Waitzmann House. Prisoners in grey on the grey surface of the yards, with their narrow shadows thrown before them, passed the windows of the car in almost identical attitudes and haphazard groups, stopping foolishly to look into it, 'without,' as Carin unintentionally told herself, 'knowing a word of the language'.

Their foreign faces were thrust upon her; their bodies, like those of dead men, seemed to be propped against the walls of the building yet they seemed to hang in the sunlight with each flat-eyed head surrounded by a plume of breath. Something absurd about them offended her so much that she became instantly furious with both Nicholas and the corporal for having let her in for this experience; yet she could not forbear turning deliberately round to look out through the back window to see what the prisoners did when once the car had passed. They stood on their hollowed trouser legs as if too surprised to move; then one of them laughed and raised a hand, a second began to feel the outsides of his pockets as if he were expecting to find something bulging inside it. Two others moved together secretively, joining first their hands and then their faces in a series of quick containing movements until from between them a little puff of blue tobacco smoke rose into the air.

The car drew up in front of the porch, white against green creeper. She searched her handbag for her compact and glanced at her wavering face. She became steady immediately and greeted the housekeeper. The hall, the staircase leading up to the drawing-room, her glimpse of the drawing-room itself, seemed each as quiet as some room in which she had awakened from illness; each object posed as by some placatory hand; the statues frozen, the pictures leaning out of vacancy.

'I would like to wash,' she said and was led to a bathroom with frosted glass windows which shut out the view of the factory. Beside the lavatory there was a ruled calendar on which Frau Waitzmann had noted Onkel Fritz's birthday as occurring on the twenty-third of that month. Over the heated towel rail there was an empty toothbrush rack with clips labelled in capitals:

ALFRIED. RUPRECHT. COUSIN ILSE.
BABY GUSTAF. COUSIN FRED'K.

There were small embroidered guest towels lying neatly folded on the edge of the basin and a piece of coarse war-time soap in the soap tray. When she picked it up she found that it had the thin wafers of three earlier tablets adhering to its back. The broad groove-marks of fingers which had squeezed them together were still apparent at the edges of the cake and one of the grooves bore the imprint of a wedding ring on the third finger.

She turned on the hot tap and scalding water from the factory gushed into the basin. She added cold to it too late; the cold water penetrated the hot and sank immediately to the bottom of the basin which was now so full that it was not only over-flowing down the waste pipe but slopping over the edge on to the floor. She turned off the cold tap and put her hand into the water to pull out the plug which had no chain attached to it. The steaming layer on the top scalded her fingers and she took Frau Waitzmann's toothbrush from a tumbler on a glass shelf below the mirror and stirred the water with its handle. Then she was able to release the plug and let out some of the water; but her tiny gold wrist-watch was soaked and so she undid the clasp with one of her nails and took it off and patted it dry with a corner of the dry towel. She dropped it on to the shelf beside the tooth glass. She washed her face vigorously with the coarse soap as though she were again a schoolgirl and rubbed at her lips and eyebrows. Her make-up stained the soap pink and blue and most of it came off but not cleanly enough to satisfy her, so she took some pieces of paper from the holder beside the lavatory and rubbed at her lips and eyebrows with them, flushing away the used tissues as soon as she had finished. From her bag she fluffed a little pale powder on to her face and then once more studied herself in the mirror. The edges of her tinted hair which showed beneath her hat were wet and darkened; but she left them like that, looking at the lines beneath her eyes and at the nakedness of her lips; at the muscles, the swellings and bracelet-creases of her neck.

In the drawing-room, shafted with light from its gauzed windows, Frau Waitzmann smiled briefly from her place on the sofa and then turned back to Nicholas to catch the end of his sentence:

'– held up for a time by the Minister, but eventually, just before we left, the authority came through; so it's now up to Ruprecht again.' Nicholas looked over to him and then smiled stiffly at Carin. 'Ah, my dear, we were awaiting you.'

Ruprecht kissed her hand glumly and retreated to his place by the piano.

'Good! Good!' said Frau Waitzmann. 'You have made out a Works Order?'

'The papers are all in the office, Mama.'

'You had better send over for them.'

'I've already done so.'

'Then that is settled. Perhaps the Baronin would like a chair. She is still standing, is she not?'

'I prefer to stand, thank you, Frau Waitzmann. So much driving.'

'Carin does a great deal of it,' said Nicholas. 'Goebbels has given her a car for her lectures.'

'So?'

'One has to do something, Frau Waitzmann.'

But Frau Waitzmann appeared not to have heard her. She turned her blind head to Nicholas: 'With the raids, Baron, I should imagine that it is quite dangerous to get about in the streets after the blackout. Does your wife drive alone or have they given her a chauffeur also?'

'Heavens, the car is far too small for a chauffeur,' said Carin, more loudly. 'It's a dreadful little box with hard seats.'

Frau Waitzmann smiled to herself. 'Such responsibilities wouldn't suit me at all. My younger son, Ruprecht, may have told you that nowadays I seldom leave the house. The yards and streets are too busy. We have a railway in the factory. In our whole history we've never employed so many people. There are not only the lorries and trailers, there are the wagons and locomotives too.'

'So much noise, Frau Waitzmann.'

'For many years after my husband's death I kept an eye on things. I'm now reduced to keeping an ear on them and there's a great deal too much to hear.'

'But you do it magnificently!' said Nicholas. 'Your mother,' he told Ruprecht, 'grows always shrewder. Her letters to me are models of clarity and foresight.'

'This is our second war, Nicholas. We would be fools indeed if we'd learned nothing.' Wilhelmina paused. 'Ruprecht tells me that your own Leo leaves tomorrow.'

'Only for France,' Carin said.

'The doctors discovered his chest trouble during his training,' Nicholas added.

'He's courageous to go anywhere. Your son Leo has always made light of his troubles, I think.'

Nicholas took his brief-case from his knees and dropped it beside his feet on the floor. 'Wilhelmina, my dear, we have had news of Alfried.'

'Yes?' She turned to Ruprecht. 'Perhaps you would ask for the coffee, Liebling. I can't think what's delaying them all this morning.'

Ruprecht did not move. He remained exactly where he was, glaring at his mother from his place by the piano.

'He is in good heart,' said Nicholas. 'We've heard that he's in excellent health.'

'You heard, Mama? Nicholas is telling you that they have news of Alfried.'

'But no, I've heard nothing for perhaps six months. I think there's not been a letter in that time, has there, Ruprecht?'

'There have been no letters, no, Mama.'

'And you say he's in good health?'

'In good heart too,' said Nicholas. 'Carin, you heard through the young Grunwald that Wilhelmina's elder son . . .'

'Ah, the Baronin knows Alfried too?'

'It must be years since I last saw him, Frau Waitzmann. But through this friend I've been assured that he is well cared for and in no danger.'

Frau Waitzmann said something to herself and looked up again, waiting.

'Ruprecht will have told you,' went on Carin, 'that we did what we could at the time. I'm sure he must have told you how distressed we all were. My husband and I had kept in touch with him almost directly. There was even to have been a party but unfortunately –'

'A party? He was difficult about them, wasn't he, Ruprecht.'

'The party for his release,' said Ruprecht, spacing the words viciously.

'Alfried was a strange child. I never fully understood him and for that reason, perhaps, I was especially fond of him; but I'm not at all surprised that he should have proved to be so difficult. I wonder what he's doing?' She looked across to the Baron. 'You didn't hear, I suppose? I'd so much like to know that he had something to do.'

'He's been transferred to useful work, Wilhelmina.'

'So?'

'Wilhelmina, it's difficult to get firm news; but I understand that Alfried has been given work in a hospital.'

'A camp hospital?'

'One of the better camps.'

'God be thanked! He'll like that. Ruprecht, the coffee.'

'Mama!' He moved obediently, slowly.

'You might also ring across to the office for the files we were discussing. The Baronin will, I know, forgive us if we conclude these business matters as soon as we've had our coffee. Perhaps she would like to tour the factory?'

'How kind of you, Frau Waitzmann.'

'Ruprecht tells me that his new processes are of interest. We are employing a lot of foreign labour too.'

'I'd love to see it all; but I've some things to get for Alexandra. Saturday you know.'

'Family shopping,' said Frau Waitzmann.

Carin went over to her chair. 'Frau Waitzmann —'

'Yes, my dear?' Wilhelmina spoke easily. 'Ruprecht, give some coffee to the Baronin. I hope Kegel hasn't forgotten the milk. She's getting very absent-minded. She has remembered everything?'

Without replying, Ruprecht passed Carin a cup that tinkled and rattled in its saucer. 'Mama, Carin is trying to tell you something. You are being ungracious.'

'It is very kind of the Baronin to have made such a long journey.'

Despite all she could do to control the little muscles in her cheek, Carin's voice sounded old. 'But Frau Waitzmann, I feel for you! I'd like, if I could, to comfort you, to assure you that —'

'That what, Baronin? Let us be truthful with one another. You, through no fault of your own, can scarcely remember Alfried and I have the impression that you can tell me very little about him.'

There was silence. Frau Waitzmann found and touched Carin's hand briefly with a ringed finger. 'Even if he were dead, I, who knew him so well, know that Alfried would not have wanted anyone to waste emotion over him. Since he was imprisoned I have had to trust him entirely to God and it's painful for me when others intervene. I hope you'll forgive me for my bitterness.'

Carin wept a little; glassy tears. But Frau Waitzmann reached for her coffee cup with quick fingers. She drank with satisfaction.

'And now,' she said, 'the matter of the Swedish pulp contract. Ruprecht, perhaps it would be polite if you were to let her chauffeur know that the Baronin will be leaving in a few minutes?'

Ruprecht stood by the open door waiting for her, and she could see the curled iron balustrade above the stair well and beyond it the upper part of the long window through which a boiler-house stack smoked white. Nicholas had followed her but she could not hear what he was saying.

'My wrist-watch,' she told him coldly, 'I left it in the bathroom, I think.'

'Carin, my dear –'

'You won't forget, will you, that Leo and Alexandra are expecting us back at one-thirty?'

Ruprecht asked her, 'Your watch? You remember where you left it?' but she did not answer him. When she returned from the bathroom, still trying to fasten it, he took her wrist and did it for her. He had a trick of speaking very slowly, almost inaudibly, when he was annoyed; and now he lagged behind her as she descended the staircase past the high window.

'My mother's not well,' he said in that low voice. 'You must realize that she . . .'

But she did not hear what she must realize. It was, in any case, she believed, impossible for her to feel any more resentful than she already did.

'I should have thought,' she heard him saying, 'that it was quite unnecessary: for you: to have come: at such a time.'

He had caught her up and she stood aside for him to open the inner door of the hall.

'You agree? You agree with me?' he insisted.

'I have been humiliated.'

'No, not really. My mother . . . .'

'Such hatred,' she said. 'That old woman has been –'

'My mother is not capable of hatred.'

'She blames me, she knows everything.'

'So I've always told you.'

'To talk of your brother, to speak of it all in that way! As if she were beyond it all.'

'You shouldn't have come,' he repeated.

'I wasn't told what to expect. Remember that I've only met your mother two or three times in my life.' She laughed. 'And to think one blamed America for Alfried's opinions, that one imagined that one could help.'

'It was quite unnecessary; a great mistake. But you are making a bigger one if you think that my mother has had any influence over Alfried.'

'Or over you, I suppose?'

'Carin, I'll see you this afternoon. We cannot discuss it here.'

'No. I don't want to see you.'

'You must expect me. I have to see Nicholas.'

'But Leo and Alexandra will be there.'

'Oh yes?'

'You wish to see them too?'

'Certainly.'

'It will do you no good, Ruprecht. They were together until very late last night. They will probably announce their engagement when we get back, that's why I'm in a hurry.'

'Then I shall enjoy congratulating them.'

Her restraint broke. 'You fool, you understand nothing! You've too many irons in the fire.'

'You are one of them. Don't forget that you played a part in all this.'

'No longer.'

'Then why did you wash your face before you came into the drawing-room? For my mother? Why did you make yourself such a sight?'

She opened the outer door, the corporal was waiting in the car. She did not reply because she did not know herself. It had been an impulse connected with those young, ageless men in the night shift. The prisoners.

'My mother is a woman who has constantly to be considered,' went on Ruprecht. 'You see that now, don't you?'

'I do,' she said, smiling away from him.

'And I am very like her.'

She smiled at him. 'That, perhaps, is your greatest mistake. You are not in the least like her.'

She saw him blanch; then, for the benefit of the corporal, she said: 'Well, we'll expect you in time for a drink, at about five.'

In the car she opened her handbag and made up her face again very carefully.

That afternoon Ruprecht drove out to Schönform in Alfried's open Lincoln. Wearing a white doe-skin flying helmet to offset a tension headache which had been threatening him ever since lunch, he drove fast. The golden sunlight of autumn, the cool air of the hills would exhilarate and whip him up, he believed; but he must, if possible, avoid stress. 'If I start a migraine I'll be as blind as Mama and absurdly sick. I shall look ridiculous!'

He left the car in the courtyard of the farm and set off in search of Leo and Alexandra, whom he knew would be out somewhere on the estate. The question was, in which direction would they have gone? To the lake and the timber stands? Or across to the corn fields on the other side of the valley? As he paused to consider, jays were robbing a group of chestnuts, their foliage piled high in golden canopies in the golden light of the sun. Metallic-looking leaves glittered against the sky. The jays flew into the crowns silently, their blue-spurred wings flashing against the blueness beyond them. Fluttering to keep their balance, they settled stealthily on small branches which bent immediately to the weight, while with their beaks they cut at the clusters of green-gold fruit beneath them. Chestnuts fell bounding from boughs. Hands of leaves, softer than gold, floated after them as the birds moved round away from him. In the distance he could half-hear the conversations of women and old men working in the fields. A squadron of Messerschmitts touched like silent flies a horizon of pines, their sound drenched out by the distance.

He would soon discover Alexandra and Leo; if he were not delayed by some chance encounter with Nicholas, whom he did not want to see until later, instinct would lead him to them. But he must be careful; Carin had accused him of having too many irons in the fire and had meant, perhaps, that he was unsure of himself, indecisive. She was wrong: he knew exactly what he was going to do. It was a question only of the order in which he did it; and, first, he must get rid of his headache. He stuffed his helmet into his pocket and watched the jays again, breathing deeply as Nicholas might have done. The birds were flying off in relays burdened with encased fruit which they would have to split open against the branches of their own roosting places. They shared the crop with the red squirrels who worked just as silently, tearing off the chestnuts with their hands, leaping with trailing tails, black against the radiant sky.

Perhaps, he thought, it might be tactless to avoid Nicholas. Later on it might look sly. He had better find him and tell him that he was anxious to get some fresh air and have a word with Leo before he left for France. Nicholas would invite him to stay for dinner and, if necessary, he could make some excuse or leave it vaguely open. His decision would depend not so much on Alexandra as on himself. Leo did not affect it at all.

He ran back to the Lincoln and drove on to the castle. Nicholas was in the courtyard awaiting him and Ruprecht asked him at once where Leo was.

'Ah, my dear fellow, I've been expecting you. I can't settle to anything. That affair this morning. I'm afraid we handled it badly.'

'A storm in a teacup, sir. I hope Carin has got over it?'

'She's lying down. She never says much, you know. But tell me about Wilhelmina, Ruprecht. My heart went out to her. The whole trouble was that we should have consulted first. I thought Carin would be helpful; but now that things have misfired she blames me for not having briefed her more fully.'

Ruprecht was impatient. 'Very good of you both; but I'm afraid you don't really understand my mother. She's not in the least angry or hurt in any real sense. She's simply irritated by your sympathy. She feels it's a disservice to Alfried.'

'A disservice?'

'I think so. In these last months she's learned to accept Alfried's imprisonment. She's not concerned by it. She wears black, you know.'

'Wears black?' The Baron was astonished.

'I'm sorry if I can't make myself clear; but I've got the devil of a headache. What I meant was that since she lost my father, my mother's always worn black. She doesn't consider it an imposition. She says it's simply a reminder of what she is. It's not even a sign of mourning as far as I can gather; even though they were so devoted. Why, sir, you should see her study. She keeps every present my father ever gave her in there. It's like a religious gallery.'

'My dear boy, I don't follow you at all.'

'I'm afraid it's this confounded headache. There are so many things on my mind. The labour problem at the main mill for one thing. My mother's becoming more and more hostile to our plans and the sickness rate amongst the Poles is climbing every day. You know how it is? I haven't had a chance to discuss anything with you and that's why I was so anxious to get out to see you this afternoon.'

The Baron was relieved. 'That's quite understandable. It's precisely why I've been awaiting you with some impatience myself. Pressure is being exerted to make me relieve you of your duties for the time being. That Luthmann fellow is suggesting to Goering that it's about time you did some flying.'

'Oh, is he?'

'I'm afraid so, but –'

'In certain circumstances I shouldn't mind in the least,' Ruprecht interrupted him. 'In fact, for the time being it might suit me admirably. For one thing you get on so well with my mother.' He glanced at the courtyard clock. 'But if you don't mind, I really can't think about it just at the moment.'

'Of course not. These matters seem so trivial in relation to the larger issues.' The Baron too was looking despairingly at the clock, its pale blue face and freshly gilded numerals. 'My God! Ruprecht, this Russian Front show's enough to send anyone out of his mind. We're getting bogged down out there. A bad winter and it could be 1812 all over again.'

'It doesn't worry me. I think only of our industry. So long as we have that intact we'll never be beggars.'

'I'm not so sure, my boy. Look here, let's break away somewhere and get down to work. My upper room perhaps?'

'Impossible. I simply have to clear my head first. I thought I might take a gun and stretch my legs.'

'An excellent idea. We'll go together. No fear of being overheard.'

Ruprecht frowned. Nicholas quite distinctly saw him scowl swiftly. He was more than merely pale. His eastern blood was showing in his anxiety; he looked a lightish green and a little hooked about the features; but a good fellow just the same. No question about that. He patted him a little hesitantly on the shoulder and said: 'Well, well, perhaps you're right. I shouldn't be adding to your worries like this. You've too much on your back as it is. You'll probably find Leo and Alexandra down by the cornfields. Ostensibly, they're seeing about the harvesting.'

'The engagement hasn't been announced, then?'

'Neither officially nor unofficially; but it's distinctly in the wind, you know. I don't mind telling you I'm delighted at the prospect.'

'A splendid match,' Ruprecht agreed.

They separated and Ruprecht went on his way carelessly; but as soon as he was out of sight of the castle he began to run.

He found Alexandra by a large wheat field which extended away from him to the edge of a shallow ravine. She was walking along the edge of the far end, a small figure almost uniformly pink in the evening light. Between them, like a rosy carpet, the deep crop stretched to the margins of the pine forest which threw jagged inky shadows across its surface. Alexandra was quite alone and making slowly for the woods. He watched her move into the shade of the massed trees and then began to run up his own side of the field. He ran fast, stooping a little until he reached the trees when he stopped to regain his breath. He moved deeper into the woods which at this point had been thinned by the foresters. His steps were muffled by the yellow moss of autumn; he moved so silently that a pair of young buck, cropping an inlet of wheat in the shadows, did not hear him until he was close upon them. One of them cannoned into the other and stood dazed for a moment. It watched him with its black shining eyes as he strode past it, turning its head to follow him as though hypnotized, not trembling at at all, strangely pale-coated against the blue trunks of the trees and the cindery-coloured wheat. Then with sudden recollection it leapt for safety, slipping away, faint sounds as of wood against wood signalling its passing. He paused, following its flight, the barring of its body as it crossed from light into shade and shade into light again.

He came upon Alexandra suddenly. She was sitting upon Leo's mackintosh with a gun and a pair of binoculars beside her, drinking coffee from a small Thermos flask and eating sultanas from a little silver box on her lap. She spilled coffee at the sight of him, her eyes as still and bright as those of the buck. He smiled at her and then kneeled down, bringing out a larger handkerchief to mop the coffee from her skirt.

'Where's Leo?' he asked her.

'He is looking for a boar. I was hungry.' She moved away from him. 'He said I was to make no noise.'

'You have some on your knees. Here, take my handkerchief!'

'Leo thinks there's a young sow somewhere in these parts of the wood. If she hears anything he won't be able to track her.'

'We have to whisper then?'

'It would be better not to talk at all.'

'I may smoke?'

'I think it would be better if you didn't.'

'I hear you're engaged. My congratulations!'

'Thank you.'

'Are you?'

'I haven't decided.'

'No, of course not. You only know that you're not.'

She had ceased to chew the sultanas. She closed the little box with a snap.

'That's why I came,' Ruprecht went on. 'I knew exactly how you'd be feeling, because I love you.'

'Leo too loves me.'

'But *you* know that you don't love Leo. That's why you've decided not to marry him.'

'I'm very fond of him.'

'And you want to help him, to make him happy? I know. In your position anyone so innocent and dutiful would feel the same and spend the rest of her life regretting it.'

'No.'

'Alexandra, you must marry *me*. You'll never regret it. You'll have no time, no energy.'

She was not surprised. Her acceptance of the conversation appeared to him to be the acceptance of himself that he had always expected. He pressed home his attack.

'You find it impossible to forget me. You were waiting here for me as I knew you would be. But the reason you are keeping Leo waiting is different.'

'Oh dear, that's true,' thought Alexandra. 'But how does he know things I don't know myself until after they've happened?' She began to feel hungry again for something, as though she might shiver with appetite, and said, 'Leo needs me.'

'Yes he does.'

'You see that?' She was a little dismayed by his ready agreement.

'Certainly. He needs you to hang in the hall.'

Though he sounded so serious, he might be joking; and she had to look at him to know. How ill he looked, as if he were going to be sick. He was trembling like a patient with a rigor. He looked so nauseated that she could no longer bear to see him at such a disadvantage and turned away.

'I'm not joking,' he said, as slowly as someone ill. 'Leo wants to decorate his house with you, Alexandra. He loves you as he loves his buck and water-fowl, his little hen pheasants. The hunter remains always a very young man; and Leo is like this – he will never mature. Once you're his wife he'll never need to forget you because you'll always be there, a part of his home; that is why he'll forget you just the same.'

'How can you say such a thing?'

'Because it's true. Some women can accept such a marriage. I think you may be like that; but I love you and I don't want to see it happen to you. I know that once you've accepted him you'll have been for Leo a good season, one of the best. All your foolish compassion will have been wasted.'

This was exactly what she had been thinking herself. She had not forgotten Leo's kiss, the sense it had given her of being furred, a trophy larger than the huntsman. She had not forgotten his opening the door to the bedroom and then slipping away like that, safe and satisfied, while she undressed, shivering amongst his possessions.

'But I'll need you always,' went on Ruprecht swiftly, 'now and for ever, all my life, alive.' He was speaking fast, his voice shaking with intensity. 'My love may ruin you but it will never insult you. Alexandra, I love you.'

She looked at him, waiting. 'More,' she was saying to herself over and over again. 'More, more. Go on, don't stop.'

'You could save me. Already, you realize, I've betrayed my brother? I'm beyond my mother's forgiveness too; that place where, if they do believe, they put you when they abandon you to God.'

Alexandra was appalled; she shuddered with the excitement of his accusations and hints: 'Your brother!' she said. 'But how did you betray him? Surely you must be blaming yourself unnecessarily?'

He was crouching beside her. He might touch her at any moment, take her hands, hold her.

'I don't care. I no longer think about either of them; but you I have to have. You're what I've always wanted. You must marry me.' He took her hand gently and kissed it in the centre of the palm, letting his lips rest there for moments so that she could feel his warm, cool breathing in her head, on her face, over her whole body. The wheatfield rippled and rustled like a calm ocean.

'You must help me,' he whispered.

'But we're still strangers. There's poor Leo, there's Nicholas.'

' "Who if I cried," ' he quoted, ' "would hear me amongst the angelic orders?" '

'And your brother Alfried,' she said, clutching at a straw she did not really care about. How could she when she had never met him? Perhaps she ought to care.

'What can you think you have done to your brother Alfried?' she asked again.

He left her hand and replaced it on the stuff of her dress where it covered her warm thigh.

'I might save him yet if I had a reason,' he said. 'I might spare the energy.' Suddenly he drew her closer, she saw his exhausted face, his dry lips, his despair; and she leaned back under his fine springing weight.

Chapter 8

For nearly six months, ever since the management of the Waitzmann Group had fallen to him in February 1943, the Baron had missed his former way of life. By that time Ruprecht and Alexandra had been married almost a year and as soon as Ruprecht's long-expected posting came through, he had invited them, together with Frau Waitzmann, to move out into Schönform. 'Under the circumstances,' he had told Wilhelmina, 'Leo will not object. He's enjoying himself in France and, in any case, it will assist my liaison with you, my dear!' And he had added: 'With the air-raids and the labour troubles you'll both be happier and safer in the castle. It needs its women-folk.'

Ruprecht, leaving for operational duty in the Mediterranean, was delighted by the arrangement. He had seen exactly what Nicholas meant. His mother's conscience might rest easier away from the daily reminder of the siding and the women's camp, now established in the factory garden. Alexandra would be less distressed by her mother-in-law's silences, and as far as he himself was concerned, the social implications of the move were most acceptable; a tribute to the rise of the family, something that would stand whether the war were lost or won. Already the Baron had done well enough out of them, he thought; whether or not he liked the idea of recognizing their social worth, his invitation proved he had come to realize that the castle and the factory stood or fell together.

When Goering's time limit for a hand-over expired – Nicholas had managed to get it postponed until after that Christmas – Ruprecht had left with a good grace, Nicholas telling him, 'Don't worry, my boy. Under your guidance I think I've got the hang of the job and with your mother's counsel no doubt we'll be able to keep the wheels turning until you return.'

But now, six months later, in the autumn of '43, he realized that he had not envisaged all that the young man's departure would entail for him personally. Ruprecht had managed to get only one short leave in all that time and had used it to upset his mother about the falling production and to make Alexandra pregnant. Increasingly, during the six months of that eventful year, Nicholas had come to regret his change of rôle in his eagerness to get his finger further into the Waitzmann pie. More and more, he had found himself getting out of the swim, constantly trying and failing to find the time to run up to the capital and keep in touch with policies which changed so fast that he was always a week or two behind them.

A landscape of thunderclouds, he told himself now on this sunny, late August morning as he strolled out of the Schön-form dining-room. Political weather that summer and winter alike was always *orageux*. In February, he remembered, coinciding with the start of his new life, there had been the epic disaster of Stalingrad; and that after the brilliant German offensive of the preceding summer. In May there had been the Anglo-Saxon conquest of Tunisia, followed by the landings in Sicily. Then in July those two shabbily dramatic meetings between the Führer and the Duce, to say nothing of the bombing of Rome and of that bombastic bull-frog's arrest and imprisonment by King Victor Emmanuel.

'Thunder-clouds,' he repeated to himself as he moved out of the courtyard for a little deep breathing in the water-garden. A man needed lightning conductors all over the place. But how was he to know where to erect them if he were kept constantly in the dark? 'No,' he corrected himself, 'on the contrary, insufficiently in the dark; a dangerous twilight.' There had been attempts, he remembered, to sound him out, a remark or two in those last Berlin weeks from persons whom he suspected of more than mere dissidence; the suggestion of a fateful question. And since then, following Stalingrad, those telephone calls coming from

God knew where to the inner sanctum of the Waitzmann Administration.

'Colonel von Hoffbach?'

'Speaking.'

'Are you for it or against it?'

'Who is that?'

'Yes or no, Colonel?'

Silence, the receiver replaced; but an hour later, a different voice through the buzz of a longer distance, the same military mode of address:

'Colonel von Hoffbach?'

'Speaking.'

'Identify yourself. You must decide. Yes or no?'

'What do you mean? Who is that?'

'You must decide. You will be called again.'

Finally, the new cordiality of the Prince Hohenheim, a bumbler if ever he knew one, whose hints of something chivalrously dark afoot had almost persuaded him that it might in some ways have been better if he had ceased ever to hanker after his former way of life in the country.

'I have paid enough,' he decided as he stopped now, by the very pool into which he remembered lobbing a stone more than three years earlier. 'I've paid and continue to pay enough to hold what is in any case my own, even to this new day itself, which is only just beginning.' And, as if to confirm him at this moment, the forecourt clock struck. As always, he checked his wrist-watch against it, a wrist-watch given him by Carin who had been sent it from Paris.

Seven o'clock and misty, the water-garden under a haze, the bronze notes rebounding between the enclosing walls on the far side of the castle, leaping its high roof in reduplication before merging into the lesser chimings of the streams against their shingle. Near at hand there were primulas and yellow marigolds, a confetti of green waterweed shining like cloisonné within the circle of his vision; while somewhere out of sight a bird slapped its wings in a shallow pool, making smacking sounds as though a child were at play.

He hurried back to the dining-room to find Alexandra

pecking at her breakfast; his brief-case beside her, bulging with papers signed overnight by Frau Waitzmann. The girl, he saw, was morning-pale and he took her to task about her failure to eat. All the way in the car to Bergedorf he lectured her about the advisability of giving up her work at the clinic.

'Not that I wouldn't miss you, my dear, in these early hours of duty; but surely you of all people should know that with a baby well on the way there does come a time when . . .'

But beside him Alexandra surreptitiously clasped her stomach, her faintly tanned hands pressing gently against its grey-skirted bulge as if she might bless it away. She was feeling ill, sitting bolt upright with her hair scraped back beneath her uniform cap, a tortoiseshell comb jammed into the lank braids at the back of her neck. She was wondering if she were going to be sick, whether yet again she would have to ask him to stop the car while she walked sedately into the woods with dozens of paper handkerchiefs and supported herself against a pine trunk.

Everything made her feel sick. As the mist, nausea rose out of the morning to swathe everything she experienced; everything except the baby, so separate and selfish, rumbling about inside her with elastic jerkings and knockings. The dangling dashboard keys not less than the hurriedly swallowed coffee and the swinging road disgusted her; yet nothing affected her quite so much as the factory gate and the tall, pink chimneys of the boiler houses. Always, as they drove past these to the Dollmannstrasse clinic, she closed off her mind, wishing that Nicholas would drive a different way; and always she suspected that he shared her discomfort. As the moment approached they each stiffened, they had a dozen subterfuges: to cough or touch their faces, to look in at the factory yard in an open, interested way, to go on with what they had been saying without any perceptible pause, to stop talking or to start afresh; but so soon as they were past began the lesser ordeal of having to be polite, sanguine and collected. Outside the clinic, Alexandra, her big handbag held in both hands in front of her stomach, stepped out on to the pavement, smiling wanly in at him before dashing up the stairs to the cloakroom, while he shouted after her, 'Six o'clock then, my dear.'

He did in fact collect himself at this instant. He collected his body and his mind together like a swimmer about to plunge into suspect water, actually restricting his awareness of everything outside himself; filling out his shoulders, expanding and contracting his middle. He acknowledged the gate-keeper's salute crisply, 'in the line of duty', patted his pre-war Homburg further down over his eyes, or else threw it off behind him decisively or nonchalantly, the decision as to which being taken in the moment of throwing. Then he shot over the sidings, rarely used now save for the dispatch of the ailing or sick, or else he drove across slowly, casting alert observant glances round him in all directions. Then he parked the car in front of one of the notice-boards whose wording he knew as well as that of a hunting text in his personal lavatory at Schönform:

Workers no longer have the rights to complain and no complaints will be accepted.

The visit of churches is strictly prohibited.

Visits to theatres, motion pictures or other cultural entertainments are strictly prohibited.

Sexual intercourse with women or girls is strictly prohibited.

He saluted various personnel, unless he chose to ignore them. He walked past the garage lines and the chemical pounds to the narrow chasm between the office block and the first processing mill. No matter what his mood he rarely did more than glance at the garages and the pounds. They were less his concern than the kennels at the rear of the urinals, or the temporary female accommodation in the garden. Occasionally he saw that something was going on in these places, the mustering of the ailing or the turning out of a shift; but unless he were officially requested or had to carry out some unrelated inspection, he avoided if he could all contact with this aspect of the factory. Indeed it had been the decision of Herr Speer's Labour Front to billet the workers on site which had decided him to offer Schönform to Wilhelmina even before Ruprecht's departure.

But it had been the staffing of the packing shop which had troubled him most; a mixed detachment of Hungarians, Rumanians and Ukrainians which had arrived soon after Christmas. They were all women and most of them detested one another. Though they worked bitterly, handling the delicate machinery more deftly than the men, they never ceased their quarrelling. Here in captivity they carried on the feuds they had begun in transit; and when they were not quarrelling they were singing. They sang at all hours, a few of them at a time, and he was never ready for the sound of their voices. Though they ignored his tours of inspection, everywhere he met their quick, vindictive eyes. When he entered the department, the movements of their hands changed as they worked; they walked past him coldly, slanting themselves as if to suggest they were avoiding the corpse of some animal. When he left the shop their choruses rose above the noise of the machinery like the cries of birds.

'I should see into this whole business,' he had decided. 'The replacement-rate is appalling. There must be something wrong somewhere.' But the German staff were unexceptionable; middle-aged women of good character, many of them the wives of service men on the Eastern front, a few of them already widowed. He had summoned the personnel manager.

'Frau Neff, I see that you have put in for ten replacements in the past fortnight.'

'I've completed the forms, Herr Baron.'

'Yes, yes I see you list ten cases of pregnancy, too. Are the night staff not patrolling efficiently?'

'Abortion, sir; not pregnancy. We are always having blockages of the water closets due to this trouble. The inmates arrive in this condition from the Camp.'

'And these cases of facial injury, Frau Neff? Are the women not observing the safety precautions? Is it the machines?'

'This is due to the rioting between the Rumanians and the Ukrainians, they go for each other's eyes. If the camp could be persuaded to send us drafts of the same nationality, sir. . . .'

'Then why do you not make these points clear in your reports?'

'I thought it might save us embarrassment if I did not specify the cause of the injuries.'

'In future kindly do so, Frau Neff.'

'Yes, Herr Direktor.'

'Confound it!' he thought now as he walked over to his office. 'That was three months ago and there's been no improvement whatsoever.' He was chilled by the morning shadow thrown across the yard by the wall of the processing mill. At the far end he could see the green sunlight of the factory gardens, the figures of the women moving about under the dark trees of August. There was a breakfast queue at the canteen, he saw, and a row of figures seated in the new lavatories. Above him, white poplars of steam rose from a row of galvanized stacks beside the colour kitchens. From grilles in the wall came the sound of the machinery and over it the high songs of the women in the garden. They had seen him approaching already and their singing ceased for a moment. On their thin legs those in the queue swivelled round to watch him, others in the lavatories drew their skirts down lower, then a new song began, sharp and thin. He hurried up the stairs to the vestibule attached to his office.

How was it, he wondered, that nothing had yet been done about those lavatories? He remembered the correspondence distinctly, the last letter he had received from Berlin:

The provision of unnecessary refinements for foreign labour is neither consistent with the present situation nor with national policy. If the area has been screened from the public view it is sufficient that the inmates should realize that they are not entitled to facilities which they were not in their homelands accustomed to.

He had replied to this at once and there would be a copy in the files to prove it. He would have it out with someone this morning. Something should be done immediately. 'By God!' he swore to himself in the cloakroom mirror, 'it's barbaric! A woman, as hairless as a turnip, exposed in all her weakness to her sons. It's an insult to one's own mother, to all mothers, to Germany. What can we have come to?' This evening he would take old Hohenheim up on the matter of those telephone calls, and find out what he'd been driving at all these months. He would make up his mind.

At the far end of the typing pool, Fräulein Seitz, virginally nervous and not young, was waiting to greet him. It was traditional that he should exchange a few remarks with her before going into Ruprecht's spacious study. How celibate she looked, poor girl: all her movements lacked conviction: the little run she made to open the door into her own office. He turned his back on it and faced down the length of the typing pool. Morale was bad, he must lift it up.

Before him, all the typewriters were tapping away on both sides of the aisle. The sunblinds had already been lowered; there was a faint smell of face powder in the room, of austere femininity. With the exception of Fräulein Seitz all the girls looked very well: two rows of shining braided heads, plump hands hovering over the keys, and the well-filled white blouses. How sharp were the deferential glances of a dozen pairs of young eyes.

'Another fine morning, Fräulein Seitz.'

'Yes, Herr Baron.'

'And the news? I haven't seen a paper yet.'

'Oh, it's not so good, no, Herr Direktor.'

'Ah, not? A landing on the Italian mainland perhaps?'

'No sir, the Eastern front, a Russian summer offensive.'

'Don't let that worry you, my dear Fräulein, they had to start sometime and the sooner they get it over and find we can't be dislodged the better we'll be pleased.'

'Oh yes, sir.'

He gripped her by her thin arm: 'All will be well, never you fear. After this protracted stalemate, a trial of strength is just what our generals have been praying for.'

'Yes, sir.'

'Any other worries?' he asked.

'Frau Mittelhof was anxious to see you. She's in dispatch, shall I tell her you're in?'

'In ten minutes, when I've done my maps.'

'Of course, Herr Direktor.'

'Now cheer up.' He raised his voice: 'All of you. Remember that Rome wasn't built in a day.'

'Heil Hitler.'

'Heil Hitler.'

He picked up the newspapers on his desk, he was glowing with excitement himself. How right had he been in his prophecies of the course of events on the central front? What wouldn't he have given to be there facing those clean issues instead of fiddling about here in the equivalent of a home posting? He saw it clearly for a moment: one was either a victim of the soldiers or of the politicians; and what was one to do when a vulgar little demagogue like the Führer took over the general staff?

But peace stole over him as he read. In place of the factory, those women in the lavatories and the painful image of Schönform, he saw the Russian steppes: the tips of the Bolshevik 'pincers', fluid as molten metal, spilling over the pale horizon, moving ever faster from the blue distances into the nearer, greener middle-ground. Retreat! The Fatherland's armies pulling out, racing backwards on their supply lines to prepared positions. In the sky above this giant landscape the brown smoke of burning villages and towns, the black of flak, of barrages and bombs.

Frau Mittelhof knocked and came in: 'Good morning sir, I waited fifteen minutes but I thought that after the telegram –'

'Telegram, you say? Where is it?'

'On your desk beside the newspaper, sir.'

It was headed: Confidential. High Priority, and was addressed to the Frau Kommerzienrat Waitzmann:

IT IS REGRETTED TO INFORM YOU THAT TECHNICAL DIREKTOR WAITZMANN. R. HAS BEEN REPORTED MISSING ON OPERATIONAL FLIGHT. YOU WILL BE ADVISED OF FURTHER INFORMATION AS AVAILABLE. UDET. COLONEL RESEARCH DIVISION.

He got up: 'I shall be at Schönform for about an hour. I shall not be returning directly as I have to see one of my neighbours. Refer only the most important matters to the Frau Kommerzienrat in my absence, anything else to Herr Luger.'

'Very good sir. Heil Hitler!'

'Heil Hitler!'

Three days earlier, Ruprecht's plane, a converted Heinkel, had hit the water at dawn somewhere off the coast between Rome and Monte Circeo. The fuselage had fractured cleanly, the front end in which Lieutenant Pöhl, the pilot, had been sitting, sinking immediately; the longer tail section, in which Ruprecht had been navigating, filling with water more slowly like a tilted bucket: giving him just time to free himself from some of his flexes before it too submerged and carried him with it.

He reached the surface quickly and floated there, treading water, with the smooth surface ripples lapping his chin. Now that he knew he was still alive he was unreasonably angry. Water had run into his ears and deafened him so that he could hear his own breathing loudly in his head. His mouth and eyes stung with the brine and petrol into which he had surfaced. Everywhere was the lifeless silence which accompanies a yawn.

He splashed a little, bewildered by his anger; then he rested, trying to find some emotion more appropriate to disaster. The silence settled in again, no longer a dead soundlessness but a kind of attentiveness in which he expected some voice to speak. He shouted, 'Pöhl! Hello! Pöhl, where are you?' Then he pulled a handkerchief from his trouser pocket. He wrung it out over the surface of the sea and screwed a corner of it into each of his ears. He mopped his burning eyes and blew his nose on it before throwing it away.

He shouted again, angrily: 'Answer me, Pöhl!' and this time heard his own voice clearly. Methodically he began to discard some of his clothing; his flying boots and overalls, his jacket and the baggy ginger-coloured pullover knitted for him by Alexandra; but not his socks nor his trousers. He swam in a slow circle, a circle within the circle of visibility allowed him by the sea mist; and as he swam he tried to recall the moments preceding the crash. There must be some sort of connection between the two situations. So long as he lived, a man had a continuity of some sort; he was not to be treated as a beast, with each moment of its present cut off from its past and its future. If he did find Pöhl, if that fool ever surfaced, he would have it out with him, he would say: 'Don't you realize you were flying *me*, Pöhl; not just your fat-bottomed self? It was your job to take me up and bring me safely down again.'

They had been flying low, only a few feet above the surface mist, as an anti-radar precaution. Pöhl had been singing *Lili Marlen* over the inter-comm., and talking about breakfast. He himself had been thinking about the letters he must write that evening from the new H.Q. at Pamezia. The last batch of mail he had received from Schönform had been most disturbing. At the exact moment the Heinkel had dipped into the mist he had been trying to decide whether he'd risk a wire to the Baron suggesting a meeting in Rome as soon as possible.

'My God, Pöhl,' he went on to himself, 'by your inattention to your altimeter you've not only drowned yourself, you've affected a great design: my grandfather's, and my son's too – when he's born. You've put the whole Waitzmann Group into the Baron's hands at the worst possible moment.'

Ahead of him, an apple floated; beyond it he saw four or five more, like small red marker-buoys. They had been sent to him by Alexandra just before the German army abandoned Sicily. They were not quite ripe because Alexandra was not good at that sort of thing, but he swam after them and collected them, eating the first one, which against the salt of the sea tasted quite sweet, and stuffing the surplus into his pockets. He had moved into the area into which the Heinkel's flotsam was surfacing. There were twenty or thirty of Pöhl's cigarettes sliding about in the smooth ripples of the dawn wind; some paper bags, a box of matches and a chianti flask up to its neck. He caught it and drank the cupful of wine it contained. He did not feel in the least tired and the surface water was quite warm to a depth of about half a metre. Below that, it struck cold. He decided that he must have a programme: he would tread water as little as possible because he was not sure about his circulation. He had always believed it was poor and normally he rarely went out of his depth. As a child Mama had warned him that all the curly-haired Waitzmanns were liable to the sea-cramps.

The cigarettes and matches made an apron pattern in the water. He floated on his stomach to watch them slowly moving away from him and tried to work out in which direction he ought to swim in order to approach the Italian coast. He had to distinguish between the effects of the light wind and the surface current which was probably tidal in origin. The wind, he knew, had been from the south at the time of the crash but he did not know whether the tide was flooding or ebbing, so he began a calculation based on his remembrance of his last morning swim at Palermo.

He was beginning to think about Alexandra and his mother now. The baby was due in about four months. Alexandra had wanted to be confined in Schönform; but he had insisted that when the time came she should be admitted to the clinic. When the sun rose higher, the mist would clear. It would be a hot, bright day, the visibility would be excellent, the baby would be a boy. Alexandra was not the sort of woman to make much of the business of childbirth, she was by nature a motherly creature. She would make a religion of the child.

He had radioed their position about ten minutes before the crash; a search plane would be sent out in about another hour. He had only to keep afloat for two hours to be sure of rescue. He must conserve his energy but he must not get chilled. He would continue to swim gently east with the wind on his right cheek and chance the direction of the current. Pöhl had had a compass in his wrist watch; but that, together with Pöhl, was by now at the bottom of the sea. After ten minutes' swimming, say two hundred strokes, he would float for one hundred and fifty breaths, approximately five minutes if one were breathing at the rate of thirty to the minute. The mist was already thinning, the range of his vision was widening fast. If there was any other debris from the Heinkel he would soon be able to see it: a suitcase perhaps, even one of the two life rafts which had been stowed in the tail unit.

Something wrapped itself round his wrist and he stopped swimming to investigate it. It was Pöhl's lavatory paper which he always kept tucked under the pilot's seat, and now it had unrolled in the water, a grey sodden streamer floating along on the surface for about ten yards then gradually descending into the depths at an angle of about thirty degrees. The weightier cardboard at its nether end had acted as a sinker and the paper indicated that the current was easterly, exactly the direction in which he was swimming.

He ate another apple and became angry again. He bellowed for Pöhl three or four times and raised his right fist above his head at the thought of his life depending on a roll of lavatory paper and a handful of apples. At this moment he saw Alfried. As if one shutter had fallen and another been raised, he saw Alfried by daylight; 'My brother!' as he said to himself when he thought about it an instant later. What did it mean? That he was about to die? Or was it the effect of the wine and benzine he had swallowed: Alfried's face had not been looking back at him; secretively, it had been gazing in some other direction, the light green eyes watching something quite near to them. The whole face, blanched and frowning, greatly concentrated, was seen by him more clearly than if Alfried had been actually present, swimming at his side. After a moment of panic, the experience subdued him. He had no further thought of anger. He was a single man in the sea, full of guilt.

He moved sluggishly through the water in the thinning mist. For several minutes, he saw nothing, his eyes were as sightless as if they had been closed. Then he heard a coughing somewhere ahead of him, a man coughing and groaning. He took no notice of it, only continuing to go

224

through the breast-stroke motions, absorbed in avoiding the dismay which the sight of Alfried had called up. The picture he held in his mind was that of a child, frog-naked in the water, jerking itself forward in near-darkness; and, for moments more, nothing would disperse this image which progressed as he did himself in absurd spasms through the long bright surface. Then, when Pöhl groaned again, only a few yards ahead of him, he saw the fair head in the flare of the sunlight. The head was in silhouette with the sun blazing on its hair. It was beside what appeared to be a floating bed, a long shape, more than half inflated, riding quite high in the water; a life raft of bright orange fabric with a scalloping rope round its edge. Pöhl in his life-jacket, was holding onto it with both hands, his head rolling to each of the movements of the raft. His face was blue-white as a fish's belly and the water round his legs was smoky with blood.

Ruprecht climbed into the raft. He blew up the cylindrical wall until it was hard then rested inside it for a minute or two. He rubbed his cold legs and did some breathing exercises to get warm. With an eye on Pöhl, still clinging to the rope, he wrung out his trousers and socks and spread them on the side to dry. Then he kneeled down and slid his arms beneath Pöhl's arm-pits, locking his hands over his shoulder blades. Beneath the fabric the surface of the raft heaved against his knees like a breathing stomach. The side flattened dangerously but he got the head and shoulders safely over it. Pöhl vomited on the floor. He took up a lot of room. His left leg showed scarlet through a rent above his flying boot. Blood jetted into the water. Working from the side, Ruprecht manhandled his buttocks carefully inboard and then rolled the whole body on to its side, collapsing the thighs against the stomach to bring all of it into the raft. There was little space left, Pöhl's was a big body with hips as rounded as a woman's. From some point just below the knee the uppermost leg was still spouting blood into the red water in the bottom of the raft.

Under his flying overalls and boots Pöhl was wearing trousers and beneath these a pair of long pants. It was quite impossible to roll them all up and get at the severed blood vessel. The bone seemed to be broken as well; every time Ruprecht lifted the leg to slide his rolled vest a little higher into the hollow behind the knee, there was a crepitus and Pöhl groaned.

'For God's sake, Pöhl, can't you help me? At this rate we're both going to drown.'

This was what he first said to him, hoping perhaps that he might answer; but he didn't. He was beginning to bubble through the blood and water in the bottom of the raft, so Ruprecht had to bale it out with his hands. The leg was still bleeding and Pöhl was no longer blue, he was a cindery colour, his lips dark mauve; but his heart was still beating persistently and he still groaned and grunted loudly.

There was a small leak in the bottom of the raft and the pressure of two bodies was making it worse. It was sure to be somewhere underneath Pöhl. Reluctantly, Ruprecht took his own trousers from the side of the raft and stuffed them, rolled tightly, beneath his head to keep his mouth out of the water. As far as he could judge, Pöhl might die within half an hour. He looked as though he had very little dying to do and it was quite impossible to stop him bleeding even externally. If he were expertly tended he might live an hour; in a hospital, with blood transfusions, the night; it would depend on the origin of the other blood; but in the raft he was an ugly complication; practically anything would have been easier: a basking shark or a small piano. It was just possible he might keep on breathing for an hour or two if the haemorrhage could be stopped; so Ruprecht went through his pockets.

There was a wallet with some letters and snapshots; two of his parents on a Strength-Through-Joy cruise of what looked like the Isles of Greece; three of different girls, two ugly and one pretty; a small white-metal flask half full of Italian brandy; a bunch of keys; three Swiss contraceptives; a comb, a fountain pen, a service identity card, a half-eaten slab of rubbed chocolate and two handkerchiefs. There was no pen-knife, nothing with which to cut the trouser legs or make an efficient tourniquet. Ruprecht knotted the handkerchiefs together and tried to pull the trousers off without upsetting the raft. The leak at once increased so he enlarged the holes in the trouser leg and slid his pressure bandage round the inside, drawing it close over the largest wound. For additional pressure he slid the fountain pen into the knot and twisted it tight. He held it for a full minute but the bleeding still continued so he slid one end of it beneath the bandage and left it there. He opened the flask and drank half the brandy himself, pouring a little of the remainder into Pöhl's mouth, holding his lips open as if he were giving it to a sick dog. Pöhl brought it back immediately, mixed with blood.

The leak was increasing. Burying Pöhl was going to be difficult; if it were delayed much longer it would sink the raft altogether. Ruprecht baled out as completely as he could and blew up the sides again. He leaned down over Pöhl's oyster-coloured ear and said: 'Have you any messages, Hans Albrecht?' He had learned his christian names from the identity card and thought he might be more likely to respond to them. But Pöhl's eyes remained closed. Though his breathing was barely perceptible, Ruprecht could feel the jumping of his heart inside the breast of his wet jacket: fast, powerful still and quite regular.

'Hans, have you any messages? You're dying.'

There was no reply and Ruprecht spoke urgently, his mouth close to the ear: 'I'll see your parents for you as soon as I can. If you've anything you want me to say make a last effort to tell me because I've got to put you back into the sea again.'

Pöhl's lips never moved; nothing happened in his throat muscles: the blood continued to flow out at the same rate over the green trouser legs, the heart to convulse at the same intervals.

Pöhl was an agnostic; it was marked in his particulars; but from some scruple, perhaps because of his earlier vision of Alfried, Ruprecht felt bound to pronounce the words of absolution remembered from his school days, over his grey, short-cropped, scalp: 'Indulgentiam, absolutionem, et remissionem peccatorum vestrorum tribuat vobis omnipotens et misericors Dominus. Amen.' He unstrapped the watch and compass from the left wrist, made the sign of the cross on the forehead and, as gently as he could, bundled the big body back over the side. Pöhl floated face down, held up for several minutes by a round of air trapped in his flying jacket. His legs straightened slowly and sank, the shallow swell rocked him, lapping over the flat back of his head and refreshing the sides of the snared air bubble. Around him he began to stain the water dark again as he sank a little lower, fractions of an inch at a time, into the sea. The bubble escaped from his loins, and head first, he began to tilt downwards.

The raft was drifting slowly away from him, the mist was thinning perceptibly and the light wind scored the calm surface. Ruprecht baled out, examined the leak in one of the seams and plugged it with the toe of a sock. He ate Pöhl's chocolate and drank another mouthful of brandy. He wrung out his trousers thoroughly and slid them on again and then he propped his feet on Pöhl's side of the raft and leaned back against the circular wall. The sun's heat was pleasant on the back of his head, his trousers were unexpectedly comfortable. He was content to wait.

He heard the voices of the fishermen suddenly: voices carrying across water, intimate and mysterious. He had been thinking about Alfried, resolving that he must do something about him, trace him and so prove to his mother that after all he himself was not yet lost, that he had still a 'good heart'. But he saw clearly that a man might do a thing in only two ways: with a full intention or without it. Even though he succeeded it was certain that, if he didn't really intend it, then it didn't 'count'.

His eyes, as he thought this, were on the pale morning sky, that vacancy of southern blue against which the sight runs like a film gone blank. Dots and lines appear, small white constellations of starshapes, glistening worms of light that are within the brain through which the mind is peering. He was sufficiently tired and hungry to become immediately superstitious. For an instant that left its taste behind it, he was exalted by the knowledge that it was not Frau

Waitzmann he had to satisfy but Heaven itself. He was a little light-headed, he realized, enjoying one of those moments of well-being unknown to the rested and healthy: an ecstasy of the intellect in which fleetingly, by unifying the private world, it makes sweet the public one. When he remembered that he had resolved to do something about Alfried he believed he had taken the decision rationally but euphorically; that he had not, in any sense, been trying to bargain with Heaven. He even excused his superstition by arguing that it would only be an unreasonable man who would not be superstitious under the circumstances; and at this moment he heard the Italian words carrying over the water.

The boat, short-masted with the sail reefed, was drifting well inside the Western horizon; a boy squatting in the bows talking to two older men in the stern sheets. When they heard Ruprecht's cries they started the engine and came over and picked him up. They gave him a mugful of fish broth, a hunk of bread and a flask of white chianti. The Captain asked him questions which he spoke Italian well enough to answer. He told them that he was a scientist whose plane had crashed through engine failure. 'My pilot, poor devil, was so badly injured that he died almost immediately, through loss of blood.'

The boy, who was the Captain's son, began to laugh and his father, a scarred man with mutilated hands, silenced him. He replied to something Ruprecht had said earlier: 'So you think the work you're doing is going to help us to win the war?'

'Undoubtedly.'

The boy laughed again, louder than before, and the Captain apologized for him. He began to explain himself:

'You Germans live inland, if you were really seafarers you'd realize that when a man's on the water he changes. The sea washes the eyes. Even Giorgio here, who's a Communist in the village, sees things differently when we've been out for a few days; and the young get carried away completely. They treat all politics as a joke. Your Hitler should never have allied himself with fisherfolk.'

The man Giorgio said, 'It's the workers who are going to win this war, secret weapons or no secret weapons.'

'Tell the Tedesco about the Duce,' said the boy suddenly. 'Tell him how we saw him this morning, and that we know this man's no scientist but a spy or a messenger.'

'You saw Mussolini?' asked Ruprecht.

'On an island walking about in the garden of a villa.'

'You're sure?'

'Who could mistake that pumpkin?' asked the Captain. 'Even through a telescope as small as this? We got fired on by sentries. A patrol boat put out; but when they saw us pulling off they put back again.'

'What island was it?'

'He's a spy,' said the boy. 'Don't tell him anything more. He'll have us all executed.'

His father threw him a gutting knife and sent him up into the bows again: 'It was the island of Maddalena.'

'Italy's finished,' said Giorgio, 'and you're finished too.'

Ruprecht ignored him and asked the Captain what Mussolini had been doing.

'He was walking about among the bushes like an old bull.'

'Skin and bone,' said the boy.

'Finished, like Italy, Tedesco!' said Giorgio. 'And it won't be long before your Führer will be in Joe Stalin's hands; but he won't be on an island.'

The Captain became serious: 'The boy's right. We've talked too much to you. It's true we've saved your life, so I'll ask you not to give us away when you get ashore; but I'm not going to take you into harbour. That'll mean too many questions. Instead we'll let you off as near the beach as we can and from there you'll have to make your own way.'

'Perhaps he can't swim,' said the boy. 'That would be a fine thing, Father, to put the Tedesco back into the water and let him drown.'

'It's what I myself had to do before you came,' said Ruprecht with a sudden impulse to confession. 'My pilot was unconscious and bleeding to death. So although I'd saved him I had to put him back into the sea again or we'd both have drowned.'

'Mother of God!'

'It all came to the same thing,' said Ruprecht. 'The raft or the sea. He'd lost nearly all his blood so what else could I do?'

'You could have waited,' said the Captain.

'For what?'

'For us.'

'But I didn't know you were coming.'

'Ah, but you didn't know we weren't. That's why a man waits.'

'It would have made no difference. By the time you did come he'd have been half an hour dead. It would have been all one to him.'

'But Signor,' said the Captain, addressing him officially for the first time. 'Is it all one to you?'

Ruprecht saw that the boy had crossed himself. He had picked up his gutting knife and was busy opening and cleaning the fish. It was a reproach which made him feel he had not sufficiently explained himself.

'My pilot was within a few hundred heartbeats of death,' he told the Captain coldly. 'The raft was leaking. So long as I shared it with his corpse my own life was in danger. Surely as a seaman you can see that?'

'And you pushed him over the side?'

'I took his papers – here they are. I told him I'd contact his parents personally; and, though he was a non-believer, I said a prayer for him before I buried him.'

'Alive!' The Captain was thoughtful. 'It seems to me that a man who'd do that to his comrade would do it to his own brother.' He looked over at his son and then back at Ruprecht. 'Signor, I'm afraid you're going to have a long swim.'

'Throw him out here,' said the boy.

Giorgio spoke: 'That way we'll make an enemy of him. If he gets ashore he'll set the navy on us. What he did was quite natural. It was a question of survival. To my mind it was his duty.'

'That's Communism for you,' the Captain said. 'It makes men behave like ants.'

'I happen to be a Christian, like you and your son,' Ruprecht insisted. 'I buried my pilot with a clear conscience or else why would I have told you of it?'

'No, Tedesco, if you'd had a clear conscience, you *wouldn't* have told us! But that's your own affair and I'll have to be just to you.' He rubbed his scarred face. 'The closer I take my boat inshore the greater the risk of identification, so I'll drop you a mile out where the current's in your favour. If you make it you'll know God's forgiven you for chopping off the end of a man's life. If you don't . . .'

'By that argument He's already forgiven me, by sending you.'

'By sending me,' agreed the Captain. 'Me with my doubts of you and of all Tedeschi. That's His way. He sends the wrong man at the right moment; because the wrong one's often the right one in His view.' He pointed to the mountains on the horizon. 'In half an hour we'll be within a mile of the beach. Rest yourself; eat what you like, while we get on with our work. When the time comes we'll put you over the port side where you won't be seen from the land.'

'I could report you for this.'

The Captain looked at him intently. 'You could, but you won't. You're too clever for that.' On his naked feet he walked over his clean nets and rope coils and sat down cross-legged beside his son.

The boat throbbed on towards the mountains.

Ruprecht did not reach his new headquarters at Pamezia until late in the evening. After a swim of nearly a mile he had flopped ashore on to a small semi-circular beach thirty miles south of Rome. The beach was stony, made up of oval, flattened pieces of granite which sparkled silver in the intense light of the sun. A field of ripe wheat stood nearly down to the water's edge and for some minutes he lay there with his naked stomach pressing against the hot lozenges of granite. He stared into the golden wheat as into a crystal. He felt as if he had been born again and made up his mind to waste no more of his life by indecisiveness.

Chapter 9

It was December 1943, that deadly winter when the news from all fronts could scarcely have been worse. The Baron was trying to persuade Ruprecht to take some part in what he referred to as 'Operation Overcoat', the plan of his friend Hohenheim's group to assassinate Hitler. After one of his increasingly frequent and prolonged absences from Schönform he had returned on this bitter Saturday morning to make yet another attempt to get Ruprecht to take some part in the affair.

'We don't want you to do very much, my boy; but we do want to get younger men interested. You've got to help our generation to atone for its mistakes. With a few fellows of your age to help us the next attempt might well be the last one.'

Ruprecht at that moment was scarcely listening to him. He was reviewing the immediate past. On his arrival at Pamezia his report of the island prisoner to a high-ranking Italian admiral had soon borne fruit. Hitler, brooding over his maps in Wolfsschanze, his East Prussian headquarters at Rastenburg, had been delighted by the chance of aiding Mussolini and so confirming his own shaken destiny. He had received the report of his 'loyal friend's' whereabouts as a sign from Heaven and at once devised 'Operation Oakleaf' whereby, despite his transfer to the Campo Imperator, the Duce had been kidnapped and flown to Vienna in a Fiesler Storch. Almost simultaneously, Ruprecht, too, had been rewarded. After a short term under house-arrest in Pamezia, he had been given leave to return indefinitely to Bergedorf and to resume, if he wished, direction of the Waitzmann Group.

Now, as he listened to Nicholas in the privacy of the

Schönform pig barn, where, at least, it was warm, he wondered if his own excellent stroke of fortune, so quickly recognized, was to be undone by this red-faced lunacy. For the whole affair was, perhaps fortunately, absurd; even the pseudonyms of the other members of the 'Hohenheim cadre' sounded more ludicrous every time the Baron mentioned them.

'Only three nights ago,' he was saying, ' "Walküre" told me that if I was successful in persuading you to join us, he had a couple of young staff officers who would immediately follow your example.'

Ruprecht looked disgustedly at the noisy pig-pens by which they were surrounded. The smell in the place sickened him and he could not think how he had allowed himself to be driven into such a corner.

'I'm sorry, but I can't help in any way whatsoever.'

'But my dear fellow, the factory business takes you everywhere. You've an ample fuel-allowance and there are no questions asked. You'd make an ideal courier at very little risk to yourself.'

'Impossible. The whole thing's far too risky; in fact, it's preposterous!'

Nicholas smiled. 'We're not such a lot of bunglers as you might imagine. We've had bad luck, that's all. Take that last attempt at the Veteran's Dinner at the Adlon. "Spengler" had planted his own waiter with the right sort of poison and "Goethe" had taken care of the food taster – you know by the way that Hitler's taken to employing one since the Russian defeats? Well, what d'you think happened? The Führer didn't arrive! He's taken to what he calls "irregular irregularity" and never more so than in his social engagements. He told Canaris that he's stumbled on the one lesson the Borgias never learned, the secret of simply not turning up.'

Ruprecht moved down the aisle between the pig-pens and Nicholas followed him.

'I'm afraid that affairs at the factory occupy all my attention, Baron. Our turn for an air-raid is bound to come sooner or later and I haven't even enough deep shelters yet.'

'Nothing to what your problems are going to be if we don't bring it off soon,' said Nicholas. 'Defeat is staring us in the face already and it won't be long before everybody's wanting to play their part in seeing that it's an honourable one.'

'It's property that's going to count, not honour.'

'No, not in the long run.' Nicholas looked round at his pigs and lowered his voice. 'Unfortunately, Ruprecht, you've got to be made to realize that you'll be involved whether you like it or not.'

'That's exactly why I'm objecting.'

'Because,' went on Nicholas, 'next time it's going to be my turn. We cut the cards at our last meeting and I drew the ace.' He paused. 'A little bomb, practically unnoticeable, very flat. I've simply got to slip it into the Führer's pocket and then get out of the way.'

Ruprecht strode towards the door of the barn and the Baron followed and caught him up. 'Stop. Let me give you a demonstration.'

'What do you mean?'

'Try your left-hand pocket. No, no.' Nicholas slipped his hand in and drew out a brandy flask. 'You'd better let me remove it. It's not armed, but one has to be careful.'

Ruprecht was shaken. 'It's madness. You'll only end up by killing yourself.'

'Exactly! And that, my dear fellow, is why I've had to come down here yet again for what may well be my last look at Schönform. My instructions are that if I find it impossible to slip it into that madman's pocket, then I'm to keep it in my own, get up as close to him as possible, arm the weapon and take him with me.' In the cold wind sweeping through the farmyard Ruprecht looked at the healthy face opposite him as if trying to see it for the first time. He said something about Carin but the Baron ignored it.

'And good bait too; we can't fail. "Goethe" has laid on an exhibition of looted pictures from Rouen, a private collection. If only to enrage Goering and Ribbentrop, the Führer will never be able to resist them. What about that?'

235

'When is this to be?'

'I can only tell you that it should be some time before Alexandra's confinement in February.'

'But don't you realize that you'll not only be endangering your wife and Leo but every single one of your associates?'

'Yes, I've thought about that a good deal. We all have, and we've decided it's a risk that simply has to be taken.'

'But Carin; your wife!' Ruprecht repeated.

'I'm afraid she's rather gone to seed, poor girl. I'm not sure we all haven't. We're strangers really.'

'Strangers?'

'There's your brother Alfried, for example, isn't there?' Ruprecht was sharp: 'I'd rather not discuss him.'

'Naturally. We'd all prefer not to. All of us with the exception of your mother.'

'For God's sake, sir!'

'No, no, I'm afraid you've got to listen to me. Your brother was our first real mistake, the first particular case in which we might have done the right thing. And close enough, my dear fellow! Right under our very noses, as near as you are to me at this moment.' He gripped Ruprecht by the forearm. 'Whether we bring it off or not, your brother's honesty, the honour of a single honourable man, will have been justified by his fellow Germans. That is all that matters.'

'The whole scheme's preposterous. The best way we can help Alfried and Germany is by surviving ourselves. It's the practical view that matters. It's all this damned dreaming that's responsible for our defeats, whether personal or national. The one way in which we can win this war is by living through it.'

'Wouldn't want to.' The Baron dropped his arm and led the way back to the castle. 'I'm sorry to have bothered you so much. In an affair of this sort everyone has to follow his own conscience. If that's not troubling one there's not much one can do about it; but I wish you'd try and have a word with Wilhelmina. I haven't confided in her myself but I'm quite certain that if I did, she'd approve.'

Ruprecht had no intention of doing any such thing.

Though, recently, his mother had been much warmer to him, he had found it increasingly difficult to understand her. Since his return from the Mediterranean her disapproval of him seemed to have been absorbed in a steady but detached affection. Watching her and failing to find any trace of the, occasionally bitter, amusement which she had so often displayed in the past, he had at first been shocked and later resentful, persuading himself that she had let him down. A mother, he believed, should never give up her reproaches. One had a right to her anger. For so long as she was alive she had no case to fill one with remorse that instead of being painful was only vexatious.

Increasingly, he tended to mock her subtly, both for her religious devotion and for her influence over Alexandra. Ever more frequently they had taken to attending Father Guardini's Mass each morning in the castle chapel. Although Christmas was so near they observed a perpetual rule of collations and ate scarcely anything. Ruprecht resented this obtrusive fasting and allowed them no peace.

'In wartime it's ridiculous, in pregnancy it's a sin,' he told them. 'Alexandra, I order you to eat more.'

'But it only makes me sick, Liebling.'

'Ruprecht is quite right,' said Frau Waitzmann. 'You must try, dear.'

They had become immersed in works of charity. Several days a week Alexandra made the rounds of the tenants, distributing her own badly baked cakes from a flat-bottomed Italian basket, while Frau Waitzmann spent hours in the Schönform greenhouses potting tulips, hyacinths and crocus bulbs which Alexandra also distributed all over the estate and as far as the nearest village. There was scarcely a cottage that had not its quota of the Frau Kommerzienrat's spring flowers already promising Easter in its dark interior. The castle too was full of them; the window-sills lined with pink and blue hyacinths, golden crocuses and showy tulips, so crookedly planted that they ascended at angles and had to be propped up with sticks. When Ruprecht returned early from Bergedorf he might find the two women making the rounds with green watering-cans.

'Good God, you both have red noses. You've been too long in the greenhouses.'

'Don't be so unkind,' said Frau Waitzmann.

'You look like Sisters of Charity. I come home from the factory where I see nothing but an army of scrawny female workers and what do I find but a mother superior and her postulant? Assuredly the war's lost!'

'You look tired, Ruprecht.'

'I am tired; but I'm serious too. When women take to their rosaries and let their faces go to hell, defeat is certain. It ought to be a treasonable offence.'

'Now eat up your soup,' said Alexandra.

He glared into his plate. 'Even Carin has decided to look her age. She has given up dyeing her hair.'

'Really?' Alexandra was momentarily as wide-eyed as in the old days. 'However do you know?'

'I heard from her this morning. A letter at the office. She's after a job for her latest protégé, that little beast Grunwald. She asks if we couldn't find something for him in the advertising room.'

'You mean immediately?'

'No, in the event of what she calls, "a change of policy".'

'How strange! And she's decided to look her age when she was always so elegant?'

'Yes, but apparently it doesn't discourage young Grunwald. He's staying with them at Rastenburg.'

'She gives news of Alfried perhaps?' asked Frau Waitzmann.

'None whatsoever.'

'So!'

Ruprecht looked at his mother quickly. 'It may be a good sign. No one has heard anything; neither Carin nor Grunwald nor Nicholas.'

'Nicholas is away so much,' said Alexandra. 'I'm sure he's doing something for Alfried. Every time he comes home I expect him to have news. We've prayed so hard.'

Frau Waitzmann finished the last of her soup and there was a silence which Ruprecht interpreted as critical of himself. He would have liked then to tell them of his most recent conversation with Nicholas; observing their sad feminine faces, their air of waiting, he felt suddenly brutal about his own danger. 'Nicholas is not bothering about Alfried,' he would have said. 'He's after the Führer. At any moment it might be me you're losing; and then where will you be with your piety and patience?' A most blasphemous idea of shocking them like this, of making his child jump in Alexandra's womb, occurred to him and was rejected; but it was rejected only because, amongst other things, he did not want his mother comforting his wife; so he said:

'Alfried, if you remember, wanted the solitude of service to the world. Well, he's got it. He's still in his camp hospital attending the sick and dying. He'd be no happier, no less unhappy, if he were working in Berlin or Hamburg or here in Bergedorf with the air-raid victims. What difference does it make that he's in a camp when the whole country's a camp?'

'Perhaps that's true.' Alexandra was near weeping.

Ruprecht smiled coldly. 'The only difference is that he might not feel so heroic, such a martyr; but God is good. He's given Alfried what he's always wanted. Your prayers have been answered.' They made no reply and Ruprecht ate a piece of toast. 'If I sound cynical, it's because I feel cynical. One can't mourn for ever in wartime – and there'll be my own child to think of.'

But they neither of them took him up on this and he became angrier than ever. He thought that he might take Alexandra back to Bergedorf to break Frau Waitzmann's influence over her. He saw himself as being up against what he called 'a damned old age', and saw it as washing Alexandra to a standstill like something being rolled on the edge of the ebb tide.

He was surprised by the immediacy of the metaphor. For a moment he imaginatively 'saw' what he was thinking and said to himself: 'The sea reflects the last of the sun. Long after it has sunk from our view it is illuminating the face of the waters.' He realized at once that this was an insight into his feelings for his mother's detachment and her influence over Alexandra and rebelled against it. He did not wish to see Frau Waitzmann's life as an illumined ocean, bathed in the light of an invisible sun, calming down and bringing all to calm upon its surface. He wished to reduce her to human proportions and see her only as an ageing woman, benevolently senile. If he were to be certain of his victory over her, he needed his self-confidence and must persuade himself that if he could no longer trouble her then it was not because she was wise but only because she was old. From that evening onwards he became even sharper with her, more tense and contemptuous.

The Anglo-American air-raid they had all anticipated took place a fortnight after Christmas, the first severe one the town had experienced. From one of the Schönform turrets the women watched the Bergedorf searchlights stitching the dark horizon, the ochre glow of the fires and flashes of the barrage. Ruprecht, who had spent the night at the factory, did not return until six in the morning. He was calm with anger over damage to the power-house and did not seem to be in the least disturbed when at lunch time Alexandra went into labour, three weeks before her time.

Out of patience with her distress over the bombing of the Dollmannstrasse Clinic he told her that she must put everything but the confinement out of her mind. In Carin's seldom-used bedroom he stood over her as she lay on the stripped bed and studied her irritably. Frau Nietern, one of the only two senior midwives to have survived the bombing, had warned him that Alexandra was brooding over the selfishness and luxury of her confinement after such a disaster.

'The first hour is always the worst,' the nurse had said. 'They have too much time to think in between pains, Herr Direktor.'

'You can give her something, no doubt?'

'It's better not at this stage. It slows things up and in any case Frau Alexandra's own training has made her a little difficult.'

He spoke to Alexandra affectionately, concealing his

anger at the nature of her further confidences about her 'selfishness'.

'So you think that God's not contented with allowing so many women to die in the town. He requires your guilt too?'

'Liebling, you don't understand.' Alexandra sat up beneath the big crucifix which Frau Waitzmann had put above her bed. 'If I were taking my chance in a cottage with only one nurse instead of all the staff and doctors you've engaged . . .'

'A cottage! Did your grandmothers have their babies in cottages? How dishonest you are.' He gestured at the room. 'You've stripped this room of its fabrics, no hangings on the bed, sheets everywhere against the dust, even the curtains removed. Yet in their place you must have the luxury of your guilt. Thank God for His providence, for Frau Nietern's night off duty. Thank God she's not delivering babies in purgatory with the rest of the clinic staff.'

She kissed him confidingly as he stooped. On an impulse she slid an arm about his neck as if to draw him closer and he saw that she was still weeping. 'Darling,' he said, 'you must be as simple as a cow – but an aristocratic cow.' And he left her to return to the factory.

In the banqueting hall he was caught by Frau Waitzmann. She had heard his noisy descent of the stairs and was awaiting him in that cold chamber, looking, as he saw, 'most insultingly' a widow; a woman without the simplicity to be bitter as was Carin's mother, that other widow in East Prussia. At sight of her, so cut off from everything by her blindness, so useless in the face of his own preoccupations, he addressed her even before he had got down the last of the stairs.

'Well, Mama?'

'You've been with Alexandra?'

'Of course. I presume you'll be here to show the doctors upstairs when they arrive?'

'But couldn't you have stayed here yourself? Just today.'

'After the raid! Now how could I possibly? Heaven knows what will have been going on at the factories in my absence. You know how inadequate Luger is in a crisis.'

'Alexandra would be so much happier to know you were near.'

'Alexandra? But haven't you always told us that a woman in childbed is alone with God?'

'That doesn't mean she's alone with her marriage.'

'Mama, I've no inclination for doctrine at the moment. Quite apart from Alexandra and this damned raid, there's Nicholas. I sent a telegram to his last address early this morning. If he rings up will you let me know at once?'

'What is it, Ruprecht? What is all this about?'

'If Nicholas hasn't told you, how can I?'

'He telephoned ten minutes ago. He told me to tell you that he'd be calling for you at the factory at five o'clock.'

'What! Anything else?'

'He said he'd failed to secure "the contract". He said you'd know what that meant.'

He stood heavily before her a moment. 'Well, thank God for that.'

'Ruprecht, I know as well as you do there's no new contract in the files at the moment. Won't you tell me what Nicholas has been doing these last months?'

'I can only tell you that if you did know you might understand my single-mindedness better, Mama.'

He saw the flicker of her distress before he turned to leave her; but she followed him down the length of the room and from good manners alone he was bound to wait for her. Her broad hand on his arm, the embroidered black sleeve like a shackle to his impatience, she went beside him along the corridor and out into the courtyard where she kissed him goodbye.

Alone in his car the recollection of her gesture bewildered him, making him feel more impotent than he had when he had been in the sea. She had guessed everything, he saw. She knew that Nicholas had for long been actively plotting and she sensed that he himself was now only waiting for her to die before he could 'get on' with his life. Yet she had been gentler than ever. That's grace, he thought. She behaves as if the world were still undamaged. But how are the rest of us to get on without indignation and anxiety? The world would die on its feet!

Punctually at five o'clock Nicholas arrived at the office. After his four weeks' absence he was initially more ebullient than ever, filling the large room with his presence, stretching himself in front of Ruprecht's desk 'to get the creases out of his flesh'.

'Well, come on. We'll drive straight back to Schönform and stop on the roadside for a confidential talk. But first tell me the news.'

'You mean Alexandra? We're still waiting. I spoke to the doctor five minutes ago. They expect the baby within a couple of hours.'

'Splendid! We'll be able to do justice to the occasion at dinner tonight. I managed to pick up half-a-dozen bottles of champagne in Bonn and I have them in the car.'

'I can't possibly leave for at least another hour.'

'You're funking it, Ruprecht. We all do. We like these things to go on in our absence. We like the Christmas parcels to be safely delivered before we climb out of our cots.'

'I'm sorry,' said Ruprecht flatly, disliking this reference to his 'birthday' grievance.

Nicholas's expression changed. 'I have other news for you too, but I can't give it you here: first, the matter of the contract which I mentioned to Wilhelmina this morning; and, next, news of your brother.'

Ruprecht got up. 'Very well, I'll come with you. I'll have to return again after dinner in any case. They may well follow up with another raid tonight.'

The Baron made no comment. He had won his point and half an hour later they drew up in the bare woods outside Hanau where he pushed back the seat and told Ruprecht about Alfried.

'Your brother was recently transferred from Dachau to one of the Reichsführer's special projects. I've done my damndest to find out more; but all I can discover is that they've been hand-picking subjects from the camps for experimental work in aviation medicine.'

'Subjects? You mean that Alfried is a subject?'

'I'm afraid so. It's possible that your brother is now one of the Party's guinea-pigs.'

'But that's not possible! I know about these places. He'll be working in the laboratory on the technical side.'

'I'm afraid not.'

'I have contacts,' Ruprecht insisted. 'I know all about it. As a matter of fact I had no alternative but to send off half-a-dozen Ukrainians only last week. They wanted some healthy young Jewesses for genetic research.'

The Baron flushed. Hatred seized him as he sat there with his hands on the steering wheel. For an instant he thought that he might remove those hands and strangle young Waitzmann where he sat. Then, involuntarily, as he waited for this emotion to pass, he entered a region of ferns. In his mind's eye, a full grown forest of fern trees stood over him, motionless and silent: green crowns and fronds on massive stems fountaining from columnar trunks covered with diamond-shaped bark, horny as alligator skin. 'But, my dear boy,' was all he could say. The fern trees, which had vanished as quickly as they had come were replaced now by the memory of his mother's fernery, that place of his childhood.

'I've told nobody else,' Ruprecht was saying. 'There's war, destruction everywhere; but I've not avoided anything with my mother. I told her only the other night that I wasn't prepared to mourn Alfried for ever.' He looked at the Baron and saw that he was not attending. 'You hear, sir?'

The Baron's mother, in her heyday, in those gentle seasons of a gentler century, had filled a conservatory with sub-tropical ferns in tubs and terra cotta vats so large that she had needed a small step ladder in order to water them. Why! he remembered, the pots were there to this day, rained upon through gaps in the glass; but in his childhood all had been sealed against the weather.

'I don't deny that Alfried probably detests his work, particularly if it's degrading,' went on Ruprecht. 'In the natural sense he may be as close to despair as any of the saints he always longed to be. But which of us isn't? Ask yourself, sir, who hears of your complaints or of mine? And we've not got Alfried's grace. In fact, I don't mind telling you that ever since our enemies forced us into war the future's appalled me, while the past, if ever I think of it, was nearly always unsatisfactory.'

But the Baron was seeing his mother in a long-sleeved grey dress of some gleaming material with the sleeves fitting close about the wrists, a ring shining like a water-drop on her marriage finger, as, rapt, she smiled to herself in her world of ferns. He forced himself to try again, saying:

'You have to consider Wilhelmina's feelings, your mother, Ruprecht.'

'She knows nothing about this new development and the more sure I was of it the less inclined I'd be to tell her. Can't you see, sir, that I've had enough? For years, as you should remember, Alfried's been a bone in my throat. I can't dislodge it and so I've got to get used to it.'

At one time Nicholas might have thought of repairing that particular conservatory despite the great expense of the curved glass. Until recently the intention might have given him pleasure; but what did he care now for those lacunae in the roof and walls, the clinging film of lichen on the undamaged panes? I've no plans for the future of my house, he told himself, astonished. Dear God! Without knowing it, for months, I've intended to die! Still half-buried in the largest of the pots, he remembered sharply, was the corm of one of those defunct ferns, harbouring woodlice and threadlike worms beneath its papery cortex; the earth dry and tired, white with revealed pebbles and stones as if it too were in dissolution.

'I've got to live with it and forget the discomfort,' went on Ruprecht, dropping a cigarette-end out of the window. 'We're waiting, every one of us, to get on with our real lives when this war's over.'

'Are we?'

'And that's precisely what Alfried and ten thousand others are doing; and don't forget that I myself have done research for aviation medicine – involuntarily. I was three hours in the water with no one to take my pulse or feed me.'

'That's the point; in your case it was the will of God, in your brother's, the will of man.'

'I don't agree. These things are relative. One can suffer as much in a large prison like Germany . . .'

'A rotten box, my boy,' said Nicholas suddenly. 'That's what Germany's become – a rotten box. Soon it will collapse.'

'In that case, instead of reproaching ourselves why don't we concentrate on saving something? If I were in Alfried's position I should want something to return to at the end of it all.'

'What we must save must be something of the heart, Ruprecht.'

'And what is that? In Germany we're always referring to the heart. It's a favourite word of the Führer's and I don't mind telling you that where I'm concerned all my worst wishes have sprung from it.' Ruprecht struck his breast pocket with his fist. 'From the heart, sir! Here in my breast!'

'No good at all,' said Nicholas, giving up. 'I was never a good talker, I'm afraid.'

Ruprecht at once became conciliatory. 'Tell me about Operation Overcoat, what went wrong?'

'The weapon failed to detonate. At five minutes to the appointed hour I broke the capsule in the gentleman's lavatory and hurried back to the salon. The acid never ate through the firing-pin wire. We're having the metal analysed before the next attempt.'

'You didn't get as far as transferring it to the Führer's pocket?'

'Unfortunately not. He was wearing a greatcoat when he arrived; but he took it off as soon as he entered the place; so there was nothing for it but to retain my own. And, would you believe it, this did not escape his attention? He actually turned and asked Bormann if the "Baron von Hoffbach were unwell?" I replied that I was suffering from a circulatory disturbance – which was perfectly true; my feet were like ice; I kept as close to him as possible.'

'And you had the bomb in your pocket the whole time?'

'In my inside breast-pocket. I had transferred it when his coat was removed. I thought it might do more damage up there.'

Ruprecht studied his face. 'And what did you think of while you were waiting?'

'Of the time.'

'You prayed?'

'You forget that I was supposed to be taking an interest in the paintings – they were not religious.'

'Yet you're going to make another attempt?'

'Certainly. Next time with two bombs – in case of accidents, you might say.' Nicholas smiled at his own joke and became serious again. 'We're very concerned, though. "Walküre" has heard of a rival group. We can't discover their identities and so we cannot get into touch with them. They appear to be well organized.'

Ruprecht relaxed. 'That's the best bit of news I've had since the war started.'

'But they may leave it too late,' said Nicholas heavily. 'The execution of this upstart must be brought off long before the Wehrmacht is finally defeated; before, in fact, the Anglo-Saxon armies invade Europe, as they will do this summer.'

'But there's a chance the rival group may beat you to it?'

'Of course.'

'Then, my God, I can now wish you success in your intentions.'

The Baron smiled. He was thinking that Ruprecht might be more approachable when once he had seen his child; and Ruprecht too was romantically advising himself of this in different terms: 'I'll be looser when I've seen my son,' he was saying to himself. 'Everything will be looser. The whole world will be shaken for me. The mountains!'

For the mountains were just visible on the horizon; light beyond the trees; a solidity in the sky, an opalescence less likely than cloud.

Frau Waitzmann was sitting with Alexandra. That upper room drew her as a grave draws a mourner. It was a place of reflection, of exaltation; as if it had been some white circlet of *immortelles* on swollen turf, or the Altar of Repose at Easter time, sheathed in white and green, locked and full. The watery, cellular, flowers of spring scenting the air.

She was certain that the child would not be born until it was dark. 'It will be a night-child, who'll not trouble you until the evening has gone,' she told Alexandra.

At five o'clock, she fitted the blackouts into the stone embrasures of the deep windows and refuelled the stove. She busied herself refilling the hot water jars and searching Carin's cupboards for woollen coverlets for them. Her own phrase delighted her; nothing could destroy for her the memory that Alfried too had been a 'night-child'. The kettle sang on top of the stove as it had sung so many years ago for her own confinement. And what does my blindness matter now? she was thinking. I had Alfried in the dark. He was one of those that crept into the world under its cover.

Each prayer she made was for him too; for the infant, perfect-limbed in the lamplight, for whom, at that time, she had had no other coherent wish at all than that he should love God. Really, it would have given her such pleasure to tell all these things to Alexandra; to beguile her, if she might, with the nature of her reassurance; to say, 'You mustn't think I grieve for Alfried. Who was I to think I could prevent such things for him?' But, of course, she could not bring up this subject either now or at any foreseeable time in the future. Alexandra, being so young, might find it too hard to forgive her for not continuing to suffer. And how could she ever explain that she was far more concerned for Ruprecht who had been born in full sunshine? A birthday king.

He was hardening, she thought. Ever since his rescue from the sea he had been horrible. Lately, there had been moments when she had found it nearly impossible to love him, no longer needing or even wanting to see his face or her own anger. Her capacity for anger, as her sight, had gone and she no longer missed them. Both indeed at this time were a disadvantage; anger certainly, at her age, as unseemly as carnal love. To kiss him as she had done that morning, recoiling from touching his face, yet nevertheless doing so, had required an even greater impatience on her own part. It was a mystery, she believed to have loved even momentarily that little so much.

When the doctors arrived she left Alexandra and went along to the Lake Room where Nicholas and Ruprecht were listening to the night news from Berlin. She heard Ruprecht leap from his chair even before she had opened the door.

'She's all right, Mama?'

'A little slow, but Doctor Brille thinks it will not be very long.'

He left them. They heard him descend the stone stairs slowly. Nicholas turned off the wireless.

'He can't stand her cries,' he told Wilhelmina.

'She's stubborn, she won't take the gas.'

Nicholas fumbled about in his ignorance of obstetrics. He was trying to recall what he had known of Lister, of Pasteur, of Vienna and childbirth fever. Then he remembered the Ukrainians in the Bergedorf gardens and his interview with Frau Neff about the abortions.

'In the factory last year . . .' he began.

'Please don't talk about it.'

'The camps too, Wilhelmina.'

She looked at him a little coldly; on behalf of his own mother, he thought.

'On Friday I talked to Father Guardini,' she went on. 'He told me of his time in the Indian Mission.'

'Ah, of course,' he said, comforted. 'He reminded you perhaps that there's poverty there too, appalling conditions? That despite it all the babies get born just the same?'

'He reminded me that there was no comparison,' said Wilhelmina. 'He said that in the hell we've made of Europe abortion and stillbirth might be holier than new life itself.'

They saw it: the kingdom into which those new flocks broke.

'It came about so slowly,' he said.

'Or so quickly.'

'And soon it will be history, Wilhelmina. Soon the whole world will know of it.'

'Then I envy it.'

'Envy, you say?'

'I envy the whole world for learning of it from the outside.'

He was unable to see her as either old or blind. Looking at his contemporary in that draughty room he was aware suddenly that his life was as new as if he had just fallen in love with her, as old as if they had together endured from the beginning of the world. They spoke no more. Sometime, later on, they heard the first cry of the child, impersonal as an animal's, threading the corridors of the castle and Ruprecht came in to them.

'She's done it, Mama. Nicholas, we've a son! Where's that champagne?'

They were embarrassed by his shout, as if he had made them both grandparents. They felt old now at this intrusion of a son about his business, yet they were glad for Alexandra and for the baby itself. They wondered how they could behave joyfully; for as well as feeling old they were made young too, by unaccustomed guilt, that realization of a cracked world into which, hopefully, the new-born tunnelled.

Frau Waitzmann kissed Ruprecht and the Baron shook his hand absently, saying only, 'My dear boy, my dear boy!'

'Alexandra –' Frau Waitzmann began as, without even her glass, she made for the door; '– I must go to her.'

'But you have not drunk, Mama. You have not even a glass.'

'Ach no! I am so happy for you, Ruprecht.'

'Magnificent news; magnificent!' The Baron felt that his turn was done, that he had come round full circle and must die now that a child was born in whose birth he could not believe.

They raised their glasses and drank.

At the end of the week the Baron left for Frankfurt and as soon as he was out of the way Ruprecht rang up Carin at Rastenburg.

'Are you alone?'

'Apart from my mother, entirely.'

'Can you put me up for the weekend? I must see you.'

'As many weekends as you like! If you don't mind sharing your evenings with Hubertus.'

'He's still with you, is he?'

'Off and on. He's handling the publicity at Rastenburg. He sees the Führer regularly.'

'Oh.'

She sounded amused. 'But if you want a heart to heart talk there'll be plenty of opportunities. Hubertus doesn't get in until fairly late.'

'We must not be disturbed.'

'Of course not. I know all about it and I'm a little worried myself.'

'Good! Then I'll be with you soon after lunch tomorrow.'

'Thank you for your telegram, by the way. How is Alexandra?'

'Wonderfully well.'

'And you've a son?' Carin sounded politely amused. 'Who does he look like? You or his good, sweet mother?'

'He has a strong face,' he told her shortly, hearing the harsh sound of her laughter as she put down the receiver.

The next day, trim in a cardigan over a creamy silk shirt blouse tucked into narrow uhlan-style trousers, especially cut for her in Paris, Carin greeted him in the driveway. Standing slender and old on the steps of the weathered porch she covered her cheeks against the bitter Baltic wind.

'You're as punctual as ever. Have you eaten?'

He kissed her hand. 'Yes, thanks. This is so good of you, Carin.'

As they went up the staircase she looked at him. 'You're older, you know.'

'I feel it.'

She patted her brindled hair with a bloodless hand. 'Here-with Mother I feel like the grandmother I could so easily be. And this time I've been here far too long.' She opened a door on the landing. 'Now this is your room. I'll open the shutters.'

He looked at the unaccustomed view. The double-glazed window was filled to a third of its height by the frosted East Prussian plain. Irregularities on the horizon suggested dunes, and, in the distance, clumps of fir trees, sloped evenly by the wind, appeared to graze like herds of thick-coated animals. An invisible train seemed motionless beneath a skein of steam.

'At night, if the wind's in the right direction, you can hear those trains,' she said. 'In my 'teens I used to lie here thinking about the Russian front. And that was before you were born, you realize?'

'You were frightened?'

'Not a bit. I was dreaming of the young Czarist officers being slaughtered by our troops.' She did not miss his smile and went on, 'I'd been reading too many Russian novels, you see, and there were times when I was sure the house would one day be surrounded by Cossacks; bearded, vigorous young men.'

He was looking round the room. There was a washstand with embroidered towels and a tablet of French soap beside the basin. The old-fashioned wallpaper was rising at the edges and in several places there were patches of dried mould flowering black above the wainscotting.

'French soap,' he said. 'You still get your little presents from Paris?'

'I had none from you in Rome, Liebling!'

Smiling, she had moved back to the door and he saw that she was no longer looking old. Her streaked hair, swathes of the still-dark red mingling with the grey-white strands, framed her unmade face.

'You've come about Nicholas, haven't you?'

He shut the door behind her. 'He's got to be stopped, Carin.'

'Of course he has; but do let's try and be light about it all.'

'Light?'

'Men always become so heavy. They betray themselves from the outset – by their solemnity. My only concession to events has been this –' she touched a hand to her hair. 'Apparently, it doesn't inhibit Hubertus; but in other quarters it makes them trust me. The Führer and his men don't like old women to look too young, it makes them feel a little uneasy.'

'You're in touch?'

'Why do you think I left Berlin? We're a sort of half-way house here for Wolfsschanze. Tired generals spend the night on their way to or from a talk with the Führer. His head-quarters are only three miles away.'

She appeared to him now to be a discovery; her opportunism gave her a quality as surprising and inconstant as beauty. With excitement he wondered how he could ever have been so crass as to imagine that their first meeting was a casual event. He saw himself as having been destined to be in her scheme of life from the beginning.

'You've said nothing to Hubertus, I hope?'

'Not a word. His head's quite in the clouds – fortunately.'

'Fortunately?'

'He's intuitive, you know; a wriggler. It's hard to keep any secrets from him when he's bored – somehow one doesn't want to; and that could be risky. But at the moment he's not bored. He's quite dizzy with his closeness to the Führer. He still pretends to believe fervently in eventual victory.'

He was impatient with her. He frowned as he said: 'You realize that if Nicholas doesn't drop this nonsense of his immediately . . .'

'We shall all be corpses? Don't worry. I've great plans for the peace.'

'How much has Nicholas told you?'

'He doesn't trust me, I'm afraid; but it hasn't been difficult to put two and two together.' She sighed as a bell rang vexedly in the hall. 'My mother. This is the time when we usually have a little wine and a biscuit together. She always comes into the hall. This has to go on, you see, or she might begin to fear we were losing the war.'

Frau de Luce, erect as a candle, was standing in the hall looking up the stairway as she awaited the introduction to whoever it might be: a general of this war or the last, a contemporary of her long-dead husband. Ruprecht, winding down the three-sided stairway behind Carin, was uneasy. These white-headed women of quality always affected him in this way. 'Be wary,' he told himself, 'a mother awaits you.'

But Carin was laughing. 'She may be disappointed that it's not Hubertus. She dotes on him. I really believe the little beast has made her fall quite in love with him.'

'She's senile?'

She lowered her voice. 'I'd rather say she was quite in possession of all the facts that no longer matter.'

Frau de Luce spoke fast in a low rough voice as if she were tired of words and regretted all her inquiries. Her grey eyes, still black-lashed, regarded Ruprecht and her daughter with equal disapproval. She asked whether Ruprecht were in the Wehrmacht or the Luftwaffe and when told that he was a scientist, said only, 'They've become important, is that not so?' After this she appeared to lose interest in the conversation until Hubertus was mentioned, when she leaned forward again and asked: 'Is he too coming this evening?'

'Now you know he'll be here quite soon, Mother. Be patient.'

Frau de Luce asked Ruprecht if he knew 'the young Grunwald'. 'He is a very polite young man; but a little "jumped-up", is he not? I sometimes wonder why he comes here so often.'

'What a turncoat you are,' said Carin.

But the old lady in her grey shawl sat composedly in her tall chair munching her water biscuit and sipping her wine as if she had been quite alone.

Carin now behaved as though this figure were some glass-cased possession, a part of the means whereby she was enabled to keep her predicaments 'light'. Her voice and manner changed as a child's may change on the arrival of its parents at a party. Since what she was now discussing was not some physical passion on which her character might have depended, but her husband's treason, on which their lives might be at stake, Ruprecht became progressively more tense. He could not rid himself of an idea that Carin wished her mother to know at least of their adultery. Speaking of Nicholas she was saying:

'It's always the middle-aged who get conscience trouble, don't you think? and then only when things are beginning to go wrong. The moment their bank balances are threatened or they find an unusual lump in their stomachs, they begin at once to brood about God and Germany.'

In all the little social arrangements which had accompanied her infidelities, he was thinking, she had always been so fastidious.

'Each time I've met him in Berlin,' she was continuing, 'I've had to listen to Nicholas's protestations about being a gentleman. I've had two long letters from him about "womanhood".' She laughed aloud. 'Nicholas and womanhood! And all because he saw some of your female workers using the factory lavatories on a sunny morning.'

Pointedly, Ruprecht passed Frau de Luce the biscuits. 'Is this quite the moment for such a discussion?' he asked Carin.

'You've never taken much interest in my family, have you, Mother?'

'I've only met the Baron von Hoffbach once,' said Frau de Luce in that rough voice.

'But Grunwald,' persisted Ruprecht, addressing Carin. 'You tell me he's here a great deal and that you find he tempts you to indiscretions.'

Carin looked at her mother speculatively. 'They've much nicer things to discuss. You don't waste your time talking politics with Hubertus, do you, Mother?'

'We play chess. Herr Waitzmann is not a great judge of character I fear, or he would know that I am not a garrulous old woman.'

'Frau de Luce, I'd no intention of being rude.'

'Then perhaps you won't let me interrupt you further, Herr Waitzmann.' She smiled icily at her daughter; and Carin, as if she had received that little parental pat on the head she needed, became more direct than ever.

'You'll have to confide in me, Ruprecht. If I'm to give Nicholas the fright he needs, I must know everything.'

'But he won't be directly compromised himself?'

'Don't be dense. If he were, we would be too. None of us would be spared. Even my garrulous old mother would be strung up by the S.S., wouldn't you, dear?'

Frau de Luce laughed – a throaty titter. Ruprecht thought she was about to speak; but when he looked at her he saw that her face was full of hatred; yet she was testing her lower lip with her teeth as if in some way she relished her daughter's suggestion.

'You have a plan?' he asked Carin.

'Some third person, I think, will have to contact Nicholas unexpectedly. Somebody completely in the know might be very disconcerting. All I want from you is the names and as much as you know of the plan.'

'The names are all in code.'

'All the better,' she said.

'You realize we've only got a week or two at the outside? How soon can you act?'

'Very quickly, once I know the facts. You must get into touch with Nicholas the moment you get back to Schönform. He doesn't know you've been up here?'

'He was away when I left. I told my mother and Alexandra that I was going to Hamburg.'

'Then as soon as you can get hold of him tell him that you yourself have had a warning that the Gestapo are taking an interest in you. Delay him by any means you can.'

'Your mother,' said Frau de Luce, suddenly. 'I remember her well. She was always more beautiful than I – and somewhat younger. We met at dances and dinners in the old days. There was a magnificent ball in 1910 when we were still in rivalry – such wealth! A banker, of course. A Jew. We ate off golden plate and then threw his flowers – they were orchids – out of the windows to the people in the square. Tell me, how is your mother now, Herr Waitzmann?'

Carin sat back amusedly and he was irritated.

'My mother is still vigorous, Frau de Luce. For some years now she's been almost completely blind.'

Frau de Luce looked at him blankly. 'And she's become very religious, is that not so?'

'She was always devout; but with age of course . . .'

'With age, Herr Waitzmann, we weaken.' Her lips, between the deep lines running up to her nose, repeated the words, 'We weaken,' and her hand went to the side of her chair where there was a stick which he had not noticed before. Her hand grasped the gold handle as if it were a powerful lever and brought it round to the front of her knees where she held it sloping upwards and backwards towards her chin.

'It's Nicholas's age too,' went on Carin. 'Nicholas's glands always controlled his conscience. It wasn't easy for men of his class to accept Hindenburg's decision in the first place; but then Hindenburg himself was old and in those days Nicholas was still young enough to be bold.'

Frau de Luce was impatient. She gave her stick a little twist and then pulled it back against the stuff of her dress to hold it between her long thighs.

'And then, of course, your mother and Alexandra getting so thick,' said Carin. 'I see it all. Women in his beloved Schönform again. A baby!' She paused at the sound of a car drawing up outside. 'That must be Hubertus.'

Frau de Luce propped her stick back against the chair and crossed the hall until she was mid-way between the foot of the stairs and the front door. She waited there.

Carin said, 'Now remember, won't you, Liebling? You must be just a little patient. It's a question of discretion, of extreme discretion. You can leave everything else to me.' She looked across at Frau de Luce. 'Aren't you going upstairs to your bedroom, Mother?'

She took her over the stick and shepherded her to the bottom of the staircase. 'Hurry up!' she bade her. 'Make yourself look very pretty.'

She returned to Ruprecht who was standing with his back to the tiled stove. He was looking ill-tempered, she saw, as she smiled at him. She felt so much better now that her mother had gone. She was really enjoying this encounter and its wicked complications. 'Don't worry so much,' she told him.

'What's keeping Grunwald? Why doesn't he come in?'

'Because he never can resist exercising his charm. He'll be making up to the maids, getting them to stoke the boiler for his bath; or he'll have gone up by the back stairs to tease Mother.'

'His charm? I hope you're proof against it.'

'Mentally, I am.'

'Tell him nothing. Let him think that this is purely a business visit. You can say if you like that we're going to pay you a director's fee to save Nicholas's tax.'

'That would annoy Hubertus dreadfully. He's a little beast about money. Sometimes I long to give it to him so that he'll feel safe. He's so anxious to be on the right side.' She paused, looking to see how Ruprecht was taking it. 'You do see, don't you, that each of one's lovers has a different requirement?'

'I only see that Grunwald is dangerous. Even without your infatuation, he's a threat to us.'

'Liebling, you're sweet.'

'Don't be frivolous, Carin. Remember the other business. You always blamed him for Alfried's relegation, and I believed you.' He turned away. 'I wanted to.'

'I had hoped you might be jealous.'

'Not now, not at the moment. How could I be – with everything at stake?'

She kissed him, smiling to herself. 'Trust me, Liebling. I know what I'm doing. I know Nicholas a good deal better than you. I'm not frightened of Hubertus. He's really very sweet. . . .'

'I excel! This is my especial gift!' was Hubertus's thought as, ten minutes later in her bedroom, he swept Frau de Luce into his arms. Gracefully he kneeled beside her at her escritoire and lobbed the dull book she had been pretending to read on to her bed.

'Reading these racy French novels!' he teased her. 'Get up, Granny Eva, you impostor. Make your hair look prettier than ever, put a little powder on your breast and come down to us for a hot toddy in the hall.'

The old lady was breathless. She told him that besides

nearly giving her a heart attack by bursting in like that, he had bruised her dreadfully; but she kept her lips close to her teeth because they were yellow and crooked; and he hadn't disturbed the little additional coil of her own hair made up for her in Berlin from her hoarded combings. He was so gentle. She did not even drive him out of her room with her stick; after such an assault she did not feel old enough to justify such a burlesque of age.

When she stood up she was laughing. She simply could not keep those sad lips in place. Long after he had gone down to the hall again she trembled by her bed, full of a starry pride for something she had never really forgotten.

Hubertus, descending the stairs to Carin and Ruprecht, seemed to fill the chilly hall with himself. He had been dryly feverish all day, awaiting with the most prickly curiosity this moment of reunion with 'old Carin' and her former lover. His hands were warm and damp, his beautiful face was as soft and moist as a ballroom girl's and his black breeches clung to his groins like a dancer's tights. He did in fact spring round the hall as he talked, artlessly telling them of his day at Rastenburg, 'close to the Führer', watching them and putting them off their guard so that they might give away their secrets. For he knew that they had such secrets; that Waitzmann would not have come all this way at short notice 'just for sex'; that there must have been developments of some sort, either in connexion with Alfried or with von Hoffbach. Something told him, as it might have told his mother, 'Musch', that Carin would not have been so cold about the telephone call, the day before, if something had not been 'going on'.

At last, flopping on to the horsehair sofa beside the stove, drawing up one narrow leg on to the rexine so that his boot-heel rested in a dimple, he told them of his glimpse of the Führer at tea-time that day.

'Considering the news, he was in magnificent form. I admit that today I'd have sold my soul for him. His confidence! His eyes! One simply doesn't know what they're looking at; something he sees beyond everything, a glimpse of the gods – the gods peculiar to Germany and to eventual victory. In this mood, I honestly believe we all fulfil our dreams in those eyes. Anything's possible because they're the eyes of a man who's more than a man; but they're the eyes of a woman, too! That's the secret! Possibly he transcends it all. Possibly he's a demiurge. And I'm not the only one. At Wolfsschanze we all feel it. They tell me that he revivifies everyone that comes there. A general, completely down in the mouth, aggressive even, arrives from the Russian front, goes into conference; and, two or three hours later, leaves again – a different man! His powers are restored to him, his confidence, his faith in our destiny.'

Carin laughed and, after a pause, Hubertus with her. For he did not want applause. He wanted only to 'find out'; and this was one way of doing it; to adopt an attitude wholly and with complete conviction, and then to dissolve it, to knock it down. This behaviour amused people, it astonished them; eventually it unnerved them. Before they knew where they were they were letting things slip: private thoughts, secret preoccupations.

'What do *you* think?' he asked Ruprecht now. 'I heard from Carin how you were instrumental in putting the Führer on to the whereabouts of the poor old Duce – and how generously he treated you. You, surely, must be on his side?'

'On his side? I am on Germany's side of course.'

Hubertus nodded as if to say, 'That's what I meant. No need to take offence.'

'Of course,' he went on, 'there's no doubt he's having a lot of injections and drugs from Dr Morrell. One could attribute the whole thing to strain and treatment. There's no doubt it's taking all his strength to absorb the present disappointments in Russia. One or two of us are inclined to think that his fixation about Mussolini isn't altogether a good thing. It smacks a little of nostalgia which can be a sign of weakness in a man – at any rate, according to my father. At teatime, for instance, he's inclined to dwell on the old Munich days at some length. It's the only trace he ever gives, though, of any uncertainty.'

'No one in his right mind,' lied Carin calmly, 'would expect things to go quite so smoothly now as they did in the first two years of the war. While you were upstairs with Mother, Ruprecht was telling me that he's quite given up the habit of looking ahead.'

'He has? I think he's right.' Hubertus gazed at Ruprecht with the greatest affection. 'It's not honest. It's not even loyal.' He turned to Carin. 'But what were you worrying about, that Ruprecht had to reassure you? Tell me, please! You both know, or Carin does, how I love these explanations.'

Ruprecht spoke: 'I was discussing the future of my factories, Grunwald. A private matter which really concerns only von Hoffbach and myself.'

'Ah, the Baron!' said Hubertus, without faltering. 'That reminds me, Waitzmann; something I meant to tell you earlier, something about your brother Alfried . . .'

There was one of those tiny pauses; cracks in the temporal flow which seem to give on to eternity, moments in which new decisions are suddenly taken without any thought whatsoever: passions of love as whole as new-born infants, hatreds and suspicions as old as mankind, flower in the mind or fall into people's heads like executed corpses.

As Hubertus tried to find the best way of putting whatsoever it was he had not really forgotten at all, he discovered an old and permanent loathing of Ruprecht. He was so startled to recognize it that what had been initially an artificial pause now became a genuine one in which he knew that he had detested both the brothers Waitzmann from the start. He saw himself clearly as an outsider, a plaything of the new establishment who had not really got anywhere at all. He could be thrown over, he saw, in an instant whether the war were won or lost. He was in with the 'wrong set', whereas the Waitzmanns could not lose. They, by their wealth, were to become a part of the aristocracy which had always ruled Germany and the Germanies.

Simultaneously, though for different reasons, Carin and Ruprecht, in this hiatus, experienced warmth for one another. They saw that their 'lightness' over Nicholas's absurd plot against the Party was a 'game' no longer and that the tree beneath which they had conspired held a real serpent in its boughs. Carin, in her moment of insight, hardened at once. She saw Hubertus as a 'dangerous boy'. He seemed to her to hang in her excitement and sensuality like the most venomous snake; and, before she could stop herself, she heard her mind say: 'But this one has fangs: Ruprecht was right. If I make a mistake *here*, I'll not merely be nipped, I'll be poisoned at last.' She did not know why, after so much familiarity with the risks of adultery and perfidy, she should have thought 'at last' like that and she was dumbfounded to realize that despite her misgivings she would not yet abandon Hubertus; that on the contrary she would go to bed with him that night too and chance a dozen indiscretions about Ruprecht's visit and her husband's plans. Perhaps, she thought, as Ruprecht once said to me over my treatment of Alfried, I've been beyond despair and am delighted to taste it again. In a horrible yet an exciting way she could visualize herself confiding in Hubertus, as once she had confided in the man Luthmann; all her scorn of her way of life and the defeats of the war might find satisfaction in such inexcusable behaviour; as if she might reach 'rock bottom' and start again if she went down deep enough.

For his part, Ruprecht, completely deceived, believed himself vindicated as never before. He felt warmth for Carin because he perceived for the first time since it had happened that it was not they who had betrayed Alfried but this creature, sinuous and empty, who had interfered in a quite innocuous plan and thereby ensured disaster and false guilt. By having betrayed Alfried, whose friend he had become, Hubertus had moved a step nearer towards destroying Ruprecht himself – and thus exonerated him. Therefore he might now hate him as others hated and distrusted the Jews. He would give him no change at all; and he suspected that Carin might soon get rid of him.

In that infinitesimal moment, insufficient even for the first syllable of a spoken word, each of them became more comfortable and relaxed, sure of their findings. All three leaned back upon new and fateful conclusions, becoming as politic and careful in their speech as in their physical attitudes.

As Hubertus explained that he had had a letter from his father in which the 'old man' had hinted that Alfried was now almost certainly a Himmler protégé – a V.I.P. prisoner singled out for preservation – neither Ruprecht nor Carin betrayed more than the most social interest.

Easily, for perhaps half an hour, they talked on into the winter's twilight. Beyond the window, a massive moon, the colour of bonfires, rose and lay upon the flat horizon. Night birds stirring restlessly in the windbreaks of pine surrounding the front of the house whistled their first hunting calls as Hubertus, growing uneasy, left them with a yawn. They turned to watch him as, with a thudding heart, he ascended the staircase to take his bath before dinner.

Chapter 10

The Baron was arrested in his pyjamas on the night of the twenty-second of August, 1944, in Bonn; exactly a month after the failure of Count von Stauffenberg's attempt to slay Adolf Hitler by depositing a bomb beneath the map table in the Wolfsschanze Lagerbaracke.

It was a hot night and Nicholas had been sleeping soundly. He dressed slowly in the bedroom of the small flat he had been using as a headquarters ever since Hohenheim's group had succeeded in contacting those acting with Stauffenberg.

While he put on his clothes, two of the Gestapo men guarded the door and a third stood with his back to a blacked-out window which overlooked the Rhine. When he was ready they handcuffed him and he walked down the stairs with them into the placid moonlight. Across the road a car waited by the river parapet beyond which the water was as black as polished marble; blacker and brighter than the car on which the moonlight gleamed. It picked out faces, weapons, the steel of the handcuffs and the metal strap of Nicholas's wristwatch. A few people, all men, were going home at the time. There was a group of three singing a little drunkenly down the road; and on the other side of the Rhine, wide and relatively shallow at this point, some others shouted across the surface to them, as if they had recognized peace in the singing.

The engine was started and Nicholas got into the back between two of the Gestapo. They ignored him and smoked continuously, one of them using Gauloise cigarettes, so that every now and again, as he nodded on the long drive to Berlin, he was reminded of Carin. He had been a fool, he supposed, to ignore her earlier warning given him in the drawing-room of the Berlin flat.

'I thought at first I might give you a fright, Nicholas,' she had said in that February, 'but it was too dangerous to confide in a third party. Surely the fact that, though I was in Rastenburg, I knew so much of your plans, should be sufficient to make you abandon them?'

'You have seen Ruprecht?'

'Not for months and months.'

'He wrote to you, then?'

He heard again her laughter: 'Now you know my rule with my men when they marry, Nicholas. I was never immoral. I leave them to their little wives.'

'Who gave you all this information?'

'You did, most of it. The rest was simply a matter of asking questions. I'm a woman, you know. We need only very little to go on. You're too old for conspiracy, it's like passion: men have to be born to it.'

He had looked round the room in which he was penned with her.

'In any case, it's too late,' he had said.

'It's not too late for you to save yourself and Leo. Let me get into touch with Keitel when I return to East Prussia.'

'You must be mad.'

'Not madder than you, ready to sacrifice everything you've worked for at Schönform.'

'You imagine that I would betray my friends?'

'Is it so very different from your betrayal of Waitzmann, your friend Wilhelmina's son?'

'I did not betray him, Carin!'

'Are you sure, Nicholas? Quite sure?'

His captors were talking. There was an air-raid in progress over Cologne, so they would leave the Autobahn and circle the city on the rotten dirt roads of the countryside. In ten minutes they would draw up to eat sandwiches. The Baron von Hoffbach might get out to empty his bladder.

'I may stretch my legs a little?'

'It is forbidden.'

'Come now, how many guns have you between you?'

'If you wish to take a walk then you must be accompanied.'

'But my dear fellow, it's the proximity of your men that I wish to avoid.'

The senior man, dark-cheeked and haggard, stared at him. 'You realize, Herr Baron, that if you attempt to escape you will not be shot?'

It had been a little too obvious, perhaps, Nicholas thought, but a good idea just the same.

'There's to be a trial?' he asked.

'The People's Court.'

'I said a trial, not a public denunciation.'

'You will be tried by the People's Court in Berlin.'

'In that case you will give me ten minutes to myself in the open. I'm a countryman. You have my word that I shall not embarrass you by attempting to escape.'

'You cannot escape.'

'You realize that I could have shot myself while I was dressing? My revolver was inside a shoe.'

'We know that suicide is forbidden by the rules of your organization. You are the last on the list, Herr Baron.'

'Ah.'

When they drew up they all got out and separated a little, as if they had been in convoy: each man standing apart from his neighbour to micturate in privacy. The Baron walked up and down the road as he had promised. He imagined that he was in command, that they were his staff officers returning from a conference in the field. The billet was not far off; tomorrow the battle; and this time, not Ypres but the Don basin or the country round the Pripet marshes. This time the historic enemy was in sight, the mechanized hordes from the East, the barbarian. 'I must die well,' he decided. 'Quietly, with all the humility my pride gives me. At the trial before that bounder, Freissler, in the People's Court, I shall, as they say, hold my peace. I shall make only one request: a firing squad.'

He took his last look at the countryside: some acres of oats, a dark village in the distance, a shoulder of pine forest, black beneath the moon.

In the car, despite his handcuffs, he smoked a cigar. The senior policeman extracted his case for him from his breast pocket, struck the match and lighted it. He tried to talk to them of their families, of the progress of the war and the air raids, of the future of Germany. But they were sour and cautious and he soon gave up.

'They've gone,' he realized. 'They are no longer here. No one can reach them. They are men; they are my fellow countrymen. One of them, by his accent, is certainly a Bavarian. He might well have been round Schönform with his wife on a Sunday tour: the muniment room, the great hall, the chapel; glad to shake the hands of all of us until we betrayed them.'

He had been wise to avoid returning to Schönform after that last visit in February. He had not compromised them all too badly. Wilhelmina and Alexandra certainly would be safe, Leo too, still in France. He had even fewer fears for Ruprecht, presumably still high in the Führer's favour, than for Carin. They both knew how to look after themselves and Ruprecht certainly had cause for an old personal grievance. Nicholas's attempt to 'rescue' him had come too late to redress the influence of those earlier discussions when he himself had been carried away by the rotten Hohenzollern dream of European supremacy. 'Yes, yes,' he saw, 'while there's still time, death's the answer for us. If they remember us, they'll remember that too.'

The paving stones of the execution block at Plötzensee had at one time been part of the Wilhelmstrasse. They were coffee-coloured and on first seeing them on the morning of his transfer from the Lehrterstrasse prison, after his trial before the People's Court, Doctor Ronald Freissler presiding, the Baron believed he recognized them. There were windows in the corridor leading to his cell and these threw barred rectangles of sunlight on to the rectangular stones, showing that they were still wet from their morning's hosing.

He walked carefully, the Gestapo escort behind him, the warder clicking along in front. When the cell door was thrown open he saw that the stones continued into it and that they too had been freshly hosed down. There was a chair and a table but no bed and no window, only an electric light bulb above the door behind a cage of galvanized wire. The warder switched on the light after he had closed the door and then, speaking softly to the Gestapo men, walked back down the corridor, his voice growing louder as their footsteps receded.

Nicholas sat down at his table and looked at the somehow familiar stone stretching uninterruptedly to the brown painted walls and the varnished door. A shallow pool had collected in the centre of nearly every stone, where, over the years, the crystals of rock had flaked away. Around the margins of the pools there were even shallower terraces of stone, and beyond these, ring upon ring, to the edges, shallower ones still; as if each, while still molten, had borne an enormous finger-print. In the corner by the door, where the mark on the wall paint suggested there had once been a bed, the stones were just as evenly worn; but four fresher hollows surrounded by white chisellings, showed that the bed had only recently been removed. The stones, he now realized, were similar in colour to those of the pavements in Weimar Berlin, before the building of the new Chancellery, when they had been replaced by moulded concrete; and they were similar, too, to the stones of the Schönform vault where lay the bodies of his parents and their forebears.

During the trial, Dr Freissler, at one point, had said, 'We and Christianity, von Hoffbach, have only one thing in common, we demand the whole man.' This remark he had made as an aside so that only Nicholas might hear it. He had then smiled at him so quickly that to anyone else, to the public gallery, to his own court officials, the gesture might have appeared only as the habitual grimace which preceded his other tone, his 'market-shout'; when, his breath constricted in his larynx, then expelled fast, his voice had reached out to the four corners of the room. At the conclusion of the trial he had yelled:

'You with your kind, the traitors of July, have shitted on the Führer's victories, the sacrifices of the Fatherland's sons.' Pause. 'Or should I perhaps say *some* of the Fatherland's sons? Those who, unlike your own by-blow, had to die where they were sent whether they were strong or not.' Pause. 'Rats grow fat! Rats look after themselves whether they are old or young. An old rat is just as dangerous as a young rat.' Pause. 'Sometimes more dangerous.' Pause. 'Herr Baron, you dirty old lecher, hold up your trousers.' Pause. 'This court needs no proof of your virility: no further proof of your guilt.'

Nicholas held up his trousers now as he walked the stones of the cell. It came into his head that at some time he had heard that hanged men died with passion, looking as if they had been about to make love. There was, he had remarked, no bed in the cell. He would not be able to hold up his trousers as he died. Since there was no bed for him it was probable that he would die tonight, and that these reflections were to be his last on earth. What an exaltation they begot; that image of man, of an aristocrat, hanging without even the trousers of a felon; the declaration of the régime experienced at first-hand, the satanic absurdity of it.

From this great distance he now prayed for and blessed his son Leo and blessed his own approaching death. 'I may have lapsed from the brightness of my youth when the world and my faith seemed so full of promise,' he thought. 'But please God, I may yet make a good preparation for the old age I'm foregoing. Under the circumstances these moments may do the trick; for my soul and my house if not for my country.'

Kneeling by his table he prayed, with intermissions, throughout the remainder of the day.

At nightfall the S.S. officer on duty entered his cell and told him that he had an hour in which to make his final dispositions and communicate with his next-of-kin.

'Is there any likelihood of such a document reaching its destination?' Nicholas asked him.

'That depends on to whom you address it.'

'I shall address it to my business parter and friend, the Frau Kommerzienrat Waitzmann. I haven't seen her for many months – as your torturers knew. But she is at present living in my castle of Schönform and I wish to appoint her my executrix.'

'It will not be my decision.'

'Then there's little point in my writing.'

'I've been instructed to tell you that a signed confession of your treason is the best way of ensuring the delivery of any letter.'

'As a postscript? So that it may be cut off for the Reichsführer's files and be incorporated in as many lies as he cares to leave behind him? A magnificent legacy for my son in the Wehrmacht and for his heirs.'

'If you wish to add such a confession as a postscript you may do so.' The S.S. man paused. 'I should also warn you perhaps that all your conversation will be repeated to my superior, Captain Maisler.'

'I don't believe in postscripts.'

'That is your affair. You've one hour.'

'I may have the handcuffs removed while I write my letter?'

'It is forbidden. This afternoon one of your number succeeded in killing himself. You too might weaken and try to do the same.'

'Leave the pencil and paper,' Nicholas commanded.

He therefore had to write on the paper with both hands at the same time, finding it easiest to clasp the right with the left as if the pencil had been a chisel and the paper a tablet of stone on which, with all his might, he were carving out his last words so that they might endure. When he was half-way through the letter he heard the sound of footsteps coming up the corridor, the tread of four or more men marching fast. His hands trembled so much that he lifted them from the surface of the table as he worked; but the detail passed his door, marching on down the stone gallery with a ringing of keys and chains to some cell farther along his landing. He heard the giving of the command to halt, the door of the cell being unlocked, a sound as clean as the opening of a rifle breech; he heard the order to the prisoner to step out and the slower crescendo of the marchers returning. At some distance the prisoner shouted out in an old voice:

'Walküre here! Long live the Fatherland.'

'Sigard! von Hoffbach here. God be with you!'

'And with you, Nicholas Leopold.'

'Silence!' ordered the guard.

'Long live our sacred Germany!' shouted the Baron.

'Silence!'

'Good night, and God bless you,' came the Prince Hohenheim's voice.

'For the last time, *silence*!'

'Good night, and God with us.'

'Good night.' A pause as the distance increased and then once more, strongly, the old man called out: 'Good night.'

'Good night,' said Nicholas, alone again as, at the far end, a door closed and the sounds resolved once more into total silence. Stiff with terror: the dread of the man he would see, a sudden knowledge that even Hitler himself was not his executioner, he completed his letter. He waited now as he had learned to wait for all emotions to pass, praying inexpertly, until once again he heard the approach of the detail and, with relief, stood up to face the open door.

Between his guards he descended three flights of steel stairs, bright with use, to the basement. Along the broad passage to the execution chambers came the sound of several voices, of a general activity being carried on no less noisily than if it had issued from a repair gang at work in a cathedral. The passage was well lighted by bulbs set into the ceiling at regular intervals. They illuminated the white-washed walls and a scarlet line painted at shoulder height down the length of the passage. The embrasures of the doors, too, were numbered in scarlet and there were scarlet admonitions on the opposite wall:

ENTRY FORBIDDEN
ALL PASSES TO BE SHOWN
S.S. AND S.D. PERSONNEL ONLY

In room 3, high-ceilinged and dazzling with light from photo floods on stands, the Prince Hohenheim's body, pink as a baby's, hung suspended by brass piano wire from a butcher's hook in one of the beams. The grey trousers lay telescoped about his ankles over an upturned stool. His face, swollen as a bursting plum, the veins ruptured in the cheeks and nose, looked through its engorged eyes over his right shoulder – gazing upwards as if at some astonishing sun. Below his hips, his wrinkled white hands hung meekly.

The Baron looked at the young S.S. man beside the mounted camera facing the body.

'You are taking photographs?'

'It is the Führer's orders.'

'*Moving* pictures?'

Behind him, Captain Maisler interrupted in the same impartial tone of voice: 'It is the express wish of the Führer that all the July traitors should be photographed at the moment of death.'

The Baron smiled. At this astonishing uniformity, never before encountered, his smile curled his mouth quite involuntarily: a response not of merriment but of extreme realization, as if he were gazing at his first monster, a creature in whom the special comedy of the flesh itself defeated the satanic principle. The captain saw and mistook his reaction; imagining it to be less than the detached insult it was, believing it to be only a personal mockery of himself and his office, he tensed with rage.

'It's not an easy death,' he said. 'It's not quick. A snapshot would not suffice.'

'But you will hang me also?'

'Not hang you, von Hoffbach, your friends are not being hanged. The Führer's orders are that you are all to die by strangulation.'

'I may pray?'

'Two minutes, please.'

Nicholas had recourse to the Memorare, the prayer of his Faith reputed to sunder mountains, to unite a man with his mother, with all mankind, through the wholly human Mother of God: the Jewess whose flesh He had taken for His own: 'Remember O most Gracious Virgin Mary,' he prayed, 'that never has it been known that anyone who has sought thy intercession, implored thy aid or flown to thy protection, has been left unaided. Inspired with this confidence I fly to thee, O Virgin of virgins, my mother. To thee I come, before thee I stand, sinful and sorrowful. O mother of the Word Incarnate, despise not my petition, but of thy clemency hear and grant it.'

A metre from the body of his friend he mounted the low stool beneath the hook. His wrists were secured behind his back, his ankles tied beneath his fallen trousers and the noose was placed round his throat. Extra floodlamps were switched on, the camera was focused and set in motion. Before the wire was tightened by the man on the stepladder beside him Nicholas looked at Maisler standing in front of the closed door.

'My last request, Herr Captain, that you allow me to kick away the stool myself?'

'If you can, Herr Baron.'

'If I can,' said Nicholas.

He turned to his executioner: 'Ready!'

Just before the noose was tightened he drew in his breath. He felt the wire whip into his flesh, he thanked God for his weight, little diminished by four weeks of skilful torture, for his heavy bones, his paunch, his thick, obedient muscles. He leapt up high from the stool, nearly hitting his head on the hook just above; and came down like an ox, neatly subluxating his neck; dying nearly instantly and without great agony.

Nearly seven months passed before a copy of Nicholas's letter reached its destination. Each word of it had been studied at R.H.A. Berlin – the nerve centre of the S.S. and S.D. – and photostats had been taken for further study and any necessary action by one of half-a-dozen of Himmler's immediate subordinates. It was a clerk in one of these offices, a man whose father had worked in the Waitzmann colour kitchens for many years during the directorship of the Frau Kommerzienrat, who smuggled the copy out at Christmas time and after some further delay posted it in the collecting box adjoining the West Kreuz Station.

Now, in early March, 1945, on a morning black with rain,

when the Baron's 'rotten box' was at last collapsing, Wilhelmina in her Schönform bedroom waited for Alexandra to come in and read the letters handed to her only five minutes earlier by Maria.

Alexandra had taken to wearing grey: old clothes kept from her training days in Berlin with the buttons changed and the badges removed. With the coats and skirts she wore grey flannel hats round as a schoolgirl's and large ankle-boots lined with synthetic fur. In these, so prudently conserved against the rationing, she went coldly about the castle and the farm with Wilhelmina and the servants, organizing its quota of refugees.

As the American General Patton's Third Army struck ever deeper into the Reich the number of homeless steadily increased. The bombed out, the liberated from camps and prisons, fugitives from the West, the East and the North, fled like fire-crazed herds to the shrinking but still safe territory in the South. Already more than forty women, children and old men were quartered in the barn and every day added to their number.

At first Alexandra had been appalled. She had appealed to Ruprecht on one of his flying visits from the factory, which in extreme discomfort he was now administering from the cellars of the house.

'Whatever are we to do?'

'Do? Hand-pick them, of course. Take them in whilst it's still a matter of choice.'

She followed him along the corridor to the ice-cold bathroom. 'But Schönform isn't ours. With poor Nicholas dead –'

'You've written to Carin and Leo?'

'Three times.'

'Then watch the posts; and in the meantime, take the people in, the strongest first. That is my policy in the town.'

'But it's the weak ones who are so pathetic.'

He was throwing off his expensive, dirty clothes, his smooth-skinned body steaming in the cold air.

'It's the greedy ones we have to consider,' he told her.

'Last night, for instance, my cousin Ilse arrived at the factory. She looked like a gypsy crone, disgusting. She'd thumbed lifts all the way down from Oppenheim with a case in her hand, and wanted to put up with us indefinitely.'

Alexandra stared at him with ardent astonishment. 'Really!'

'Yes, really.' He took off his shoes and socks and stood before her in his dusty black trousers, naked to the waist. 'She inherited a fraction of the share capital and in the old days was always badgering Mama about her rights. I said nothing about Mama's whereabouts; but I took her in and there she sits like an old spider in my cellar counting her gold. Every time the woman moves she drops a coin or a brooch.'

'But you did take her in, Liebling?'

'Of course, what else could I do? But understand that Ilse is an exception. In general you should take in only the fittest. Later they drive the dangerous and the greedy away.'

'But Wilhelmina thinks –'

'I've already spoken to Mama. We, the Waitzmann Group, will pay the bills later if the Americans don't do it for us. In the meantime the best way to protect our property is to organize the refugees. Turn them into small private armies against the swine and the looters who will inevitably follow.'

'But Schönform isn't our property.'

He looked at her blackly. 'Isn't it? Do you realize that Nicholas was up to his neck in my debt when he died?'

'But, Liebling!'

'It's beside the point. I'm not interested in Schönform at the present; but this is a war we can't lose. If we're clever, all of us will be richer at the end of it than we were at the beginning. It's a question of property and ideology only.'

'I don't understand you,' said Alexandra sadly.

'Of course you don't. But you will later. Darling, you really must go. I want to take off my trousers and have a bath.'

'You'll be staying to dinner?'

'No, I have to get back to the factory.'

'But your cousin Ilse. Don't you think that you ought to tell her where Mama is? She'd be so much more comfortable out here with us.'

'Certainly not. And don't tell Mama about her at all. I'm doing all that is necessary, and, incidentally, I'm charging Cousin Ilse for it. She's lived off the firm for years and gold never rusts. It's as popular with the American as with the Russian.'

'When will you be back again?'

'Soon, soon.' He kissed her. 'Now go, please. Go and make your plans to fill the farm with refugees; but select them carefully. Within three months this business will be over and then the bargaining is going to start.'

She had obeyed him, finding to her surprise that her training in obstetrics had given her an authority which got results in the quite different purposes for which she now had to use it. The people obeyed the sad-faced, hesitant young wife of the Herr Direktor implicitly. Individually they went absorbedly about the business of survival, being as obedient at meal-times in the big barns as at the occasional confinements in the other outbuildings, now hastily converted into dwellings. From among their number Alexandra appointed leaders, deputies, to whom she gave orders each morning at eleven o'clock after she had taken coffee with her mother-in-law. She had even found Wilhelmina a secretary, a war widow from Bergedorf who had once worked in the Waitzmann typing pool. She was an experienced book-keeper and kept note of every pfennig expended on 'the Emergency'; so that later, the Frau Kommerzienrat might know how much she owed Leo and Carin for the hospitality she was extending on their behalf. She moved now about the castle and the farm as formerly she had walked about her factories: a black-dressed woman with white hair, striding like a long-legged man, her stick swinging about in front of her.

'It's like the old days,' she told Alexandra. 'When there was a struggle to keep them in work and ourselves in pocket.'

'You are happy, Grossmutter?'

'Not happy; but I'm busy again. It's good after so long to want to work. And what is more, between us we're saving a baby or two. Isn't that so?'

'Oh yes, there have already been three confinements – quite normal ones.'

'There are more?' asked Wilhelmina eagerly.

'Two, quite near. So many of these poor women are starting their labour early after the dreadful things they've suffered.'

'That is good, good,' repeated Wilhelmina. 'The more babies we can rescue the better. Germany is going to need them. I've a little superstition that if we save enough then I might see my Alfried again.'

On entering the big bedroom over the south side of the courtyard, Alexandra kissed her.

'Six letters,' said Wilhelmina. 'And one of them crackles as if it were official. It feels like one of those Gestapo communications we've had in the past.'

Alexandra caught her breath. 'Which one, Grossmutter?'

'There, there, on the top.'

Alexandra tore open the flimsy envelope clumsily and took out the photostat. 'It's from Nicholas.'

'Nicholas? Not Alfried? It's not about Alfried?'

'It's Nicholas's last letter to you, Grossmutter. It was written months ago.'

Frau Waitzmann sat back in her chair, she crossed herself and sat upright again. 'What are the words? What does he tell me?'

But Alexandra could not reply for a moment. She was seeing isolated words. The sense of the page, quite independently of its consecutive sentences, was irradiating her like heat or light. She could not weep. She could scarcely breathe. The gross handwriting, the unsteady signature at the end, pale photographs as they were, bound her like ropes.

'Please, dear, if you can,' begged Frau Waitzmann.

Alexandra began to read:

My dear friend,

The day has been dark and rainy. I have been given permission to instruct an executrix and with gratitude I request you to accept that appointment. I have been told to be brief as I am to be executed within the hour – and not, I understand, by the firing squad I demanded as my right of rank at the trial.

The Prince von Hohenheim zu Godesburg has already gone. Greet for me, I beg you, his noble widow and tell her that despite his infirmities he called out strongly to me as he passed my door. Pray see Father Guardini for us about Masses and instruct him that I wish my body, if later obtainable, to be placed beside those of my mother and father. Their catafalques are on the newer ledges at the far end of the vault and are clearly inscribed.

Embrace my son Leo for me on his return. Also my wife, Carin, whose whereabouts are at present unknown to me. Tell Leo that my will – made last year – is in the safe keeping of the family lawyer in Munich.

And now, my dear friend, accept my adieux in that Faith which neither of us wholly betrayed. Greet for me your son Ruprecht Alöis. Tell him that I entrust him with the single codicil which I must now add to my will:

Amongst the many matters which I was unable at the time to confide in you or in any of your family, I learned that the authorities at the camp which supplies the factory's labour needs were burying their victims on my land. Tell Ruprecht and my own son, Leo, it is my desire that in that part of the gravel beds in my forest of Schönform where these victims are laid to rest, a very high oaken cross be erected as soon as the conditions of time permit, with the following inscription:

Here lie from three hundred to five hundred Christians and Jews. May God have mercy on their souls and on their murderers.

Kiss Alexandra for me and your grandson, Nikolaus Ruprecht. Ask them always to pray for me.

In steadfast affection,

Nicholas Leopold von Hoffbach.

Chapter 11

On the morning of the second of May, in the house in the Schellenstrasse, Kommandant Grunwald and his wife Gudrun prepared to carry out the suicide they had planned after the collapse of Rundstedt's offensive in the Ardennes. Hubertus had tried over and over again to dissuade them from such 'a ghastly decision'; but they had not listened to him; or rather, with some satisfaction, they had. During those final months of increasing raids and the horrors of the Russian advance into the Eastern sector of the city, they had argued the point for hours on end all over the house at every end and turn of the disrupted days of that period. Hubertus, on indefinite leave from the Ministry, was supposed to be working on a cultural history of National Socialism for Dr Goebbels; and his father had encouraged him in this.

'Normality,' he had said. 'Under the circumstances it's the only thing. I'm delighted that the Reichsminister should be so consistent. He's obviously a dedicated man. And what's more, he sees you, Hubertus. He understands you.'

'God! Father, it was only a bribe to get rid of me. Ever since I tipped him off about the von Hoffbachs months ahead of the Stauffenberg putsch and was ignored, he's found me an inconvenience. I know these things.'

But the Kommandant had kept this all to himself. Refusing to become involved in these tricky arguments, he had pursued his own policy of normality to the end, determined that whoever ultimately took over the city should find him officially beyond reproach. If the prison should continue to escape major damage from shelling, then whether Russian, American or Anglo-Saxon, the 'new authority' would find it in good order: the files straight, the survivors in reasonable shape and the staff well-disciplined. It did not worry him in the least that he himself would not be there to 'hand over'; and it did not worry Gudrun. Apart from the question of Hubertus, their only concern had been the timing. It had to be right; and, as he had so often said during those hasty meals in the kitchen or in the long nights in the brightly lighted cellar, 'Something will turn up. We'll be given the hint. So long as the Führer's alive he'll remember those who've remembered him.' Gudrun had agreed. 'An astonishing woman,' he reminded himself, repeating it too to Hubertus, many times: 'Your mother's an astonishing woman. She has unexpected resources.'

And Hubertus had agreed too that he loved her and that she was astonishing. Without noticing it himself he had ceased referring to her as 'Musch' and now called her 'Mother', always. She had taken on a new lease of life and he found it galling that there was nobody to whom he could tell this. He would have loved to have had his friends back again: Carin, Alexandra, even Waitzmann Junior, so that he could have explained this change to them, saying, 'My mother's amazing. She's taken on a new lease of life. Ever since she and my father decided that they'd die for the Reich, she's become a new woman. She's a wife to him again, and a mother to me.'

But there was no one to tell. Everyone was scattered all over the place. Berlin was like a barrack brothel under fire from the enemy; and everyone who could do so had left it months ago. Hubertus could not leave. His friend, Dr Hans Hagen, who had gone to Bayreuth in October to work on a thesis entitled 'The National Socialist Guidance Question', had written to him several times asking him to join him while there was still time; but Hubertus had always declined by return of post and at considerable length, spelling curiously as ever:

I can't, dearest Hans. God knows it would appeal to me to be buried down there with you in creative work while the churches tople and the gods wrestle with our Nazi youth in the smoking streets. But this place draws me. The artist in me has only to put his nose outside the door for my whole soul to be filled with life and death. It's a masterbation of the spirit to be here in these latter days. The streets swarm with prostitutes. All Berlin has become a brothel. Every woman of seventy or under is preparing to take off her knickers for a carrot or a turnip. It's a city of women and old men and boys with the Russian at the gates, and even at the risk of my life I must stay, as the Führer stays, to see it thru'. Thru' to what? I don't know. But if I emerge unscathed, as I feel I will, I shall be a living flame. I compare myself to Shadrek and the other two who danced in the flames. I shall have Matterial.

But even to so close a friend he did not confess his other conflicts. An artist has to keep some of his processes to himself, he believed. He can't really, at this stage, explain to anyone about his parents and his feelings for them, because he doesn't really know what they are himself.

His mother had become so very elegant. Now, at last, she used all her hoarded clothes; appearing each morning in a new white blouse with a black skirt, each evening in some dated dinner-dress of her Nuremberg period. Chaste and clean, with her shining hair parted in the middle and coiled over her ears, she would preside over the coffee-watches in the cellar. She had re-taken to cooking again, too; serving them as nearly as possible the food of her own girlhood: country dishes of offal, mounds of sauerkraut helped out with steamed nettle and nutmeg in place of pepper. She had uncovered for them a secret hoard of old tins and bottled meat-balls which she had put by in 1939, priding herself on her foresight and the efficiency of her methods. There were jars of beetroot in home-made vinegar, a little black at the top, still good at the bottom, of apple-pulp and sliced aubergines, sealed boxes of dried apricots, prunes and apple-rings buried in miller's bran.

She smiled often to herself in her kitchen and went humming about the house. In the mornings when the Kommandant was at the prison, Hubertus helped her with the housework and then went off on a foraging expedition with the ration cards and a round basket. He charmed the tradesmen and cajoled the bitter Berlin women. At night he robbed vegetable gardens discreetly or visited the black markets where it was still possible to trade in a silver spoon or two for measures of flour or lard.

But always in the end he returned home to keep a watch on everything, to prepare himself for his next probe on his parents' feelings.

The argument over their impending death-pact developed quite slowly. There was no particular occasion on which it could have been said to have begun. It was rather a climate in the house, like one of those family jokes whose beginnings are often obscure, an attitude born of dozens of remarks which in themselves had been nearly innocuous. But now it was as much a fact as an approaching wedding or a holiday journey; and Hubertus was as horrified and fascinated as if they had both developed cancer. He could not, as the Kommandant so often said, 'drop the subject'.

If at news-time in the cellar they themselves started to talk politics without reference to their own plans Hubertus would attack them at once, asking, 'What difference does it make what the Russian does? Or the American? Why are you so interested when you won't be here to take part in it? And what about me?'

'Hubertus, pass your mother another cup of coffee. I'll not have you upsetting her again.'

'He doesn't upset me, Felix. He only upsets himself.'

'Well, himself then. The whole question devolves upon the Führer, upon his official attitude. Whatever happens, we must continue to take our lead from the top. At this stage we must be concerned only with what we have done today and propose to do tomorrow, *not* in six months nor the month after that.'

'We must have faith,' said Gudrun, 'as we did when we were young.'

'But *I'm* young!' shouted Hubertus. 'How can I have faith when I know that you two are going to shoot yourselves if the Bolshevik takes over Berlin?'

'You should work,' said his father. 'Follow my example, Hubertus. Get on with your writing so that come what may, you'll leave something behind you.'

'It's by what we've done that we shall be judged,' said

his mother, 'when the Tartars destroy the city and deflower our German women.'

'*If* they destroy and *if* they deflower et cetera', the
Kommandant corrected her.

'What the hell does it matter?' cried Hubertus. 'If we're
all going to be corpses? Who cares whether a corpse is
virgin or not? And what's the good of having worked if the
damned democracies are going to let Jewish Bolshevism
destroy it all?'

They composed themselves to sleep, one on one bunk and
one on another; and Hubertus, defying the air-raids and
occasional Red Army salvoes falling in the distance, went
off on a tour of the cellar-bars, not returning until the
following morning when things, for once, were relatively
quiet. The Kommandant had gone off to the prison and he
found his mother resting alone on her bed, composed and
lush-looking. Grey-green as he was after so many foul
drinks and cups of malt coffee, he started into the attack
immediately. 'You can't do this thing to me, Mother! You
can't! You're all I've got.'

'What thing, dear?'

'You've trapped me. You face me with an excruciating
decision.'

'As your father says, you must have faith. It mayn't be
necessary.'

'I could kill him,' said Hubertus. 'How dare he threaten
you, my own mother, after all these years?'

'He's not threatening me. Nobody is, Hubertus.'

'So you're not going to kill yourself?'

'Not necessarily.'

'Mother, answer me. If the war's lost, if the Führer
demands it and father shoots himself, will you die with
him?'

'I am his wife.'

'Well, that's it then. You are going to. You put me in an
impossible position, Mother.'

She lay smiling at him with shining eyes. 'I know!' she
said; and he saw the comfortable movements of her arms
beneath the coverlet. He flung himself across her. 'Mother,

283

I know I've been a disappointment; but you're all I've got. You can't go on torturing me like this.'

She did not embrace him as he lay there with his grubby-nailed hand clutching her big shoulder. If he could have seen her face he would have seen that it was as greedy as someone holding back a caress until the last possible moment; but his own eyes were screwed up like a child's. 'It's unfair!' he was sobbing, over and over again. 'It's unfair!'

She took fire from his grief. His shaking body moved her supremely. She had a vision of herself as a matron-heroine, a sudden idea that these moments might be historical in the larger sense and that she was not doing them justice. She sat up and made him sit up too. She confronted him with small burning eyes as she had done in his guilty infancy.

'Unfair?' she asked. 'Would you rather see your father and myself executed by the Bolsheviks?'

Hubertus blinked. He had always resented his mother's taking over of his own scenes; and it was so long since she had attempted it that he was even more nonplussed than usual.

'Executed?' he repeated foolishly. 'By the Bolshevik?'

'Yes, tortured and executed as we would be by the minions of the Jews, either Russian or American.'

'But they can't execute everyone. There are too many of us. You can't eliminate a race!'

She was suffused with nobility. 'And what about *our* Jews?' she asked.

'Our Jews?'

'You know, Hubertus! You know! So do I and so does your father. In five years we've eliminated them. In Germany there are none.'

'But that was different.'

'Of course it was; but do you imagine that our enemies will see that, our Jewish enemies? And who do you think they will hunt down first? Anyone who has had anything to do with the Führer's measures, anyone who remained loyal to his vision.'

'But we've had nothing to do with it, directly. Father's a

prison specialist, that's all. He's been a Kommandant for years and is still one. They can't accuse him of anything.'

'An eye for an eye,' she said.

'Why, it's on the record, he wouldn't even go to the camps. It would have meant more money; but . . .'

'A tooth for a tooth!'

'Stop it!' shrieked Hubertus. 'Listen to me, Mother. We're safe! This is all your imagination. We can burn things, but we don't need to. Father's record could clear him. We could hide, wait and hide, and then help *them*!'

'Not imagination,' she said. 'Oh, dear me, no! I may have lapsed from the Jewish-inspired religion of my youth; but I haven't forgotten it. Did you ever hear this, Hubertus? "And the sins of the fathers shall be visited upon the children unto the third and fourth generation".'

Though he was looking at her he could scarcely see her. She had ceased to be his mother. She was an oracle, suddenly, a voice speaking out of the peculiar German past. Though he did not know it, he was at this moment fulfilling an earlier intuition of his father's: that moment when the Kommandant had seen his wife standing between Hubertus and the prisoner Alfried Waitzmann.

'Children?' he said. 'You mean *me*! This is the end of home.'

'Facts are facts, Hubertus. We can't escape them. Children have to grow up, parents to die.'

What a room it was, Hubertus was seeing, what a moment! He felt as if she had suddenly cut the cord with her own hand; the 'artist' in him was correlating a thousand impressions; those recent meals of her girlhood when so often, as she served them, she had said: 'This is what we ate at home in the Black Forest – this is a country dish.' In a few months she had relived the whole of her marriage for them: the Missionary dresses, the later Nuremberg styles, the stuffy, suggestive, honeymoon nightdresses of the once new century; and now, his own birth.

He could not bear her satisfaction any longer. He stood up.

'It's guilt, not loyalty, Mother darling,' he said. 'You and Father are impelled by guilt and it's driving you on to your deaths. My generation knows all about it; but your one doesn't, because you're the last of the pre-Freudians.'

She smiled to herself. 'What long words, Hubertus.'

'And you're trying to frighten me; but you can't, because I don't feel guilty. I've done nothing to the Jews, nothing to anyone. I've simply grown up in this big house, in this city, with my friends – artists – who've done only what they were told to do and believed the same.'

'Well, go then,' she bade him. 'Make your own plans. Don't forget, though, what I've told you today.'

But Hubertus couldn't go. He was beginning to enjoy himself again. It had occurred to him that the thing had possibilities; it was Material. He might even 'do it' when the time came. If he had it 'out' with her he would later be able to write it all down, imperishably, in a letter or a book. If he wrote it down with the possibility of joining them in their death, if he convinced himself that this was his intention as he wrote, then he might be inspired to a unique work; imperishable. But first he must explore their guilt.

In the weeks which followed this conversation he explored the 'big house' of Berlin. His earlier imaginative letters to Hans Hagen were turned into truth as the Red Army, after liquidating General Heinike's army to the North, moved further into the city. Amid the increasing chaos Hubertus led an ever more exultant life, moving about through a landscape which he could not define, 'because of its dynamic qualities'.

'It changes hourly,' he wrote in the journal which was to survive him. 'It's all Dadaism, Surrealism, Cubism and Abstract art in one. Vistars of our wide streets open up overnight in the residential flat-blocks. As I walk or run, the city-scape is changed for me as if I were again a child, full of fire and distruction. How often then did I wish that I might mowe down buildings with my glance or machine-gun passing buses and train windows with my little gun. Now it happens for me. The sky is full of smoke and the air of noise. I am become an apostel of distruction. I only have to wish for a building to colapse for there to be a good chance of it happening.

And the people! We are all one big family taking our chance. We can go into any open door and ascend the stairs to any room. There is no property any longer. A Bolshevism has already been achieved; for we who survive are lords of life and death.

I call on various groups of women of all degrees, all equally dirty and dishevelled. They all manage to get hold of 'sleep-food' and 'rape-money' and will make love at the drop of a hat on a fine bed or a bare floor, being excited by the approach of the Russian.'

But his trips, though frequent, were never prolonged. He was too fascinated and involved in his 'home situation'. No matter how exhilarating his forays and adventures, he always returned to the battered house in the Schellenstrasse in time for the cellar meals which were served, more formally than ever, by Frau Grunwald. Punctually at one o'clock he would bring back his purchases and barters, beet sugar, precious vegetables, small packets of ground lentils. He would put them in the larder, wash his hands and go down to the cellar where his parents would be awaiting him. Afterwards, when they had drunk the ceremonial malt coffee, heated by Frau Grunwald on an old-fashioned table stove which had been among her wedding presents, the Kommandant would return to the prison and Hubertus to his journal:

'Time has been teleskoped for me,' he wrote. 'I am living at a furious pace in the knowledge that I shall be buried with my parents – and simultaneously. An artist has always looked forward to this event, the foreshortening of his life when he too must rejoin them in their coffins who gave him to life; when, as Shakespeare said, "The rest is silence." But in my own case it is for me a curtainty; because I have, after all, a loyalty of the blood and of their guilt, having been feathered in the same nest of dropings in which I was begoten. I have come to see that I owe this to them after all, my death as well as my life; and it is good sense, since, as SHE says, the jews will have no mercy on the least one of us.'

The journal grew longer as the days of late spring lengthened into those of summer.

'What news of the Führer?' wrote Hubertus on the afternoon of April the 30th. 'The wireless in our cellar is silent on this point. I know that my chief is with him in the Führerbunker as the s.s.

are still on duty there. A week ago I made one special visit down that road past the ruins of the Adlon, taking with me my father's binoculars. I observed that a Hauptsturmführer was on inspection and that someone had struck a large potatoe in the ventilator in the top of the tower. It is a pity that it is now too dangerous for me to make a second visit as I have a presentiment over that place, a sence of their voices in the ground, from which eventually the word must come to decide our own hour for us!'

The voice did come, at two or three minutes after ten o'clock on the following evening when they were sitting beneath the low, freshly whitewashed, vaulting of the cellar. The Kommandant had not attempted to visit the Prison that day, as the shells were falling too close. Instead, he had consumed the morning by transferring his entire library to the cellar as a 'reinforcement'.

'Against the bombardment, Felix?'

'Against the bombardment,' he had agreed with a significant smile.

Between the three of them they had built a double wall of print, of calf, morocco and cloth-bound books which completely spanned two sides of the cellar from floor to ceiling. Now, after the evening meal, as Hamburg radio played a recording of Bruckner's Seventh symphony, they sat in silence, the Kommandant reading peckishly from the row of volumes nearest to hand whilst Gudrun, sewing, rocked to the music with her small eyes half-closed.

'We are waiting here,' wrote Hubertus in his last and longest entry. 'It is evening, nightfall. Overhead the gods are lose. The city is wrocking to its doom and the people to its decline. Music sweeps over us, those counterpoints of Bruckner imaged above in the bitter air; those sounds of unimagined tempests and trumpets best caught perhaps by the Führer's favourite composer, Wagner, whose art anticipated this magnificence and majestie. I throw my mind up to the white heavens, to the pure radiance of the Nation's fallen endeavour, where the stars crackle still. I throw my mind down and along through acres of earth to the Führerbunker where those we have followed to this appauling destiny wait likewise for a particular moment to be born.

I am proud at last to have found myself the apatheosis of my parents' generation, feeling thick with the loyalties of death, alive and warm to my Führer and my chief who, even as I write and breathe, might at this moment, less than a mile away, be sharing my emotions and my thoughts.'

But Paul Josef Goebbels had written and breathed his last an hour and a half earlier. Deep below the ground surface the bodies of his six children, the little girls in their best white dresses, lay cooling on their beds, poisoned by injections similar to those given to the Führer's Alsatian dogs. Up above, his own gasoline-drenched body, lying beside that of his wife Magda, smouldered half-consumed in the Chancellery garden, as, in the Kommandant's cellar, the symphony faded into a roll of military drums and the Reichminister's last words were transmitted from Hamburg:

Our Führer, Adolf Hitler, fighting to the last breath against Bolshevism, fell for Germany this afternoon in his operational headquarters in the Reichchancellery.

On April 30th the Führer appointed Grand Admiral Doenitz his successor. The Grand Admiral and successor of the Führer now speaks to the German people.

'Stand!' ordered the Kommandant, dropping his book as he got up.

Frau Grunwald, too, suddenly roused from her hypnotic sewing, swayed slightly on her unaccustomed high heels; Hubertus noted that at first her face was white as the ceiling; but that as the speech progressed her cheeks reddened and thickened religiously.

'It is my first task,' the Grand Admiral said, 'to save Germany from destruction by the advancing Bolshevik enemy.'

'Sit!' said the Kommandant. 'Silence!'

'For this aim alone the military struggle continues,' went on the Grand Admiral. 'As far and as long as the achievement of this aim is impeded by the British and American we shall be forced to carry on our defensive fight against them as well. Under such conditions, however, the Anglo-Americans continue the war not for their own people; but solely for the spreading of Bolshevism in Europe.'

Hubertus sat as if paralysed, not by fear but with excitement. He looked at his noble father – suddenly ennobled by doom – and at his mother, tranquil for the first time in his remembrance of her. The moment was so beautiful that he was quite unable even to consider writing about it. Dead! He kept thinking; but alive now, knowing it all; and no need for words. Death sitting down in our lovely bodies, proud and blanched, letting us know that everything is possible.

His father spoke: 'It is now twenty minutes past ten.'

'And the Führer has fallen,' she said.

'Tomorrow morning at the same hour,' said the Kommandant, 'we too will make our peace with History.'

'Tomorrow morning,' repeated Gudrun, 'the city will fall too.'

'There can be no compromise,' said the Kommandant.

'There will be no compromise,' said his wife.

'Let Doenitz and the others parley with our enemies before opening the gates to them.'

'To the barbarian and the Jew,' added Gudrun. 'Let those traitors speak while they still have their heads to speak with.'

'We shall follow the example of our leaders,' went on the Kommandant. 'And we won't be alone in this decision.'

Hubertus spoke: 'Are there others? Good God! I hadn't thought of that. Of course there will be. Even in death we won't be alone. All over Germany –'

'I received this letter from my chief officer, Halstedt, yesterday morning on my last visit to the prison. Your mother first, Hubertus.'

'I don't want to read it,' she said. 'He may have it. I never liked that man. He was a hypocrite, he bullied his wife and family.'

Hubertus took the letter from his father and read it to himself.

Herr Kommandant, Sir,

I regret my delay in coming to a decision with you over the matter you were good enough to discuss with me at the commencement of the month. I am glad to say that at long last my mind has been properly composed for me and I am now able to tell you and my dear wife and little ones that I shall no longer be a burden to them and their many friends in the future, since I have retained safely the means of our Reichsführer which you distributed.

Having surmounted the rough passage of recent events with the help of so excellent a pilot I now look forward to calmer seas, when with 'God's' help I shall at last reach that honour of which you spoke to me and the rest of the staff. I would like to take this opportunity to send you, your good wife and 'family' the very respectful greetings of one who has shared with you so many trials and tribulations of civil service employment.

Heil Hitler.
Signed Gottlieb Halstedt.

'Why does he put "God" and your "family" in inverted commas?' asked Hubertus. 'It seems like an insult to *me*.'

But neither of his parents answered him, though he noticed that his mother smiled to herself.

'And "the means of our Reichsführer"?' asked Hubertus again. 'What's Halstedt referring to? Did Himmler give you something, Father?'

'Tomorrow, please,' said the Kommandant. 'No questions at the moment, if you don't mind.'

'But I want to know. I've got to know. You forget that I'm young. If I'm going to die in the morning I must know how as well as when. I'm an artist, Father; I can't just die any old way. I've got to select my means and think about it first, like a character out of Dostoyevsky.'

'Tomorrow,' repeated the Kommandant. 'And we shall wear uniform.'

'Father, unless you tell me I'll do something rash.' Hubertus was dancing with excitement. 'I'll kill myself here in front of you both. I won't wait. I can't. You've never understood me. I've been loyal to you both but I've got a different kind of soul and it's got to be considered.'

'Give him his capsule, Felix,' said Gudrun.

The Kommandant took a small black and white pill box out of his pocket and placed it beside the coffee cup on the table. He put on his spectacles, removed the round lid on which a number was stencilled in violet letters; and extracted one of three quite large, translucent, capsules. He handed this to Hubertus, who nested it in his palm, his face cold with emotion. He gazed at it and his parents watched him as intently as if he had been in his infancy again, shining and tremulous over a new present.

But they were as quickly bored and got up together to make up their bunk beds and lie down upon them fully clothed except for their shoes. The Kommandant switched off the main light so that the cellar was now only illumined at Hubertus's end where his father's heavily shaded, Nubian, desk light stood on the little table on which he wrote his journal.

In the city above the street fighting went on. Bombs and shells tore down masonry and disrupted, like rats' nests, whole groups of people crouching in cellars and shelters. Tanks slewed across pavements and butted through half-demolished buildings like metal elephants. The black night blazed with sound; but Hubertus continued his final entry with his capsule sitting on an ash-tray in front of him:

'My parents sleep,' he wrote, 'I watch them from the height of my youth as if I were their father and mother. Their light is out but mine is on. It shines on my hands which are dirty but active, it shines on the capsule of death which I know contains hydro-cyanic acid, the almond poison that is so quick. If I were about to live instead of to die I could make a new philosophy out of this unique situation. In it I have attained completion greater than any son of Oedipus. I now know all that there is to be known of life, poised as I am beneath this growning city, between those who made me and who tomorrow will feed me my milk of death. I am become Art itself, that scrible and daub of hope which speaks of heaven while his feet are in the grave. All my plans are gone from me. I thought I was cuning and full of guile; but now I know that I am too old for the world or philosophy. While my freinds ran on death and many of my freinds died well in the Luftwaffe and Wehrmacht, I was left here alone for this which at last gives me the resolve I never had before. Tomorrow or the next day, when the first living person enters this hole and sees my stretched-out self with his stiff face, he will carry away with him for ever this image of beauty and yongness and accomplished purpose. He will be my mirror of the world in which my own reflection shines as I would have it shine, silent and youthful, older than Art, as are all poets; as was Rilke when he wrote: "Us the most fleeting of all, just once, everything, only for once. Once and no more, and we too once and never again; but this having been once, though only once, having been once on Earth, can it ever be cancelled?" And with these words I close my journal and my life.'

                    Signed. Hubertus Mark Grunwald.'

In these last months Frau Grunwald had been making a soft leather cushion of black-and-white scraps cut from hoarded gloves. She had many pairs left over from the old days, some of them long and buttoned for evening wear and others short. At the beginning of the collapse she had taken a drawerful of them down to the cellar and cut them up into triangles and squares, sewing them together during air-raids in an exact harlequin pattern, with strong black stitches.

Now, on the morning following Doenitz's announcement, as they ate a small breakfast, she had the completed cushion beside her. It lay on a square of tissue paper next to her chair; and she looked at it often.

After the meal, when they all three went upstairs into the empty house with its leaking roof and fallen plaster, she took the cushion with her and put it on her chair in the kitchen whilst she and the Kommandant washed up the breakfast things. Then as soon as this was done she carried it through into her shattered drawing-room and put it in the middle of the sofa, propped against the back. She dusted the drawing-room furniture, brushed away the fragments of the Meissen groups from the mantelpiece and the carpet and drew open the curtains just a little. She swept up the window glass and the fallen plaster, then rattled the stove which she had lighted the night before and opened its doors to warm the room. Ten minutes later, she went upstairs to her bedroom to change for the last time.

The Kommandant had scarcely spoken that morning. He had kept a close eye on the time, constantly glancing at his wristwatch as if everything he did were being assigned to some strict pre-arranged schedule. He disconnected the wireless sets and the telephone, carried a selection of books upstairs to his study and rearranged various photographs in the drawing-room. Then he, too, returned to his bedroom to change into his '14–18 uniform of full Colonel. At ten o'clock he emerged again and went downstairs to the drawing-room where Hubertus was already awaiting him.

Hubertus was wearing the Death's Head uniform which did not belong to him and to which he was not entitled. His father had always suspected that his possession of it had been a transaction of one of his love affairs in the early days of the Régime; and, usually, he objected to his wearing it. But this morning, after a quick glance, he made no reference to it, and Hubertus was a little disappointed. He was burning with pride for his father that morning, seeing him for the first time as a 'Veteran' and finding himself surprised that until now he had never realized that he was himself the son of a soldier. He was in an extraordinary state of mind, in a way apathetic but at the same time seeing everything as if it were enormously larger than life. He no longer resented the clichés of his immediate thought, finding it unnecessary now to go beyond them, saying to himself in this instance: 'But it's true. Life *is* larger than Life.'

He sat on the damp sofa beside his mother's round black-and-white cushion, waiting for her to arrive and complete the family circle. He had stowed his journal beneath his father's bunk in the cellar. The note which he had attached to it requested the finder to take it 'as soon as the war is over, to any reputable publisher, together with my books of poems and the press cuttings of all my articles published for the Ministry of Propaganda'. In addition, he had written a number of letters: one to Carin von Hoffbach, one to Dr Hans Hagen in Bayreuth, a third to Alexandra and a fourth to be conveyed to the commander of the occupying forces, whether Russian, American or British. He had not bothered with the craven French.

He had no very clear idea as to what exactly he had written in each of these letters, they were a composite protestation which, when put together, might add up to some final statement; to emotion and respect for Carin's good breeding, to aesthetic appreciation of his death-pact for Hans Hagen, to a form of apology to Alexandra for the necessary betrayal of Alfried and the Baron. He had hoped, in fact, when writing this particular letter, that it might be read both by the Frau Kommerzienrat and by Ruprecht himself. He had given it a little defiance and much subtlety. Sealed with his death it must surely convince its readers of his 'all-along sincerity'. They would be bound to say: 'He was real. We see now that Hubertus did believe from the beginning.'

But in the just-warm room, with his letters and his journal behind him in time, he was now concerned with the manner of his death. In a few moments his mother would come in and there were questions he had to have answered first.

'Father,' he now asked at last, 'I want to be quite clear that I'm doing this of my own free will. If I chose to walk out now, you and Mother wouldn't reproach me?'

The Kommandant frowned. 'Your mother's late,' he said.

'I know she is. That's why I'm having to talk to you. I could have stood it if she'd been on time; but this is our last chance and there are things you've got to tell me. You owe them to me.'

'You are free to go or stay. You came of age four years ago. Your mother and I no longer have any claims upon you.'

'And you've no doubts about the rightness of our action?'

'None.'

'You realize it's something we can't even regret when once we've done it?'

'I am a soldier.'

'But how do we know we won't regret it *while* we're doing it? Quickly Father, before Mother arrives, tell me; how long does it take?'

'Three seconds.'

Hubertus had his capsule in his hand. He looked at it and asked:

'Are you going to bite yours or swallow it, Father?'

'Be quiet,' said the Kommandant as the door opened.

Frau Grunwald was in her black and white again, low heeled shoes, sensible grey stockings, a thin string of artificial pearls round her neck and a single scarlet rose made of silk pinned to her blouse.

'Well?' she said, as she waited for her husband to kiss her. She moved over to the sofa and Hubertus got up and saluted her hand. They all stood there, hearing for the first time that morning the traffic of the battle for the city.

'It is time, I think,' said Frau Grunwald. 'My capsule if you please, Felix.'

He handed it to her and she sat down upright on the sofa, carefully adjusting her cushion behind her shoulders.

'The stove,' she said to Hubertus. 'Close the doors, please, we don't want a fire.'

'We will recite nothing,' said the Kommandant. 'We shall die as our fellow Germans have died, on the field of battle, on the seas, in the air and under the seas. We shall die as our Führer died, wordlessly, in the face of the enemy we despise.'

'And together!' added Frau Grunwald. 'Hubertus. What is the matter? Why are you so uneasy?'

'I don't know that I can do it. I can't get it straight. I don't want to be hurried like this.'

'I have told him, Gudrun, that he is free to go,' the Kommandant explained.

'No music,' said Hubertus suddenly. 'Nothing, only gun-fire.'

'And isn't that enough? It was sufficient for our Leader and for tens of thousands of our men in this war and the last.'

'Of course he is free to go,' said Frau Grunwald. 'We all are. We are free to be hunted down amidst the ruins of our country by a pitiless Jewish enemy.'

'By the Bolshevist barbarians who will carve up Europe under the flags of the Allies.'

'Father, answer me. Are we doing this because we've lost the war or are we doing it because of the revenge of Judaism?'

But Frau Grunwald answered for her husband. 'We are doing it for our faith, Hubertus. I am only a woman; but *I* do not falter.'

'We're not frightened?' asked Hubertus. 'There's no moment like this; but if there were, one would want to be sure one wasn't doing it because one was frightened,'

'Death isn't frightening to anyone but the coward,' said his mother. 'If you are frightened, Hubertus, you had better leave us.'

'Leave us,' repeated the Kommandant, 'but quickly. In thirty seconds I shall give the final command. You must make up your mind.'

'Make it ten seconds,' said Hubertus as the house shook to a nearby salvo. 'Make it ten and I shan't hesitate. Good-bye, Mother. Kiss me once. Good-bye, Father. It's coming true; I see it now; we'll die together as secretly as we've lived.'

The Kommandant sat down in a big chair. His eyes followed the second-hand of his wrist-watch as it jerked up the face to the hour.

'Now!' he commanded; and with closed eyes they all three slipped their capsules into their mouths.

Hubertus screwed up his eyes tightly. He held the gelatine sphere between his teeth. He stroked it once gingerly with his tongue, waiting for and dreading the first bitter taste. Behind his front teeth, he pressed his tongue far down into the ditch of his lower jaw, waiting for some one essential thought to come into his head before he clenched them. Then, as the seconds went by, he heard his mother's breathing change. He heard his father gasping, they both filled the room with their hunger for air. Someone began to drum on the floor with shoe heels – a spasm of thumping, faster and faster. His mother cried out in a young, unrecognizable voice; a phrase of human sound which was cut back suddenly. Deeply his father groaned, hiccoughing and panting like a sick beast. They whimpered together, tiny travailing noises as in Hubertus's mouth a thread of almond taste, thin as silk, touched his tongue. He spat, he leapt past them blind to the door; out through the hall to the cloakroom tap, spitting all the way, letting no drop of his saliva down his throat before he filled his mouth with running water, over and over again.

He sat down on the lavatory seat, leaning crooked and nauseated against the cistern. The gas, he thought, I must have inhaled a little of the gas, too much. This may be death. He staggered out of the cloakroom. He would not die in the lavatory; it would falsify everything, his notes and letters, his journal. Better the staircase or cellar, anywhere; but not the lavatory or the drawing-room where his parents were still sitting. His legs bandied beneath him and he collapsed at the bottom of the staircase, closing his beautiful eyes, breathing as tormentedly as they had done. It was extremely uncomfortable to lie on a staircase, he found; and he found that he was still thinking fast and clearly. Fresh air! A doctor! Telephone call – no good; disconnected; but fresh air – a superhuman effort to reach the bolted front door.

He reached it quite easily, drew the bolts and stood on the top step, slouched against one of the round pillars of the stuffy little porch watching the horizon drunkenly. Daytime fires were blazing, fawn-coloured smoke and dust-clouds of grey puffed up against the sky as fresh salvoes of Russian shells pounded the centre of the city. Across the road in a similar house a party of city women had taken over. They were tending a fire of wood debris on a metal balcony, cooking. Beneath budding trees a respectably dressed old man was dragging a branch across the garden. The distance across the road seemed immense. Beyond the thin privet hedge the figures of the scarfed women looked tiny.

Unnecessarily gulping at the spring air Hubertus believed he was too weak to wave to them, to shout or otherwise attract their attention. He expected still to slump beneath the porch at any instant. He wanted violently to speak to someone, to explain; but he was paralysed by the poison he believed he had inhaled. Fear made him vomit on the steps, on the polished black jack-boots and creased black trousers of his uniform. He was delighted and exhilarated by the experience. To vomit was a sign of life. He was not perhaps going to die. He was going to get better. He was going to live. He felt for his wrist pulse but could not find it. He undid the breast buttons of his uniform jacket and slid a hand in over his chest to feel his heart bumping away furiously beneath the whiskers of his left nipple. Shells were screaming overhead, machine guns clattered, grenades exploded in the distance. Someone was tolling the bells of a church and every now and again tiles slipped from the damaged roof of the house; but Hubertus, kneeling now, gazing into the pool of his own vomit, was weeping with the joy of knowing himself alive. A thousand ideas burst in his mind like the shells and grenades. He felt as if everything were saluting his birth, the new life rising out of the old like the deathless phoenix of myth. He realized that he wanted no one to see him, that far from wanting to speak to the group who had moved in over the road, he was going to slip back into the house, a living ghost invisible to all, planning a future in his renewed and tender flesh.

In the cellar he made himself a cup of malt coffee and opened a bottle of his mother's soup, heating it up in the saucepan and drinking it all carefully and gratefully. Things tasted sharp; hot was hot, the water in the kitchen tap, still functioning, cold and clean. The air, rich with the scents of battle and spring, was sweeter than that of his childhood and he was filled with astonishing energy. He took off his uniform in his bedroom and put on his oldest civilian clothes: a sporting jacket, a peach-coloured pullover with an American roll-top neck, and a pair of narrow, horsey trousers. Then he started to work on the plan which it would take him until nightfall to carry out.

First he removed everything combustible from the cellar; books, bedding, wooden furniture and clothing. Then he methodically ransacked the house. He fetched tin chests from the attic and filled them with his father's valuables: silver, glass, cutlery, pictures and first editions, clocks and two cameras. He filled a hand-case with loose money, bank notes and coin, from the study desk and the safe in which the prison funds were kept. Then he collected his mother's few pieces of jewellery – an amethyst brooch, two rhinestone necklaces, some hatpins with turquoise and moonstone heads, lockets with blue enamelled edges and ancient hair inside them, a collection of gold rings mounting little rubies and seed-pearls, a golden swastika studded with tiny diamonds and a silver reticule filled with old foreign coins, including two English sovereigns and some American silver dollars. All these he put in the case and then carried it to the outhouse behind the kitchen. He dragged the tin trunks down to the cellar and walled them up with bricks taken from a pile in the garden. He locked the bottom door and sealed the cellar stairwell with a wire mattress, covered it over with two barrow-loads of earth and stone. He collected such food as was left in the kitchen and stowed it with his father's last fifty cigars in a second suitcase which he also stored in the outhouse.

When he had done this he piled his parents' clothes and his own uniforms in the cupboard under the stairs, going meticulously through the pockets in search of keys, loose change and ration cards as he did so. He had worked all afternoon and through into the evening and yet he was not tired. He believed that if necessary he could have continued as energetically throughout the night without either food or sleep; but it was getting dark and at any moment an air-raid might begin. By ten o'clock he intended to be established in one of the deepest cells with a particular group of resourceful young women. With his foodstuffs and currency he knew he would be welcome and later, after the surrender, he would start his new life with someone. They would accept the Russians to begin with, willingly. They would explain that he was a non-combatant, recently discharged from one of the sanatoria with lung disease, that his identity card and all his personal documents had been destroyed in the battle. In a few weeks' time, when the Americans entered the city, he would if necessary go over to them, acting perhaps as an interpreter or guide, even as a batman to some senior officer. Eventually he might work his way down south to Munich and trace Carin von Hoffbach. It all depended on the circumstances. In the meantime he was alive and provided for. He had his own strong-room in the cellar and before he set fire to the house there remained only the final visit to the drawing-room. He had avoided entering it all day and now he wished he had not been so cowardly. There had been no electricity for several days and his torch batteries were flat. He had a strong impulse to knock on the door before he entered it. He was by no means sure that one of them might not reply, weakly, patiently; or out of desperate sickness. Perhaps he had been callous not to think of it sooner; but he could not really blame himself. He had always had such faith in them, and if they said they were going to die then surely they must be dead.

He threw open the door and waited for a moment, shining the dull beam of his torch into the interior. He saw the back of his father's head over the top of the armchair, his mother's black-and-white body posed comfortably on the sofa with her harlequin cushion still behind her shoulders. Their mouths were open and their eyes. They seemed to be yawning at one another in the twilight, yawning simultaneously as if one had 'caught' the yawn from the other and might at any moment acknowledge it and apologize. He expected this to happen for some moments, he expected to see his mouth close or hers and to see them smile; perhaps. Then he realized that he could not remember having seen them smile at one another for many years, that it was not among their communications.

His father's upper teeth lay in his lap just beside his clenching fingers, his mother's shoes had come off and lay on their sides beside her pretty stockinged feet. As his father's, her head had tilted back in her swift death throe; but only a little because of the cushion. Beyond her, between the parted curtains, the twilight was blue in the broken window panes and now that his eyes were accustomed to the light, Hubertus switched off his torch. He was still standing in his original position. He wanted to feel a great deal more than he was already feeling. He wanted to be 'moved' to a poem later and wondered if there were not something he ought to do in order to make himself feel more 'shaken'. He tried looking at his father; but what he saw only confirmed his first impression; that unfortunate yawn, indefinitely prolonged as in some maladroit photograph, as if it might by mistake have revealed a lasting secret.

'That's it,' Hubertus thought. 'It's not my fault I feel so little. His death has shown him up. He was bored. They both were. They must have been bored for years without my ever knowing it, and there must have been thousands like them, practically the whole of that generation, the Führer's generation. If we'd won . . .'

But he knew it all. He'd had one of his intuitions and would turn it into his journal later; a shining analysis of the old Germany. He might even write a novel called *The Kaiser's Children*. The Americans would publish it. It would end on a note of hope; the new Germany: 'our qualities harnessed for peace and democracy. We were led by a goat into the wilderness. We are the true orphans of Europe, we need an uncle, Uncle Sam.' No, that wasn't good enough, not true enough. They needed nobody. Just a little self-determination and some money to build things up again. A new faith in themselves, a relegation to the historical process of Hitler's mistakes, the mistake of 'that Child of the Kaiser'.

Hubertus slipped his mother's two rings off her fingers. He had noticed that she was wearing her 'big' diamonds for the death-pact and had thought it foolhardy even at the time; some damned looter or Gestapo man pocketing that ring as if it had been a perk on the finger of a camp Jewess! He unclipped her pearls, too, from her warm neck, her little gold wrist-watch and his father's Swiss Rolex with its complicated date and correction mechanism. He even searched the Kommandant's breast pocket and found inside it his best fountain pen and a morocco wallet containing five hundred marks in notes and two sepia late Hohenzollern photographs of his grandparents on their wedding day. There was nothing else in the room worth taking away with him; but he was loath to leave it. He fussed round them both, not daring now to touch them but convinced there was something more he ought to do for them. At last he overcame repugnance and reluctance and set about posing them more comfortably. He kneeled and put his mother's shoes back on to her slender feet. He drew his father's knees together and with his handkerchief picked up his false teeth and slid them back into his mouth. He tried to close his jaw but it was already too stiff to move, so he put his other hand into his lap and then crossed over and did the same for his mother's spreadeagled arms. He straightened her head a little and stroked back a lock of her dark hair which had fallen across her cheek. Then he kissed each of their foreheads, hoping that he might at last weep.

The gesture moved him profoundly. It was more than 'magical', it was 'atavistic'. 'Thoughts that do lie too deep for tears', was the quotation that came into his mind, when his lips touching their cool brows, something did move in his breast. It was a heart-cry so violent and silent, so reproachful, that it shifted his heart a fraction, some organ in his chest, as the note of mourning was yielded from a deep place in his soul; as if, for an instant, there were a real connexion between the two.

He closed the door on them reverently and then became brisk again, ready not to disparage his 'moment of truth' but to define it as an aesthetic experience. He brought in a tin of kerosene from the outhouse and tipped it over the pile of his parents' clothes in the cupboard under the stairs. He took his handcase of small valuables round to the front porch and made a second journey to collect his case of food-stuffs. He filled a basket with sufficient food for twenty-four hours and then hid the case in the bushes behind his mother's rose arbour in the private garden at the back of the house. There were still a number of fires burning in different parts of the city; and one more, out here in the suburbs, would scarcely be noticed. He doubted very much if anyone in the other inhabitable houses of this area would trouble to call in the fire service and was unsure whether they would trouble with such a fire even if they were notified. He would be all right. His plans were excellent. By to-morrow morning he would have ceased to exist. He would be the new Germany; young, betrayed, hopeful and useful. He would be guiltless and his parents would have justified the history for which they had died.

He slipped back into the house and with his cigarette-lighter set fire to one of his mother's many pairs of grey stockings. Soaked in kerosene it flared up swiftly and he threw it on to the bundle of clothes in the cupboard. He left the cupboard door open and, as the flames began to roar inside it, ran up the staircase unclipping all the rods on the first flight of stairs. Then he pulled the end of the carpet over to the cupboard door and sandwiched it between two of the hall chairs, pouring the last of his kerosene over them. The blackouts in the hall windows were still in place, the front door was locked and bolted. If he left open the kitchen doors and the back door, there would be sufficient draught; yet the flames would not be seen. So he left by this route. He picked up his case and basket and hurried away down the Schellenstrasse before a flame had showed in the blazing house.

Chapter 12

Alfried remained at his work for several weeks after the unconditional surrender on May the 7th. He was in fact reluctant to leave the camp at all now that he had a free hand. He had seen the joy of the prisoners when they were liberated; he had watched those who were able leap on to the lorries ferrying them to the new camp a few miles away and seen others staggering out blankly on their own feet with no certain destination in mind. Many of these had been chased by American transport over the flat countryside before they could reach the nearest bombed and battered towns. They had been rounded up and driven back into the camp and allotted new huts until such time as 'normal procedure' could deal with them effectively.

The ditches and verges of the road at this time were full of small pink and blue flowers and blossoming grasses, harbouring moths and butterflies; and the prisoners in their striped camp wear, tiring too soon, had sat down among them in groups looking like hundreds of clowns escaped from a giant circus. A number of them had died where they sat or lay; of joy or sadness or of simple dysentery which had been rife in the camp for months. Others, when the gates were opened, had started fights over the American rations and cigarettes. A soldier only had to throw a cigarette or lob a tin of Spam on to the concrete for half-a-dozen of the stronger prisoners, 'black badges' usually, to be prepared to kill one another to get possession of it. But gradually as the weeks passed and the Americans 'evaluated the problem', as they put it, order began to prevail. The huts nearest to the hospital block, which was no more than a group of larger huts connected by roofed stretcher paths, were turned into annexes for the sick from other parts of the camp. An American medical unit moved in with supplies of drugs and field hygiene and 'theatre' equipment. Alfried, together with two other orderlies whose relatives had all been exterminated in the gas chamber, volunteered to remain on under the command of the 'medics' who were glad to avail themselves of interpreters and inmates with a knowledge of the camp layout.

One nurse, Fräulein Emma Bernd, also volunteered to remain; but Alfried warned her that if she did so he would report her crimes to the doctors.

'You have no proof,' she said.

'You gave injections to the patients,' he retorted. 'I have the night book with entries in your own handwriting.'

'I gave injections only on the orders of Doctor Brand. The drugs I used were those specified by the Superintendent.'

'Benzine is not a drug.'

'You are scum, Waitzmann!' the nurse said. 'You hope to ingratiate yourself with the Americans and get yourself clothed and fed; but you object to anyone else doing the same.'

'You are a murderess,' Alfried replied. 'You slaughtered indiscriminately with a needle under the cover of darkness and your uniform. You murdered Poles, Germans and American airmen, Jews. I myself saw you poison a little Dutch priest who prayed for you when he was dying and gave you his rosary.'

'If that was what you saw, why didn't you stop me?'

'I'm stopping you now, when I may,' said Alfried. 'Go! Get your case packed and find a new life for yourself somewhere else in Germany.'

'I'll remember this, Herr Jew.'

'You'll be too old, Fräulein Bernd. It can't happen again in your lifetime or in mine.'

Fräulein Bernd, with her two suitcases, left trimly in an ambulance provided by the Americans and Alfried put her out of his mind. He hated the hatred with which she and many others had filled him and forcibly suppressed many of his memories, being sure that the practice was good for his health. When specific events such as that of the priest's murder came into his mind, he sometimes succeeded in extracting a kind of joy from the certainty of them, the certainty of his years in the camp, where everything had been so simple. Occasionally, when he had completed his rounds of the annexe he would wander about, visiting those areas of the camp which had formerly been out of S.S. bounds. He walked down the long alley-ways between the hut-lines, stood for a moment at intersections looking at the distant coils of barbed wire and the empty watch-towers with their machine-gun mountings and floodlights still in place.

One evening he walked down to the crematorium adjoining the gas chamber. Spring weeds were growing up through the cinders, a zig-zag crack had started down one of the brickwork sides of the square chimney. The mortuary, too small for the dysentery epidemic, was not in use. The Americans had taken over one of the factory buildings on the other side of the camp roadway and he noticed that they were themselves wiring this area off. The Stars and Stripes was flying from the mast outside the former Kommandant's house. There were notices up in German and American:

OFF LIMITS TO ALL BUT HEADQUARTER'S STAFF.
ALL PASSES TO BE SHOWN ON DEMAND.
ENQUIRIES THIS WAY.
NO PARKING.

Alfried walked across to the extermination unit. It had been effectively tidied up in the weeks immediately following the surrender. The traces which the S.S. had been unable to eliminate themselves in the rush following Eichmann's final directives had been dealt with by local labour under American supervision; yet in some way the place still seemed to be 'warm'.

Against the walls of Bunker 2, rows of primitive hand trollies were drawn up, their handles slanting upwards to the sky as if they had just been rolled there and dropped.

One pair of the crematorium's double doors was open and Alfried walked in. His shoes smote the concrete and echoed up into the rafters where the hooks shone from their polishings of rope. In the floor the staples, chains and shackles of the stokers were still in place in running patterns or neat piles. The doors of the six retorts were all open, a metal-wheeled stretcher in place before each of them, each with its long-handled iron fork resting beside it. There was no sound in the building, not the drip of a tap from the adjoining mortuary nor a catch of the summer wind through the open doors. Alfried moved through into the death chamber he had so often heard described by the regulars who had worked in them in other camps; men who in order to prolong their own lives for a few weeks had led the new drafts into them with words of reassurance and protestation. He ran his finger into one of the blind shower nozzles on the low cement ceiling. It was very dark in the small chamber, concrete grey.

Joy seized him to be still alive, a thousand startled faces of men, women and their children shone for him in the grey-green darkness, locked bodies, all safe now, the faces and bodies of friends and enemies, of bold Jews and cowards, of strangers being dealt with in this hollow concrete cube. He wept for the beauty of his certainty, for the conformity of the ugliness, the sameness of the designs of destruction after so much history. The bunker, shielded by evergreens and formal shrubberies, had been a rumour close as the smoke which floated over the remainder of the camp; it had given dignity to everything else, to despair and foolish generosity, to the dirty century itself. Now, with not a single voice left, with ten thousand stories never to be told, the silence, the stained concrete and the tidiness proclaimed a victory. Kneeling, he prayed his rosary and then walked out through the changing room where they had all undressed by the radiators. He stepped out into the open evening.

From the headquarters, across the wire, came the familiar American commands:

'Picket, attention!' 'From the right, number!' 'Form threes!' 'Quick march!' Jeeps were rolling towards the command post at the entrance, white summer's dust billowing up behind them.

Colonel Burkhardt, the officer commanding the American detachment, decided to interview Alfried about a month later. His security branch had been combing the German personnel and had come up with the hospital orderly's true identity. The Colonel, a New Englander of German descent, was impressed. He told his A.D.C. that he would talk to this particular man himself.

'He's one of the few survivors you might get some sense out of,' he said. 'My old man did business with his firm prior to the war. Fix an appointment for the morning.'

A security man contacted the hospital and Alfried's chief, Captain Sweet of the Medical Division, dropped him the hint over a cup of Maxwell House coffee in the hospital residence.

'It turns out that the Colonel wants to talk to you, Waitzmann. It looks as though you'll be leaving us.'

'When?'

'Very soon, I should say. You never told us you had a family in the offing. We thought you were in the same position as the other two, nowhere to go.'

'I was fortunate. Have my family been enquiring after me, Captain?'

The Captain was facetious. 'Your family certainly have; but don't blame it on them too much for wanting you home. Security would have caught up with you pretty soon anyway. Nurse Bernd dropped them the hint before she left.'

'What did she say?'

'Oh, it wasn't too nice. She didn't like you a lot.'

'She had her chance,' said Alfried.

'She suggested you were a second Krupp, slave labour in your family's factories and so on. Somebody pointed out that Krupp didn't get himself into a camp and she clammed up pretty quickly.'

'I hadn't thought of that. I shall have to get back.'

'You're pretty reluctant, aren't you? What's the matter? Have you got camp apathy?'

'I don't think so.'

'This place has become a kind of a home to you, is that it?'

'In a way. I've been here two years; I'd a lot of friends. I kept expecting to die the whole time; I felt I ought to.'

'Don't let the "Psych" hear you talking like that. He'll want to start in on an analysis.'

'I knew what the dangers were,' went on Alfried. 'In a way I grew fond of them simply because nothing could be worse.'

'Things are a good deal better now.'

'That's what I mean. It's not going to be so easy for me. I shall certainly have to go.'

'You oughtn't to reproach yourself for surviving,' said the Captain suddenly. 'Perhaps I oughtn't to tell you this; but your escape wasn't an accident, you know; it was a design. It turns out you were on Himmler's special list. If things hadn't gone wrong somewhere along the line you'd have been pulled out of this camp months ago. You were scheduled for bargaining at the Armistice with other V.I.P.s.'

'I should be grateful, I suppose.'

'Why not?'

'I enjoyed the work here. I forgot about things.'

'But there's your family. Don't you want to get back to them?'

'I do, of course.'

'Maybe they're going to need you. If they ran things the way Nurse Bernd suggested they did, you could turn out to be the one white sheep.'

'They'll have made mistakes,' said Alfried. 'My younger brother's an opportunist. I'm not looking forward to meeting him again.'

'You're sore?'

'I suspect he betrayed me – to the Gestapo.'

'Well, then, rejoice, man! It's going to be your turn now.'

'You don't really believe that?'

Captain Sweet looked at him.

'It was an idea, that's all. You must realize how hard it is for us to put ourselves in your position. We just can't get any idea of what really went on in these places.'

'It was just the same as ordinary life,' Alfried said. 'But it was speeded up. Everything happened very quickly in the camps. You ate quickly, slept fast, worked hard. If you were beaten then you were beaten quickly and most people died easily. We were filmed from the watch towers a lot of the time; if we worked slowly we were "selected" at once. A grudge at once went all the way. You could see it take shape in a man's face, a prisoner's or a guard's, in a matter of seconds and make him kill, wound or betray straight away. On the other hand, if someone wanted to save someone else's life, to take their place in the selection for the chambers or give away their soup, they acted then and there.'

'It's an interesting idea.'

'The slowness,' said Alfried. 'My old life was slow and confused. I had too much time to think.'

'You've made a point.'

'That's why I can't altogether blame my brother if he did what I suspect. I kept him waiting too long for a certain decision. I did nothing. I thought that I had a vocation.'

'For the Ministry, you mean?'

'Yes.'

'And how do you feel now?'

'I was not expecting this to happen.'

They laughed. Captain Sweet said, 'You'd better take the day off and get yourself ready for Colonel Burkhardt. He's a tough cookie and it's my guess he's going to want to know an awful lot about you.'

'He will have to answer my questions first,' said Alfried.

He thought about the conversation again that evening as he undressed in his room in the hospital annexe. There was something he had been unable to explain to the captain, not morbid, not self-conscious. It was an impatience impatient of interference, massive, as if he were about to take root: a tree which if it were not dislodged would grow where it stood, a thing of life which could not go wrong in the landscape of stones for which it was made and which was made for it, so that it might flourish and never die. This knowledge justified for him his reluctance to move out of the camp, his vexation at the journey which was being imposed upon him from the outside. He believed it might deprive and defer him from his certainty for ever, from his vocation which, as the tree, had grown amid rock.

Before he put on his hospital pyjamas he looked at his body for the first time in many months: at the scars, the outward slope of his stomach, the heads of his bones, the coarsened, newly grown, toe nails. He prayed that he might continue to be what he was no matter how long he might have to wait and decided that he would take up no advance attitude towards Ruprecht and the future of the Waitzmann Group.

In the morning he presented his pass to the command post and made his way through the American half of the camp. In the preceding weeks they had greatly extended their own area. In addition to the S.S. administrative buildings they had now taken over the entire factory and the parade ground where the prisoners had been mustered for selection and punishment. Their wire mesh fences bit into the original area behind the extermination bunkers like new salients. They had opened a vehicle repair shop in one of the old warehouses and turned Canada House, the clothing depot of the dead, into a filling station. Soon, he thought, only the hutted section might remain and it was said already that this too might shortly have to be used as emergency housing for local refugees.

In front of Colonel Burkhardt's headquarters in the former Kommandant's house there was an elaborate garden laid down in 1938 by S.S. Obergruppenführer Eicke. Theodor Eicke, the first inspector of concentration camps, had formed a Death's Head division of the S.S. in which he had later died the soldier's death he had always desired. In his early days at this, his first camp, he had been a relentless spoiler of his men. Unlike Kommandant Grunwald, whose promotion he had consistently opposed, he had never in any sense been a 'prisoners' man' and his officers had loved him. He had given them ruthless hearts, luxurious quarters and fine gardens such as these, his first experiment in formal layout. In off duty hours they had been able to stroll wide gravelled paths between green lawns and watch 'Papa' Eicke's magnificent cultural fountain playing continually on summer's days.

It played now as Alfried walked towards the yellow building above which the Stars and Stripes fluttered from the masthead. In the centre of the cement-walled pool a solid sphere of great girth made of white concrete received a dozen powerful water jets against its sides. The jets vaporized into finest droplets and floated away again as dew, a flame-shaped curtain of mist forever shifting in the light breezes, keeping the lawns green and veiling the buildings and palisades of the railway sidings. There were evergreens and trees, too, between the sidings and the bunkers, so tall now and overgrown that they completely hid the crematorium chimney from which, on windy days the smoke had swept grey as the fountain mist. But now, no engines from the north drew up steaming white beyond the palisade, no buffers rang, no commands were shouted from the other side of the wire and trees. American personnel whistled or sang, walking or hurrying irritably on different assignments. They glanced at Alfried disinterestedly or they ignored him as he moved past them. He had a conviction he was on the wrong side of the wire, that he belonged to the deserted section of the camp where the empty huts stretched row upon row, where everything rusted.

'Because it was true I can afford to forget it,' he told himself. 'Things are as they should be.' But a story came to him as he went up the steps to the headquarters. A sentry asked for his pass and showed him into some room to wait, a kind of drawing-room ante-room, half German, half American. A 'mauve-badge', a Polish Jew, had told him the story of two children playing outside the bunker on a fine day. It had been sunny like today. It was a big draft and they had a long journey and waited about for hours under the trees for their 'de-lousing' and 'baths'. Their mothers had gone ahead with the crush as if it had been a rationing queue and undressed in the dressing-rooms and followed everyone into the 'showerbaths'.

'They knew,' the Jew had said. 'They wanted to get it over, all together; as families; but they couldn't find their two children. They became frightened and angry and started shouting their children's names. The S.S. shouted too. The gas chamber was full and the prisoners who had led the rest of them in there had wanted to get out before the door was screwed up. The mothers had been unable to come right out of the showers because they were stripped and it was anyway forbidden; but they did come as far as the doors of the dressing-room – as if it looked out into a street, as if they were ashamed to come further. They stood there calling their children over and over, but the children were playing by the wood in the shadows of the trees. They had stones and sticks and were playing a sort of croquet.

'The S.S. had lost their nerve by now. I saw it all from where I was sitting in Canada House – they ran over to them and stood in a circle round them. The children ignored them, they called back cheekily to their mothers that they didn't want a bath until they'd finished the game; and no one could pick them up. They were quite young and dark-haired, about five and six, a girl and boy in big clothes. The Kommandant came over and the men waited to see what he would do. He got down in among the boots and picked both the children up. They struggled and screeched to begin with and then began laughing to each other, the way children do when the game's up.

'He carried them all the way back to their mothers – not running or hurrying – and the women thanked him and went ahead of him, naked, between the guards into the chamber. The children followed in their clothes. There was no time to undress them because it was such a big selection. They screwed up the door on them all. No one got out that day, not even the dummy prisoners who began to scream to be let out. The S.S. came to themselves and everything went on as normal. . . .'

There were *Time* and *Life* magazines on an occasional table beside the sofa. The boots of Americans thudded on the tiles of the corridor. They walked differently from the Germans, less precisely. Through the window a detachment could be seen mustering for coffee-break, shuffling back into line with innocent faces, younger than Alfried. Seasoned as they were, they saluted their officers laconically and appeared to take a certain pride in their slackness. It was hard to believe they had crossed the Atlantic and won the war, that they had conquered Europe as far as the Soviet limits.

Somewhere in the building a wireless was spilling out jazz, typewriters were tapping and through an open window wind, moist with gusts of the fountain, fluttered a poster.

'Colonel Burkhardt will see you now,' an officer announced in good German.

'Thank you.' Alfried got up and followed him to the Colonel's office.

'I suppose he knows that I speak English, Captain?'

'The Colonel speaks both.'

The Colonel stood behind the Kommandant's desk. He was almost as tall as the twin flags hanging cone-shaped on either side of him, the Divisional colours and the Stars and Stripes. He wore a crew cut and had a short thick face with green eyes in between smooth lids. He was young and stern, in his early forties. He did not smile.

'Alfried Waitzmann?'

'Yes, sir.'

'Colonel Burkhardt. We'll talk English if you don't mind.'

'Thank you.'

'Why did you give a false name at your examination by Security?'

'I didn't wish to be moved from the hospital for the time being.'

'You realize that this is an offence against the mandate of General Eisenhower?'

'Yes, Colonel; but since I was in some ways assisting your medical division I cannot see that it was important.'

'It's the principle that matters. You might have been someone Security was trying hard to find.'

'I understand that I was.'

'Don't be facetious with me, Waitzmann.'

'No, Colonel.'

'What was your real reason for wishing to remain in the camp when you have relatives only ninety kilometres away in Bergedorf?'

'I've given you my real reason.'

'You may speak frankly to me, Waitzmann. I'm not myself hostile to you or to your decision. I'm interested personally, that's all.'

'In what, Colonel?'

'In the reason that will make a man remain, after long imprisonment, in the same prison in which he was allegedly tortured, constantly threatened with death and starved into the bargain.'

'Sir?'

'I've only recently been appointed to this command. It's my business to get to know everything that went on before I took over. My commission here is almost as much political as military.'

'You did not see the camp at the beginning?'

'I saw nothing. I fought my own war in the Pacific until I was wounded in the Philippines, after that from the Pentagon. I've done my best to improve the place in the past few weeks, I've extended our wire and gotten the services working. Maybe you noticed the fountain on your way across from the hospital?'

'What exactly do you want to know, Colonel? How can I help you?'

'You can tell me the truth.'

'The truth about the camp?'

'It'll help me to size up my own commitment, the political issues, my personal liaison with the civilian authorities over here.'

'You don't wish to hear atrocity stories?'

The Colonel shifted stiffly in his chair. 'Now look, Waitzmann, I've fought against the Japanese. As military opponents they stuck at nothing. But this is Europe, my own father was German; as a matter of fact he did business with your subsidiary in Baltimore. Now do you understand me? Can we work together – or can't we?'

'I think so. But we can't alter facts, Colonel.'

'This is entirely off the record. You're half German and so am I; there are things we could discuss.'

'I have Jewish blood also, Colonel.'

'That's a point! You can't be much more than an eighth

Jewish though, the rest of you is pure German like myself. You're a wealthy man, pretty soon you'll be having to do what I'm doing, picking up the threads and trying to make this country work again.'

'You feel that I'm to be trusted?'

'I'm not joking; I've been through your record. I know everything there is to be known about you personally and about your family's connexions.'

'From my records you say? That is a Gestapo delusion.'

'Now look, Waitzmann, this war isn't over yet. This was simply phase one. Whether we like it or not we Americans and Germans have got to learn to speak the same language.'

'I will answer your questions if I can.'

'This was a small camp as camps go, I understand?'

'Yes, it was.'

'And how many people are the authorities supposed to have wiped out here?'

'I've no accurate idea.'

'Round figures, Waitzmann. Five hundred, six hundred, a thousand, two thousand?'

'Ninety thousand, I should say.'

'I'm not referring to deaths from natural causes. I'm not even referring to the medical casualties, Waitzmann. I want the hardest figure you can give on the official executions, the gassings.'

'Then it's ninety thousand. That is the least estimate I can give since nineteen thirty-eight. There have been a smaller number of executions before that in the peacetime.'

'Right. And what percentage of this ninety thousand would you say took place in the last four years inclusive, nineteen forty-two to forty-five?'

'Probably about seventy per cent.'

'Yes, that agrees with my own estimate. That is to say that for approximately eleven hundred days continuously the Kommandant and staff here are supposed to have liquidated Jews and others at the rate of just under one hundred a day?'

'Yes.'

'Well, they couldn't work at night, not after nineteen

forty-three, the air raids got too severe. Also there are only six ovens in that crematorium, the gas chamber over there holds only thirty people standing upright, I've measured it and I know. Tell me, Waitzmann, did you yourself witness any of these executions?'

'I was not employed in that section of the camp, Colonel. Entry was forbidden.'

'As I thought.'

'The dog squad was quartered in the kennels between the extermination unit and the southern section of the hutted area. To approach this area meant instant detection and probably death.'

'I've seen the kennels, Waitzmann. I didn't see any dogs.'

'You forget perhaps, Colonel, that not all the executions at this camp were by means of the gas. There was the rifle range and the blood ditch, also not all the bodies were cremated. There were large communal graves.'

'Where?'

'I don't know where they were situated, since I did not work there. Recently, too, the S.S. received orders to re-open the graves and grind up the bones.'

'And what's happened to the prisoners who did work there?'

'They were executed.'

'And the S.S. staff?'

'They have gone.'

'Exactly, Waitzmann; and I've seen the records of those Security picked up and questioned. Their estimates do not match up with yours.'

'I am sorry.'

'Don't think I blame you. You pass on only what you were told. Propaganda, like charity, begins at home and back in the States we were fed even taller stories than you raked up for yourselves here on the spot.'

'I must remind you, Colonel, that it was because I was supposed to have disseminated enemy propaganda that I was imprisoned here in the first place.'

The Colonel clasped his left wrist with his right hand.

'I'm being tough on you, Waitzmann, but it's because I respect you. You've got to credit me with a point, though. No doubt you believe that the real policy we've been discussing was carried on elsewhere; at Auschwitz say, or Belsen?'

'I was never at either Auschwitz or Belsen myself.'

'Well, neither was I, thank God. I'm only just trying to point out that if we're going to make a fresh start we've got to be freed of any damned fool illusions. This was as much my father's country as yours, Waitzmann. If you and I are going to start off against the real enemy, phase two of the world struggles, we've got to have something to offer and we've got to have clean hands to offer it.'

Colonel Burkhardt stood up. 'You might like to know that I've sent a dispatch-rider off this morning. By now your family will know that you're on your way back to them.'

'Thank you.'

'You've made yourself useful here. Doctor Sweet spoke highly of your work for the sick and dying in these last few months. He's offered to run you back home himself in the hospital jeep any time you like to leave.'

'It's extremely kind of him.'

'Shake hands, Waitzmann. I don't expect you to take all I've said right now; but this has been a good moment for me. Later on, when you're in business again, maybe you'll remember my point of view. It's one I hope to disseminate throughout this whole area; but I'm not in any hurry.'

Alfried shook hands and the Colonel walked with him over to the tall double doors. 'Your family are going to get an awful shock when you come rolling up in that jeep. How long is it since they saw you?'

'I've been in prison since early nineteen forty-two.'

'It'll be like Lazarus,' said the Colonel. 'Like Lazarus rising from the dead. Your mother'll scarcely believe her own eyes.'

'My mother is blind, Colonel.'

'Oh well now, Waitzmann, I'm sorry to hear that. Good luck, and I hope we meet again in happier days.'

319

'Good-bye, Colonel.'

'Good-bye. Orderly! Take Herr Waitzmann over to the hospital.'

Twenty-four hours earlier, in bright sunshine, Ruprecht and Onkel Fritz had met nearly fortuitously outside the battered white front of the Waitzmann House in Bergedorf. Onkel Fritz had been back in Bavaria a fortnight, having flown into Frankfurt with an advance secretariat of the American Control Commission stationed in Munich. His credentials were impeccable, his local knowledge and contacts unique, and his bewilderment no greater than anyone else's. As he had told Wilhelmina and Ruprecht:

'Everything is under the finger of Providence. Anything and everything could happen here and we must allow for all eventualities. You must try to understand the Allied point of view.'

'Well, go on, tell us,' ordered Ruprecht irritably.

'More particularly, since we ourselves are in the hands of Washington rather than those of Paris, Moscow or London, the American point of view.'

'And it is what?'

Onkel Fritz was unruffled. 'There is no American point of view, no single one, that is. There are elements only. First the military element; the sooner they can get the population back on their feet the better. They don't want to be responsible for their subsistence a day longer than necessary; therefore they're inclined to be more approachable. Second, the civilian-political; they would wish to take over all the industrial complexes of the nation and control them themselves for a time. Heavy industry would be wiped out, light industry managed by their own representatives. Broadly, they would institute a policy of form-filling and pastoralization.'

'What's that?'

'Cows, ploughed fields, sheep and pigs.'

'My God, a nation of peasants!'

'Then there is de-cartelization,' went on Onkel Fritz, 'and dismantling, the British policy; or dismantling and slaughter, the Communist policy, or two hundred per cent reparations, the French policy!'

'If this is all you have to tell us I can't help wondering why you troubled to secure the appointment.'

Onkel Fritz lighted a cigar. 'That is the worst of it, Ruprecht, and the best too. There are grounds for optimism. There always are when one is faced with a conflict of opinion. My boy, one day you may learn that stability is the only economic force that the capitalist need fear. That is why the Communists have espoused monolithism: before it, the individual is as helpless as a worm in the path of a steam roller.'

'Then what is the plan?'

'The plan is to behave exactly as if this were peacetime, a normal peacetime. In other words, we should have a dozen plans, all based on the assumption that what we own will always remain ours, that sooner or later property will continue to exercise its basic functions in society.'

'But what are you going to do?'

'I'm going to do all that is possible; but a little at a time. Now Ruprecht, you mustn't question me further. Discretion, even in a democracy, still has its uses. I think your mother may still have something to teach you, you may have noticed she hasn't asked me a single question this morning!'

'I don't need to,' said Frau Waitzmann, concluding the conversation. 'Your return was sufficient answer in itself, Fritz.'

True to his own advice, Onkel Fritz had at once set about this particular and private aspect of his duties. For the third morning in succession, with Frau Neff taking his notes, he had been touring the factory-holdings, totting up the capital expenditure that would be needed to carry out the rebuilding scheme. He was in excellent spirits on that particular day. His after-breakfast cigar tasted especially good and by this time he was sure of his figures.

'The Herr Direktor will be delighted,' he told Frau Neff. 'We may now assure him that he was right when he suggested the bombs had fallen in all the correct places. We've had an expert demolition free of charge and one day we shall have modern buildings to rehouse up-to-date plant.'

'The Herr Direktor has carried his plans in his head so long, sir.'

'Then this morning we shall give him the good news. If you can get the balances typed over the weekend, Frau Neff, I'll take the figures to Munich with me on Tuesday when I report to the Commission.'

'They'll be ready in triplicate, sir, by Monday evening.'

They walked past the cleared foundations of the old boiler houses. 'A strange role to play at the end of such a disaster, Frau Neff. I've spent five years worrying about the future of the Group and now I find myself appointed by our late enemies to help restore economic order to the whole area.'

'It's almost as if the war had never taken place in some ways, sir.'

'Yet one has only to look at the skyline to see that – ' he broke off as Frau Neff paused beside him.

'There *is* the Herr Direktor, Herr Ruprecht, sir.'

Onkel Fritz hurried off to meet him as he walked slowly across from the office block to the house.

'A dispatch-rider is coming in with a message from some American,' he called out, waiting beneath the shade of a damson tree.

'For me?' asked Onkel Fritz.

'No, for Mama or myself, I understand.'

'Not my doing, I've not had time to send them on anything this week; but you'll be glad to hear that your own estimates are a little pessimistic. The Baltimore profits should be able to cover the damage twice over as soon as the dollar loosens up again.'

'I'm not worried about the money, Fritz, it's the time factor.'

'War is always quicker than peace, my boy. One has to be patient.'

They waited together for the arrival of the man on the motor-cycle; but he was some minutes passing the gate and getting over the disused sidings. There was time for the older man to see that his young cousin looked ill in the mornings.

'Peace is like this tree,' he said. 'One season it may be bare, the next laden. One has only to wait and then shake it. In the meantime one must preserve one's strength.'

'What's keeping him? It's that damned fool at the gate. He telephoned me five minutes ago that he'd arrived.'

'Where's he from?'

'I'm not sure; some Colonel Burkhardt.'

'Colonel Hans Burkhardt?'

'I don't know.'

'If so it might be very good for us, Ruprecht. We did a lot of business with his firm in the thirties.'

The motor-cycle came up the drive fast, the rider dragging his high boots on the gravel, riding slackly. He got off his machine slowly and came over to meet them, reaching his hand into his pocket for Colonel Burkhardt's letter.

'Can you tell me where I can find Frau Waitzmann?' he asked.

'I am Ruprecht Waitzmann. I am her son.'

'A letter from Colonel Burkhardt of the United States Third Army. I was told to deliver it personally to Frau Wilhelmina Waitzmann.'

'You may give it to Herr Waitzmann.' Onkel Fritz spoke in English.

'Will there be an answer?'

'An acknowledgement only,' Ruprecht said in German to Onkel Fritz. He handed him the open letter. 'It says that they have found Alfried, that he is returning tomorrow.'

'Alfried? Alive?'

'Apparently.'

'Nothing else?' asked the rider.

'We must tell Wilhelmina,' said Onkel Fritz in English, adding to the rider:

'Wait a minute, if you don't mind. Frau Waitzmann may want you to take a reply. She'll certainly want you to take our thanks to the Colonel.'

'I'll come with you unless you'd rather see her alone,'

said Ruprecht in German. He turned stiffly to the American. 'There is nothing more to say. Our thanks to your Colonel.'

The American kicked his engine to life and rode away.

'You must of course come with me,' said Onkel Fritz. 'In fact it would be more accurate to say that I will come with you.'

'This is something that I cannot do. You must tell Mama for me.'

'It is a shock, that is agreed. But if you can't take this in your stride – '

'At the moment I can't.'

'You must think ahead.'

'I am thinking ahead.'

'Do not think of the past.'

'I shall be leaving Bavaria,' said Ruprecht.

'We mustn't keep Wilhelmina waiting longer.'

'Mama doesn't know she's waiting. There is time for me to tell you of my intentions. I can show you that I'm not thinking entirely of the past.'

'We are a unit, don't forget that.'

'It was always on the cards that Alfried might turn up again at any moment. Alexandra believed he would. Mama won't be in the least surprised.'

'True, perhaps.' Onkel Fritz felt as if he must steady the young man. He must allow him to talk and then convince him of the necessity for small sacrifices, the necessity for a magnificent pride.

'What is your principal worry?' he asked him.

'There is the question we discussed the other night. You admitted yourself that your influence had its limits. You mightn't be able to clear me on the question of the camp labour force during the shortage.'

'Von Hoffbach claimed the responsibility for that.'

'But not Leo. He'll have his father's letters. There is Carin also.'

'You've heard from her?'

'She's in Paris living with an important American. If it suits her she will betray me instantly the moment I come up for de-Nazification. Also there are the Party's records. They are very accurate.'

Onkel Fritz took his hand. 'Very well, then. Wait until the time comes and if necessary let them sentence you. Leave the rest to me and to our friends in industry and to the Americans themselves. These proceedings are a formality. They're totally unreal on three counts. First, the war is not over; Communism remains the real enemy and a country can't do without its shrewdest men. Second, to be imprisoned on the instigation of a conquerer civilized enough to leave the sentence to the conquered is no great hardship. It only makes a man more popular in his own country. Third, there is Alfried who, like myself, fought on their side.'

'You suggest they'll make fools of themselves, is that it?'

'They cannot make fools of themselves nor of us.'

'They'll imprison me and you and Alfried will take over?'

'For the time being.'

Ruprecht was silent. Onkel Fritz dropped the stub of his cigar on to the dry gravel and put a neat heel over it.

'We are not defeated,' he said. 'We cannot be. We are more than German or Jewish. We are more than capital. We are Europe, we are Christian. The war is yet to be fought.'

'For me it is over,' said Ruprecht with finality. 'When I said I could not take it in my stride at the moment I meant now. As a natural man. I am what I am and I cannot be changed any more. There are no sides here, you have proved that to me.'

'True, true.'

Ruprecht pointed briefly over the pink stump of a factory chimney. 'But there is a side over there – beyond the division which bisects us in the East. I made plans long ago, I've been offered work over there by the Russians and I can take my choice, physics or management. Alexandra and Nikolaus will come with me.'

He moved away back to the office block. Onkel Fritz followed him and caught him up. 'You don't yet know what Alfried's decision might be.'

'I have never known, I no longer care.'

'I'll see you later, my boy. I must go to your mother now.'
They moved away in opposite directions.

In the night, Alexandra had an attack of night fears.
Beneath the bedclothes she prayed a rosary with damp
fingers over the pit of her stomach. In between the decades
she asked God: 'What sort of a life will it be for little
Nikolaus?' She had asked God's Mother: 'What about my
mother getting old and wanting us to be near her now that
the war is over? What did you do when your husband
ordered you to make a journey into pagan lands?' But
Ruprecht, sleeping in his anger beside her, was not at all
like St Joseph. He never prayed; he was a tower of wrath,
young; the stubble of his beard blackening his white jaw at
one o'clock in the morning of the day that would bring back
his brother.

After his conversation with Onkel Fritz he had remained
over in the office all day, not reappearing in the house until
the frugal evening meal which in this instance had been
supplemented by some of Leo's Schönform vegetables.

'There is nothing to discuss,' he had told Onkel Fritz in
the middle of a discussion.

'Mama, though I'm not tired I've every reason to be,' he
had told Frau Waitzmann, stern and watchful with all but
her eyes. 'Tomorrow I'll come over to meet Alfried at
eleven-thirty; but I can't spare the time for talk, I leave
that to the three of you.'

'As you wish. There is no hurry.'

'If I am to leave things in order for some sort of production by the autumn time, there's a hurry for you and for the
Group.'

'There is plenty of time – plenty,' added Onkel Fritz.
'Things are going very nicely with the Americans. The
Military, at least, seem to want to get light industry going
as soon as possible, if only to stop the drain on their own
finances.'

'Where I too am concerned,' went on Ruprecht, 'there is
very little time. Alfried's return, splendid as it is for every-

326

one, will draw attention to my own position. Though the prospect of my trial before one of those damned de-Nazification courts doesn't greatly worry Fritz . . .'

'Alfried had no trial,' Frau Waitzmann interrupted him. 'He has spent three and a half years in prison without any trial whatsoever.'

Ruprecht ate for a few moments; but Alexandra put down her knife and fork. She had a sick headache and wanted to go upstairs to the old nursery where the unrepaired roof leaked; but where two-year-old Nikolaus and his nanny would be eating happily.

Ruprecht spoke to no one in particular: 'Already it is becoming a memory, Alfried's sacrifice. Though it is not yet even ended, already we are being asked to remember it.' He drank a little wine. 'I shall not be here to be reminded of it very much longer nor shall I be here to be tried and imprisoned.'

'I have such a headache,' Alexandra said over her broad beans and potato.

'There's no clear policy as yet,' Onkel Fritz reminded him. 'Morgenthau is quite sympathetic and though there are some hard men on the civilian side. . . .'

But Ruprecht ignored him: 'The Russians want all the physicists they can get. I've been told that every week their offers over the radio go up by several hundred marks. One doesn't need to go to Moscow either. Posts may be had in East Germany, in Leipzig, even in Berlin itself.'

'I feel so sick,' said Alexandra.

'You would be able to visit your mother and father in Upper Bavaria in the summer holidays,' Ruprecht told her. 'You'd be able to visit them outside the summer holidays. From East Berlin you'd be able to go to the Mass if you wished. Nikolaus could have his first communion.'

'Liebling, if you don't mind, I'll go upstairs. I can't eat any more.' Ruprecht got up and opened the door for her and went up the stairs with her as far as the top landing. She caught at his hand there but he only smiled at her and withdrew it before he hurried back to the dining-room to finish his meal in silence.

327

Alexandra did not go to her room to lie down. She spent the whole afternoon with Nikolaus and Helma Kolbe, one of the Schönform refugees who had proved clever with children. Without actually speaking she told Nikolaus that he had wonderful little teeth, sharp and pointed like his father's; that he was a gay baby, very strong; that there were no countries in the world without churches, that he would be able to pray anywhere. 'You'll be a praying baby,' she mentally told him. 'You'll pray for me and for both your Grossmutters and for your daddy. Where we're going, *if* we go, it may be dark; but there'll be snow for you. We'll keep Christmas and Easter while we're there and one day we'll come back. I know we'll come back – like Alfried, your uncle.'

She hated Alfried; but only because she loved Ruprecht so much. Nikolaus couldn't hate anyone yet; he was too young; but later he too might grow to hate his uncle. She played frantically with the child: 'hand-pats', 'walkie-walkie', 'knock-down-Hansel', a game of their own invention. 'Ruprecht's had Alfried in his life all the time,' she thought. 'I've never even met Alfried. I defended him from the beginning; but why hasn't he ever done something about his life? Poor darling! After all his work. . . .'

And of course she meant Ruprecht; but she had insight. She knew it was wicked to think of Alfried so maliciously; but gave her thoughts their 'head' for the time being. She knew that by doing so she was entertaining evil and that she would have to confess her sin to the new priest at the Jesuit House; but, really, she got into such states! In discussions at Schönform she had several times explained this inner turbulence to Father Guardini. 'Each family, each nation has its characteristics,' he had said in his Roman accent. 'You are German. Germans are very innocent and obedient, easily perverted. Like children, how brutal they can become! Like children, how little interest they take in their government until someone starts shouting at them. Children are easily outraged. Outrage is always present for all of us; but it must be expressed in judgement, political or otherwise; there it may cleanse.'

'But Italy too, Father, was easily misled by Mussolini?'

'We are children of the South, we have our own defects. You Germans are God's children of the North. We didn't follow Mussolini so far in any direction. Adults make bad soldiers and poor torturers and we tend on the whole to indolence. Few of us take anything to extremes, not even our religion. There was no alternative at the time of course; but if there had been St Peter might well have chosen Paris or Madrid in place of Rome.'

'Then if I am angry and worried, what am I to do besides pray?'

'See what the reason is and if it is a good one, be angry to some good purpose. If only you had been an angrier nation you'd not have been so in love with the false rages of Hitler.'

'If Ruprecht goes on like this.' Alexandra thought now in the darkness of the bedroom, 'then for once in my life I might be angry with him. But then I am so annoyed with Alfried.'

That afternoon she had dressed little Nikolaus up in his prettiest clothes, a pair of tiny grey lederhosen, a long-sleeved silk shirt and the white sandals sent her from Paris by Carin.

Carin, according to Leo, had had a most dreadful time at the end of the War. She had been at home nursing her mother when the Russians invaded East Prussia. The Red infantry, advancing faster than anyone had predicted, had come over the snow during the night and were less than a mile from the estate wall. The two women had heard noises downstairs and Carin, bravely, had gone to investigate. Her mother, only just recovering from pneumonia, had followed her. She had refused to go back to bed and they had argued in whispers in the lamplight.

'Take this!' 'Get that!' 'Be sure you don't forget the jewellery,' Frau de Luce had implored. And then there had been a terrible scene in which the old woman had accused Carin of wanting to leave her behind too. For over an hour she had refused to go back to bed, following Carin all over the house in the darkness, waving her stick and saying: 'This is the excuse you've been waiting for all your life,

329

Carin. You want to leave me and go off with your lovers. You'd let me die here, you'd let me be raped, you'll go off in the sledge in the morning with the servants and both the horses.'

And this was exactly what Carin had been forced to do. After that night her mother had been too ill to move. Working furiously with the two maids and a few old men, they had harnessed the horses and sledged off to Danzig with all the valuables, leaving Frau de Luce, half comatose, in the big bedroom with a message pinned on her nightdress.

With a pass supplied by Hubertus who had got it direct from Dr Goebbels at the Ministry, Carin had crashed the refugee queue for the boat at Danzig and even persuaded the Captain, a Party member who was somewhat in awe of her, to take all her belongings on deck as well.

She had soon found herself a job, working in an American canteen, and later had moved to Paris with a Major who had protected her and treated her very generously. She sent many parcels to Bergedorf and Alexandra was particularly glad of the luxury clothes which occasionally arrived for Nikolaus. Completing his costume that afternoon with the little white sandals, she had taken him down to the Marienkirche to light a candle and made him say a prayer each for Ruprecht and Alfried.

As they were leaving the church, standing at the top of the steps, where pigeons fluttered over the rubble of the square and flew high above the shattered towers of the old Archbishop's Palace, they had met Frau Waitzmann coming up the steps with the chauffeur's widow. She had not seen Alexandra; and Frau Höth, who had only recently heard of her husband's death in a Russian camp, had been too sad to speak to them. Nikolaus had trotted down the steps fluttering out his arms as if he were about to fly. Frau Waitzmann, all in black; and Frau Höth, in black too, had passed Alexandra outside the West doorway and nobody had said a word.

Alexandra had gone back to the house for tea. She had played the old musical box in the nursery; putting on record after record, metal perforated circles larger than dinner plates. The upper floor of the house resounded to the waltzes of Strauss and the tunes of the Kaiser's Germany. Fräulein Kolbe had danced with Nikolaus and swung him on the landing swing until his bedtime.

Alexandra herself had gone to bed early, hoping to be asleep before Ruprecht joined her; but her 'state' had been too pronounced to allow of her slipping away like this; and she never took sleeping tablets. The factory too was noisy at nights. Ruprecht had managed to get floodlights erected so that the work of clearing the rubble and completing the demolition of damaged shops should go on without interruption. The bedroom shook to the full tremors caused by falling walls. Swivelling lights penetrated the net of the unblacked-out windows and slid across pictures hanging crooked. In the distance, workmen could be heard shouting at their labours.

Standing against the lighted doorway, Ruprecht switched on all the lights in the bedroom.

'You are awake?' he demanded.

'Yes, Liebling, but I am very tired.'

'You must support me.'

'I always have.'

'Tomorrow, I mean, in the morning. We must let it be quite clear to Mama, to Fritz and to Alfried that we are going, that there is nothing left for us here.'

'But it's not true; there is so much.'

'On the new terms, nothing.'

Alexandra sat up, pretty and pale against the frilled pillow slips.

'What are your terms, Liebling? What exactly do you want?'

'I want what I have worked for, what I have inherited by interest and determination.'

'Haven't you loved your work?'

'Love doesn't enter into it. Has Alfried loved it? Has Onkel Fritz, Mama? No. To them it has been only a way of life; but to me it is more than that. My work and everything the Group represents is me myself. I am a man who is his inheritance, who is that or who is nothing.'

'Liebling, take off your clothes and come to bed. We can talk about it in the morning.'

'There will not be time.'

He sat on the end of the bed, richly suited, his manicured fingers resting in his lap. 'Damn these political men. Damn Alfried and von Hoffbach and Onkel Fritz. Damn the Party and the Führer. I did nothing, I neither joined the Party nor fought against it, yet now that I have kept our place for us it is I who am threatened with political action.'

Alexandra was so happy. He was angry; there was a crack in his resolve, a small one, so shallow that it did not penetrate its depths; but if he had been sure of his decision he would not have been resentful, he would not have talked. She must let him talk, then, all night if necessary. She must pray that in the morning not one word or sentence would be said by Grossmutter or Onkel Fritz which might seal that crack again. She must pray, above all, that his brother returning would see him, that he would understand Ruprecht and not condemn him.

'Liebling, I've been so sad,' she said. 'I could bear anything if we could stay here somewhere near home; but I couldn't live if you were to make us go to the Russians.'

'Then if necessary I shall have to go without you.'

'But you'd never stand it. You couldn't do anything there, you'd be nothing. Think, Liebling, you're not a political man, you've said so yourself, and what would they want from you there no matter what else you were doing? Politics, all day long. They'd fill you up with it. They'd turn you into a monster.'

'The foreign Press thinks we are all monsters in Germany. The Russians whom you so despise think we are the greatest monsters of history.'

'I don't know,' said Alexandra, rinsing her fingers in the hollow of her eiderdown. 'I can't think about it, I never shall be able to; but I do know that if you take us out there we'll none of us ever come back again. I was reading something so dreadful tonight, I couldn't go to sleep.'

He was bitter: 'Oh, some pamphlet of the camps! Some new revelation about the evils of the Thousand Year Reich?'

'No, it was Goethe, Faust. It's here, I'll read it to you.'

No way! Towards untrodden ground where none may tread; A way towards the unprayed for, beyond all prayer. Are you prepared? There are no locks, no bolts to thrust aside; you will be driven hither and thither by hosts of loneliness. Do you know what void and loneliness mean? ... You will see nothing in that distance of eternal emptiness, you will not hear your own step, you will find nothing solid for your rest.

Ruprecht took off his shoes. 'The Communists have no use for dreams. Perhaps they miss something; but if one has dreams one also has nightmares.'

'I thought of your brother, of Alfried,' she said. 'I wished I'd met him.'

'You'll meet him tomorrow. Don't worry, we all will.'

'No, before, I meant; before he went away. If it's true about the camps, if everything we're being told now is true and even the guiltless aren't so guiltless as they wanted to be, then Goethe might have written that for Alfried. He must be a man who knows what "the void and loneliness" mean. He wasn't "unprayed for" and he wasn't "beyond all prayer" himself. He was "prepared"; but I don't want *you* to go towards "untrodden ground"!' She lay down. 'Liebling, I tremble when I think that tomorrow he will be looking at us all. . . .'

In the morning, while they were waiting upstairs, she confessed something of her fears to Frau Waitzmann. Ruprecht was over in the office block. Through the drawing-room window Alexandra could see him as he moved past his own window dictating his letters to Frau Neff. He came continually to the dark window like a figure beneath water, pausing to look down into the yellow sunlit space between the two buildings where at any moment a staff car might draw up or a man arrive on foot. Onkel Fritz was rustling with his brief-case, tense and cheerful, talking of the Morgenthau Plan and the confusion in high places. But Frau Waitzmann, beautifully dressed in black silk with a collar of carved ivory medallions round her neck, sat peacefully on the sofa, her face as serenely dull as the ivory.

'Perhaps it is a superstition,' began Alexandra precisely. 'But in the night I thought of Alfried so intensely. I never believed I'd ever meet him. All the photographs I've seen are so unreal that it didn't hurt me to look at them at all; but now I'm so troubled, Grossmutter.'

Frau Waitzmann made one of her sounds; dry, a little impatient. 'And well we might be,' she was thinking. 'Again, we might not; but I too am afraid.'

'I don't think Alfried will have changed,' she told Alexandra suddenly. 'He'll accuse nobody.' She found and held one of the girl's restless hands.

'He may well be very bitter,' said Onkel Fritz. 'One cannot tell. I myself feel bitter; but, like Alexandra, I have some difficulty in believing all I've been told. If *I* have difficulty. . . .'

But he said no more. They all three knew that he had fled to safety, that it had been real enough to him then.

'It's Ruprecht who's bitter,' said Alexandra. 'Perhaps that is what is worrying me so much – not Alfried at all.'

'It's more than that,' said Frau Waitzmann. 'Alfried would say that it was History. He'll be so happy.'

'We should rejoice,' said Onkel Fritz.

'Ruprecht is so very bitter,' said Alexandra. 'I've prayed and prayed about him but it makes no difference. It seems not to.'

'More than History,' said Frau Waitzmann. 'He's alive. Alfried was one of the very few who have lived through it all. He was wise from the beginning, too.'

'True,' said Onkel Fritz. 'Without him, you realize, you'd have nothing.'

'*We* would have nothing,' Frau Waitzmann corrected him.

'We, I was forgetting, Wilhelmina. Already one is so tempted to dissociate oneself from it all.'

Frau Waitzmann stood up. She was now physically impatient too; really angry that on this day of all days she could not see. The windows, so full of light, were tall blurs of gauze, even her hearing was less acute than it had been. She might not hear the approach of the car nor the sound of Emma hurrying to the door on the floor below. Instead she must listen to this wash of talk, to the speculations of the guilt from which she knew she was not herself free.

'You are going, Wilhelmina?'

'I am so angry, Fritz.'

He got up, plump and fussy. 'My dear, I did not mean that I did dissociate myself from it; merely that, after so long an absence –'

'No one can dissociate themselves,' she said, 'Not Germany, nor Europe, nor America. Dear God! I only pray that, unlike the rest of us, Alfried may not have changed and will never change.'

She found her stick and left the room confidently. They heard her going slowly down the stairs to her bedroom.